TRACI HARDING

AWOL

THE TIMEKEEPERS [3]

HARPER
Voyager

Harper*Voyager*

An imprint of HarperCollins*Publishers*

First published in Australia in 2015
This edition published in 2016
by HarperCollins*Publishers* Australia Pty Limited
ABN 36 009 913 517
harpercollins.com.au

HarperCollins*Publishers*
Level 13, 201 Elizabeth Street, Sydney, NSW 2000, Australia
Unit D1, 63 Apollo Drive, Albany, Auckland 0632, New Zealand
A 53, Sector 57, Noida, UP, India
77–85 Fulham Palace Road, London W6 8JB, United Kingdom
2 Bloor Street East, 20th floor, Toronto, Ontario M4W 1A8, Canada
195 Broadway, New York, NY 10007, USA

National Library of Australia Cataloguing-in-Publication data:

Harding, Traci.
  AWOL / Traci Harding.
  978 0 7322 9271 3 (pbk.)
  978 0 7304 9288 7 (ebook)
  Harding, Traci. Timekeepers; bk 3.
  Time travel – Fiction.
  Prophecy – Fiction.
  Science fiction.
A823.4

Cover design by HarperCollins Design Studio
Cover images by shutterstock.com
Typeset in 10/13pt Goudy Old Style

Traci Harding, best selling author of 'the Ancient Future Series', has published in excess of twenty books through through HarperCollins/Voyager Australia, Brio Books and Bolinda Audio. Her work blends fantasy, fact, esoteric theory, time travel and quantum physics, into adventurous romps through history, alternative dimensions, universes and states of consciousness. Her books have been published in several languages throughout the world.

To find out more about Traci and her books
visit her website at: traciharding.com

For autographed copies of Traci's books visit her store at:
allthingstraci.com.au

Get Exclusive Content at Patreon:
patreon.com/user?u=20034469&fan_landing=true

Find Traci on Facebook at:
"Mastering Your Reality with Traci Harding" Group -
All Things Traci Store - Traci Harding Fans - Trazling

Traci is also on:
Twitter: @tracharding
Instagram: traciharding_author
YouTube: youtube.com/c/TraciHardingChannel
& Redbubble: redbubble.com/people/traciharding/shop?asc=u

Books by Traci Harding

THE ANCIENT FUTURE TRILOGY
The Ancient Future: the Dark Age (1)
An Echo in Time: Atlantis (2)
Masters of Reality: the Gathering (3)

The Alchemist's Key

THE CELESTIAL TRIAD
Chronicle of Ages (1)
Tablet of Destinies (2)
The Cosmic Logos (3)

Ghostwriting

The Book of Dreams

THE MYSTIQUE TRILOGY
Gene of Isis (1)
The Dragon Queens (2)
The Black Madonna (3)

TRIAD OF BEING TRILOGY
Being of the Field (1)
The Universe Parallel (2)
The Light-field (3)

THE TIMEKEEPERS
Dreaming of Zhou Gong (1)
The Eternity Gate (2)
AWOL (3)

The Storyteller's Muse

To all the members of
Trazling and Traci Harding Fans FB Pages
and all my readers everywhere,
who have taken this journey with myself,
the Chosen and the Timekeepers.
Thank you for your encouragement, input,
promotional efforts and support
over the last nineteen years —
this one is for you!
ENJOY!

CONTENTS

LIST OF CHARACTERS

Ship: AMIE (Astro-Marine Institute Explorer)
Head of AMIE: Prof. Lucian Gervaise
Financial Director: Dr Taren Lennox
Lucian's Brother: Swithin Gervaise
Marine Biologist: Dr Amie Gervaise
AMIE Pilot: Zeven Gudren/Starman/Kale Tane/Bob
Zeven's Father: Mythric Zeon/Spyridon Vidor/BA Tane
Mythric's Wife: Princess Satomi (deceased)
Zeven's Wife: Aurora Gudrun
Zeven's Daughter: Thurraya Gudrun
Science Advisor: Telmo Dacre
Co-Pilot/Navigator: Leal Polson
Ship's Doctor: Kassa Madri
Botanist/Horticulturist: Ringbalin Malachi
Marine Botanist: Ayliscia Portus
Ex-Head of the MSS: Zelimir Ronan
Ronan's Son: Yaspar Ronan
Yaspar's Wife: Jazmay Cardea Ronan
Yaspar's Son: Fari Ronan 'the Thrice Strong'
Technician: Kalayna Zuri
Psychic Fugitive: Vadik Corentin/'the Hurricane'/Harry Cane
President of Sermetica: Jabez Anselm
AMIE's Nemisis: Khalid Mansur
Khalid's Father: Kaveh Ahura Mazida — Angra Mainyu
Dropa Master: Dorje Pema
Dowager Duchess: Maiara Vidor (deceased)
Custodian Vidor Manor: Trance Ducer
Phemorian Ruler: Qusay-Sabah Clarona

Phemorian Viceroy: Jalila Lamus
Jalila's Sister: Jafera Lamus
Qusay's Guard: The Valoureans
Head of the Valoureans: General Prochazka
Prochazka's Lieutenant: Sovee Puturi
Vault Guard: Captain Vishketah
Last Phemorian Prince: Chironjivi (disembodied)
First Phemorian Queen: Thurraya the Slayer (deceased)
Maladaan's President: Woodford Tallak
Ruler of Frujia: Chief Matan-tu-hoo
Rainbow Monkey: Karisha
The Being of the Field: Azazèl-mindos-coomra-dorchi

TIMEKEEPERS REINCARNATION GUIDE

AMIE	THE CHOSEN	GRIGORI	ZHOU	ANCIENT BRITAIN
TAREN	TORY	AZAZÈL (female)	JIANG HUDAN	TORY
LUCIAN	MAELGWN	AZAZÈL (male)	JI DAN	MAELGWN
ZEVEN	BRIAN	SAMMAEL (male)	JI SONG	BROCKWELL
AURORA	NAOMI	SAMMAEL (female)	HUI RU	KATREN
RINGBALIN	NOAH	ARMAROS (male)	FEN GONG	SELWYN
AYLISCIA	REBECCA	ARMAROS (female)	HE NUAN / LING HU	KAILEAH
TELMO		ARAQIEL (male)	YI WU	TALIESIN
KALAYNA		ARAQIEL (female)		
JAZMAY		GADRIEL (female)	JIANG HUXIN	
YASPER	JAHAN	GADRIEL (male)	JI SHI	URIEN
LEAL	FLOYD	SARIEL (male)	JIANG TAIGONG	TEIRNAN
KASSA	BO	SARIEL (female)		IONE
MYTHRIC	RHUN	PENEMUE (male)	JI FA	RHUN
SATOMI	SYBIL	PENEMUE (female)	YI JIANG	BRIDGIT
SWITHIN	DOC	BEZALIEL (male)		CARADOC
AMIE	VANORA	BEZALIEL (female)		VANORA
KHALID			WU GENG	
	AVERY	SACHA (male)		

PLANETS OF THE UNITED STAR SYSTEMS

Maladaan
Capital City: Esponisa
Ruler: President Woodford Tallak
Climate: Polluted
Landscape: Overdeveloped
High-rise modern cityscapes
Known as the technology capital of the USS

Frujia
Capital City: Kotan Bathaar
Ruler: Chief Matan-tu-hoo
Climate: Hot, tropical
Landscape: Scattered island archipelagos
Small tourist colonies
Known as the pleasure capital of the USS

Sermetica
Capital City: Heavensgate
Ruler: President Jabez Anselm
Climate: Controlled
Landscape: Desert, mineral-rich
Mobile-airborne cities in the clouds
Known as the mining capital of the USS
a.k.a. the Planet of Men

Phemoria
Capital City: Tonissia
Ruler: Queen Qusay-Sabah Clarona
Climate: Moderate
Landscape: Forest and ocean rich
Beautiful ancient cities, unspoilt by time
Known as the cultural capital of the USS
a.k.a. the Planet of Women

Oceane
Ethereal City: Karmandi
Ruler: Azazèl-mindos-coomra-dorchi
Climate: Wet and steamy
Landscape: Largely ocean and small rocky landmasses
Unknown to the USS

You owe me a life; I have to repay my debt to you.
From these causes and conditions
we pass through hundreds of thousands of aeons,
in a sustained cycle of birth and death.
You love my mind; I adore your form.
From these causes and conditions
we pass through hundreds of thousands of aeons,
in a sustained mutual entanglement.

\- Śūraṅgama Sūtra, Vol. 4

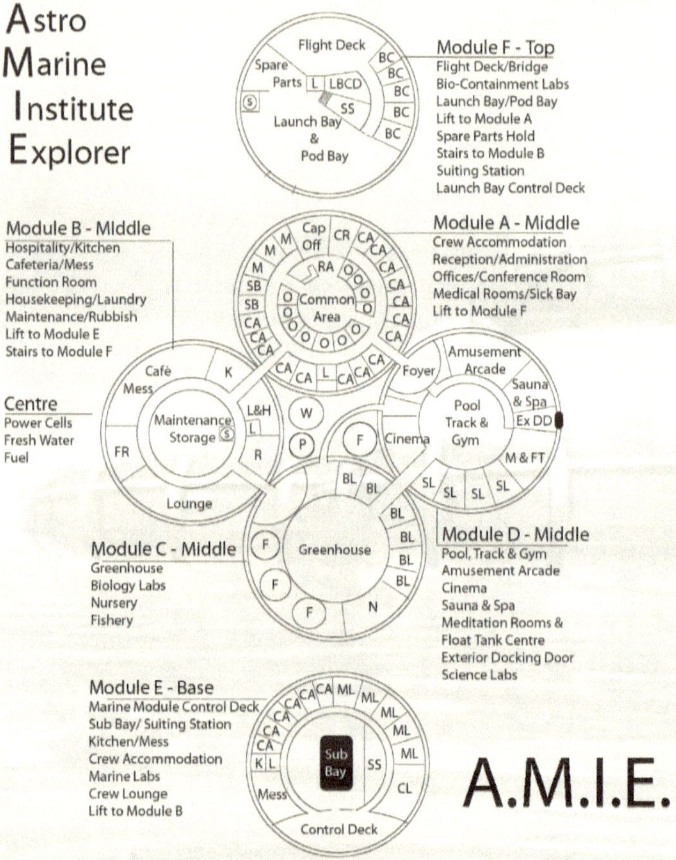
Astro
Marine
Institute
Explorer
Module F - Top
Flight Deck/Bridge
Bio-Containment Labs
Launch Bay/Pod Bay
Lift to Module A
Spare Parts Hold
Stairs to Module B
Suiting Station
Launch Bay Control Deck
Flight Deck
Spare Parts
L
LBCD
SS
BC
Launch Bay & Pod Bay
Module B - MIddle
Hospitality/Kitchen
Cafeteria/Mess
Function Room
Housekeeping/Laundry
Maintenance/Rubbish
Lift to Module E
Stairs to Module F
Module A - Middle
Crew Accommodation
Reception/Administration
Offices/Conference Room
Medical Rooms/Sick Bay
Lift to Module F
Cap Off
CR
RA
Common Area
Centre
Power Cells
Fresh Water
Fuel
Cafè
Mess
K
Maintenance Storage
L&H
FR
R
Lounge
W
P
F
Foyer
Amusement Arcade
Sauna & Spa
Pool Track & Gym
Ex DD
Cinema
M & FT
SL
BL
Greenhouse
N
Module C - Middle
Greenhouse
Biology Labs
Nursery
Fishery
Module D - Middle
Pool, Track & Gym
Amusement Arcade
Cinema
Sauna & Spa
Meditation Rooms &
Float Tank Centre
Exterior Docking Door
Science Labs
Module E - Base
Marine Module Control Deck
Sub Bay/ Suiting Station
Kitchen/Mess
Crew Accommodation
Marine Labs
Crew Lounge
Lift to Module B
Sub Bay
SS
ML
CL
Mess
Control Deck
A.M.I.E.

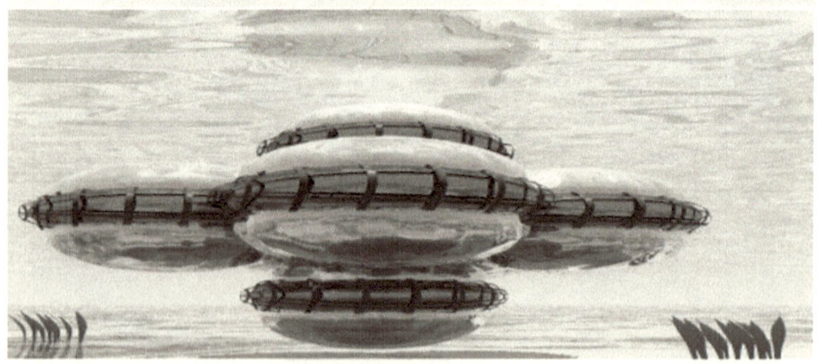

PROLOGUE

ABSENT WITHOUT OFFICIAL LEAVE

Mission Log — Day 1

What I have chosen to do is shocking. When I contemplate all I must negotiate in order to achieve the desired outcome, trepidation underpins every move I consider.

A timekeeping mission into the past of AMIE project, alone, and without the knowledge of the timekeeper and rest of the crew, is borderline insanity. I know this! Screw up, and I could drastically alter many of our past successes. The liberation of the Phemorian queen and her people from the curse of the Phemoray is a prime example of a major event that must remain unaltered. This mission resulted in three out of the four planets in the United Star Systems signing a 'psychic' bill of rights, freeing those with the Powers — like the crew of AMIE — from persecution. The time period in question will also see my parents reunited after decades in limbo, as my murdered mother is resurrected from the grave. I will see my own daughter sacrifice her life to free the souls of her tormented ancestors from a pit of despair on Phemoria. This most harrowing moment of my life I must also leave to play out as before, in the knowledge that her life will be restored by a fellow crew member.

This is where the AMIE project is unique.

Before the Astro Marine Institute Explorer launched — having secretly only recruited crew members with the Powers — psychics had never had the courage to admit to having a Power, or been given the opportunity to freely band together and use their talents for the greater good. Through our work, the bad reputation and widespread fear of those with the Powers is being turned around. Our services, always rendered in secret, are clearly beyond the scope of any other task force ever assembled, and as our identities are being shielded by the government leaders we serve, our PR is also handled by them. Hence, the evil stigma that has hung over those with the Powers since the sexual revolution on Phemoria will be all but swept away in three star systems.

The timekeepers have come to understand, via our adventures through time, universes and altered states of consciousness, that the material world is an illusion and hence there is no such thing as individualisation or personal achievement. Your actions are either to the detriment or benefit of the grand scheme, which has only one end game — make it back to source. If all are one, then service to all is the only means that will serve. Yet the greatest service anyone can perform for the good of all is mastery over the self — through which comes the realisation that there is no self.

Of all the timekeepers, I had the hardest time grasping this premise, and subsequently had my Powers revoked on several occasions until I shed all want of personal glory and was not a liability to my fellow timekeepers — or Zagriata, as we are known in this universe.

This sabbatical into the past I have embarked upon is not about me playing hero — not this time. Nor is this about me getting overly cocky due to my command successes on the timekeepers' most recent mission in the universe parallel. This lone manoeuvre is about minimising the risk to our timeline, whilst neutralising our biggest opposition to the event that the timekeepers first set out to prevent. This will be, for me, the second attempt the timekeepers have had at altering this event, and the third time I have actually lived through it. I have seen these circumstances play out, and I know what must be done to ensure our end goal. Of all the timekeepers, I am the only one who can complete this mission solo, and that is no boast.

It is a well known fact that I, and I alone, will destroy Khalid Mansur, our opposer in this event. This prophecy was spat forth by my grandmother the night I was born. The trouble is the man became a trusted ally and good friend of mine in the universe parallel. I vowed to him that I would not forsake him in that universe or this — where he is being controlled by an evil entity that attached itself to him on the night of his conception. Sadly, circumstances beyond my control prevented me from keeping my vow in the first part. He was killed and his recall of that adventure, and our friendship, wiped from his eternal memory. My recollection is perfectly intact, however. Here, in our rightful universe, I have an opportunity to make good on the latter part of my vow and completely defuse the circumstances surrounding the event the timekeepers ultimately seek to alter.

For those reasons I chose to return to this day, several years further back in the AMIE project history to where the rest of the timekeepers on our last mission will be uniting to debrief. It was agreed we would meet back in this universe one week before the event we meant to alter. I still intend to make that meeting, but by the time I do, it is my hope that we shall be facing a far more congenial situation than that we will face if I do not act.

On this day the Qusay-Sabah Clarona — Qusay being the Phemorian term for their queen — will have her curse lifted. Then my mother will rise from the grave, and the inter-system gateway to the Oceane system will re-open after eons in shut down. This is also the day that my nemesis from birth, Khalid Mansur, will escape the psychic security prison the timekeepers put him in five USS standard years ago.

This is the situation as it stands upon commencement of my quest. It is my intention that this log serve as an account of my actions to my fellow timekeepers in years to come — when they shall return to AMIE with their conscious recollection of our visit to the universe parallel intact. I trust it grants insight into why I chose to take absence without official leave, to run a mission that I was never assigned. But, to my reasoning, fate chose me for this task a long time ago. Causality will be my judge, and it is my soul intention to have her rule in our favour.

PART 1

DIVERGENCE

1

MACHINATIONS

It was bliss to awaken in his sleeping pod with his wife curled up behind him. It had been too long since he'd emerged from sleep to find himself in such a happy situation. Then the reason he felt this way dawned on him, and suddenly he was hyper-aware of being back on AMIE. If his will had been fulfilled he was now absent without official leave and was the only member of the crew who would remember anything of their last mission for several years. From this second forth he was changing history — the premise sent pangs of shock rocketing through his being. He held his breath, and mentally shook off the foggy hangover of his post-mission time-lag, as it always took a moment for the brain to process the shift in reality.

He was Zeven Gudrun, aka Starman, Kale Tane and Bob. His true birth name, which only a handful of people knew, was Zaman Vidor, of the royal House of Vidor on Sermetica. In the old Sermetic tongue his name translated to mean 'time warrior'. Taren Lennox, whose real name was Tymea Anselm, meaning 'time protector' according to the Phemorian tongue, was his cousin. Taren — the secret offspring of President Anselm of Sermetica and Qusay-Sabah Clarona, Queen of Phemoria — was *the* timekeeper, here to awaken all the *Zagriata* to their potential. But he was Taren's first recruit and oldest confidant, who had been time-hopping with her since the beginning. Zeven felt a little guilty; having made Taren vow that she would never jump time without him, here he was doing exactly that. Taren was going to be pissed at him when she found out — but then she'd never asked him to make that same vow.

I have a plan, Zeven assured himself. On the upside, he was back to being youthful and he appreciated that — having left an ageing body back in the universe parallel. *If I have landed where I willed, then all I did this morning was make love to my wife and take a shower; I can't really screw that up.* That fact helped Zeven breathe easier.

Aurora stirred behind him and gave a delighted moan, as her arm wrapped around him and her hand came to rest over his heart. 'Your heart is beating out of your chest! Feeling a bit amorous, are we?' She kissed the nape of his neck to let him know the feeling was mutual.

'Do we have anything on today?' he thought it the opportune time to query.

'Nothing until the mission brief this evening,' she peeked her head over his shoulder to advise with a grin. Her short, platinum blonde, shaggy hairdo was all messed up, there were traces of yesterday's make-up on her ivory skin and around her baby blues; but still, she was a sight for sore eyes.

'About the Phemorian problem,' Zeven supposed, trying to keep his mind in the game and confirm his landing date.

'Or stopping the inter-system gateway to Oceane being activated,' Aurora suggested. 'Only Taren knows, and we'll find out soon enough.' She kissed his cheek, and returned to snuggling him from behind.

Although the crew of AMIE had yet to discover it, the inter-system gateway had been brought back online two days ago by a couple of their future crew mates. Zeven had thought about returning to AMIE then, but he couldn't remember anything specific that happened on the morning of that day. Today was quite the opposite, and he was both relieved and horrified to discover that he'd landed right on target.

Most of this day was fairly uneventful, which gave him time to think and prepare. Such opportunity warranted taking immediate advantage of, yet, as Aurora's roving hand slid downwards towards his already aroused member, he felt equally obliged to stick to history's timetable in this instance.

As Aurora took a shower, Zeven grabbed his portable workstation and began a mission log for his own future defence. He also began noting down a list of things Taren had to know before he left and everyone started getting the wrong impression of him. It was best that no one knew the truth right now, but he wanted to give Taren at least an inkling.

'Are you *writing*?' Aurora sounded flabbergasted.

Zeven looked up to find she had emerged from the bathroom.

'I didn't think you knew there was a keyboard on your workstation!'

'Sure, I know about the keyboard.' Zeven hammed it up as he closed the device. 'I use it to play games all the time!'

'Ah.' Aurora was enlightened. 'Of course … I should have known.'

Zeven rose to kiss his wife, taking the workstation with him towards the shower.

'Why are you taking your workstation to the bathroom?' she queried.

'That's probably not the best idea.' Zeven played innocent and returned it to a desk — hopefully Aurora was not in an overly snoopy mood this morning. 'I'm in the middle of a level,' he thought to add, to discourage her meddling.

'I wouldn't *dream* of touching it,' she said, and headed into the wardrobe. 'Go, shower. I need to eat.'

'You don't have to wait for me,' he advised as he entered the wet room.

'I won't,' she assured.

She really wasn't fooling anybody. Aurora had trained in the secret service on Sermetica; of course she was going to investigate. But it wouldn't serve her, Zeven considered — hot water pelting down on him — as he'd activated the security access code function. She'd be waiting for him all right.

'Since when do you security code anything from me?' She stood, arms folded, waiting for him as he exited in a towel in search of clean clothes.

'Since you can't help but toy with my stuff,' he replied surely.

'I don't toy with your stuff!' she defended, whereupon Zeven turned from his trek to the wardrobe to serve her a cheeky grin.

'That stuff isn't security coded,' she rebuked his sidestep of the issue.

'That's right, you'll always have free access.' He winked.

'What are you up to?' Aurora's arms folded even tighter.

'I'm writing a book,' he replied.

Aurora was stunned and then burst into laughter.

'See!' he emphasised, faking disappointed. 'I knew you'd think it was stupid, so I didn't want to tell you until I was done.' It was only as the words were rolling from his tongue that Zeven realised what a truly talented bullshitter he was.

Aurora immediately backed off and appeared apologetic. 'I'm sorry.' She smothered her mirth. 'I don't think it's stupid … I'm just a little stunned is all. What brought this on?'

'Well, I've had more adventures than most,' he pointed out. 'And once psychics become more widely accepted, an account of how that came about might be a bestseller!'

Aurora smiled supportively, although a trace of scepticism still lingered in her frown. 'I can't argue with that reasoning … and I'd love to read it once you're done.' She wandered over and gave him a kiss of apology.

'When it's done,' Zeven stipulated and she nodded. 'Don't tell anyone,' he was quick to appeal.

'No,' Aurora agreed, holding her rumbling belly. 'I'll leave you to it.'

Zeven nodded and smiled in appreciation as Aurora departed.

'Okay.' He gathered his thoughts as he dressed and shoved some personal effects in a bag along with his workstation. 'Done.' He looked to his reflection in the mirror and took a moment to appreciate all he'd been through to deliver his consciousness back to this body.

Being shorter than most blokes didn't bother Zeven any more. He'd been fanatical about body building in his teens, but now he realised the body was only a vehicle — and an imaginary one at that; influence over reality lay entirely in one's intention. The soul that was a conduit to the mind had ultimately chosen the manifestation he was employing, and with good reason; what the vessel looked like mattered little. Still, he hadn't entirely shed his ego; he was still grateful that his vehicle was once again young, agile and good looking.

'You ready for this?' It was a rhetorical question, meant to strengthen his nerve, as now he was here, he really didn't have any choice but to follow through with his directive. Hence, he pulled out his communicator and put through a request for Taren to meet him in the pod bay.

'Why the pod bay?' Taren called out from the centre of the huge spacecraft hangar in Module F.

'Up here,' Zeven announced through the launch bay intercom, to draw her attention to where he was in the control deck.

Taren looked up to the command centre that overlooked the launch bay area, and with a questioning frown, proceeded to the stairs that led up there.

It was great to see Taren tromping about in her old body; he'd rather missed this personification of her. He may have been a married man, and Taren's cousin, but before he'd discovered this and wed his dream girl, he'd had a crush on Dr Lennox. As a half-caste Phemorian she was a stunning beauty — tall, slender, graceful — who had inherited her mother's exotic mauve-grey eyes and her commanding nature. Her long blonde hair was flying in the breeze as she strode towards the control deck stairs, although blonde was not her natural hair colour, she was a brunette, like both her parents. As much as Zeven had once hated to admit it, their relationship was more like siblings than lovers — and since he'd married Aurora he'd been happy to settle with being Taren's cousin.

'I've got a *wee* bit on my mind today.' Taren made her entrance. 'I really don't need one of your little dramas right now.'

Zeven was affronted. 'That's unfortunate.' He sat forward in his seat and held out a paper printout to her.

'What's this?' Taren impatiently took the note from him and read it aloud. '"On mission to Phemoria include Amie Gervaise in Anselm's escort." Why?' Taren looked to Zeven.

'Because you'll need her,' he advised, sitting back in his chair again. 'Keep reading.'

Taren's frown deepened as she looked back to the note. '"When Mythric retrieves the body of Satomi from Sermetica, he must take Swithin. Kassa Madri will go anyway, and it is very important that she does."'

Taren's expression was, as predicted, a little pissed. 'How do you know this will happen?'

'Keep reading,' he strongly suggested.

'"Kalayna and Telmo activated the inter-system gateway to the Oceane system, two days ago—"' Taren gasped and looked to him, but Zeven merely redirected her back to his missive. '"They are about to be exposed by the Maladaan Secret Service, you need to get them out."' Her words trailed off and Taren was apparently too stunned by the implications to be furious.

'Today is the last day they are going to be alone in that station,' he explained. 'By nightfall, ships will be lining up to enter the Oceane system, and the last thing we need is anyone from Maladaan discovering Oceane and the mysterious gaseous energy there.'

AMIE's discovery of this 'gaseous energy', which proved to be more of an 'entity', was exactly what had started this entire inter-universal, time-hopping crusade. This entity was a very powerful evolutionary architect, working its magic on the virgin planet Oceane — named thus as it was primarily an ocean planet. But beneath where the gaseous entity was concentrated, plant life had taken root in the muddy stone terrain. AMIE had taken a sample of this gas, unaware that even separated from its mass the portion was energetically joined to its source. Initial tests on the sample indicated that just this small amount of the gas had an unlimited potential to generate power — but this observation proved false, for the sample was simply draining power from its original mass. This was discovered too late to prevent part of their sample being stolen and transported back to Maladaan. When the huge entity detached itself from Oceane and shifted universes to tend its next assignment, it dragged with it anything attached to itself — the entire planet of Maladaan had vanished from this universe. This disaster had been reworked by the timekeepers and prevented; their arch nemesis had been dragged into the universe parallel instead. Thus began their last mission criss-crossing universes, which Zeven had only just completed.

'Either you've become a prophet, or you've pulled a time-shift without me,' Taren surmised.

Zeven winced. 'I'm not a prophet.'

But Taren was not amused. 'We promised —'

'No, *you* promised.' Zeven was quick to stomp on that protest. 'One week before D-day, your memory of our last mission will return and then you'll know why I am doing this.'

'Our last mission was to rescue my father from Khalid, five years ago!' She wasn't following.

Zeven shook his head. 'We went back to the universe parallel to warn Rhun about the threat to Kila, just like you promised him you would.'

'I've already done that?' Taren was boggled.

'It turned out to be a little more complicated than previously thought,' he appraised. 'But in the end, yes.' Zeven served her a friendly wink. 'You can cross that wish off your bucket list.'

Clearly, Taren wasn't sure if she should be sceptical, joyful, or angry. 'Is this why I sent you back?' She referred to the note in her hand.

'No,' he admitted. 'Those notes are just to cover what role I played in those events, so I can be otherwise detained.'

'Doing what, *exactly*?'

'I can't say.' He stood. 'But I know you trust me. And if you don't, well … you'll figure it out soon enough.'

'Figure what out?' Taren grabbed his arm to prevent him using his psychic ability to teleport himself anywhere without her. 'Oh!' Zeven clicked his fingers as he recollected. 'Another thing. Get a big piece of Juju into the centre of AMIE; Khalid knows what the interior looks like. A long time before you recruited her, Amie Gervaise sent him the fly-through graphic that Lucian made when he was first selling the project. And we stuck to that design —'

'But Khalid is locked up in a psychic prison.' Taren was sounding increasingly more alarmed.

'Just saying.' Zeven shrugged. 'It would be a good precaution.'

'Anything else?' Taren asked, indignant.

'Not, *under any circumstances*, should you or anyone from AMIE come after me.' He reached up under his left sleeve and removed the armband that contained the Juju stone of protection that all the timekeepers wore.

Taren was immediately panicked by the gesture, for the Juju stone prevented the timekeepers being found by other psychics. The amulet was infused with the essence of their soul source, which guided them via intuitive means and prevented them from being identified by the MSS photon camera.

This camera was an evil piece of technology used to identify psychics on the one planet that still held them in contempt. Sadly, the condemning camera had been devised by using stolen blueprints of one of Taren's inventions, a device that measured the photon count of all living things.

'What are you doing?' Taren lost her official tone and let Zeven go as he placed his protective amulet in her hand.

'Mind it for me,' Zeven suggested. 'Where I am going, I won't need it.'

'Are you going to Oceane?' Taren quizzed, knowing that was the only other safe place where a timekeeper could hide without a Juju stone, as that was where the stones had originated from.

'A good guess,' he awarded. 'But no.'

'Where then?'

'It's not important.'

'Zeven?' Her tone demanded an answer.

He was not thrilled about disobeying his timekeeper. 'You know how much this project and the timekeepers mean to me. I would never do anything that would jeopardise what you've built here.'

'Of course I know that, without question,' Taren agreed. 'But … how long will you be gone? What am I to tell the rest of the crew … your wife?'

'Tell them the truth.'

'That you've gone AWOL, and I have no idea why?' Taren was clearly frustrated.

Zeven screwed up his nose and considered. 'If you are going to stop anyone coming after me, you'd better lie.'

'I am always lying for you!' Taren threw her hands up in frustration; and it was true, she had been forced to cover for him quite a few times in their long association, especially where her husband — the captain of the AMIE vessel — was concerned.

'Well, that's because I'm always risking my arse for you and this project!' he reminded her.

Taren ceased protesting and rethought her approach. 'Why can't you just tell me?'

'Because you have to focus on that list!' He clutched the hand in which Taren held the printout. 'All of this is just as important, and is going to make for one hell of a long work day, especially without me to assist. What I have to do cannot wait, and will take some of the heat off all of this.' He let her go. 'Are we clear?'

Taren, still perturbed, nodded.

'Wish me luck then?'

'Since when do you need it?' She held her perturbed mood, and folded her arms, not wanting to condone his stance.

'Okay then.' He picked up a bag containing his personal workstation, and other personal effects. 'Just remember whose side I am on.' He closed his eyes to focus on teleporting himself elsewhere.

'Take care of yourself, Starman.'

The genuine concern in Taren's voice was reassuring — she was on-side, for now. It was too late to respond, as his physical form was already shifting location to his desired target area, hundreds and thousands of light-years away, on Sermetica.

2

GRAN MAI'S LIBRARY

The family library in the House of Vidor was very grand to Zeven's mind. How many words were contained within this huge double storey room? Not that he really cared to find out; he'd never been much of a scholar when it came to anything that wasn't vehicle or weapon related.

Bookshelves rose from the floor on three walls, through a mezzanine level and all the way to the roof of the second storey. In addition, tall bookcases ran the length of the room to form several aisles. On the only wall that was not paved in books were tall, slender feature windows in intervals, in front of which were lounges or desks. To one end of the massive room, where you entered, were other lounges and study desks that were out of the direct sunlight. Zeven stood amidst these, admiring a huge tiled mosaic inset in the polished stone floor. This depicted a feather quill crossed by a sword — the insignia of the Sermetic royal Houses of Anselm and Vidor.

Zeven knew very little of his heritage — being born into the royal lines of this nation was a precarious affair. The royal families of Sermetica were refugees of the psychic uprising on Phemoria that had struck the fear of Powers into the USS for hundreds of years. A report of a supernatural spirit force protecting the queens of Phemoria arose shortly after the female rebellion there had seen every male Phemorian banished to Sermetica. This unnatural force was known as the Phemoray and their advent served to cast a shadow of doubt over speculation that psychic power was inherent in the Sermetic royal line. The royals of Sermetica had, of course, denied this supposition fervently, insisting that the Phemoray were the sole source of the Phemorians' supernatural power. Still, it was widely suspected that the Sermetic royal lines were merely hiding their psychic potential, which indeed they were. Many Sermetic royals had resorted to placing their children in foster homes and disguising their identities for their own safety. Zeven and Taren had been two such children. As the first offspring of Sermetic and Phemorian inter-breeding for centuries, they were more pure blood than most royal progeny who, only decades ago, would have been considered a threat to humanity and thus hunted and restrained. Zeven was glad not to be entirely ignorant of who he really was any more, but like his father he was in no hurry to come out of hiding, not even for so great an inheritance as he was standing in at present. They had found a better way to serve their people and their deeds had seen psychic ill will lax on Phemoria, Sermetica and Frujia. These three planets would soon unite to protect those with the Powers; all Zeven had to do was not screw up.

It was morning here in Heavensgate, the capital of Sermetica, which was one of many floating cities that hovered high above the desert wasteland of the mining planet, where temperatures were cooler. Skylights in the ceiling allowed additional natural light into the library, through which Zeven now wandered, turning circles as he went. On one of the desks between windows, he spotted a workstation that was a relic from before he was born!

'Get with the times, Gran!' He noted there was no other technology to be seen — all this money and the House of Vidor didn't even have a decent workstation! 'Just an index file of some description would be helpful.' Maybe that's what the old system was for? 'It'll probably take ten hours to boot up!' Zeven exaggerated, turning his attention back to the bookshelves to his other side. 'How do I find one little prophecy among this lot?'

He'd never seen the document in question, so he couldn't just make it appear, or will himself to it; in fact, the truth was he didn't even know if the prophecy in question had actually ever been put to paper. Zeven desired to check the exact wording of the prophecy — as any such claim was open to interpretation. What he did know was what the prophecy was about, and maybe that was enough to see his psychic intent fulfilled?

'The prophecy of Zaman Vidor!' Zeven held out a hand in command, expecting the text in question to speed from its location and into his grasp; unfortunately that wish did not manifest. 'So does that mean I lack the power to locate it, or does that mean it does not exist?' He gave a heavy sigh as he considered, but a thud at the far end of the room drew his attention — he suspected a book had fallen from a shelf. Yet, as he moved to investigate, the sound repeated again and again.

Beyond the long aisles, at the far end of the library, there was an open cavity in the wall of books. In this annex was a heavyset door and from behind this, the thudding sound persisted, like something continually ramming against the inside in an attempt to break through. The door had security coded locks, which Zeven overrode with his psychokinesis, otherwise known as PK — the lock clicked off, the door slid aside and out flew a large volume that Zeven was quick to catch with both hands.

'Holy crap, Gran Mai!' Zeven grumbled upon impact; he'd not expected the text to be so heavy. Closer inspection revealed this was more a coffer than a book. The item had its own security measures — several spinning numerical locks, attached to an ornate metal device that wound around the treasure box like an impenetrable prison.

'I should have expected nothing less from my great-gran.'

The Duchess Maiara Vidor had been precognitive, as Taren was, and thus saw everything coming, perhaps even this event now transpiring five years after her death? The grand old dame was also a prophetess.

Prophecy differed from precognition in that the oracle slipped into a trance state, and instead of seeing glimpses of the future which could be recalled afterward, would begin spouting prophecy, none of which would be recalled by the oracle after the event.

Someone must have been with Maiara when she had made the prophecy about her grandson, or otherwise no one would have known about it, not even Maiara.

Zeven's hope was that it had been recorded word for word for posterity. For as much as Zeven respected his grandmother's great gifts, he had a hunch that she had misinterpreted her own prophecy in this instance. For he knew things about their nemesis that his grandmother did not. Maiara had raised Khalid through his formative years, suspecting there was something not quite right about the child, and even when his treachery was apparent, she had been hesitant to believe he was to blame. Maybe she'd had an inkling of what Zeven now knew to be true?

The words embossed in the lid of the coffer were in the old Sermetic tongue, which Zeven had never learned. But what he had discovered during his last mission was that the soul mind to which all the timekeepers were connected granted them the ability to understand all languages — at least it had in the two universes they'd inhabited before this. So rather than blow off the inscription as something incomprehensible, Zeven carried the weighty coffer over to a table where he could set it down and study it more closely.

As he read the words, '*Asa fide Vidor es minto gesta nata ciphis*,' in his mind, the content was decrypted into his own modern dialect and he knew the meaning. '*Any true descendant of mine needs no code.*' Zeven had a chuckle at his grandmother's reasoning. 'Too true.'

With a wave of his hand over the mechanism Zeven set the locks spinning, whereupon each stopped at a different glyph and released its ornately fashioned metal arms. The bindings coiled away into the coffer casing — like twisting vines being dragged from a tree — and the coffer opened by itself.

Inside was a memory card, which being over twenty years old was no longer in use and would not connect to his workstation. 'Damn! Hang on … Maiara is not behind the times, she is always ahead!' He grabbed the card and headed back to the old workstation he'd spotted earlier.

Once booted up, which took but a few minutes, the memory card slotted perfectly into the side. To Zeven's great excitement, the content was not a text file filled with ancient Sermetic for him to decipher, but a movie file.

'Someone actually recorded the event?'

It was too much to hope for. But upon opening the file his pessimism proved unfounded. The footage opened on the Duchess of Vidor floating several feet above her covers, whilst her maid servants struggled to tie her down to the bed.

'Are you getting this?' one of the maidens queried to camera.

'Yes,' replied the person operating the camera. A woman, judging from the voice.

'Blood!' Maiara cried out, deep in trance. 'Blood on the hands of the Old Ones, to whom the halfling of shadow harks back!' She spat the words out as if possessed. 'Not they, nor the Phemoray, foresaw the curse upon their union.'

She spoke of Khalid — he was the halfling of shadow.

'Hungry demons have an adult patron,' Maiara warned. 'Sermetica and Phemoria have a male heir; a second halfling of transcendental means — the polarity to the curse!'

In the first part of this quatrain Maiara spoke of demons — the unnatural source of Khalid's power to be found at Dead Man Downs on Sermetica. In the second part, she spoke of the event that was unfolding at the very time that she was voicing this prophecy — Zeven's birth. The son of her grandson, Spyridon Vidor, and the Princess Satomi, first daughter of the late Qusay of Phemoria. Satomi had taken flight from her home planet before the cursed crown of the Phemoray was placed upon her head and had spent the rest of her short life in hiding.

'When first they collide, blood pools in the House of Vidor. Victim and victor endure, to meet again, not so by chance.'

Here Maiara spoke of the night Khalid came after Zeven as a babe, having got wind of the prophecy. The Princess Satomi was murdered and a blade was driven through Zeven's infant body while his father lay unconscious. But Zeven had survived, thanks to Maiara, who, at her old age, had managed to summon the power to teleport herself to Zeven's crib and teleport him to the aid of a healing child she knew. This healing child was now one of Zeven's closest friends, Ringbalin Malachi, whom he'd met again through the AMIE project. In the last part of this quatrain, Maiara hinted that Zeven and Khalid's next meeting would be a well planned affair. 'And so it is,' Zeven confirmed with a confident grin.

'Time dances through shadows, to know even what the Old Ones could not. Then the victim will be victor, returning the curse to the abyss!' Maiara calmed, and floated gently downwards towards her bed.

The maid servant in charge turned to the camera. 'That will be all,' she instructed, and the image froze.

This was where Zeven felt everyone had misinterpreted the prophecy. For they all considered Khalid himself was the curse. Yet first-hand experience told Zeven that once Khalid was cut off from the influence of the unnatural entity at Dead Man Downs he had the potential to be as righteous as any of the timekeepers. Although Khalid had been counted among their ranks for a while on the last mission, he did not belong to their soul-group, and yet he possessed the same talents as the best of the timekeepers. Which posed the question — where did Khalid belong? Who were his soul kin — the Old Ones Maiara mentioned in the first quatrain? Maiara spoke of time dancing through shadows, referring to Zeven's timekeeping adventures, but where she spoke of the victim becoming the victor and returning the curse to the abyss, Zeven felt this could just as easily refer to Khalid as himself, who had equally been a victim since before he was born.

'Zaman Vidor.'

The sound of his true name being spoken struck the fear of exposure in his heart, and he turned about to find a beautiful middle-aged woman with a pulse laser weapon aimed at him. A stone, set on a chain that hung around her neck, was glowing with brilliance.

'There are only three men alive who could have retrieved that coffer: Khalid Mansur, Spyridon Vidor, and his long-lost son, Zaman,' she informed him. 'I have met the first two candidates, so it stands to reason that you are the third.'

'The lock on the coffer triggered a silent alarm.' Zeven figured that's how she had discovered his presence.

'Of course,' she confirmed, her fingers toying with the glowing jewel she wore.

'And if I am who you think I am?' Zeven queried.

'Then you get to leave this room alive,' she advised sweetly.

'Hold on.' Zeven looked back to the image frozen on his workstation. The woman before him was the same woman aiding to hold the duchess down as she spouted her prophecy.

'You were there!' He looked to the woman, excited by the prospect of some help with his queries. 'Do you know anything about the Old Ones that Gran Mai speaks of in the first quatrain of this recording?' Zeven posed.

The woman suddenly seemed disposed towards him. 'Gran Mai,' she repeated the part that had captured her sentiment. 'That was the name Spyridon called my mistress; you have had contact with your father?'

'Maiara knew that we'd found each other?' Zeven became suspicious.

'Family secrets stay in the family, and I am not family,' she replied. 'Only a humble servant of this house, here to see that my lady's legacy is delivered into the right hands.'

'Then help me solve this riddle,' he requested politely. 'Where do I seek information about the Old Ones?'

'What difference does it make, when your objective is clear?' Obviously she wondered at the point of researching the history of the man he was expected to kill.

'You've never heard the phrase, know your enemy?' he posed. 'There must be something written about the Old Ones in all of this?' He referred to the treasure trove of books all around them.

The woman shook her head. 'If the Old Ones still exist somewhere, and if one of them did mate with the Qusay of Phemoria, then only the Phemorians know how to make contact, or have any record of who the father of the curse was.'

'No,' Zeven corrected. 'The Qusay's chosen mate had no more to do with this curse than the late, mad Queen of Phemoria did herself.'

The woman frowned, having misunderstood the prophecy like so many others. 'Are you here to rid the House of Vidor of the curse that is Khalid Mansur?' she asked him outright. 'He who killed your royal mother and my duchess. He who destroyed your father's sanity and reputation, and attempted to take your own life as a babe!'

All touchy subjects with Zeven, but he chose to overlook the recount of his life's most tragic events. 'I have been from one end of time to the other, in order to know how this curse might be broken,' he began, hoping to reassure her. 'Rest assured that I will see my late grandmother's word made fact. The curse will be returned to the abyss from which it came.' What Zeven didn't mention was that he had no intention of banishing Khalid with it.

'Then my job is done.' The woman seemed, for some reason, trepidatious.

'It would seem so.' Zeven turned to retrieve the vital memory card from the old system and placed it in a zip pocket of his jacket, realising that perhaps the woman's fear came from thinking he would now kill her to ensure she did not give away his identity to anyone. Thus he held both his hands high before he turned to face her again. 'Don't worry, I would never —'

The laser gun firing startled Zeven. He swung about to see his grandmother's messenger fall to the ground, a bloodied hole in both sides of her head where the laser bullet from her own weapon had burned right through.

'Damn it! I should have seen that coming.' He was still adapting to his royal status of importance; he was used to being a nobody, and had worked hard at that after his career as a show-off, smart arse, crash test dummy, had proven not very conducive to keeping a low profile. He hated that anyone would feel their own life was less important than his, and the suicidal precaution was unnecessary in any case as he was more than capable of defending himself. With a flick of his finger he closed the coffer and returned it to its place inside the room and the door locked closed in the wake of the treasure's passage.

'What a waste.' He eyed over the dead woman. This was one of those instances that he wished he could go back in time and prevent, but too much of the day had already passed to go back to this morning and start again. A myriad of things could go wrong if he attempted to rework every instance since he awoke, so he was bound to stay his course. One of the few setbacks of time-hopping was that you could only jump into a body during its last unconscious state prior to your target day. And the more you tried to rework one instance in time, the messier causality became, the harder you had to work to make circumstances turn out to your favour.

Zeven had hoped to pause and take stock here, but with a dead body on the floor, here was not the place to pause and reflect.

He took up his bag and wandered to the foreign section under non-fiction, and browsed the titles.

'*The remote islands of Frujia,*' he read the title that captured his interest. The cover photo was of a beautiful uninhabited island close to the isle of Lappis. 'That will do nicely.' He observed the picture of the island paradise and held that image in his mind as he replaced the book.

Zeven could teleport anywhere once he had knowledge of what a place or a person looked like, and this was true of anyone with PK. All the timekeepers would eventually master this talent, although only a handful of them had learned to do so at present.

Frujia was the pleasure capital of the USS; everyone wanted to go there as the planet was kept in pristine condition, and a large part of the planet was a protected preserve, no residency allowed. Which made that part of the planet the perfect place for a psychic fugitive like himself to hang out.

The destination Zeven had glimpsed filled his thoughts, and with his will to be there, his atomic structure was excited into a higher quantum state being and swept away through the light-field to its intended destination.

AN ACCOMPLICE

The crew of AMIE were called to a meeting much earlier in the working day than expected. There were a few additional notes Zeven had made on the printout he'd given Taren, but she felt she needed to confirm the information before advising those involved.

One such claim was that Telmo Decree, whom they were about to recruit to the crew, was the brother of one of AMIE's security staff, Yasper Ronan, which meant Telmo was also the long-lost son of Zelimir Ronan, the ex-chief of the MSS. As head of the Maladaan Secret Service, Zelimir had once been fiercely anti-psychic, and had admitted to banishing his wife and unborn second child to life on Sermetica after he discovered that she had been hiding her Powers from him. Zelimir had placed them in the protection of President Anselm of Sermetica — Taren's father. Zeven claimed in his missive that her father could confirm this. This puzzled Taren, as she had spoken to her father about Telmo before, and he'd claimed to have no knowledge of the man.

Another side note Zeven had made about Telmo was that Taren's kiss would awaken the latent Power of his akashic memory. This lad had the ability to tap into all his past selves, one of whom had been the spiritual master, Taliesin Pen Beirdd, in the last universe, who had been a mentor to many of them during their past lives there. They had learned from experience that, because of the power of the Juju stone they all wore, a simple kiss, given to anyone of their soul-group, would activate their psychic gifts. But then that was true of anyone who wore a Juju, not just Taren. As a happily married woman who did not wish to give her husband the wrong impression, she had no intention of fulfilling this prediction, but she would certainly bear it in mind.

Besides herself, and with Zeven absent, there were fourteen people on board AMIE at present; twelve discounting the two children who were currently doing school lessons via visual correspondence in the office area. If Zeven's predictions proved correct they would acquire another three crew members within the next working day.

'What's the story?' Swithin appealed as he wandered in with his wife, Amie — head of their marine department.

Amie was an impressionist, meaning that she could implant thoughts and memories into the minds of others and alter their recollections. Swithin Gervaise, the older brother of their captain, was the money man behind AMIE, who in younger days had been rather self-serving. Ironically he'd developed the one psychic gift that could only benefit others — his touch brought back the dead. Zeven had named both these crew members as vital to a mission this day; and they had three missions to complete by her reckoning, only two of which she need mention at this time.

'Something's come up,' Taren told Swithin, not prepared to say more until everyone had gathered in the mess room — which had proven a better place to have mission briefs than the conference room as all food and beverages were close at hand. The mess was a rather expansive space as AMIE had originally been designed with a large crew in mind, but it was their aim to see the true purpose of the Astro-Marine Institute Explorer realised in the not too distant future.

'Always does,' Swithin grumbled, heading for the drink dispenser.

'I'm here,' Aurora announced as she breezed through the door. 'But I can't find Zeven anywhere! Do you want me to use my —' she pointed to her temple.

Aurora was referring to her Power. No one was permitted to use their psychic gifts on another crew member without permission from the timekeeper or the captain. Aurora's skill was remote viewing; this meant that in her mind's eye she could find any target and see where they were and what they were doing.

This would not bode well for keeping Zeven's movements secret, and as much as Taren was curious to know what Zeven was up to, she had promised to leave him go and so shook her head. 'Zeven has his own mission today, and will not be joining us.'

Aurora frowned, perplexed to learn this, but did not question it.

'You mean to say Zeven is forgoing our first mission in space?' Mythric, Zeven's father, was certainly surprised. 'That doesn't sound like the thrill-seeking, spotlight-hogging lad I bred?'

'If Zeven's gone on a mission,' Leal, Zeven's co-pilot and crew telepathist, followed Mythric into the mess, 'then technically he's already *on* our first mission in space.'

Mythric raised both brows and stood corrected. 'That's true to form then.'

'I thought this was a day off?' Jazmay, head of security, and her husband Yasper entered.

Jazmay was a former Valourean — the Valoureans were the personal guard of the Qusay of Phemoria. The most feared warriors in the USS, Valoureans exploited their psychic power to protect their queen and planet, and had done so ever since the sexual revolution. Jazmay was also the only shapeshifter on the crew, and she could transform herself into just about anything she came into contact with. Due to the fact she had been in contact with the timekeeper, she had also inherited all her powers and a lot of Taren's memory. Yasper, whose Power was levitation, was ex MSS, and Taren's ex as well; they had had a brief fling way back during Taren's early years in the secret service.

'For many of you it is still a day off,' Taren advised. 'At this point,' she added under her breath.

Ringbalin their biologist who ran Module C — the greenhouse on AMIE — was accompanied into the room by Dr Ayliscia Portus, their marine biologist. They were both fairly quiet types, who merely waved as they entered, and headed to the food bar.

The two biologists had become fast friends since joining AMIE, and this was no surprise to Taren as in a past timeline they'd been star-crossed lovers and the regular odd couple.

Ayliscia was Phemorian, like Jazmay, but as a secret service agent she had been sent on board this vessel to spy on Taren and the project by the Phemoray. Still, as Taren had known this from previous timelines, she had recruited Ayliscia to the timekeepers, long before Dr Portus had time to do their project any damage, and her loyalties now lay with AMIE. Ayliscia and Jazmay were two people, in only a handful, who knew that Taren was the daughter of Qusay-Sabah Clarona and thus the heir to the Phemorian throne. As Phemorians they felt they would rather protect the heir apparent than their possessed queen and her spiteful Phemoray. Ayliscia was a remote viewer, as Aurora was, and had the stunning good looks and formidable warrior form and nature shared by all Phemorian women.

In comparison to his fellow biologist, Ringbalin was rather effeminate and diminutive in stature; he was usually attired in overalls and covered in dirt. His shoulder length fair, straight hair was kept pulled back in a ponytail when he was working, but strands were always escaping and falling in his face. More boyish in appearance than manly, Ringbalin was also a good deal younger than the woman who'd taken a fancy to him. Phemorian women had a reputation for hating men, but Ringbalin had such a gentle way about him that everybody liked him; in fact, Taren ventured to say he was the most loved crew member on board AMIE — despite that he kept very much to himself. The fact that Ringbalin ran Module C and supplied them all with excellent fresh produce was only part of his appeal. An emotional sympathetic, Ringbalin could project his emotions onto others; he could heal or kill anything in his vicinity depending on his mood. Hence Ringbalin endeavoured to be happy, humble, grateful and positive at all times, and as long as he was, his greenhouse prospered.

The captain entered the mess and had a brief look around. 'Who's still missing?'

'The doc isn't here,' Leal waylaid pouring his coffee to advise Lucian.

It figured that Leal noticed her absence, for AMIE's doctor was Kassa Madri — their second telepath — who their co-pilot had been instantly intrigued with upon first meeting. Again much younger than the woman he admired, both he and Kassa had been excited to meet another telepath and although neither of them may have realised it yet, their attraction was inevitable.

'My father's not here,' Yasper observed.

Lucian backed up into the corridor to look for the stragglers. 'Here they are,' he advised upon spotting them, whereupon he finally entered the mess and approached his wife, kissing her. 'Good morning,' he said after. 'Where did you disappear to so early?'

'I had to see Zeven about an errand,' she answered.

'Anything I should know about?'

Taren shook her head. 'We have more pressing matters that you should definitely know about.' She noted Kassa and Zelimir had joined the rest of the crew, who were clustered around the group of tables closest to the servery.

Zelimir had joined the ranks of the chosen after he was arrested by the organisation he'd been heading for over half a century. After being so anti-psychic and banishing his wife and unborn child to another planet, the ex-chief of the MSS had discovered he had a Power himself — he saw auras. Zelimir's wife had died giving birth, and so he had never seen her again, nor the child he abandoned.

Today, if Zeven's intel proved correct, Zelimir and Yasper Ronan were about to get their lost family member back.

However, if Zeven had made a time-jump without her — and he'd pretty much confessed to doing just that — then they were already changing the course of events. Since meeting with him this morning, Taren's plan of attack had changed; she had to trust Zeven knew what he was doing, for she was now his willing accomplice.

Before Taren had left the universe parallel to come back in time to save AMIE and Maladaan, she had made a list with Lucian of goals they needed to achieve. There were eight items on that list.

1. Stop AMIE taking the sample from Oceane
2. Wake Lucian up to Amie and Swithin (completed)
3. Lift mother's curse
4. Reunite Taren's parents
5. Expose Khalid (completed)
6. Free Jazmay and Fari (completed)
7. <u>Return to Kila to warn Rhun about the Orions (?)</u>
8. Save Yasper (completed)

Since returning to the past Taren had managed to achieve half of her objectives — over half, if Zeven's claim that they had already returned to Kila to warn Rhun was true. Number 1 on her agenda could only be achieved with the fullness of time, so items 3 and 4 were a very high priority. One could even say that AMIE's first mission had been decided long before the vessel had ever been built. To rid her mother, the Qusay of Phemoria, from the curse of the Phemoray, and hopefully get her two estranged parents to start speaking with one another, on a diplomatic level at least, had been top priority — until her chat with Zeven this morning. Now there was another goal to add to her list.

Retrieve Telmo and Kalayna — get them to shut down the inter-system gateway they fixed, before anyone, including the MSS, come through and arrest them.

This goal was now priority number one, and fortunately the timekeepers had some time to spare before needing to report to President Anselm for their mission this evening.

'So, we are gathered here today to …?' Yasper posed to prompt Taren to be out with it.

'To be briefed on tonight's mission,' she advised. 'I have an errand I have to run myself before we leave, so in case I get held up, I thought it best to bump this meeting forward.'

'So what is our first mission to be?' Leal was curious, as he'd only just signed up to the crew, and only knew snippets of the full agenda.

'Anselm has, after four years of negotiating and pleading for a meeting, finally persuaded the Qusay of Phemoria to grant him an audience, and we shall be his guard,' Taren informed.

'I really need to speak with Anselm.' Yasper was predictably eager. 'Only he knows where my long-lost sibling is. They might be in this very room and I would be none the wiser.' He made light of his dilemma, but for his father, Zelimir, it was a gentle ribbing.

'I know you've not forgiven me,' Zelimir granted, 'but Anselm will not have let me down.'

'I can't believe you never even bothered to find out if you'd fathered a boy or a girl,' Yasper said, though without angst; his father was a very different man these days.

'Absolutely, Yasper, you are on the team,' Taren confirmed to end the affront. 'There's a good chance we'll need you to create a bit of an airborne diversion for the Phemoray.'

Yasper looked a little wary about that premise.

The only crew who were originally involved in the de-crowning of the Queen of Phemoria were Lucian and Ringbalin, both of whom were essential to this mission. They needed Lucian's etheric sight to keep tabs on what the angry female thought form guarding the crown of Phemoria was doing during their visit. They needed Ringbalin's ability to influence the moods and emotions of others to keep the Qusay's Valourean guard in good spirits.

'I have to be touching someone to pacify them.' Ringbalin was panicking upon learning this. 'I cannot do it en masse!'

Taren knew that in the future Ringbalin would learn to, but during the instance in question his talent had been no more developed than it was now.

'That didn't matter the last time we went through this.' Lucian wanted to reassure him. 'You still had hardened Valoureans pleading to their queen to spare your life!'

Ringbalin was very embarrassed by the claim, yet concerned also. 'Why was I in trouble with the Phemorian Qusay?'

The captain paused.

'The Qusay of Phemoria tried to kidnap me and wasn't happy when Lucian protested,' Taren jumped in to spare explaining to Ringbalin about a love affair that was yet to happen for him, and its tragic end — which would hopefully never eventuate. 'Of course you sided with Lucian and …' She shrugged in conclusion.

Ringbalin was looking at Taren sideways, as though he sensed he was not getting the whole truth. 'Well, if you need me, I am at your service.'

'We're also going to need a telepath.' Taren looked to Leal and Kassa.

'I'll go,' Leal didn't hesitate.

'Hey,' Kassa was offended. 'The Phemorians are more disposed towards women than men, so … I should go.'

'I don't need their permission to read their minds,' Leal bantered with a grin.

'Neither do I,' she challenged, grinning back.

'I can't risk injury to our doctor.' Lucian called it. 'Leal is trained for this kind of thing.'

'Oooh,' Kassa protested, with a big pout.

'Not to worry,' Taren assured the doctor. 'Your chance is coming.' According to Zeven's list, Kassa would run her first mission before the day was out.

'I am coming,' Jazmay assumed. She was Phemorian and Taren's unofficial bodyguard.

'Of course.' Taren felt that went without saying. 'I'll also be needing Amie.'

'Really?' Amie was surprised to be included. 'What do you need me for?'

'I have no idea,' Taren answered honestly — Zeven had called this one. 'But I guess we'll find out.'

'Okay.' Amie was pleased to agree, despite Taren's vague reasoning.

'Mythric?' Taren looked to him. 'I gather you and Satomi might like to come along?'

The Princess Satomi may have been dead, but her ghost was usually to be found in her husband's vicinity somewhere. Thanks to the captain's talent for seeing the disembodied, they had been enlightened to her presence. In life, Satomi had been searching for a means to spare her younger sister from the curse that was attached to the crown of Phemoria — today she would finally see her efforts realised.

'Definitely,' Mythric spoke for her.

'Satomi is giving that the big nod,' Lucian confirmed Mythric's gut instinct.

'The Phemorians are going to be more on guard than they were last time around,' Taren advised. 'Anselm is the man the Qusay-Sabah Clarona despises most of all, but with any luck my presence will conciliate the Qusay's wrath long enough to get the crown off her head.'

'So where are you off to this morning?' Lucian, as captain, was surprised he'd not been informed that Taren intended to run an additional mission.

'Kalayna and Telmo have fixed Inter-system Gateway Five ahead of schedule,' Taren informed him, and most in the room gasped as this was an event the timekeepers needed to prevent if they were going to keep the entity on Oceane from discovery.

'So I'm taking Mythric to get them out,' she stated, 'and shut it down.'

Lucian nodded; he didn't need to ask why she was taking Mythric — he was the only person left on AMIE that Kalayna knew personally, although she knew Mythric by the alias BA Tane. Mythric also had PK, meaning he could help transport their new members back here, rather than needing Taren to teleport him as well.

'Who are Kalayna and Telmo?' Yasper queried, as Mythric raised himself from his seat to answer the commission.

'The two babies of the crew,' Taren filled him in. 'We've been holding off on recruiting them as long as possible, but now their safety is in question, so it's time to conscript them.'

'Do they know about us?' Yasper, as security, was always concerned about new personnel.

'I suspect they don't even know they have Powers, let alone that a whole bunch of us psychic outcasts have banded together,' Taren outlined. 'But they belong on this crew, and already have been timekeepers, once upon another timeline.'

'If you say so,' Yasper said. 'You've been right about everybody else.'

Taren smiled, gratified by his faith, and indeed everyone's. 'Shall we?' Taren looked to Mythric, who gave her a wink.

'I'll meet you at Kalayna.' He vanished, and Taren followed his lead, bringing an image of Kalayna Zuri to mind to seek her out.

Arse planted on a sandy beach, a wet, salty breeze blowing in his face — Zeven had missed the Frujian lifestyle.

He'd spent years living on an island just off Frujia's capital island, Kotan-Bathaar, with his father, Spyridon Vidor, aka Mythric Zeon — a name his father much preferred. Still, the locals on Frujia had dubbed Mythric Bakar Aitor Tane, which meant 'alone good father man', thus he was also simply known as BA. At the time, Zeven had only just discovered that Mythric was his father, and he looked back fondly on those years that they been awarded to get to know one another, whilst the AMIE vessel was being built. Mythric had become a good friend and ally long before they'd discovered the truth behind their inexplicable connection to one another.

'I do believe I shall retire here,' Zeven decided, although that was every person's dream, despite what planet they were born on, and it was easy to see why — everywhere you looked the view was picturesque.

It was coming on evening here in the cooler climes of Frujia, and the beach was bathed in the long shadows of the trees at his back — Zeven had maybe a couple of hours of daylight left, which was all the prep time he would need.

What did he know about the situation he was about to pop into?

Khalid was being held in a top level psychic security prison — meaning that Zeven could teleport himself to his target, but he could not teleport them both out until the cell was opened and they were both clear of its restraint. Such a powerful prisoner would also be wearing a psychic restraining device, which effectively rendered him Powerless — this would work to Zeven's favour. From the last time he'd passed through this instance in time, and his adventures since, he knew that Khalid currently had the evil spirit, Chironjivi, who had been posing as his father, trapped inside his body with him. This was the result of Chironjivi and Khalid's ill-executed attempt to join forces to assassinate Jabez Anselm, President of Sermetica. The timekeepers had thwarted this event, and Khalid was sent to prison for the murder of the Duchess Maiara Vidor, whom he'd killed only hours prior to his arrest. Unknown to them at the time, when Khalid had been psychically restrained the evil entity possessing him had been trapped in his body with him and had been tormenting him ever since. Zeven had later discovered that the key to separating the curse from the man lay in a tiny metal amulet that had been implanted in Khalid's hand at birth to ensure his allegiance to the evil cesspool of souls at Dead Man Downs. The last time this instance in time played out Khalid had begun cutting this amulet out of his hand himself. As his cell was monitored constantly, his jailers had moved to intervene. Zeven never got the full story, but somehow Khalid had escaped custody, cut the trinket out of his own hand and then trapped Chironjivi's evil soul in a coffer. If they could do the same with all the evil souls at Dead Man Downs then Khalid would be free to discover who he really was for the first time in his life.

'Oi, you!' The voice was aggressive, but some distance away.

Zeven looked to the source to find a huge, strapping, blond fellow striding towards him.

'What are you doing on *my* beach?' The man obviously didn't relish company. 'How the fuck did you *get* on my beach?'

That was a good question as no transport came out this way, but Zeven had picked this spot because it was uninhabited, and thus he'd not been expecting to have to answer questions. He could have just vanished, but Zeven was curious about who this guy was — looking as he did, he wasn't a local, as native Frujians were shorter, and dark of hair and skin, usually.

'I wasn't aware that property out here in the protected regions of Frujia had become available for purchase?' Zeven shouted back over the evening breeze that was whipping up.

'Political asylum,' the large fellow replied. 'What's your excuse?'

'The Frujian government gave you a residency here?' Zeven found that hard to believe. Standing on a beach as he was, Zeven was paying no heed to the water pooling at his feet.

'Secret service,' the islander boasted with a grin.

'Whose?' Zeven probed, then felt the water at his knees. He looked down to find it was rising up over his body — as if filling an invisible casing around his form. 'Oh shit.'

'You ask a lot of questions, little man.' The fellow stopped just out of reach and folded his arms, smiling smugly. 'Now you have five seconds to tell me who you are and what you want, before I drown you. Go!'

'This is really not necessary,' Zeven warned him politely. 'Call it off.'

'Three seconds.' The islander grinned as the water reached Zeven's waist.

'Have it your way.' Zeven imagined a psychic restraining band clamping around the ankle of his opponent, and it was so.

'Fuck! I fell for it again!' The hulk of a man protested the restraint, dropping onto his haunches to try and rip it from his ankle. 'Get it off!'

Power impeded, his opponent's liquid casing broke from around Zeven and the water fell away in one almighty splash.

'The chick who put me here did the same thing!' the man grumbled, but then had an afterthought. 'Did she send you?'

Zeven suppressed a grin as he considered that there was only one secret service female with the ability to do what he'd just done. 'Fit, bit taller than me, long blonde hair, tenacious?'

'That's her,' the fellow confirmed. 'A bit of a rebel.'

Zeven laughed at the understatement, and the coincidence — but then, being a timekeeper he'd learned there was no such thing.

'She said that she'd send someone back to fetch me once she'd gathered her forces.' The fellow was sounding far more amenable.

Zeven nodded, suddenly realising who this fellow was. If his guess was correct, the timekeepers had first run into this guy in the universe parallel, where he'd aided Jazmay and Fari to escape

MSS custody. In this universe, however, Taren had persuaded him to abandon a vendetta he was waging against the MSS, and to retire to Frujia; this deal had in turn prevented Yasper Ronan's death six years ago. On neither occasion had Zeven met the man but thankfully Taren always gave a comprehensive mission debrief.

'Vadik Corentin,' Zeven put a name to the legend. He'd been one of the MSS's most wanted psychic rebels. Due to his mastery of the elements, they called him 'the Hurricane', thus Taren had given him another alias. 'Or should I call you Harry Cane?'

'Harry is fine,' he advised, cocking an eye. 'So she did send you to fetch me?'

'Why would you want to leave this?' Zeven considered that Vadik already had it made.

'Because the MSS are pulling some creepy shit on the psychics on Maladaan and I want to make them desist,' he seethed.

'How would you know about that, living all the way out here?' Zeven wondered.

'The elements are everywhere,' he advised, and smiled in conclusion, 'and the elements are friends of mine.'

Zeven considered this a good answer. 'And why should we trust you?'

'You want me to prove my conviction to the cause?' Vadik challenged and stood, keen yet offended. 'Take this fucking band off my ankle and give me a mission. I'll do anything you ask me to.'

'Anything?' Zeven grinned as he could use an accomplice at present, especially somewhere this remote. 'You may not like what we have in mind. In fact, I'm quite sure you won't!'

Vadik grinned. 'I'm just hired muscle, I don't have to like what I do … and despite how gruesome the task may be, I usually *do* enjoy my work.'

Zeven removed the psychic restraint from the man's ankle as a show of good faith, but was smiling on the inside. *Let's see how well he does babysitting the man who headed the very organisation he once sought to bring down.*

'So what do I call you?' Vadik queried, happy to be free of the restraint.

'Bob.' Zeven held out a hand to his new ally, who shook it gladly.

'What do you want me to do, *Bob*?' Vadik clearly recognised the simple name was an alias.

'Well, *Harry*, I just need you to *wait here*,' Zeven stressed the simple instruction. 'I'll bring your assignment to you.'

'Good deal.' Vadik looked about the island, a little baffled. 'So where is it?'

'Sermetica,' Zeven advised, and before Vadik could express his bafflement, Zeven teleported himself to his next target: Khalid Mansur.

When Mythric and Taren landed on the control deck of Inter-system Gateway Five, they'd not expected to find Kalayna alone and in tears. She was curled up in the control seat, oblivious to their arrival.

'Kalayna?' Mythric called to her gently, not wanting to startle her — but he did nevertheless.

She jumped to an upright position in the chair and, looking to him, was stunned to behold her old friend. 'BA?' she gasped.

'None other.' He held his arms wide.

Kalayna sprang from her seat to embrace him. 'Thank goodness!' The embrace brought her sobbing under control. 'You have to help me,' she pulled back to implore him.

'Of course we will,' Mythric assured her, as Kalayna looked to his companion. 'You're Dr Taren Lennox — I mean, Dr Gervaise,' Kalayna corrected herself. 'Your work is amazing! I've studied you.'

'Coming from the girl who solved this old inter-system gateway paradox, that's quite a compliment,' Taren awarded.

Kalayna was a thaumaturge. Thaumaturgy was known as the 'art mathematical', an ability to construct complex mechanical devices that are ahead of their time. It had been theorised that this was how the inter-system gateways were first constructed, so it came as no surprise to Taren that Kalayna had managed to fix this old system gateway where all those before her had failed. Still, Taren was fairly certain that Kalayna was completely oblivious to the fact that her talent with technology was a Power, and one that the MSS would arrest her for.

'What seems to be the problem then?' Mythric queried his young friend.

'And where is Telmo Decree?' Taren had thought he'd be here on the control deck if they were about to reopen the gateway for traffic.

'He's the problem!' Kalayna stressed. 'I don't know what's come over him. After working for years on getting this gate to function, we are successful! There was this *huge* media bidding war to determine who got to travel through the gate first to get the scoop and interview Telmo and myself.'

'Let me guess, EBN won.' Taren quoted another side note of Zeven's.

'The Esponisa Broadcast Network, that's right,' Kalayna confirmed. 'But how did you know —?'

'Not important.' Taren waived the query, although Esponisa was the capital of Maladaan, which explained how the MSS might have gained access to the station to arrest Telmo and Kalayna as predicted.

'We are supposed to be opening the gateway for traffic this morning,' Kalayna continued her tale of woe. 'I have the Space Corp and the network on the intercom blasting me because we are running behind schedule.'

'What's the hold up?' Mythric was grateful for it, whatever it was.

'The gateway is no longer working!' Kalayna stressed. 'I don't know what happened! I went to do a system check, and nothing is responding, so I can't even figure out how to fix it.'

'You think Telmo sabotaged the opening?' Taren suggested, thinking this was either an odd stroke of luck, or a very meaningful coincidence.

'Normally, I would say no way.' Kalayna clearly didn't like accusing him. 'But he was kind of strange yesterday. Then this morning ... the gate is no longer functioning, and he is *gone* ... what am I to assume?'

'Define strange?' Taren probed.

'Well, Telmo is normally an intelligent individual but not in a philosophical sense. But yesterday, he was spouting all sorts of deep musings. And I heard him muttering something to himself, when he thought I was elsewhere,' she recalled. 'He was mumbling something about how some guy was not going to out-time-hop him, or something to that effect.'

'Do you remember who he was ranting about?' Taren queried.

'Um,' Kalayna struggled to recall, 'some name, it started with Z, I think?'

'Zeven?' both Taren and Mythric queried at once.

'Yes!' Kalayna was surprised. 'That's it? Do you know him?'

Kalayna knew Zeven, only he'd been going by the name Kale Tane when they'd all met on Frujia.

'All too well.' Mythric looked to Taren, wondering if she wanted to divulge any more than she already had.

But Taren's mind was ticking over. 'How does Telmo even know about Zeven? They've never met. Unless —' She took her contemplation internal. *If we've been through this already, Telmo would know Zeven. They went to the universe parallel, with me, in four years' time and then crossed back into this universe to now.* 'Shit!'

'What?' both Mythric and Kalayna begged to know.

'I've got two timekeepers AWOL!' She turned away to pace out her frustration — why had two of her crew chosen to run a mission without her? 'What the fuck is going on?'

'My question exactly.' Mythric wished to be enlightened.

'So Telmo is gone from here?' Taren put the query to Kalayna.

'I know that sounds impossible,' she defended, 'when none of our transports are missing, but, before you arrived, I was the only life form on board.'

'Do you want me to go after him?' Mythric volunteered.

Taren shook her head. 'Not at this point. We have other commitments today.'

'So we just take Kalayna and run,' Mythric suggested, as everything else was seemingly peachy.

'What are you talking about?' Kalayna was suddenly alarmed. 'You have to help me get this gate functioning, BA, I'm in a lot of shit here!'

'No, you're not,' he advised her calmly, with a smile. 'We came to get you to shut the gateway down.'

'What! Why?' Kalayna was shocked to the core.

'Because the EBN will bring the MSS and once they screen you and Telmo with their new photon camera, they'll arrest you both on psychic grounds.'

Kalayna was doubly shocked. 'Not just me, but Telmo too?'

'You don't think your understanding of this hi-tech ancient system is something you picked up during your Space Corps study, do you?' Taren tried to make light of the news.

'How could you know what hasn't happened yet?' Kalayna clearly doubted the claim.

'Because I'm a pre-cog,' Taren admitted openly, which was even more shocking to the poor girl.

'Oh shit!' Kalayna began to go into shock. 'What am I going to do? My career is over!'

'No, baby, no.' Mythric moved in to reassure her and stroke her hair. 'Your career is just beginning!'

Kalayna was perplexed by this and her gaze drifted back to Taren.

Taren nodded to assure her this was quite true. 'Welcome to AMIE.'

4

BREAKING LOOSE

Zeven manifested in Khalid's cell, but he maintained an invisible state of being to observe.

Khalid looked like hell, slouched on his bunk watching the news in just his trousers, which didn't appear to have been changed in a while. The cell was so filthy, Zeven had to wonder if it had ever been cleaned. Had they just dumped Khalid in here and left him? As one of the most high profile psychics in prison, he was probably considered too dangerous to escort anywhere. It was only because Sermetica had no death penalty that Khalid was still breathing.

A news report about the opening of Inter-system Gateway Five, and a shout out from Kalayna to the crew of AMIE on interstellar TV, had been the trigger for Khalid's escape attempt this day. Their nemesis got it in his head to kidnap the two hotshot engineers who'd solved the ancient mystery and use them to devise a huge photon camera that could find the source of the timekeepers' protective power. Khalid had managed to find Oceane, and his attempt to destroy Azazèl-mindos-coomra-dorchi had seen him dragged into the universe parallel with some of the timekeepers. This quantum leap had severed Khalid's attachment to the evil forces he'd allied himself to all his life, and that's when the timekeepers realised that Khalid the man was a very different entity to the demon they took him for.

If Taren had acted upon Zeven's memo this morning then the news report that would trigger all these events would not happen.

A timekeeper could just leave the situation at disaster averted, but Zeven knew his very righteous friend, Wu Geng, was in Khalid somewhere. An extra-terrestrial metaphysical master, Dorje Pema, had whipped Wu Geng into spiritual shape over a thirty-year period — Zeven had less than four years to aid Khalid to achieve the same. He hoped he was not being egoistically optimistic about his chances of succeeding in his quest, but that was really beside the point — he had a promise to keep. Hyper-aware of the HUGE risk he was about to take, the intent was to provide a trigger for a very different sequence of events in Khalid's life.

First things first. Zeven wanted to see everything in the cell, including Khalid, spotlessly tidy.

'What the fuck!' Khalid was startled by the sudden change in environment — he actually roused the energy to sit up.

Next Zeven changed the bright yellow colour of Khalid's trousers to deep midnight blue, which had been Wu Geng's favourite colour.

'Someone is screwing with us.' He stood, gazing down at his clean, dark blue trousers in horror, and then gasped as he looked to the camera monitoring his room. 'Oh shit.'

'That's right, the guards are coming for you,' Zeven spoke and startled the life out of Khalid.

'Who the fuck —?' Khalid was irate, and wary of how vulnerable he was, he turned circles hoping to get a fix on his invisible stalker.

'A friend,' Zeven replied.

'I don't have any *fucking* friends! Never did! So fuck you!' he spat.

Zeven didn't know anyone who swore quite so much as this guy when he was angry. 'Just shut up, stand still, and take your medicine like a man.' Zeven gripped hold of Khalid to prevent him moving, and used him as a human shield when the door slid aside and several guards fired sedation darts into the cell.

'Fuck!' One planted itself in Khalid's right thigh, and Zeven deflected the rest. 'Let go!' Khalid wrenched himself from Zeven's grasp at the sight of the open door.

Feet first, he launched himself towards the doorframe and slid across the floor to use an ankle as a doorstop. When the door closed, it crushed his psychic restraining device into his ankle, effectively disabling it. With a great howl of pain, Khalid passed out.

'*So that's how you broke out of prison.*' Zeven followed as Khalid was rushed to hospital. '*I could have gotten you out much less painfully, but,*' he shrugged off the slight deviation in his plan, '*whatever works.*'

Through drowsy eyes, Khalid deduced he was in a hospital room alone. There was no guard inside the room, nor even an orderly to report on his return to consciousness — perhaps he was under visual surveillance?

Despite appearances, Khalid was never really alone — he'd not had a thought or an action all his own since the spirit of Chironjivi, the last prince of Phemoria, was trapped in his body with him — five endless years ago. He should never have allowed the entity to co-habit his body, but he'd been so filled with visions of grandeur at the time he'd not considered the worst that could happen. And even if he had, his imagining would not have matched the nightmare that had become his everyday reality. He'd thought his prior life in service to his father's bloodlust was wearisome; having a constant telepathic insight into his nefarious thought process and memory was a wretched misery that defied description. Fortunately the spirit had to rest, just as Khalid did, so they took the body in shifts. Every waking minute that he had sole occupancy of himself, Khalid dreamt of the day that he was anywhere that he might find an implement to cut the amulet out of his hand and sever his bond to the vampiric spirit of his father. With any luck Chironjivi was still unconscious and now was Khalid's chance.

'*You don't have any luck, you worthless piece of treacherous excrement! Do you think I don't know that you've been planning to be rid of me?*' His hand unexpectedly slapped his own face. '*Why didn't you mention you have your Powers back!*'

'I haven't!' Khalid growled. 'It was one of those bloody light-fuckers screwing with us! And if you hit me again, I'm going to cut off my overworked dick and there'll be no more jerking off for you!'

'*Why would one of them want to free us from prison?*'

'How the fuck would I know? But I know it was one of them, because they are the only thing in existence that makes me feel nauseous, besides you!' Just thinking about their energy made him feel queasy. Yet Khalid was more concerned with why his ankle wasn't killing him. He raised the bed sheet to take a look at the injured limb, to find that the neutraliser had been removed. The ankle itself was still badly swollen and bruised, and was a dead weight as it had been numbed. It made him smile to see the restraining device gone; it only took an hour for the effects to wear off. But a glance across to his other ankle crushed his aspiration to freedom as a psychic neutraliser had been attached to it instead. 'Son-of-a-bitch!'

'*Looks like we'll be staying together after all,*' Chironjivi taunted.

'You didn't have to go bust your ankle; I was going to free you anyway.'

'He's still hanging about.' Khalid recognised the voice as the same man who had been speaking with him earlier in his cell. '*That's* why I still feel revolting.'

'I took precautions to keep your adverse reaction to a minimum, but it will not be an issue once your curse is ended.'

'*We need to get out of here!*' Chironjivi took control of the body, ripping monitoring sensors from his skin in a frenzy. But when he planted his feet on the ground, the numbness of his foot gave way to pain, and he was forced to grab for the bed to prevent falling over.

'Argh! You idiot!' Khalid yelled at the spirit co-inhabiting him, as he seized back wilful control of his body. No sooner had he accomplished this, than he was swooped up — not by a man but a psychic force — and plonked back on the bed.

'You're not going anywhere,' their invisible company said, as the force bore down on them, pinning Khalid's body to the bed. 'I haven't finished operating on you yet.'

Khalid and Chironjivi attempted to rise against the force, but it felt like they were buried to the neck in sand. 'Go fuck your mother!' they snarled in unison, as Khalid felt his father commandeer his vocal cords.

'You already did,' came the reply.

'*Even better*,' Chironjivi's unearthly voice snarled, and he wriggled his tongue in a fashion to imply cunnilingus.

'And now it's time for a little *payback*.' The voice sounded suddenly up-vibe and uncomfortably smug.

'Wait!' Khalid regained control of his vocal cords. 'Don't listen to me! I never fucked your mother —'

'You did, actually. Her name was *Satomi*.'

The name struck a dagger of horror through his chest, not because Khalid regretted raping and gutting her, but because her only child, who they had killed that same day, was prophesied to bring about his destruction.

'You can't be Spyridon's bastard, I stuck a dagger through it myself.' Khalid rejected the claim.

'When I was flat on my back and unable to defend myself,' the voice concurred. 'Pretty much as you are *right now*.'

'*I fucking hate this little prick already! I'm going to rip his bleeding heart out and —*'

'Kill me, for pity's sake!' Khalid was beyond caring any more. 'Just get me away from this demented, dead fucker in my head!'

The invisible stalker was heard to laugh. 'I'm not going to kill you. The dark unknowable forces of this universe are just patterns unseen, *begging* to be understood.' Their captor employed a compassionate but ominous tone as he took hold of one of Khalid's hands. 'Our secret desires are but signposts to our destiny.'

As Khalid watched his palm turn upwards and his fingers splay wide apart, he realised that the hand of interest was the same one that contained the amulet that bound him to his dead father.

'One should never be put off from a defining experience by the prospect of a little suffering. All great achievement comes at a cost.'

Was their captor hinting at his intent? If he was of the mind to rip the cursed trinket from his hand, Khalid had dreamt of little else! 'Yes, do it!' Khalid implored, as he felt a tingling and a shifting movement inside his hand.

'*No!*' Chironjivi fought back, and clamped the hand into a fist. '*This is my body now, I made it and it's mine!*'

Once again their captor sounded most amused. 'You are no more Khalid's father than I am.'

The claim sent shocking pangs of anger through Khalid's being, heat upon heat. In the dark, shadowy depths of his being Khalid had always suspected that Chironjivi was lying about his paternity; and it really pissed Khalid off to think that he might have been sucked in, like the gullible infant he was when Chironjivi first made contact with him.

'Lying pissant, he's trying to divide us and weaken our position!'

'Your blood father was of the Old Ones, Khalid,' the voice insisted.

Chironjivi's laughter mocked the grand claim to crush the aspiration in Khalid before it could arise. The premise was bordering so close to preposterous that Khalid's anger broke over his disbelief — Chironjivi was right, he was surely being taken for a ride.

'There exists a recording of Maiara Vidor in a trance, spouting a prophecy that states this fact,' the voice informed. 'The same prophecy that predicted the demise of your curse. I have seen this with my own eyes, and I don't believe that I am the victim turned victor who would destroy the curse, Khalid … I believe that victor is you.'

Could he be right? Khalid's fingers began to bend to his will. If there was such a recording, Maiara Vidor was never wrong — that's why they had targeted Satomi's child in the first place.

'A fucking fantasy if ever I heard one!' Chironjivi hissed venomously. *'That is how these light-fuckers operate, by enticing you with promises of leading the life you've always dreamt of! But what you'll get will be nothing like it! You are a prince of death, forged from bloodlust and revenge —'*

'You are a lying sack of rotten corpses, Chironjivi,' the voice rebutted.

Khalid smiled on the inside; clearly their captor knew there was more than one soul inhabiting this body. As he was clearly more pissed at Chironjivi than himself, Khalid struggled to overthrow his father's will.

'Not that it matters what you are, because either way this goes, your existence ends *today*. It's time to clean house at Dead Man

Downs and send the crew of the *Insurrecto* back to their maker. Khalid can either help me with that, or join you in death.'

'*You know me?*' Chironjivi was flabbergasted; he'd gone to great lengths to keep Dead Man Downs a secret, and yet his dark ego was also flattered to be notorious.

'Make him comply!' Khalid gained the upper hand with his larynx, yet Chironjivi forced the fist to close once more; his whole arm shook with the effort of trying to splay his fingers — his hand was near as numb as his busted ankle. 'I'll do anything ... *anything!* Just get this freak show out of my body!'

'Deal.'

Khalid's hand burst open, and in a blinding flash of pain, the metal amulet ripped its way out of his palm. The blood-soaked piece of metal flew into a metal canister that appeared in midair, open at one end. The container slammed closed, locked and settled base-down on a table.

The mindless chatter and constant scheming stopped, all the stress and tension rushed from his body and Khalid was left completely wasted.

'Rest easy, buddy,' he was told, 'I got your back this time.'

Someone appeared before him, yet Khalid's vision blurred and he was forced to close his eyes and explore the silent oasis of his own mind. The peace was as close to joy as Khalid had ever come, and although he couldn't imagine why a man he'd tried to kill at birth would want to help him, he was truly thankful for the service. For even if he died the most awful death now, or went back to prison, he was free of Chironjivi.

After cleaning the wound in Khalid's hand and bandaging it up, Zeven left him to recuperate and exited the hospital room he'd conjured up. Beyond the hospital door he stepped onto the deserted beach where Vadik was waiting to be briefed.

'If there is one person I have dreamt of killing, it's Khalid Mansur.' Vadik spied him unconscious within the room, and clearly expected to be given permission to act upon his whim.

'Sorry to disappoint you,' Zeven shut down that thought to pose the challenge. 'Your mission is to protect him.'

'Pig's arse I will!' Vadik flew into a rage and the atmosphere on the beach turned suddenly stormy.

'Those are the orders,' Zeven stated plainly, unfazed by Vadik's lack of emotional control. 'We are to make Khalid feel as comfortable with us as possible, and treat him as a trusted comrade.'

'I'd rather suck dogs' balls!' Vadik repelled the notion.

'I thought you wanted to bring down the MSS,' Zeven countered.

'I do!'

'Well this is one *small* part of a much *larger* plan,' he explained. 'Screw it up and our entire strategy crumbles!'

Vadik's storm died down when he realised he might have misjudged the situation. 'Lull him into a false sense of security so we can fuck him up the arse later, is that it?'

'You're just the hired muscle,' Zeven quoted Vadik back at himself. 'You don't ask questions, you don't need to enjoy what you do, isn't that what you said?'

'Yeah,' Vadik frowned in objection with himself. 'But no one has ever employed me to be *nice* to my target before … I'm not trained for that!'

'Oh, I don't know, you've been hanging out in nature for the past five years, you must have learned a little something about living in harmony with other living creatures?'

Vadik's frown deepened. 'Little furry critters and plants, but —'

'Well, pretend Khalid is a poor, injured little critter and treat him accordingly, even if he tries to scratch or bite,' Zeven suggested.

'Are you sure this is the plan?' Vadik was completely bemused and deflated. 'Doesn't seem right to me.'

'I am absolutely positive,' Zeven vowed. 'We need Khalid, for more reasons than I am at liberty to list, but know for certain that if anything adverse should happen to *that man*, the boss is going to be really, *really*, pissed at whomever was responsible. So either step up to the challenge, or bugger off. We cannot use anyone who cannot put the greater good before their own selfish desire.'

'Is that what you are doing, Starman?'

Zeven recognised the voice immediately, and looking to the source he found Telmo Dacre. 'What are you doing here? You shouldn't even know me yet.'

Telmo grinned and raised both brows suggestively. 'But I do.'

'Who is this guy, Bob?' Vadik queried. 'Do you want me to take care of him for you?'

Zeven had to laugh at that — if this Telmo had followed him here from the universe parallel, he was one of the most powerful timekeepers of all. 'He's a friend, Harry.' Zeven set Vadik at ease. 'A nosey, distrustful, pain in the arse, control freak —'

'You released Khalid from prison,' Telmo butted in.

'He was going to break out anyway.' Zeven defended his strategy.

'Not without the transmission from the inter-system gateway opening, and I shut down the gate, so there was no transmission today.' Telmo grinned in conclusion.

'So the boss got to you in time,' Zeven figured. 'I warned her to get you guys out of there and shut down the gate earlier.'

'Nope, I haven't seen the boss,' Telmo replied. 'Isn't she reconciling Sermetica and Phemoria right now?'

'Gosh, it's all happening!' Vadik observed from the sideline.

'I told you there was a bigger plan,' Zeven commented aside to his recruit.

'Is there?' Telmo wondered. 'Or are you just flying by the seat of your pants as per usual?'

'You have absolutely no faith in me, do you?' Zeven resented being followed and supervised.

'Of course I do,' Telmo replied bluntly. 'I just thought you could use a hand. We're both going to be in trouble with the boss now, so you may as well utilise me.'

'Hey … I thought you said *she* sent you?' Vadik was alarmed.

'Listen to me.' Telmo stepped in and the big guy turned his focus to him. 'Please stop thinking,' he appealed politely.

A vague look swept over Vadik's face, and the big man sat down on the sand and shut up.

'You can do that without touching your subject now,' Zeven noted. 'That's impressive.'

'Yeah.' Telmo raised both brows and looked to Zeven. 'I perfected it on you.'

'How do you mean?' Zeven's annoyance spiked again.

'How do you think I knew what you were planning?' Telmo put forward. 'Not to say that I didn't guess. But, to be sure, I pulled you aside at Noah's lake house before we left Kila and you told me about coming back early to save Khalid.'

'That's a breach in your AMIE contract, as you're —'

'— not supposed to use my talents on any member of the crew without the captain or the timekeeper's permission,' Telmo recounted the rule. 'But it was in AMIE's best interest that someone knew what you are up to.'

'Because you don't trust me,' Zeven rolled his eyes in conclusion.

'Because I have talents and knowledge that you don't have and will need,' Telmo reasoned. 'Do you know how to return the spirits of the dead to their maker?'

'Well … no,' Zeven admitted.

'Do you know how to train someone in self mastery?' Telmo quizzed.

'Not really.' Zeven was beginning to see that his mission would be a lot less research heavy with the aid of Telmo's superconscious memory.

'I won't be required on AMIE now, as I would have been creating a monitoring system for Oceane to keep us alert to any sign of Khalid, but easier still would be not to lose sight of him in the first place,' he concluded diplomatically.

'Fair enough.' Zeven accepted that Telmo's reasons had nothing to do with his capability. 'Do you know anything about the Old Ones who supposedly built the inter-system gateways eons ago?'

'Actually, I attempted to write a paper on them in university,' Telmo advised, 'and I can tell you with all surety that there is barely anything known about them on three out of four planets in the USS.'

'Phemoria.' Zeven had already been told they were the only civilisation likely to know anything of the Old Ones; they were also the least likely to share information, especially with a man.

'Legend has it that the Phemorians still have contact with the Old Ones, and due to their inter-breeding Phemorians inherited their psychic powers.' Telmo shared the only gem of information he'd managed to find.

Zeven nodded as this corroborated what he already knew. 'Right then, I'll be off. Would you stay and watch these two?'

'Good luck, I'll be interested to know what you find out.' Telmo agreed to his lot too easily, like he already knew what Zeven's next move was and didn't have to ask, which Zeven found a little irritating. Yet, if Telmo had asked to know the plan, Zeven would have found that equally irritating — the truth was Telmo just irritated him.

It wasn't really Telmo's fault that he was carrying such an old soul in such a young persona, but the mismatch just made him seem like a know it all, even though he did really have access to more spiritual knowledge, talent and experience than the rest of the timekeepers put together.

'Thanks for babysitting,' Zeven said before he departed. He could have been referring to Vadik and Khalid as the children who needed minding, but he silently included himself in that equation.

'We are legion,' Telmo replied with a smile, 'and we all must play our part.'

As expected, Zeven found Aurora, Kassa, Zelimir and Swithin sitting around in the mess hall on AMIE awaiting the rest of the crew's return from their mission to Phemoria with the president of Sermetica. He was delighted to find Kalayna was also in attendance — her presence was confirmation that Taren had followed his directive and recruited her before today's main agenda began.

'Are we winning?' he asked to make all aware of his presence.

'Zeven!' Aurora jumped up and embraced him. 'Where have you been?'

'I've been doing other stuff for the cause.' He grinned and bequeathed a kiss to her. 'I just need a quick rundown on where you guys are at.'

'They successfully removed the crown of Phemoria from the Qusay's head, and contained the Phemoray along with their cursed crown in a case made of Osmium.' Aurora stepped away to fill him in. Osmium was the densest and strongest metal in the known universe. 'But the Qusay passed out before the situation could be completely resolved, so they are just waiting for her to awaken.'

'Kale?' Kalayna was having an epiphany. 'You're Zeven?'

'Sometimes,' he said and then conceded, 'mostly.' When his humour didn't even fetch a smile from his old friend, he was concerned. 'What's up?'

'A work colleague of mine has gone missing,' she explained. 'He mentioned seeking Zeven out.'

'I know where he is.' Zeven smiled to assure her. 'He is absolutely fine.'

'Really?' The relief of the news compelled her out of her chair to hug the messenger. 'Thank you, Kale — Zeven? Thank you so much!' Kalayna let him go and then appeared a little awkward — she'd obviously forgotten his wife was right beside them. 'Sorry ... got a bit carried away.'

Aurora waved it off as no big deal. 'I know you guys were study buddies for a long time; hugging is allowed.'

'So where is Telmo?' Kalayna begged to know.

'He's helping me out with a few things, and we may be gone a while,' he advised both ladies.

'Why hasn't Taren told us what you are up to?' Swithin was suspicious, but then he always was — thanks to his criminal days working in the black market it was second nature.

'Because she wants you all focused on the larger job at hand,' Zeven proffered.

'I am free,' Swithin offered his services.

'No,' Zeven insisted. 'Taren is going to require your aid after she gets back from Phemoria.'

'That would be a first.' Obviously Swithin couldn't imagine why Taren would need to bring someone back from the dead.

Zeven shrugged and backed up. 'I gotta motor, or I'll miss my window of opportunity.'

'I suppose asking you where you are going is pointless?' Aurora posed and received a wink as confirmation, whilst Zeven brought his PK to bear on delivering him to the throne room of the Qusay-Sabah Clarona.

In the Qusay's room of court in Tonissia, the capital city of Phemoria, Zeven arrived to find Amie working her impressionist magic on the Valourean force who were frozen stiff around the room. This was why Zeven had told Taren she would need Amie on this mission. Last time around, Zeven had teleported Amie here after the confrontation with the queen — Taren had left Zeven back at base in case they needed any additional team members brought in. But as Zeven had been unsure whether or not he would return to base in time to transfer Amie to the throne room, he'd included the directive in his notes to Taren.

So far so good, he considered; his plan was right on track.

Amie was implanting the impression in each Valourean that the council meeting they had just witnessed had gone splendidly well, that they were to forget all the details and were free to go. Unfortunately Amie's talent didn't work en masse, so she was working her way around the room, dismissing the Qusay's force one by one. Each of the Valoureans looked really pissed off, but their aggressive looks melted as Amie worked her magic, and each guard left the room in a quiet, orderly fashion.

'Zeven?' Taren was clearly surprised to see him, and approached to lead him away from the rest of the team. 'What are you doing here?'

'Research,' he said. 'How do you fancy my chances of getting access to Phemoria's Hall of Records?'

Taren was completely perplexed by the query. 'Pretty good, most likely … being that at this day, my mother has been released from her curse and is talking with my father for the first time in three decades!'

'Have you and Mythric spoken to her yet?' Zeven quizzed, to try and figure how far into this situation they were.

Taren frowned, obviously annoyed that he already knew how today's events were playing out. 'Yes, and the Qusay asked Mythric to return the body of Satomi to Phemoria, just as you predicted. We are just waiting for my father to say his goodbyes, so that we can see him safely back to his hotel and his usual security force. Then we'll return to AMIE and form a new team to carry out my mother's request.' Taren was sounding rather perturbed. 'I was rather expecting you'd like to aid your father in this.'

'My presence is not vital to the outcome,' he countered, regretting he'd miss seeing the moment his parents were reunited — but at this point only Zeven knew that the story of Spyridon Vidor and the Princess Satomi was to have a happy ending.

'Well, I have to believe you on that,' she regretted to say, 'being that you've been right about everything else today, except for the fact Telmo has gone missing.'

'Telmo is with me,' Zeven put her mind at rest in one regard, but this fact meant he was in trouble on a whole other level.

'Telmo!' Yasper's ears picked up, having just this day taken the opportunity to have a chat with the president of Sermetica about his lost sibling and discovered his identity. 'How does Zeven know Telmo Dacre?' Yasper was curious.

Taren already knew the answer. 'Yes, that is a very good question, isn't it?' She held up a hand to prevent Yasper approaching and joining the conversation — whereupon he returned to the others, clearly disappointed to be denied answers at this time. 'Or more to the point, how does Telmo know you?' Taren folded her arms, knowing that there was only one conclusion that would explain it. 'Two of you are AWOL.'

'It's not my fault,' Zeven stressed quietly. 'The little shit is as powerful and knowledgeable as Taliesin or Yi Wu ever was —'

'Who is Yi Wu?' Taren wondered.

Zeven waved off the detail. 'You'll remember in four years when your memory comes back. The point is, Telmo is super smart and I can use him. You won't need him now that —' He managed to bite his tongue before mentioning Khalid's escape. 'You just won't.'

'Isn't it about time you told me what you are up to?' Taren appealed in all seriousness. 'I have a telepath here and I'm not afraid to use him.'

'You two are acting very strange today.' Lucian approached to join their huddle; as captain of AMIE he had a perfect right to include himself — although technically Taren was in command of this mission.

'Zeven is stuck on something I need to help him out with,' Taren advised Lucian, and looked back to Zeven to query, 'Is my presence vital to the outcome of the next timekeeping mission to Sermetica?'

'Not if they take Swithin and Kassa, no,' he answered.

Lucian's friendly demeanour waned. 'Why is Zeven speaking of a future event like it has already happened?' Lucian posed. 'Has he developed precognition, like you?'

'Exactly right.' Zeven liked the sound of a premise that could explain a lot, without having to explain too much.

'But more research is needed to verify a few things,' Taren added to cover his bases.

'And the only place I can reference said information,' Zeven concluded, 'is here on Phemoria.'

'I see.' Lucian accepted that explanation, although it was clear he wasn't entirely convinced.

'If you can organise the troops to retrieve Satomi's body from Sermetica, I'll stay here and give Zeven a hand with his enquiries,' Taren proffered.

'If you are confident of your safety.' Lucian obviously wasn't entirely comfortable with trusting the Phemorians — they had tried to kidnap and brainwash his wife before today and although that instance may have been many timelines ago, thanks to Lucian's eternal memory he'd not forgotten.

'Mother and I have made our peace,' she assured him. 'She is eager to make amends for all the years we have spent at odds. We will be perfectly safe.'

President Anselm and the Qusay's viceroy, Jalila Lamus, exited the private audience chamber behind the Qusay's room of court, where Qusay-Sabah Clarona was recovering from her decades-long ordeal.

Zeven had never seen any man appear quite as humbled and elated as Anselm did upon rejoining his task force.

'The Qusay-Sabah Clarona and myself would like to extend to you all the gratitude of both our nations and our personal thanks for your part in this reconciliation — it would not have been possible without every single one of you!' The president looked to his daughter, tears of joy and pride in his eyes, when he noted Zeven beside her. 'Except for maybe you, Bob. Odd for you to miss all the action?'

Zeven grinned at the man he'd once worked for. 'You know me, Sir; I always have my own action going on.'

'Yes, you do.' Anselm grinned, seeming almost proud that was the case.

'Time for us to see you back to your hotel, Mr President,' Lucian spoke up to rally the troops, and Taren left Zeven's side to go say her farewells to her father.

Amie sent the last Valourean from the room and then joined the rest of the crew.

'Zeven.' Yasper approached him while he had the chance. 'You know my little brother?'

'I do. And better still, I know where he is,' Zeven was glad to inform.

'You gotta let me see him, man!' Yasper appealed.

'I can't do that right now,' Zeven insisted. 'But I can assure you that he's absolutely safe and well.'

Yasper, who was primarily a happy-go-lucky kind of guy, smiled broadly at the news, his excitement beaming. 'So, what's he like?'

Zeven had to laugh at the question. 'You're asking the wrong person for a character assessment of Telmo.'

'Is he an arsehole?' Yasper was suddenly concerned.

'No.' Zeven didn't want to give him the wrong impression. 'If I had to sum him up in a word, I'd say he was brilliant!'

'Well, that's cool!' Yasper decided. 'He's the brains and I'm the brawn then.'

Zeven only chuckled at this as he realised that as brothers Yasper and Telmo couldn't have been more opposite. Although the happy-go-lucky side of their nature was consistent with both of Zelimir Ronan's sons, that must have been something they inherited from their mother, as the ex chief of the Maladaan Secret Service was not so inclined.

'Thanks, Starman!' Yasper gave Zeven the thumbs up for the insight as Taren called him to teleport out of here with the president and the rest of the AMIE crew who were departing.

Once the timekeepers left the throne room with the president, Taren and Zeven were left with the one person, beside the convalescing queen, who could help Zeven with his little research project — the Viceroy of Phemoria, Jalila Lamus.

She looked to Taren in the wake of the day's events and smiled — as Phemorians rarely did — with sincerity. 'It seems you have freed my Qusay and people from centuries of the Phemoray's manipulation in just one morning. There can be no doubt that you are the next rightful heir of the Phemorian throne, Highness,' the dark-haired beauty conceded, her tone a little bittersweet. But as Jalila moved to bow before the heir apparent, Taren placed a hand on her shoulder to prevent it.

'I don't think so,' Taren opposed the viceroy's submission, secretly knowing she had once been prepared to launch a rebellion to end the hereditary rule of the Phemoray on Phemoria. Zeven knew this from prior experience also and he, like Taren, suspected that Jalila's aspirations for governmental rule on Phemoria would not end with this happy turn of events. 'As I have already advised the Qusay, I will be abdicating in favour of the formation of a governing body for Phemoria, which we would both like you to aid us to instigate, as acting prime minister.'

Jalila was telepathic, but as Taren was wearing her Juju stone her thoughts could not be read by any — hence it was that the viceroy was left completely aghast in the wake of learning that her life's aspiration had just come into being.

'I ... I am *so* astonished, and honoured, that I think I shall regret that you shall not be our sovereign. This is a monumental stance you are taking.' Jalila moved to drop to her knees in thanks, but again Taren prevented her.

'I know it is an aspiration that has been close to your heart for your entire political career,' Taren conceded. 'It must have been horrifying trying to negotiate with the Phemoray on a daily basis. You are the true heroine of Phemoria, Viceroy Lamus, not I.'

'How could you know so much about me?' Jalila had never met Taren before today.

'I am precognitive,' Taren gave the simplest explanation.

'Only one of her many talents,' Zeven added to embellish the fib and make it not so much so.

'And who are you, Sir?' Jalila queried politely, having not met him in the course of this day's events.

Zeven looked to Taren, unsure of how much she wanted the viceroy to know, but Jalila's eyes opened wide in wonder and she gasped; unfortunately Zeven was not wearing his Juju — which he'd removed to avoid making Khalid unduly ill. Taren knew this and thus they both figured, 'She knows.'

'My apologies, but the thought was so clear,' Jalila defended, sounding humbled to be privy. 'You are the son of the Princess Satomi, the halfling of transcendent means, the one the Grand Duchess Vidor prophesied would end the curse of our late Qusay's bastard child — the halfling of shadow.'

Taren frowned, having never heard the prophecy in these terms before, and was a little surprised when Zeven acknowledged the viceroy's claim.

'Correct.' Zeven winced inside — he'd been rather proud of this fact once, but now he just wanted to correct the widely spread misconception. 'I am attempting to do just that, as we speak.'

'Is that what you are up to?' Taren was suddenly enlightened.

'Well,' Zeven conceded with a tick of his head and a crooked smile, 'I'm the man.'

'Do I detect a hint of irony?' She no doubt wondered why he was not so thrilled by his destiny.

'Not at all,' Zeven had trouble dropping the satire, 'I just didn't realise there had been an interstellar memo about Maiara's prophecy.'

'I only know of it because I am head of the secret service and our agents are very good at their job.' Jalila wanted to assure him. 'We were informed you had been killed at the same time as the Princess Satomi.'

'No offence to your agents, but it would seem your intel in this instance was incorrect,' Zeven warranted. 'But as my own father believed me dead, all credit to the late grand duchess, as it was through her efforts I slipped under everyone's radar.'

'You are cousins,' Jalila realised, looking from Taren to Zeven, her eyes coming to rest on the latter. 'And you are the first true prince of Phemoria since the revolution!'

'That hardly matters if hereditary rule is to be replaced by Phemorian government.' Zeven took the defensive; he didn't want to cause another revolution and technically he wasn't the first true prince of Phemoria — Khalid was.

'No,' Jalila agreed, but was amused by his misunderstanding. 'I was not intending to have you assassinated. To the contrary, we Phemorians have a long-held prophecy that foretold when the first prince of Phemoria returned the rule of the Phemoray would end. Of course I never informed the Qusay of this.' Jalila was almost bursting with happiness. 'But, I have been searching for you my entire career, and I see now that the prophecy has been fulfilled and that my belief in it was not unfounded.'

Zeven wiped a hand across his brow. 'Phew, that's a relief.'

'For me also,' Jalila granted.

'We need your help with some research.' Taren found the perfect opportunity to get to the point.

'Of course.' Jalila smiled at the tiny request. 'What information are you looking for?'

Taren referred the question to Zeven, obviously curious to know herself.

'I'm looking for information about the Old Ones?'

With his request the joy drained from the viceroy's face.

'Do you know where I might find out about them?'

Jalila gave a hesitant nod.

'Is there a problem?' Taren wondered at the lack of forthcoming answers.

'This information is stored in a secret place,' Jalila was vague. 'No man has ever gone there.'

Taren's face lit up in epiphany, but Zeven had no idea what Jalila was talking about, and he'd prided himself on knowing everything Taren knew. 'I do believe I know the place of which you speak … I visited there myself once,' Taren told them both.

'That's quite impossible,' Jalila politely stated her doubt.

'The etheric city,' Taren informed and Jalila was dumbfounded.

'You'll fast learn that impossible is not in my cousin's vocabulary,' Zeven advised their company and then turned his attention back to Taren. 'Have you been withholding intelligence from the team?'

She merely grinned, smug in her knowledge. 'No one knows all my secrets, Zeven, not even you.'

'Well then, hot shot,' Zeven jibed her. 'Can you get me into this place, or not?'

Taren looked to Jalila, who shook her head. 'You could go in, but you can never come out. The only two-way portal to this place was controlled by the Phemoray, and can only be opened by the Qusay wearing their crown.'

'Not a good idea after all we went through to get it off the Qusay's head and trapped in a box.' Taren struck that off as an immediate option. 'What happens if we destroy the Phemoray?'

'The city will collapse,' Jalila informed. 'And all our sisters living there will return here.'

'That is certainly on my agenda,' Taren told Jalila, who nodded to agree it was on her agenda also.

'But the information stored there would be lost?' Zeven assessed.

'Correct,' Jalila concurred. 'All that would survive would be the knowledge our sisters have stored in their heads.'

'I need this information yesterday,' Zeven appealed for a better idea.

'I can communicate with our sisters in this place.' Jalila proffered a solution. 'Perhaps one of them can do your research for you?'

Zeven felt that would probably save even more time, provided the Phemorians were prepared to be completely transparent in handing over information. 'It is vital that I know all you can find on the subject, no matter how minor the detail.'

'*All* our resources are at your disposal, my prince.'

Jalila obviously knew his concerns — he had to stop thinking so loudly, and must not under any circumstance consider any other part of his mission while in her company. 'Please don't call me that.' Zeven winced. 'Just Zeven is fine.'

'Highness —' Jalila attempted to object.

'Nope, not Highness either,' he cut in. 'I've remained secret this long, let's keep it that way. And *please* stop reading my thoughts.'

Jalila nodded in accord with his wish. 'I'll have one of my agents bring you a thought scrambler, which just attaches to your clothing. Then you may rest assured I cannot read your thoughts … not even by accident. Strangely, I cannot read your thoughts, Highness.' She looked back to Taren.

'I have the protection of the *Zagriata*.' Taren gave the simplest explanation.

'So it is as President Anselm told my Qusay earlier today,' Jalila surmised. 'The *Zagriata* is a force, not an individual.'

Taren nodded to confirm. 'Which is why, when you attempt to read my thoughts, all you hear is music —'

'Yes.' Jalila's eyes lit up as the statement obviously rang true for her.

'It is the music of the spheres you hear,' Taren began, but Jalila dropped to her knees, to humble herself before the new princess of Phemoria, and it made Taren immediately uncomfortable. 'Please, prostrating yourself is not necessary.'

'Forgive me, Highness, but you are not only anointed by blood but by creation itself!' The normally hardened diplomat was overawed and teary.

'And there are many others like me.' Taren had just tried to explain that. 'Men and women from every planet in the USS. We are legion and the only veneration we require is understanding and cooperation.'

'You are probably one of us,' Zeven added.

'I wouldn't be at all surprised,' Taren agreed, crouching before Jalila.

'They all answer to you.' Jalila had probably noted this in the confrontation between the president and her Qusay this morning.

'Great leaders don't inspire followers, they inspire more great leaders.' Taren gave her view. 'And you are certainly one.'

Jalila had gone so far as to seduce and conspire with Khalid Mansur in another timeline, in the hope of lifting the curse from her Qusay, but of course Khalid betrayed her. He kept secret the little fact he was her Qusay's bastard brother whose conception had driven the previous Qusay to madness.

'Forgive me.' Jalila rose with Taren at her prompting. 'It is overwhelming.' She gasped on the statement, struggling to regain her composure. 'And it is not my nature to be so affected.'

'I know,' Taren assured her with a smile, 'but I think you will find it is in fact joy you are feeling, and you should revel in it. The nightmare of the Phemoray is over, and a grand celebration is in order, but first things first.' She brought them back around to Zeven's mission.

Jalila gave a resigned nod. 'Follow me.'

Itching!

Khalid swatted his nose and twitched it, in an attempt to allay the annoyance. He didn't want to stir from his dreams, it was so comfortable here, peaceful, *pure* bliss! *Except for the itching!*

He gave the side of his nose a proper scratch this time, but the effort woke him.

The sight of a colourfully faced creature filling the entire expanse of his vision as he opened his eyes, startled Khalid. He yelled in fright, whereupon it backed up and he realised it was only a small critter in close proximity to his own face. Khalid knew nothing about the natural world and had no desire to be educated.

The creature squawked in response to the adverse reaction and hit him in the face with the large feather it was holding.

'What the fuck?' Khalid sat up and watched the rainbow monkey drop the feather and scamper quickly up the tall bedpost to settle on a high crossbeam, continually screeching and waving its tiny hand at him in a threatening fashion. Crossbeams ran between the top and bottom of the bedposts to form a large cubed frame, and the hammock he was lying on was strung to all four posts. Clearly he wasn't in hospital any more.

Overhead the grass roof of the huge hut-like structure sloped down in front and behind him, almost to the floor, but was completely open on both sides, bar the waist-high wooden railings. This dwelling appeared to stretch the expanse of a small ravine — all he could see for miles was jungle ascending up a valley in one direction, and descending down a valley in the other. He could hear the sound of water babbling — and his curiosity urged Khalid to rise and investigate.

He took pause before placing his two feet on the floor. His damaged ankle had been strapped, and the other ankle was still bound by a psychic restraining device. This fact got him to wondering where the invisible man was. Perhaps he was here watching?

'Oh do shut up!' Khalid finally got jack of the monkey's squawking. 'I can't abide animals!'

'That is only because you fear them.'

Khalid looked to the creature who had seemingly responded to his complaint, to find it looking towards the true source of the remark.

A young, fair lad had appeared out of nowhere in the middle of the sparsely furnished treehouse, and he was holding a leg brace in his hand. 'I thought you might be needing this.'

'You are Zaman Vidor?' Khalid was confused; this was not the man known as Starman he'd been expecting. This guy appeared about a decade too young to be his prophesied destructor.

'No.' The stranger smiled at the misconception. 'He is currently doing some research on your behalf, but has asked that I take care of you in his absence.'

The monkey squawked.

'Sorry, and Karisha has volunteered to aid me in that,' the lad added to acknowledge the monkey's involvement.

'How is a bloody monkey going to help?' Khalid objected to the arrangement.

'Maimed as you are, in this place?' He motioned to the jungle around them, and then looked to the monkey to suggest, 'Perhaps a demonstration?'

Karisha leapt up to latch onto the ceiling crossbeam and scampered off across it, disappearing onto the roof.

'That's helpful,' Khalid commented dryly.

'She'll be back.' Telmo launched the leg brace in Khalid's direction, and in the split second Khalid flinched, he felt the brace clamp around his damaged leg and lock closed.

'You've got PK too?' Khalid was shocked as it used to be a rare talent and linked to the Phemorian royal bloodline.

'I don't *got* PK,' Telmo replied with humour. 'I *developed* PK. And the fact that you developed it also tells us that you are far more than you have, up until this time, appeared.'

Khalid forced a laugh at this; was he trying to compliment him? 'Hah … I'm special all right!' He gently put pressure on his sore ankle and awkwardly got himself to standing position.

'See that!' The kid startled him, having made an observation that Khalid was unaware of. 'Remorse.'

Khalid resented that implication. Yet he was surprised to note how numb he felt; there seemed to be no spite left in him — only gratitude to have his own mind back. 'What else is going to save my arse in this situation?' He covered his uncertainty with sarcasm.

'*Self realisation*,' his host replied, throwing his arms wide.

At this point Khalid suspected that his captor might have left him with a complete loon, and one that was wet behind the ears to boot. 'Where the fuck am I?'

'Clearly, you are in paradise,' he advised.

'Frujia is *far* from my idea of paradise. I hate sun, I hate sand, I hate water and I HATE animals, and bugs!' Khalid could at least guess at what planet he was being held on; the terrain was indicative of the tropical islands only found on Frujia. 'What are you planning to do with me?'

'The question is more what you will do with you?'

Was this kid playing mind games?

'But it is our intention that you learn who you *really* are, before you make that decision.'

'I've been subject to some sick shit in my time.' Khalid felt he knew the intention well enough. 'But forcing me to decide the means of my own death —'

'No,' the guy calmly insisted he was wrong about that. 'We are granting you the opportunity to decide on your own life.'

While Khalid was pondering what it could possibly mean, the monkey returned with a large pinkish fruit under one arm, which she carried down onto the hammock and held up in offering. It was about the cutest thing he'd ever seen and Khalid felt himself melt a little. 'You got that for me?'

Karisha put the fruit down and backed away from it. Reaching out towards it, Khalid noted a bite mark on his wrist — the marks matched up to the two fang-like teeth in the monkey's upper jaw. 'You bit me!' He suddenly found his anger. 'You're just fattening up your dinner, is that it?'

Again he reached for the fruit, of a mind to toss it at the creature, but the monkey did not flee. The animal launched itself towards Khalid's extended arm and clung on with all four limbs, then sank its little teeth into his arm and began suckling blood from his body.

'You … little … *parasite!*' Khalid tried shaking it off, but within moments the anger rushed away — he felt very light-headed and extremely calm. 'Whoa!' He collapsed onto the hammock once more.

'Karisha is a rare breed of monkey widely known as the rainbow monkey,' his company advised. 'But locally, they are more aptly named the vampire, or mind-melding monkey. They tranquillise their prey with a poison that triggers happy endorphins. They are extremely sensitive to the emotions of other creatures and will attack at the first sign of fear or anger.'

Karisha came up for air and looked to him, and all the amazing colours on her face appeared far more vibrant now. 'She's *so beautiful* …' The revelation brought tears to his eyes. 'Even with blood dripping from her little chin like that.'

'Yes,' his host said. 'In case you haven't guessed, Karisha's here to assist with your anger management issues. She will be your constant companion and you shall feed each other.'

Khalid drew a deep pleasurable breath; he hadn't felt this carefree ever! 'I *love* this program.'

His entire life had been spent despising the past and plotting the future; he'd never once stopped and just experienced now, mainly because he'd never lived a moment worth cherishing. But in this instance, nothing mattered beyond just being present — comfortable, relaxed and thankful to be so. Odd that, in the hands of his enemy, he'd never felt so safe.

As Zeven and Taren were led through the Phemorian palace in Tonissia, he in particular was receiving some very strange looks from the Valoureans guarding the secret depths of the ancient structure, where, he'd been informed, no man had ever trodden.

At least now Zeven had been supplied with a thought scrambler and was able to drop his mental guard. Taren could have just given him his Juju back, but they did not want to draw any attention to their amulets so it was better to just run with Jalila's solution.

They came to a long, very large, vault-like set of doors that were heavily guarded by Valoureans. They stood their ground despite the viceroy's approach — their eyes boring into Zeven.

'Step aside,' Jalila commanded, holding up the signet ring of Phemoria that the queen rarely took off her hand. 'We are on the Qusay's business.'

Upon sighting the Qusay's royal seal, all the Valoureans present dropped down onto one knee.

'Forgive me, Viceroy Lamus, but this event is unprecedented.' Despite her humbled stance, the guard in charge was suspicious.

'If you don't believe your own eyes, then by all means ask your superior once you have seen the Qusay's order granted,' Jalila suggested, before her tone became far more ominous. 'But make me wait, and I will have you all flogged and expelled from the Valoureans.'

Presented with that ultimatum, the guard in charge rose and stepped aside, whereupon the rest of the guard followed suit.

Jalila moved directly to the doors and locking the seal of the Qusay's ring into the keyhole on the doors, she turned it clockwise. There was a loud *chink* of metal disengaging, whereupon Jalila removed the ring and the large metal doors of the vault opened inwards to grant them entry.

Beyond was a grand, vaulted, stone arched hallway, eons old judging from the archaic design. At the base of both sides of each arch, the pillars curved out into a plinth, hollowed out in the centre and filled with oil. These burst into flame in consecutive order down the long hall, to light the way to a similar set of metal doors at the far end of the passage.

'You are to speak to no one but your superior about this event,' Jalila advised the Valoureans as Zeven and Taren proceeded into the passage. 'If word of this gets out to anyone, you will all be held to account.'

Jalila followed them into the passage, leaving some very bemused and agitated Valoureans in her wake. Once the signet ring Jalila was carrying entered the passage, the doors automatically closed behind them.

'How will the Qusay react when she finds out about this?' Zeven queried the viceroy, once they were enclosed in the hallway.

'She won't find out,' Jalila assured her. 'The General of the Valoureans saw our ruler hand over complete authority to me this morning when she gave me this ring to carry during her convalescence. The general is under strict instructions to refer all state affairs to me.'

'You don't think it's wrong bringing a man down here, when up until now you've been forbidden to do so?' Zeven was curious about her liberal attitude.

'I have always believed that the Phemoray are pure evil,' Jalila enlightened him. 'So any rule they made I mean to break.'

'I can see we are going to get along very well.' Taren was right with the viceroy on that count.

'We should have their crown tossed in a furnace and destroyed,' Jalila posed to test Taren's theory, and Taren was about to agree.

'No!' Zeven stressed and both women turned to him, surprised by his protest, and he was momentarily stunned to have to explain. 'That crown must be dispensed with in a very particular way, so that the curse can be dispelled, otherwise you may just as easily set the Phemoray free to wreak havoc wherever they like.'

'And you know this *how?*' Taren challenged.

'You know *how*,' Zeven suggested more timidly. 'The crown needs to be kept in a safe place until the right elements come together to release the curse properly. But I am working on assembling those elements as we speak,' he assured them both.

Taren didn't like taking anything on faith, and her expression and Jalila's were most displeased.

'Ladies, I believe that not only can the curse of the Phemoray be lifted, but the curse of the halfling of shadow at the same time.' He looked Taren in the eyes to drive home the fact. 'We have *never* managed to do that before.'

'You know who the halfling of shadow is?' Jalila was shocked.

'I suspect,' Zeven did not commit.

'Who?' Jalila pushed for an answer.

'No offence to you, Prime Minister, but the task of seeking and dealing with that curse, fate has assigned to me. It would not do to have every secret service agency in the USS confusing the issue.'

Clearly Jalila saw his point, and probably was regretting giving him a thought scrambler. 'That child was an abomination!'

Cursed from conception does not an abomination make. Zeven wished he could express that thought aloud. 'One might think so, but I have reason to believe that assumption may prove incorrect.'

'What?' Jalila was perplexed by his response.

Taren knew he'd seen more of the present and immediate future than she could remember at this point in time, so she must also realise that if they handled this correctly it would be most beneficial to the outcome. 'Considering the Phemorian prophecy about the end of the Phemoray, and the Sermetic prophecy regarding the end of the halfling of shadow, it would seem advisable to trust Zeven's word in this matter.'

'Agreed.' Jalila's frown lifted. 'I didn't imagine being rid of the Phemoray would be a simple matter. If you have knowledge as to how it can be done, then your plan is my plan.'

The doors at the far end of the passage were opened in the same fashion as the first, but what lay beyond them came as a complete surprise to Zeven.

They were on a balcony, overlooking a vast ancient vault that was filled with tall rows of pods, all lined up on vertical shelves like a library — only in the place of books there were unconscious women, whose faces could be seen through windows in the tops of the otherwise opaque pods.

'Oh my goodness.' Even Taren was taken aback. 'I had no idea there were so many!'

'Phemoria's finest,' Jalila said, sadly.

'I thought you said you'd been here?' Zeven had to wonder why Taren was so overwhelmed.

'I've visited the celestial city that the soul-minds of these women frequent.' Taren's gaze drifted back to the view. 'I knew this place existed, but …' She slowly shook her head, lost for words for a moment. 'What would happen if we just shut the system down?'

Jalila's expression became very solemn. 'That was attempted by one of my predecessors, a long time ago. The act severed every one of them from their soul-minds and they all died instantly. The one who tried to free them was executed by the Phemoray, and they re-culled our population to re-populate their celestial city. It is theorised that only lifting the curse will return these sisters to us safely.'

'Do you think they wish to come back to the physical realm?' Zeven wondered out loud.

'That is irrelevant,' Taren cut in. 'If these women were meant to spend their life as spirits, they would never have incarnated in the first place.'

Jalila found her smile. 'My sentiments exactly.'

'So how do you do this?' Zeven posed, not wanting to seem rude. 'Will it take long? I'm on a bit of a tight schedule.'

'Are you now?' Taren chided.

'Stop that,' Zeven protested. 'One day you will thank me, and on *that day* you will be very pleased not to have given me a hard time about this.'

'I'm not giving you a hard time!' Taren placed hands on hips. 'I'm helping you, or we wouldn't be here.'

'Anyone would think you were siblings, not cousins,' Jalila noted, slipping off her shoes and proceeding barefoot.

'Join me.' Jalila moved to one of several smaller balconies that annexed off the front of the main balcony, and stood upon a round plate in the middle of it. As Taren and Zeven both went to remove their boots, Jalila advised that it was not necessary for them to do so.

The little balcony had a bench curving beneath its balustrade and at first glance, Zeven had thought this just a decorative seating arrangement. But as they joined the viceroy, the plate beneath her feet lit up and the annex detached from the main balcony and began to hover.

'Telepathic control.' Zeven assumed Jalila was directing the module through her feet.

Jalila smiled to confirm, before suggesting, 'You might want to sit down?'

'Good call.' Zeven planted himself in the seat beside Taren as the little balcony began to plummet downwards into the library of capsules, before shooting off down one of the long aisles.

After an all too brief thrill ride through the massive complex, their module slowed and, open side facing the wall of capsules, they came to hover before one in particular. 'Lock,' Jalila said out loud, to prevent her passengers panicking as she stepped off the control plate to approach their subject, who was the spitting image of the viceroy in their company.

'Your sister,' Taren stated what was all too obvious.

'*Twin* sister,' Jalila said sadly. 'The Phemoray split us up on purpose.'

'She is telepathic, like you?' Taren supposed.

'Because we were so strongly linked, we had the best chance of forming a telepathic line between the worlds, *were* it ever required,' Jalila said with a good serve of spite.

'And was it ever required?' Zeven asked the question Jalila was begging to be asked.

'They tested the link when they first split us up, that's how I know it can be done. But no, *not once* did the Phemoray require our services in over a hundred years.' Jalila's voice went raspy as she looked back to her slumbering sister. 'That abnormal apparition of spite and hatred tore us apart for a backup plan it never used, and now that indulgence shall be its undoing.'

She placed her hands on the metal plate positioned beneath the window in the capsule and closed her eyes.

Over the next half an hour Jalila didn't utter a word, but Zeven witnessed the viceroy run a whole gamut of emotions. This was an odd and rare event, as Phemorian women were usually externally emotionless.

When Jalila finally stepped away, she appeared completely exhausted, and Zeven waited for her to return to their company and be seated.

'Was she able to help us?' Zeven queried.

Jalila drew a deep breath, appearing overwhelmed, but nodded to confirm. 'She told me that the Old Ones are a celestial race who can still assume a solid form but rarely choose to. Our sisters in the Phemoray's city know them as the Dropa, and have had dealings with them in the past —'

'The Dropa?' Zeven cut in, stunned by the mention. That was the name of an extra-terrestrial race that had crash landed in ancient China, until the timekeepers changed the timelines of that universe and the event never happened. *But how could they have ended up here?* he wondered. *The Eternity Gate, perhaps?*

'Does that mean something to you?' Taren queried.

'It does.' Zeven nodded. Khalid had once had a deep affinity with the last of the Dropa people on Earth, Dorje Pema, for she had been the spiritual master who had aided Khalid to self realisation. 'I think we are definitely onto something here.'

'I'm sorry to inform you, but the Dropa severed all communication with our sister city following an incident that happened during our last Qusay's reign.'

'Ah-huh.' Zeven had suspected this. 'The Phemoray arranged a pairing between the late Qusay and a male of the Dropa kind,' he hypothesised, 'just as they had many times before. That's how psychic power became inherited through the Phemorian line. Then what happened?'

Both women in Zeven's company were staring at him, stunned speechless.

'A son happened,' Jalila ventured to say. 'Our Qusay was not treated with all due respect during the conception. The prince the Dropa chose abused her in ways thought inconceivable to the Dropa. Not only did he overpower her physically, but to a point that she lost all control of her psychic sensibilities and conceived a son.'

'The halfling of shadow,' Zeven deduced.

'But —' Taren was about to query Chironjivi's involvement, for they had always assumed Khalid was born of an evil spirit and had no earthly father.

'Shh!' Zeven didn't want to get off track. 'What happened to the Dropa Prince?'

'He was seized and thrown in prison, and eventually went as mad as our late Qusay did. But when our sisters refused to release him, the Dropa cut all communication with us.'

'Thus the next time a Phemorian Qusay needed impregnating, you were forced to look to the royal House of Sermetica.' Zeven motioned to Taren, who was the issue from that pairing.

'That's right.' Jalila was stunned. 'But how could you know all of that, when even I did not?'

'Ditto,' Taren concurred.

'Where is the Dropa Prince now?' Zeven sidestepped the query and remained focused on Jalila.

'Still in prison, or dead, I suspect,' Jalila outlined the only two options.

'We need to find him,' Zeven stated in no uncertain terms. 'He has been wrongly incarcerated and I can prove it.'

Jalila gasped, Taren did not. 'I believe I understand Zeven's reasoning here, and he is absolutely correct.'

'If he is still alive,' Zeven instructed, 'we need to repair him, physically, mentally, emotionally, spiritually.'

'How?' Jalila felt the request impossible.

'You find him, clean him up, and we shall take care of the rest,' Zeven advised.

'We?' Taren noted her inclusion in his plan.

'If you could get Ringbalin to pay him a visit, that would help a lot,' Zeven said. 'Then Telmo and I can take it from there.'

'Okay,' Taren agreed warily.

'Excellent.' Zeven stood. 'I have to get moving, but I'll be back in touch soon.'

'Be careful.' Taren raised half a grin, seeming more inclined towards trusting him.

'Don't do anything with the crown for now.' Zeven made them both swear. 'We need to get this right this time, 'cause it's our last shot at this.'

Taren nodded, understanding his meaning.

'And if your mother decides to have a family dinner party, delay it until I've assembled all the elements we need to dispose of these curses,' Zeven cautioned.

Taren gaped at the suggestion. 'That's hardly likely —'

'In fact,' Zeven spoke over her, 'ensure my daughter, Ray, does not visit Phemoria before the said event either.'

Taren frowned as she fathomed his reasoning. 'Ray has a part to play in all of this?'

Zeven grinned, and at the risk of taking the module he was standing on with him — and the two ladies besides — he decided to jump ship.

Plummeting feet-first into the void was an excitement rush the like of which Zeven had not felt in some time. In the past he would have waited until the last possible second to set his intention on his next destination, to enjoy the ride and the shock of his onlookers. But these days too much was riding on his memory.

Khalid. The thought swept his form into a quantum stream of light, before his company had time to gasp.

5

ANGER MANAGEMENT

By the time Taren returned to AMIE, the third mission of the day had been completed. She had teleported herself to her husband, and she joined him in the captain's office — Lucian was alone.

As the captain was already seated behind his desk, Taren took a seat to be debriefed.

He reported that the AMIE team who had gone to Sermetica to retrieve the Princess Satomi's body from the Vidor family crypt had found her not entombed as expected, but in a stasis module, where she had been kept in a state of suspended animation since the time of her death. Due to Zeven's directive, Swithin was present to resurrect her, and Kassi Madri — the ship's medical officer — was on-hand when the princess returned to life and began bleeding anew from her death wounds. The patient was immediately transported to the medical quarters on AMIE, where Ringbalin Malachi was called in to heal her wounds and restore her to full health.

'Good grief!' Taren smiled at the wonderful news, and at what could be achieved when psychics were permitted to pool their talents. 'So Mythric has his princess back.'

'And Zeven has his mother,' Lucian added, dryly.

'Maiara foresaw all of this,' Taren imagined. 'And in the end, managed to save them all from Khalid.'

'Yes, quite the little miracle.' Lucian's tone turned cynical, and he leaned forwards onto his desk to advise, 'Only now Khalid has escaped from prison.'

'What?' Taren's heart began racing in panic.

'He was apparently spotted on security camera performing psychic feats in his cell, *whilst restrained*. When the wardens tried to sedate him, Khalid managed to jam his ankle in the security door and crush his restraining device.' Lucian conveyed what President Anselm had confided in Taren's absence.

'But why would he want to smash the neutraliser, grievously injuring himself in the process, if he already had his Powers back?' Taren challenged.

'He thought he was under psychic attack,' Lucian voiced his conclusion.

'You think someone broke Khalid out of prison?' Taren didn't think Khalid had any allies.

'Well, you and I both know it takes at least an hour for the effects of a psychic neutraliser to wear off.' The irony in Lucian's voice increased. 'So … with a broken ankle, under sedation, and with his psychic powers still dumbed, Khalid vanished from his top security vehicle in transit to the hospital. You know what that means, don't you?'

Deep pangs of shock were shooting through her body as she realised. 'He either mysteriously got his Powers back and crushed his ankle for no good reason, or he had psychokinetic help.'

'Exactly right,' Lucian awarded, sounding most displeased. 'Needless to say this does not bode well for the psychic freedom act your parents are hoping to pass through the USS senate.' He stood, frustrated, and then took a few deep breaths to calm himself. 'Fortunately your father is altering the story to one that indicates Khalid acted on his own.'

In this case Lucian was absolutely right to be angry; she was angry too! She did not appreciate feeling like a scolded child.

'There are only a handful of people living with such a talent, all of whom are on board this vessel. But at the time Khalid escaped, Zeven was mysteriously absent.'

Taren was feeling ill; surely Zeven had not freed Khalid! Yet it could explain his interest in the father of their nemesis.

'In light of all this,' Lucian appealed kindly from behind the desk, 'do you want to tell me what is really going on? As I am certain Zeven did not suddenly develop full-blown precognition, without at least his wife finding out about it?'

Taren stood up to confess. 'The truth is I have two timekeepers AWOL and I have no idea why, nor do I know what they are up to.'

'What do you mean, AWOL?'

'I mean, they have executed a time-jump without me.' Taren threw both her hands up in question briefly, completely bemused. 'Apparently they … we,' she included Lucian in the equation, 'have already returned to Kila to warn Rhun about the threat to the Chosen. Upon completing that mission the plan was to return to the week before the Oceane incident. But for some reason Zeven and Telmo jumped back to this morning. So I shall be unable to verify Zeven's story until just before D-day.'

Lucian sank back into his seat. 'What did Zeven say he was doing?'

'He wouldn't say. Told me to trust him …' She reached into her jacket pocket and retrieved the memo outlining Zeven's instructions. 'And gave me this.' She handed the missive to Lucian, who upon reading it learned that it outlined every essential component of the missions they'd just run. 'Zeven did say that under no circumstance was anyone from AMIE to come looking for him.'

'Including you?' Lucian clarified.

'Yep.' Taren raised both brows, baffled, and then frowned as she considered. 'Oddly, he also returned his Juju stone to me for safe keeping.'

'That confirms it then,' Lucian reasoned. 'The Juju stone would have repelled Khalid and made him violently ill.'

Lucian was right about that. Taren slapped her forehead into her palm. 'No, I can't believe it. Why would Zeven do such a thing?' Taren's head shot up as she gasped. 'Unless he means to kill Khalid and fulfil Maiara's prophecy? But then why the interest in Khalid's father?'

'Chironjivi?' Lucian assumed.

'No,' Taren confused the issue. 'It seemed Chironjivi did not use his old corpse of a body to rape the late Qusay of Phemoria. Instead, his evil spirit possessed the body of the Qusay's chosen mate. Zeven must have uncovered information pointing to the Old Ones as the source of the male of this coupling, as we have confirmed this claim is quite true.'

'Your research trip on Phemoria?' Lucian guessed.

'What an education that was!' Taren felt her eyes bulging, as she considered how much work there was to be done on that planet in the wake of the Phemoray.

'So Khalid is fully human?' Lucian was shocked to learn this.

'And if separated from his demons ...' Taren was having an epiphany. 'We might even be able to —'

'Rehabilitate him.' Lucian reached the same conclusion.

'Zeven came up with such a plan? Really?' Taren felt this notion sounded as odd as Zeven planning to kill Khalid. 'But that would explain why Zeven is seeking Khalid's father, to be part of that process.'

'Or to be used to torture his enemy further?' Lucian had not ruled out the darker possibility.

'This is Zeven we are talking about.' Taren defended her cousin.

'A Zeven who has gone through who knows what since you saw him yesterday, ' Lucian reminded her and Taren was forced to concede the caution. 'Revenge would explain why he doesn't want any of us going after him. Why he's not wearing his Juju, as it would not allow him to take a life.'

'Zeven wouldn't risk the Grigori revoking his powers again.' Taren knew that in her soul. 'And why the desire to heal Khalid's father? If he wanted to shock Khalid with the sad truth, he'd just drag his father before him raw from prison and not have him healed first.'

'Wait?' Lucian was sure they'd missed some information here. 'They imprisoned the Prince of the Old Ones? The Old Ones who built the inter-system gateways?'

'Well the Phemoray thought he had raped their Qusay,' Taren defended her people. 'They don't know anything about Dead Man

Downs, apart from what the legends say about it being haunted and no one ever returning from there. If Khalid's father is still alive, Zeven has asked me to return to Phemoria with Ringbalin to heal the fallen prince.' Taren was thoughtful a moment.

'Well,' Lucian assessed all the information. 'From what I can tell, Zeven seems to be doing good work so far. All today's missions went smoothly, thanks to his intel, and a tonne of new information has come to light about Khalid.'

'And many other things,' Taren conceded with a smile, thankful that Lucian was awarding their pilot the benefit of the doubt. 'I shall get some shut-eye, and then take Ringbalin to Phemoria. Zeven will be returning there to collect the man in question, and I shall be waiting. No more sidestepping the issue; we need to know exactly what his intentions are.'

Lucian, who could read her like a book, seemed appeased; clearly, he knew that he now had the full story. 'Agreed.'

Upon his arrival at Vadik's treehouse on Frujia, Zeven found the top floor abandoned. He approached the railing and looking over it, spotted Telmo and Vadik lying on the small beach down below, in the shade. Khalid was wading around in the river, arms folded, and not very happy.

Zeven headed down some wooden stairs that gave access to the upper bank on one side; here a lean-to housed a kitchen. Stone stairs led under the top floor and down the bank, where the stairs forked.

To the left a set of wooden stairs led to a lounge area, suspended from chains that hung from the upper level of the dwelling. These chains attached to all four corners of the large, square basket-like construction, which had lounges running along underneath the taller banisters at the edges. This suspended area provided excellent views of the river that ran beneath the hut, while being high enough above it to avoid the damp. The lounge was protected from the weather by the level above, but was always well shaded and breezy.

To the right of the fork, the stone stairs continued down the bank to a pathway that led along the river's edge. Zeven followed this down to the little beach that sat in the shade of the hut during the warmer afternoon hours.

'You stay away from me, you little blood-sucking freak!' Their patient was yelling at a colourful little monkey that was screeching at him from the bank, unwilling to enter the water. 'What? You can't get me in here?' he goaded the animal. 'Well … suck shit!'

'Making progress, are we?' Zeven commented on the scene that greeted him.

'Well, yes.' Telmo sat up upon realising they had company. 'We've got him liking the water.'

'I don't like it! I hate all the fucking elements!' Khalid waved his arms about, accidentally splashing himself in the process.

'Oi!' As a master of the elements, Vadik was offended.

Zeven placed one hand on Vadik's shoulder to calm him, but addressed Khalid. 'That hatred is born from fear, which is due to ignorance.'

'Well I'm pretty damn intimate with water at the moment, and I still *hate it!*' Khalid staggered about thigh-deep in the river, getting used to balancing with his leg brace. 'But it's the only place I'm safe from that little blood-sucking devil, making me stoned out of my mind!'

'And what's wrong with that then?' Zeven queried, removing his jacket.

'I can't think straight!' Khalid emphasised.

'You can't scheme, you mean?' Zeven corrected, stripping off his T-shirt and boots. 'You spend too much time plotting the future or cursing your past. You need to spend a little time in the present, my friend; the monkey's venom aids you to do that.'

'What are you doing?' Khalid was immediately affronted to note Zeven heading towards the water.

'I'm coming in.'

'Why?' Khalid staggered backwards into deeper water.

''Cause you need to remember how *not* to be such a sour-face, whingeing, pain-in-the-arse, sorry for himself, motherfucker!'

Telmo and Vadik cheered Zeven's response.

'What do you plan to do?' Khalid was on edge as Zeven dived beneath the water. 'Where is he?' Khalid turned circles, awaiting his fate. But after a few moments when the attack never came, he dropped his guard, fed up. 'Just fucking kill me then!'

'Boo!' Zeven startled the life out of Khalid as he appeared behind him and then turned invisible.

It must have appeared odd to those onshore when Khalid shrieked and began contorting wildly. 'Stop! You're a dead man!' he threatened, while evidently suppressing an urge to laugh. 'I won't crack!'

'Is Bob ... *tickling* our prisoner?' Vadik queried Telmo, confused.

'Our patient,' Telmo corrected, and Vadik served him a wink in response. 'But yes, it would appear so.'

Vadik grinned at this. 'Payback. Come, Karisha.' He held out his hand and the monkey ran up his arm and perched itself on his shoulder, whereupon Vadik waded out to join the rumble.

'Oh, fuck off!' Khalid noted Vadik's approach, but couldn't restrain his laughter any longer. 'This is fucking torture!' he squealed, gasping for breath as Vadik brought his considerable weight to bear on the matter. Karisha was quick to bite into Khalid, whereby his protests ceased, and he let loose his laughter. 'You rotten fucking bastards!'

'Oh, really?' Vadik lifted Khalid clean out of the water and the monkey returned to Vadik's shoulder.

'Well, I have been known to make rash judgements,' Khalid attempted to retract the statement.

Vadik only laughed as he cast him backward. 'Are we learning yet?' he hollered before Khalid landed in the river, and disappeared under the water.

'How deep is the water there?' Zeven queried, knowing Khalid couldn't swim.

Vadik shrugged. 'Should we care?'

'You'd let a team member drown, would you?'

Vadik frowned but couldn't bring himself to care. 'If he was a little insufferable prick —'

Khalid resurfaced in a huge spray of water, arms waving about wildly, as he gasped in air amid laughter. 'Ha-hah! That was … fun!' Khalid seemed surprised.

'If you ask me to do it again …' Vadik pointed a finger at him in warning, 'I'll flatten you!'

'Yes! Do it again!' Khalid waded back towards them.

'He thinks we are playing?' Vadik was annoyed by this.

'That is exactly what we are doing,' Zeven advised, lifting Khalid out of the water using his PK. Their patient squealed with delight as Zeven cast him backwards into the water once again. 'Khalid never had a childhood, he's never played, had fun, been loved, or had anything or anyone to be grateful for.'

Vadik was deeply bemused by Zeven's statement. 'My childhood wasn't exactly ideal either —'

'But you were not possessed and controlled by abhorrent, disembodied demons since the day of your birth.'

'And he was?' Vadik challenged, pointing to where Khalid was surfacing in a fit of laughter.

'*Yes*,' Zeven confirmed, forthrightly. 'I can, and will, prove that claim in due course.'

Vadik frowned, looking back to Khalid laughing like a lunatic as he splashed water around. 'That's pretty horrific,' he had to admit.

'I do believe this is the first time in his life that Khalid has been free to feel anything at all,' Zeven said as he walked them both back to shore, out of Khalid's earshot. 'You and I recognise bad times because we've had good ones, Khalid has not. He's never had anyone on his side, nor has he had anyone to side with.'

'You could be talking about any psychic ever born!' Vadik cried.

'Of all the psychics in existence, including the boss …' Zeven hypothesised, 'I believe Khalid may be the most significant.'

'Why is that?' Telmo was curious.

'What is the easiest way to hide a great treasure, and protect it from discovery?' Zeven posed.

'Have it housed in something impenetrable,' Vadik replied.

'And guarded by something vicious.' Telmo grinned, bobbing his head in understanding. 'But you are acting on more than a hunch, I can tell by your surety.'

'True, but I have a few more pieces of the puzzle to fit together yet,' Zeven waived that topic for another time. 'What is of paramount import is that we fill Khalid up with as many emotionally stimulating experiences as we can. This island is the best place in the USS to experience the many wonders of life, and you know this place better than anyone!' Zeven put it to Vadik. 'Show Khalid the joys of being alive.'

'And what if he chooses to return to his evil ways?' Vadik argued.

'Then he does so with a balanced perspective on life, and in full knowledge of the damage he is doing,' Zeven reasoned. 'That has not been the case before now.'

'You really think you can rehabilitate the most vindictive agent that the secret services ever commissioned?' Vadik was finding the truth of their mission hard to swallow.

'I've been to the future, I've seen it done,' Zeven advised Vadik, whose jaw dropped open at the claim. 'And the boss is counting on us to accomplish this.'

'Why bother? Why not just kill him?' Clearly Vadik couldn't let that aspiration go.

'Then we would be no better than the MSS that you seek to bring down,' Zeven explained.

Vadik began nodding. 'I see the boss is very wise,' he awarded, and Zeven grinned, quietly proud of himself.

'Certainly is,' Telmo added, and Zeven was stunned by his rare praise.

'But?' Zeven knew there was always a 'but' as far as Telmo was concerned.

'No but,' Telmo assured with a grin. 'I would hardly become involved in a plan that wasn't ethically sound.'

'Of course you wouldn't,' Zeven concurred, realising the truth of that statement was a boost in confidence. 'So, you guys have got this?' He indicated Khalid.

'You know me,' Telmo stated, needing to say no more.

Zeven looked to Vadik, who was now viewing Khalid as something of a curiosity. 'Can you do it?'

Vadik looked to Zeven, uncertain. 'You've seen what he's like when he is in his right mind — he's an ingrate who sees the beauty in nothing!'

'Exactly,' Zeven concurred. 'So we need him feeling like this …' He pointed to Khalid who was still laughing at his own clumsy attempt to wade out of the water. 'When he's not high on monkey venom.'

Vadik's frown deepened. 'I don't know if that's possible?'

'I know it's a tough assignment,' Zeven granted, 'but it's a vital one. If you doubt your own patience in this matter —'

'No,' Vadik insisted. 'I want in on your rebellion, and if this is what it takes …' He looked back at Khalid as he collapsed back on shore exhausted from the outpouring of joy. 'I accept the challenge.' Vadik was grinning like he knew he could garner some satisfaction from the exercise, which was a worry.

'I'll be here to supervise,' Telmo reassured Zeven, who with a thought was dressed and dry once more. 'Where are you off to?'

'To finish piecing the jigsaw together,' he advised.

'Don't *go*,' Khalid demanded — the venom must have been wearing off. 'I want to talk to you.'

'And I you,' Zeven replied. 'But first —' He mentally honed in on Jalila Lamus, and willed to join her.

'Don't fucking disappear again —'

Zeven joined the acting prime minister of Phemoria in her office and Taren was with her. These two women had a lot to talk about, but oddly they were both seated, lost in quiet contemplation when he arrived.

'So what's news?' He announced his arrival, whereupon they both snapped to attention and rose. 'Did you find him?'

'We did,' Jalila said in a circumspect fashion, 'and he lives …'

'But?' Zeven invited Jalila to voice her concerns.

'Understandably, he is mentally, emotionally and physically scarred from his stay in prison,' the Phemorian leader explained, as Taren approached to show him some footage of the subject that she had stored in her communicator.

The man appeared completely feral, emaciated, and there was not one part of his body that was not covered in festering wounds.

'How is this man still alive?' Zeven was shocked by the images.

'Apparently, if the Dropa take a physical human form, they are immortal and cannot die.' Jalila implied that she had only just discovered this.

'So he would have remained imprisoned in this sorry state forevermore?' Zeven was a little riled to learn this, and Jalila appeared regretful too.

'This is not the prime minister's fault, or anybody's; the Phemoray were the only ones privy to this information,' Taren politely reminded him, but Zeven was still hot under the collar.

'Valoureans did this to him?'

'No,' Jalila refuted the blame. 'All the festering wounds you see were self inflicted.'

'Ringbalin is with him now,' Taren advised, 'so at least his physical scars can be healed.'

Zeven scoffed, and shook his head. He didn't buy the self-inflicted injury part of the tale. 'Does this unfortunate have a name?'

'Kaveh Ahura Mazida,' Jalila informed, 'which in the old tongue means royal lord of light, truth and goodness. But following the *incident* with our late Qusay, he was known as Angra Mainyu, the evil spirit. The name change was of his own choosing, I am told.'

Zeven was even more sceptical, but calmed down, realising that laying blame was not going to be beneficial. 'May I see the man in question, please.'

'I need to speak with you privately first.' Taren waylaid the proceedings.

'I'll leave you my office.' Jalila moved to exit.

'That won't be necessary,' Taren politely declined — no doubt

fearing the office might be bugged or under security surveillance —
and looked to her cousin. 'Follow me.'

'To the end of creation.' Zeven wanted to roll his eyes, knowing
he was in for a grilling.

'We'll be back, presently,' Taren advised Jalila and vanished.

'I am very sorry about this oversight,' Jalila said to Zeven before
he departed. 'I intend to have the entire prison system reviewed in
the wake of the Phemoray, as I realise there will be others who have
been wrongly incarcerated at their command.'

'Good will come of all this, no doubt.' Zeven wanted to
encourage her efforts.

Knowledge of Khalid's heritage and his true father had not come
to light the last time they had all lived through these events, and
the silver lining was that it only confirmed to Zeven that he'd done
the right thing taking on this personal mission. Now to convince
Taren of that.

With no clue where Taren was leading him, Zeven was rather
surprised to find himself in Taren's security apartment on
Maladaan — they hadn't been here since becoming involved in the
AMIE project.

'You still keep this place?' Zeven ran his finger along a side table
covered in dust. 'It hasn't changed a bit in what? Six years?'

'About that.' Taren was clearly not in the mood for a trip down
memory lane. 'Did you assist Khalid's escape from prison?'

'Yep. He was going to escape anyway.' Zeven shrugged off the
event and headed into the kitchen. 'You got any coffee?' He turned
about to find a freshly made cappuccino in a take-away container,
floating before his eyes. 'Oh, cheers.' He took hold of the beverage,
and had a sip.

'Do you plan to kill him?'

Zeven was so shocked by the question, his coffee near came out
his nose. 'What? No!' he spluttered, between gasps for breath.

'Sorry.' Taren seemed delighted to see how abhorrent he found
the premise. 'So what *is* the plan?'

'To rehabilitate him, of course.' Zeven put the coffee down and flicked the spillage from his person.

'You are psychotic!' Taren appealed with dramatic flair. 'This is the man who tried to kill you as a baby. Do you really expect me to believe —'

'*Yes. I do*,' Zeven roared, in his own defence. 'That was not Khalid! That was Chironjivi and his horde. Khalid has been cursed since the day he was born … don't you have to wonder *why*? And I'm talking in the greater scheme of things here … why did creation choose him to carry such a horrific burden?'

Taren was obviously surprised by the gusto he put into Khalid's defence. 'You're right, that is a very good question. And that's why you are seeking Khalid's father?'

'You got it.' Zeven retrieved his coffee to take another stab at drinking some of it.

'How did you find out about him?' Taren conjured herself up a cup of tea.

'Ah yes.' Zeven pulled the archaic memory disk from his pocket.

Taren laughed. 'I haven't seen one of those in a long time! What's on it?'

'Maiara spouting prophecy the night I was born.' Zeven watched Taren's eyes light up with curiosity.

'Someone recorded the event?'

'Indeed.' Zeven was not as excited by the fact now. 'The same woman who saw to it that the item reached my hands, before taking her own life.'

Taren gasped. 'In front of you?'

Zeven winced. 'Your quest for detail is really morbid sometimes, just saying.'

'Sorry, I didn't mean —' Taren waved off a full explanation, not to be sidetracked. 'Whose plan was it to save Khalid's soul?'

'It was mine,' Zeven admitted. 'You didn't send me on this mission, I chose to do this on my own. But then, I was the one prophesied to do so.'

Taren couldn't argue. 'And Telmo?'

'He believed in the cause and followed suit.' Zeven took a seat on the lounge in a puff of dust. 'See, Khalid got sucked into that other universe with us. Severed from his demons, he was a different person and was recruited by the timekeepers. But there was —'

Taren burst out laughing at this point. 'I'm sorry,' she attempted to rein in her amusement. 'But do you know how improbable that sounds?'

'I don't care!' Zeven stated frankly. 'Khalid has been a good friend to all of us in the future, and you not remembering that doesn't change the fact that this is the right thing to do.'

'What about Chironjivi?' Taren probed — Khalid aside, she knew they still had the curse to contend with.

'That entity is contained for the moment,' Zeven was happy to report. 'And I know what is required to lay that ghost to rest permanently. But you have to give me some time to pull all the elements together.'

Taren mused upon his appeal, and sipped her tea. 'Anything we can do to assist?'

'No,' was Zeven's first reaction, but then he reconsidered. 'AMIE might want to explore Oceane's star system in a bit more depth, however.'

'What are we looking for?'

Zeven shrugged. 'Of all the inter-system gateways, that one was the first built, and the only one the Dropa shut down. Why?'

'To protect Oceane and the celestial architect at work there,' Taren supposed. 'But admittedly we've always been so caught up in what is going on on Oceane that we've not explored the rest of the system.'

'This could be a good opportunity,' Zeven explained, 'as the next few years are fairly uneventful for AMIE, especially now that Khalid is under watchful eyes.'

'But what about the psychics being tracked down and persecuted on Maladaan, thanks to a photon counter I invented?' Taren was clearly not prepared to let that ride.

'Kalayna will come up with a clever way to solve that problem without anyone ever having to leave AMIE.' Zeven finished up his coffee and tossed the container aside, where it vanished.

'Serious?' Taren was impressed by the claim, and disposed of her cup in the same fashion.

With a nod to confirm she had nothing to worry about, Zeven stood to appeal, 'So may I please get on now?'

'This project of yours could take years, you realise?'

'Even that's a little optimistic, especially if you keep delaying me,' Zeven quipped, and Taren served him an unamused look. 'But worth it, if we can get through D-day on Oceane without incident.'

'So there was an incident last time,' Taren deduced, 'with the being's departure from this universe?'

'That has already been averted by my actions … sheesh!' Zeven threw his hands up.

'Sorry!' Taren raised both hands in truce. 'I have Lucian on my back and we owe him some answers.'

'Then let's get some, shall we?' Zeven forced a grin and vanished back to Phemoria, eager to meet with the Kaveh Ahura Mazida.

When Zeven and Taren rejoined Jalila Lamus, she was consulting with Ringbalin inside the mental institution that sistered the Phemorian prison in Tonissia. Ringbalin was wavering in his stance, appearing completely exhausted as he noted their arrival.

'I've done what all I can, and physically he is healed,' he reported. 'But I cannot fix his mental anguish; perhaps you should call in Amie?' The healer's legs nearly went from beneath him, and Taren and Zeven were quick to support him and guide him to the closest seat.

'Healing doesn't usually take it out of you like this,' Taren noted, sitting beside him.

'Usually patients want to be healed, but this man was fighting me all the way,' Ringbalin said. 'No sooner had I healed him than he was scratching his wounds with his own fingernails.'

'We've had to strap him down,' Jalila advised.

'Has he been sedated?' Zeven was concerned.

'No,' Jalila said. 'I thought you would like him coherent. Or at least as coherent as he can be … I am afraid he is quite mad.'

'We can't bring Amie in to rework his horrible memories,' Zeven was sorry to inform Ringbalin. 'I need his memory intact.'

'Then I don't know what to suggest.' Ringbalin barely had the energy to keep his eyes open.

'You've done well,' Taren advised their botanist-cum-biologist. 'I'm going to take you home to rest.' Taren took hold of his arm to teleport Ringbalin with her. 'Zeven can take over here.'

'Before you do,' Jalila addressed Ringbalin, 'I just wanted to thank you for staying my hand earlier today. You were right, you are all the answer to my greatest wish.'

Zeven had not been present when most of the AMIE team had lifted the Qusay of Phemoria's curse earlier today, but obviously Ringbalin had worked his charms on Jalila; the healer's gentle ways seemed to cast a spell over every woman, even when he wasn't trying.

'It is an extraordinary man who can dissuade a Phemorian from her sworn duty,' the prime minister awarded, obviously quite taken with him.

'As you now realise, I have an unfair advantage in that regard,' Ringbalin downplayed the praise, as was his way. 'But all shall be well with your people, as promised … I believe your good self and …' he looked to Taren, 'the boss, will see to that.'

'You have played a very large part in today's events.' Taren would not allow him to forgo his due. 'So much so, that we've utterly drained you!'

'I am grateful to be finally able to use this talent for the greater good and not just my own personal advancement,' he insisted. 'My vitality will be easily replenished in my greenhouse.'

'I should love to see your greenhouse in space,' Jalila posed. 'It must be quite something to be so invigorating.'

'It would be my honour to give you the tour, Prime Minister.' Ringbalin was being polite, but Zeven was not entirely sure that was the message Jalila was receiving.

'I shall look forward to that,' she accepted, and even Taren was looking a little concerned.

'We should go,' Taren decided, for even jaded as he was, Ringbalin was suddenly exuding a very amorous vibration.

At this point in time Ringbalin had not been on board AMIE long enough to realise that their Phemorian marine biologist was slowly falling in love with him, and Ringbalin was far too modest to aspire to seducing a Phemorian. He felt it was his ability to influence emotions that had women falling at his feet all the time, and could never truly believe he'd won their affection fairly. What Ringbalin failed to take into consideration was that it was the fact that he had the capacity to exude such emotional love and healing that was the big attraction. Phemorian women had a common belief that all men were emotional amoebas — Ringbalin was clear proof that this was not the case, and Zeven felt this was why Phemorians in particular seemed to find the young, effeminate horticulturist so attractive. Two Phemorian women fighting over the same man was completely unheard of in this day and age, and Zeven imagined it would not be a pretty sight to see. He felt Taren was thinking exactly the same thing.

'Keep me informed,' she requested Zeven, ahead of vanishing with Ringbalin and effectively removing him from the new prime minister's emotional sphere.

Still the good mood lingered on the leader's face after their departure, even when Zeven no longer felt Ringbalin's attractive influence. 'Your crew are truly extraordinary; wherever did you find and recruit them all?'

'You could say a higher power brought us together,' was all Zeven would say. 'Some things are just fated.'

'Indeed,' Jalila agreed, suppressing her good mood. 'This entire day has seemed most serendipitous.' She said this as though she was not entirely sure that these events were just a happy coincidence; perhaps she'd drawn more from his thoughts earlier than she had let on?

After passing through several security doors, they came to stand before the cell of the Kaveh Ahura Mazida. 'I can take it from here,' Zeven informed her. 'I request this man be released into my protective custody.'

'Might I ask what you intend to do with him?' Jalila was understandably curious.

'Repair him,' Zeven answered simply. 'Then perhaps Phemoria can make peace with the Dropa.'

'Why is that so important to you?' she probed.

'It is the quest of the *Zagriata* to restore peace and order everywhere, not just within the USS,' he advised cryptically.

'But you only learned of this rift today.' She found the response perplexing.

'Better late than never,' Zeven concurred, but Jalila was still ill at ease.

'Very well,' she granted, 'but I wish to be kept informed of his whereabouts and progress.'

'Taren Lennox is the one to discuss terms with, I am only acting on her behalf.' Zeven attempted to avoid causing offence, but the look on the Phemorian's face told him he had failed. 'But if your sisters, trapped in the celestial realms, are to be released, Taren will not allow that portal to be closed before this injustice has been rectified. Understand we have no political aspirations; the *Zagriata* are only concerned with the affairs of the spirit and of humanity's evolution as a whole. All that is needed to achieve our ends is to bring to light the misdeeds and lies of the past, then the USS can secure a more well-informed future for all.'

Jalila was only mildly appeased by his assurance. 'You have no idea what this being is capable of. If he returns seeking vengeance —'

'He will not.' Zeven was quite sure about that. 'And you are wrong, I have a very good idea of what this being is capable of and it's all good.'

'What is that supposed to mean? Were you not listening when I spoke of what he did to our late Qusay?' Jalila challenged.

'He was possessed of a curse at that time,' Zeven enlightened her.

'How —'

'— do I know he is not still possessed by it?' Zeven pre-empted her query, and Jalila nodded. 'Because I have the curse contained elsewhere.'

Jalila gasped, stunned by his claim.

'So, although you may find it difficult to trust me, perhaps you could at least trust that I know what I am doing, or your new princess would not have given me charge of this matter.'

'Far be it from me to obstruct the plans of the *Zagriata*,' Jalila finally conceded, opening the security coded lock of the door for him. 'The prisoner is yours.'

'Gratitude.' Zeven pushed the door open, whereupon the ramblings and anguished cries of the sole occupant could be heard.

'Good luck with your quest.' Jalila backed away to depart, with an air of cynicism in her smile. 'I think you are going to need it.'

From the initial sound of it, Zeven conceded she was probably right.

The cell was dimly lit, which was no doubt due to the fact that this prisoner had spent fifty years in isolation and near darkness. Still, Ringbalin's healing would have corrected any damage incurred by Ahura's body during his incarceration, so this allowance was probably unnecessary.

The Dropa Prince had been laid out and fastened to a metal table with cuffs that were all bloodied from his frustrated attempts to free and harm himself. He appeared to be in a mental delirium, babbling and screaming in anguish.

'Kaveh Ahura Mazida.' Zeven's address temporarily silenced the prisoner; it must have been some time since he'd heard his true name spoken.

'Angra Mainyu,' he insisted, as he resumed his fruitless struggle against his restraints once more, bloodying his wrists further.

Zeven lost his patience and forced the man via PK means to lie still, leaving only his head at liberty. He wasn't entirely sure that the Dropa Prince even spoke his language. 'You are not evil and never were,' he told Ahura to test the waters.

The Dropa Prince screamed and shook his head to protest the claim, which led Zeven to conclude that he understood well enough.

'Listen to me!' Zeven lifted the steel bed into a vertical position with a thought, then gripped hold of the taller man's face to gain his attention. 'You were cursed right before you coupled with the Qusay of Phemoria.'

Ahura rejected the claim by refusing to look at Zeven as tears rolled down his face.

'That curse *left you* immediately following the incident and since then it has been controlling *your son.*'

With a gasp of disbelief the prince turned harrowed eyes to Zeven. 'A son was born of my wretchedness?' he whimpered, even more distressed.

'It was not you who —'

'It was me!' Ahura roared, repelling Zeven backwards into the cell wall with a burst of energy conjured by his will. 'What I did to her …' The prince did not elaborate, but wailed out his remorse.

Winded from the impact, Zeven peeled himself off the wall. Ahura was at least as powerful as himself and could have broken free from his imprisonment at any time — just as he could now.

'I am dangerous.' Ahura's gaze turned back to Zeven, and there was a caution in his tone. 'I have no control.'

Zeven noted the prisoner was wearing a restraining device that still appeared to be working. 'Does your device not hinder your Power?'

Ahura began to laugh hysterically, before his expression fell deadly serious once again. 'Nothing hinders it.'

'Whoa!' The mind boggled; Khalid was probably far more powerful than he'd ever imagined. Maybe instead of empowering him, the entities at Dead Man Downs had been suppressing Khalid's power?

'My offspring is evil,' Ahura assumed.

'No,' Zeven insisted, 'the curse is evil, the man is good.'

'In another place, another time perhaps?'

Was Ahura reading his mind? 'Same soul,' Zeven argued. 'My friend —' His voice wavered upon recollecting Wu Geng and the time they'd spent together in the universe parallel. 'He died to save my life, and I shall do the same, if need be.' He assured the prince that his view on the matter would not be swayed. 'Now, I can put you back in that cell to wallow and rot for all eternity, but consider this ... you suffered that curse for but *one night*; your son has suffered it for *fifty years*!' Zeven paused so that he might absorb that premise. 'Do you want to do something to correct the damage done him or not?'

Ahura was wide-eyed at the prospect, and seemed to be having a sane moment. 'I am damned,' he hissed as if Zeven was daft.

'You are only deceived,' Zeven appealed, whereupon he found himself airborne again as Ahura responded with force.

'*You* are deceived! I was there ...' The prince exhausted his anger and began to weep once more.

Frustrated by a second winding and losing patience with diplomacy, Zeven decided it was time to take action. 'This place sucks.' Zeven strode towards Ahura, not prepared to accept psychosis as an excuse.

'Sucks?' Ahura appeared concerned by Zeven's intent.

'I believe a wee change in scenery is in order,' Zeven advised, gripping hold of Ahura's shoulders. 'Then I'm going to give you a brief lesson in Phemorian history.'

It was way too soon for a father and son reunion, so Zeven delivered the Dropa Prince to the coast at the opposite end of Lappis Island to where Vadik based himself. Here the sun was sinking into the ocean and streaking brilliant colours across the horizon. Two of Frujia's three moons were already glowing brightly in the evening sky above, and Ahura could only gasp as he took in all the beautiful elements around him at once.

'Argh!' He released a cry both pained and exulted, and then breathed deep the sea air. 'So, so long.' With a shake of his head, he closed his eyes — perhaps to deny himself the beautiful sight, maybe to give silent praise for it, or take in the sound of the lapping waves and the lively jungle behind them. 'I am not deserving,' he said at last.

'I have indisputable proof that you are.'

Ahura, finally calm and coherent enough to be curious, focused his sight on Zeven. An intense moment followed as Ahura siphoned everything Zeven had learned about Khalid, over three timelines and two universes, right out of him.

'ARGH!' Zeven cried under the strain of the information flowing through his mind via no will of his own. Yet he attempted not to impede the information flow — that was like being caught up in a wave you couldn't surface from — but this was certainly easier than a verbal explanation.

'You are right.' Ahura released his hold over Zeven's mind, and Zeven was a little dizzy in the wake. 'I was compelled by a force beyond my reasoning, but I fathom it now.' He looked to the darkening ocean with renewed hope. 'All can be amended.'

'Yes!' Zeven was excited to note that Ahura seemed to have joined the program.

'And my son is on this very island!' He threw his arms out wide and moved towards the water.

'He's not ready —'

'I know.' Ahura turned back briefly to assure he knew all that Zeven did about the situation. 'But this doesn't suck,' he added, having fathomed the meaning of that term in the process of their mind meld.

Zeven grinned to agree. 'So glad we concur on —' But he'd already lost the prince's attention.

The prison clothes were abandoned on the beach, as Ahura ran for the water and dived beneath the waves.

'I remember!' he cried as he surfaced in a great spray of water, laughing like a lunatic.

'Now I see the family resemblance,' Zeven uttered under his breath, but it was more than this that had him smiling in this instance; it was knowing that, for once, he was lost in the right direction.

In honour of the Princess Satomi's recent resurrection from the dead, those on board AMIE had decided to hold a special dinner, so that she, along with Kalayna, could be formally welcomed aboard the project and be introduced to the rest of the crew.

As daughter-in-law to the guest of honour, Aurora had decided to cook for everyone, and Kalayna had insisted on lending a hand. Aurora was one of the few people on board Kalayna knew, and she was keen to cultivate their friendship.

When Taren arrived to check how things were going, she found Kalayna and Aurora dancing and singing away together as they worked. It was not at all surprising to see them getting along like a house on fire — they'd been lovers once upon another timeline.

'You can summon everyone to come and be seated,' Aurora told Taren when she spotted her by the door.

'Can I help?' Ray, Aurora's six-year-old daughter, entered and immediately began eating leftover pieces of pastry off the bench.

'Don't get all covered in flour before dinner,' Aurora appealed, just as Ray was about to wipe her fingers down the front of her clean dress. Ray froze, unsure how to dispose of the excess pastry sticking to her hands.

'I haven't seen you since you were a baby.' Kalayna came forth with a kitchen towel to wipe the child's hands clean. 'I can't believe how you've grown!'

'I'm nearly seven,' Ray said proudly.

'Smells fantastic in here.' Jazmay stuck her head in the door.

'Look.' Aurora pulled a tray from the oven and having to get by several people to find a clean space of bench to put it down she took charge. 'Why don't you all go and set the table?'

'I'll help!' Ray wriggled her clean fingers at her mother for inspection, and then took hold of Kalayna's hand.

'Very good, you do that.' Aurora smiled at Kalayna, thankful for her aid.

'You can show me where everyone sits.' Kalayna allowed Ray to lead her out into the mess room.

'I usually sit between my mum and dad, but I think I shall sit between Grandma and Grandpa tonight.' Ray outlined her plans on the way out the door.

'It would be nice if Zeven were here,' Aurora commented to Taren just as she turned to leave.

'Yes, it would,' Taren agreed, 'but there will be other dinners.'

Aurora was not usually sentimental or argumentative, but obviously she felt compelled in this case. 'What could possibly be more important than meeting his mother who has not seen him since he was a newborn?'

Taren understood this was an extraordinary circumstance. 'I wish I could tell you.'

'But you can't.' Aurora tossed her tea towel aside in a huff, and then calmed to appeal for more information. 'Is he in danger?'

Taren considered the query carefully. 'No. No, for once I think Zeven is in full control of the situation.'

'In control? Zeven?' Aurora forced a laugh. 'I'd pay money to see that.'

Taren grinned. 'Perhaps he'll surprise us all.'

'If you say so.' Aurora's disappointment lingered. 'Still, it would have been nice to have a normal family life for just one evening.'

'Well, to have a normal family life, one needs a normal family,' Taren posed in jest. 'Never going to happen.'

Aurora gave up the bad mood and laughed. 'It must be time for a drink then?'

'Yeah!' Jazmay cheered from the door. 'Let's get this party started!' With a wave of her hand, music began pumping through the loud speakers all over the ship, and Jazmay began to dance around. 'That will save you paging everyone.' She grinned at Taren, as the rest of the crew began entering the dining hall, some inspired to dance in and some not so much.

'Whatever works.' Taren decided that she liked the music and began swaying around.

'And for you.' Jazmay manifested a bottle of mescaline and a bunch of shot glasses.

'Goodness.' Aurora boggled at the challenge and Taren had to laugh, knowing that Aurora wasn't that much of a drinker.

'Or?' Taren conjured them up a nice bottle of Frujian passionberry bubbly as an alternative, which Aurora pointed to as her choice.

'As I'd like to make it to dinner.' Aurora held out a fluted glass to be filled, as Taren popped the cork.

'Chef's choice.' Jazmay shrugged off the rejection and, spotting someone who was surely going to join her, she grabbed her bottle and held it up for him to see. 'Hey, Mythric!'

Mythric excused himself from the guest of honour as Satomi was led to her seat by their granddaughter, and ducked over to the kitchen doorway to say, 'A lovely thought, Jaz, but I am trying to be on my best behaviour.'

'Well you're all no bloody fun.' Jazmay looked from Mythric, who frowned apologetically, to Aurora and Taren.

'I know Kalayna likes to indulge,' Mythric suggested.

'Oh yeah, the newbie.' Jazmay grabbed a couple of glasses and wandered off to get better acquainted.

'I *will have* one of those.' Mythric entered the kitchen proper, as Taren poured the bubbly, and when she handed him a full flute he emptied it faster than she'd filled it.

'You're nervous,' Taren guessed the cause of his thirst.

'First night with my wife in thirty-odd years, yeah, a little,' Mythric admitted, and held out his glass for a refill. 'And she is the same age as our son now!'

'Satomi adores you, that's why her spirit stayed by you all these years.' Taren gave him another half glass, and he polished it off too.

'Aww, it's so adorable that you would doubt yourself.' Aurora squeezed his cheek to emphasise her view. 'Are you sure Zeven is your son?' Her joke made them all laugh, but Mythric sobered first.

'I could use a pep talk from him right about now.' Mythric lowered his head but raised his eyes towards Taren in quiet appeal. Aurora mimicked him.

'Oh come on, guys!' Taren didn't like disappointing them both. 'If Zeven could be here, he would be. Still, I know what he would tell you, Mythric.'

'And what's that?' Mythric let his wish go, as it was obviously going to be denied.

'He'd tell you that Satomi has been your soul mate throughout every timeline we've known you in. She doesn't know how to love any other man, so you have nothing to be anxious about.'

'How lovely.' Aurora toyed with her drink, wafting away in a little romantic daydream.

'Would he now?' Mythric obviously didn't think the advice sounded very much like Zeven. 'I rather thought he'd say something like … "just focus on how hot she is!"'

Aurora nearly spilled her champagne as she burst into laughter. 'Now that sounds more like my man.'

Taren couldn't argue that either, but assured Mythric, 'It's all true.' She served him a slap on the back as Zeven might, and joined the growing party around the table.

It wasn't until after dinner that the subject of Zeven arose again, as Taren stood to make a toast on his behalf. 'Dearest Aunt.' Taren raised her glass to Satomi, and repeated the gesture in their new crew mate's direction. 'And Kalayna. I know Zeven wanted to be here to welcome you both aboard AMIE —'

'Where is Daddy?' Ray tugged on Mythric's jacket.

'Sweetie.' He placed a finger over his lips to let the child know this was not the time to ask.

'Zeven played a vital role in delivering you both safely to us,' Taren continued, 'and although other vital work prevents him delivering these good tidings to you himself, please know that we could not be more thrilled to have you both alive, well, and with us on board this craft. To the Princess Satomi and Kalayna!' Taren held her glass high.

'Just Satomi,' the princess insisted, as they all rose and raised their glasses.

'To Satomi and Kalayna!' they all repeated, ahead of drinking and being seated once again.

'Hey, where did Ray go?' Fari, the only other child at the dinner table noticed her missing from between Mythric and Satomi, and with a quick check under the table, he reported, 'Nope, she's not under there either.'

Aurora's jaw dropped. 'I know where she is. That little minx! That's why she wanted to be seated between Mythric and Satomi — they both have psychokinetic ability!'

Ray had no Power of her own. She was known as an adaptor; she assumed the power of any psychic in close vicinity to her.

'She's gone after Zeven!' Taren realised, quietly panicked.

'Ray has been asking where he is,' Aurora explained, 'and as we keep fobbing her off, I guess she decided to go find out for herself.'

'I'll go after her,' Satomi was happy to volunteer.

'No,' Taren forestalled her. 'I'll go.'

The princess obviously didn't appreciate being overruled by her young niece. 'I have been waiting decades to see my son —'

'I realise,' Taren sympathised, 'but Zeven specifically requested that no one from this crew follow him —'

'I am not on your crew,' Satomi served Taren a stern reminder, and then vanished in pursuit of her grandchild.

'Holy shit!' Taren freaked out, suspecting Satomi was about to come face to face with her murderer.

'What is it?' both Aurora and Mythric appealed to know.

'I have to go.' Taren willed herself after Satomi but found she was unable to follow. 'What the hell?'

Mythric winced. 'She's cast a physic shield in her wake,' he informed Taren. 'It's this little trick she perfected when running from the secret service. Even I have no idea how she does it.'

'Bitch!' Taren cussed, frustrated by the delay.

'What?' Mythric didn't like her attitude.

'How long will it last?'

'Long enough for you to give up,' Mythric warranted, not seeing the harm. 'She wants to be with our son and granddaughter, what is wrong with that?'

For the first time in a long while, Taren was angered speechless. She just threw up her hands and walked away to compose herself.

'What's the problem?' Mythric appealed to the captain.

'Taren doesn't give orders just to piss you all off; most often they are for your own *protection*,' Lucian explained.

'Is Ray in danger?' Aurora panicked.

'Not with her father present,' Lucian advised, 'but only the universe knows what she has just interrupted!'

'She's just a baby,' Aurora defended, as Lucian was clearly vexed. 'She didn't know —'

'Ray and Satomi *must* understand that as long as they are on board AMIE, they follow orders like everybody else!' Lucian was not going to be lenient in this matter. 'When the princess and Ray return, they are to speak to no one before I debrief them.' Lucian directed his order at both Aurora and Mythric. 'AMIE is not a family holiday resort; we are not playing games here! This is a *huge* breach in USS security … *that's* the problem,' Lucian enlightened Mythric, before joining his wife in the hallway to have a quiet word about how to proceed.

Zeven had re-assigned Vadik to babysit Ahura on the other side of the island; this was mainly to watch that the fallen prince didn't regress into self harming. He seemed high on life and fairly coherent at present, so Zeven didn't think there was much danger of a relapse. He left Vadik a communicator and a warning — if his charge did anything odd he was to call at once, as Ahura was far more powerful than any of them and could quite possibly seem a little nuts.

'He couldn't be any more insane or unpleasant than our other *patient*,' Valik had resolved, quite happy for the change of assignment.

Back on the upper level of the hut, Khalid was awaiting Zeven's return with Telmo and his monkey, and when Zeven showed, Telmo took a walk.

'We have some business to attend to, you and I,' Zeven opened the proceedings.

'Finally! Death! Thank fuck!' Khalid opened his arms wide in acceptance.

'I've already told you, no one is going to kill you.' Zeven stripped off his jacket and tossed it aside. 'No one I know, anyway.' He took a seat to make this discussion less confrontational.

'The prophecy —' Khalid contested.

'— is about you ending the curse, not me ending you,' Zeven voiced his belief. 'I am hardly going to kill the greatest human psychic ever born.'

'What?' Khalid obviously thought he'd lost the conversation somewhere.

'Your father is one of the Old Ones, Khalid,' Zeven informed, and Khalid rolled his eyes in disbelief. 'I know it is true, because I have met him.'

'What?'

'So if the *Zagriata* was a single magnificent being, that being would be you,' Zeven stated with all sincerity.

'Have you lost your fucking mind!' Khalid roared, yet his tone lacked its usual venom.

'No. I just asked the right question,' Zeven asserted. 'Why pick you to curse? Answer: because you are the most pure blood Phemorian psychic ever born, and you're a man!'

Clearly Khalid was processing a whole bunch of emotions he'd never experienced before — hope, insight, compassion, clarity, kinship — all overshadowed by a good serve of doubt and scepticism.

'There is another prophecy, of Phemorian origin, that has been a secret so well guarded by the Phemorian Secret Service that not even the Phemoray know of it.' Zeven added a little spice to the tale, and Khalid was intrigued enough to sink into a chair to listen.

'Go on.'

'The prophecy foretells that when the first prince of Phemoria returns to that planet, the rule of the Phemoray will end. It is my belief that someone on Phemoria really didn't want you ever discovering your own power and origins, yet they did not wish you dead either. That someone must have been brave enough to go into Dead Man Downs and negotiate a deal with Chironjivi that would ensure this miracle baby never came to light.'

'But why not kill me?'

'Well, obviously whoever it was is keeping you as an insurance policy because you are the only thing they know of that will destroy the Phemoray,' Zeven posed.

'Fuck!' Khalid stood and kicked the chair he'd been seated in with his sore foot and his monkey sprung up, alert, but did not attack. 'I am *sick to death* of being used!'

'I have a plan that will put a stop to it,' Zeven advised.

Khalid was seized with suspicion and pointed a finger at Zeven. 'Why have you done this?' he demanded. 'What's in it for you?'

'Intergalactic peace,' Zeven said simply. 'But in truth, you died to save my life once upon another universe, and I am in your debt … in fact all the peoples of two universes are in your debt.'

Khalid was frowning in disbelief, and was about to contest the story when Thurraya suddenly appeared before them both.

'Daddy!' Ray threw her arms up in the air and ran at her father for a crash cuddle.

Zeven's heart was pounding in his throat, having his daughter in sight of their one-time nemesis. If he showed this panic Khalid would see that distrust, and befriending him would be near impossible. 'Good to see you, pumpkin, but I don't think you are supposed to be here … Daddy's working.'

'Wow!' Ray looked around at the hut and spotted the monkey. 'She's so cute!'

'Don't let appearances fool you,' Khalid warned, keeping his distance as he pointed out the bite marks on his body. 'But she only bites bad people.'

Ray eyed over Khalid in a discerning fashion. 'You don't look so bad to me.'

Zeven was amazed to see a sparkle of a tear in the corner of Khalid's eye.

'He is a *very* bad man,' Satomi stated with thirty years of pent-up anger suddenly pumping through her veins.

'Mother!' Zeven was shocked to see her, and devastated by the situation that was way beyond awkward.

'Is this the night of the living dead?' Khalid was stunned to see another of his fatalities still living and breathing.

'I am no ghost any more, thanks to Maiara,' Satomi seethed. 'And you!' Her rueful gaze shifted from Khalid to Zeven. Words failed her a moment. 'Why do you sit in friendly conversation with this murderous *animal?*'

Zeven sympathised with how this must look to his mother, but he was sick of the ignorance. 'He is a human being —'

'You *dare* to defend *it* to *me*?'

The betrayal on her face thrust an emotional dagger into Zeven's chest; choosing a side was impossible between these two people, for Satomi had also laid down her life protecting him.

'And to expose your daughter to this foul creature!' Satomi, incensed, manifested a dagger. 'Get her out of here.' Satomi commanded Zeven to take Thurraya and go.

'No, Grandma!' To the shock of all present, Ray took a stand in front of Khalid and pointed to the monkey that had positioned itself in the rafters above Satomi's head. 'You are the one being bad!'

The desperate tears streaming down her granddaughter's cheeks snapped Satomi out of her shock-induced psychosis and she allowed the knife to vanish.

'Mother, you need to hear me out —'

Satomi held up a finger, not prepared to listen at present and approaching Zeven, she eyed him over and slapped his face with all her human force. 'You are not my son.' She grabbed hold of Thurraya's hand, of the mind to vanish with the child.

'I don't want to go with you.' Ray pulled away and ran back to Zeven.

Satomi's anger was tinged by sorrow, until her eyes returned to Khalid. 'I don't know what evil trickery you've cast on my family, but I will end it, and *you*.' She vanished, whereupon everyone present drew a deep breath in the wake of the tension.

Zeven was quick to drop on one knee and address Ray. 'You have to take yourself back to Mummy now. But you are not to tell anyone what happened here, besides the captain and the boss, you got that?'

Ray nodded, obediently. 'When are you coming home?'

'Not for a while.' Zeven was honest, and Ray was not happy. 'But when I do come back, you'll be the first person I come see. 'K?'

With a smile of acceptance, Ray looked to Khalid. 'I'm sorry my grandma said those awful things about you.'

Khalid was quite placated by her view. 'Awful accusations are not so hurtful when they are deserved.'

'People change,' Thurraya told him. 'And no matter what others decide about you, only you know what is in your heart.'

'I shall remember that,' Khalid respectfully conceded.

Zeven couldn't believe that he was witnessing Khalid being gracious — it seemed this terrible turn of events had been of some benefit.

'Off you go,' Zeven prompted his daughter, and with another hug, she vanished.

'I've never been defended by a kid before,' Khalid joked. 'I've never been defended by *anyone* … least of all, to their mother.'

'It was not the reunion I imagined.' Zeven touched the side of his face, still stinging from Satomi's slap.

'She's right though,' Khalid warranted. 'Everything I touch turns to shit! That's a bitchin' kid you've got there —'

'Her name is Thurraya,' Zeven said.

Khalid shook his head, seeming annoyed by the show of trust. 'And I suspect you married that equally bitchin' blonde you found singing in a band on Sermetica.'

'I did,' Zeven confirmed.

Khalid was frustrated. 'You're an *idiot* to risk the perfect life you've built for yourself on my account!' he warned.

'I know.' Zeven accepted that. 'They used to say I was insanely brave, but I think I've turned that around — now I'm just bravely insane.'

'This is no joking matter.' Khalid almost cracked a smile, but he endeavoured to be serious. 'Keep your precious things *away* from me! Already your doting mother despises you on my account; pretty soon that will be the case with your entire family!'

Zeven took the very fact that Khalid cared at all as a promising sign. 'Unfortunately my precious things have a mind and will all their own.' He made light of the threat, though it was far more real than he cared to admit. Still, mutual trust needed a foundation and Khalid had no idea how to build one, so Zeven had to take some risks. 'What I am more concerned about at this point is securing your safety, and I need your cooperation to do that.'

'My safety!' Khalid thought him joking, until Zeven conjured forth the coffer containing the amulet of Chironjivi.

'We need to discuss Dead Man Downs.'

When Satomi reappeared on board AMIE she was deeply distressed.

'Satomi!' Mythric was at her side in a heartbeat.

'Where is Thurraya?' Aurora was alarmed to see the princess returned alone.

'Still with her father.' Satomi's bitter tone surprised everyone bar Taren and the captain. 'Do you know what he has done?' She put the question to her husband and everyone.

'That information is classified,' Taren was quick to butt in. 'Divulging classified information will put you in breach of USS security and I will have to arrest you and everyone here.'

'You are worse than both your parents put together!' Satomi confronted Taren. 'Why would you condone such a crime?'

'Crime?' Mythric queried the choice of word, the implication of which spread like a virus to unnerve the rest of the crew. 'What is she talking about?'

'She doesn't know what she is talking about,' Taren countered. 'No one but Telmo and Zeven know the whole truth of the matter.'

'Telmo?' Both Kalayna and Yasper's interest were piqued.

'Ha! Then even you cannot say what the truth is!' Satomi challenged.

'I have Zeven's word.' Taren was really struggling to remain civil. 'That is all I need.'

'Hear, hear,' Lucian seconded that motion, as did everyone on the crew, until the round stopped at Mythric, and Satomi looked to him for a modicum of support.

Taren felt for him, caught between his son and his wife, when he had no idea what they were arguing about.

'Our boy is no fool,' Mythric gently appealed to her sense of reason.

She slapped his face. 'You are a fool,' she told him, and backed away to distance herself from everyone. 'All of you *be* damned!' She vanished from their midst, just as Ray reappeared and embraced her mother.

'Thank heaven!' Aurora squeezed Ray, and kissed her cheeks. 'Never do that again! Are you all right?'

Ray began whispering in her mother's ear.

'Ray,' Lucian cautioned his youngest crew member. 'You are not allowed to speak about your daddy's work to anyone.'

Aurora comforted Ray, and looked to the captain. 'She didn't say anything about Zeven, she's just scared that Grandma has turned bad.' Aurora looked to Mythric, who was now completely bemused.

The questioning looks on the faces of the crew were all aimed at Taren and begging for answers.

'What the hell have you got Zeven doing?' Mythric demanded.

'If we couldn't tell you that twenty seconds ago, we cannot tell you now either.' The captain was as tired of questions about Zeven's doings as Taren was. 'I need Ray to come to my office for a little debrief.' Lucian held a hand out to the child.

'Must you do that now,' Aurora entreated him. 'She's been through something traumatic —'

'No, Mum,' Ray shot in. 'Daddy said I had to tell the captain some things.' She left her mother to go with Lucian to his office.

'I'm on damage control,' Taren announced, but when she focused on her subject she had no success pursuing her. 'Damn! Satomi has cast another shield in her wake.' Taren mused about her aunt's options. 'There's only one other place that I'm aware of that Satomi would go for support … I'd best get to my mother before she does.'

'Let me track her down,' Mythric waylaid her to petition.

'Don't you start! That will only widen the breech.' Taren refused his request, which frustrated Mythric. 'I'm sorry —'

'You're sorry!' Mythric bit out. 'No sooner do I finally get my family back together than some USS fucking secret service agenda is tearing them apart. We've changed nothing!'

'If the princess had followed my directive —' Taren bit her tongue; seeking to place blame was a waste of time, and Mythric was storming from the room in any case.

'Well, this has been quite a bash,' Swithin broke the tension. 'It's like one of those "whodunnit" parties, only in this case we have to guess "what's he fuckin' done this time?"'

'He is saving our arses, as usual!' Taren made her view known. 'Unless his mother throws a spanner in the works.'

'She seemed pretty distraught.' Aurora was looking a little that way herself. 'And whatever upset her, Thurraya was privy to as well.'

'Thurraya seemed to think that Satomi was in the wrong in this case, and so do I.' Taren ended the discussion. 'This project has had a dream run thus far and you all are the best damn crew in the known universe! But lose faith *now*, at the first sign of bad weather, and there is little hope for freedom for those with the Powers in the future of the United Star Systems.'

'I got faith.' Jazmay held up her shot glass to Taren in a show of support, and everyone present followed suit, although Swithin — ever the sceptic — was the last to do so.

Although Taren was grateful for the sentiment, she knew that if they discovered what Zeven was up to she'd have a full-scale rebellion on her hands. Just about everyone here had cause to detest Khalid — including herself. It had been a battle for Taren to wrap her head and heart around Zeven's compassionate stance in this matter; it demonstrated a spiritual mastery that surpassed that of anyone she'd ever known. She was proud of her cousin, and was looking forward to remembering the journey into the universe parallel that had awarded Zeven and Telmo such great insight. It was now all too clear why Zeven had endeavoured to keep his movements secret; he was truly risking everything he held dear in an attempt to redeem his worst enemy. But if Satomi shared what she knew with anyone, this profound act of mercy was liable to turn round and bite them all in the arse.

All her adult life Satomi had known no home.

Her childhood as a young Phemorian princess had been happy enough. Heir to the throne, she'd been given everything she desired, while being kept blissfully unaware of the heavy price she would pay for that privilege upon being crowned Qusay of Phemoria. At age ten her life took a dark turn as she bore witness to her mother's decline into insanity following the shameful conception and birth of a son. It was Phemorian law that no male of royal birth was permitted to live, and the guilt of having the child killed only compounded the fragility of her mother's mind. The prince's execution was also revenge, aimed at its father and his people — whoever they were. Satomi had never learned those details, nor even who her own father was. Phemorians were considered fatherless. In the years that followed, Satomi's own psychic powers developed and she came to see the curse lurking behind the crown her mother wore. This mysterious force, known as the Phemoray, had been assembled from the tortured spirits of her great foremothers and gathered unto the service of the Phemorian crown by the mighty Thurraya. Thurraya was considered the first true Qusay of Phemoria, as she was the first female to rule in her own right, having banished all the men from their planet. Her first act in office was to slay her husband the king, before she banished her only son, Chironjivi, to a slow death en route to Sermetica — hence earning this Qusay the name Thurraya the Slayer. The fleet of vessels that had carried the last men from Phemoria had crash landed at Dead Man Downs and created the most feared and avoided location in the whole of the United Star Systems — for no one who went to investigate the crash ever returned. Yet despite her history lessons and being assured that the Phemoray were there to serve the Qusay, Satomi observed her mother's own disdain of the force. In her increasingly abstruse moments towards the end of their association, the Qusay would accuse the Phemoray of controlling her and she seemed to revel in the abandon that overtook her during those moments of madness when she forgot to fear her demons. For eight years Phemoria suffered at the hands of a schizophrenic ruler, and Satomi knew that the Phemoray were only waiting for her to come of age so they could do away with her mother's unpredictable services and replace her with a younger, saner woman who was easier to manipulate. Fortunately Satomi had found sympathisers among Qusay's close advisors, those who knew the truth about the crown and its curse. They had conspired to aid the young princess to escape her sad destiny that, four years later, was regrettably passed on to her younger sister, Clarona, as soon as she came of age.

After fleeing Phemoria, Satomi had spent many years on the run, learning to protect herself, cover her tracks and stay one step ahead of the Phemoray and the queen's Valoureans, who never gave up their pursuit of her. In Spyridon Vidor, Satomi found a haven for a short while — just long enough to fall in love, start a family and have it all torn away. The moment she fell pregnant, Satomi knew that it was only a matter of time before her past caught up to her. For this was not just any baby, but one of the first children born of both the Phemorian and Sermetic royal lines in a thousand years. And the child was *male*. Despite Spyridon's complete dedication to the protection of his family, and as powerful as their combined psychic powers were, it was never going to be enough to keep every secret service agent in the USS at bay. If not for Maiara's prophecy, they may have had more respite to bond as a family. Had retribution come in some expected form, Satomi would have had a fighting chance. But Khalid Mansur, who had been raised as a member of the Sermetic royal family, had caught her off-guard. No male living should have been her psychic equal, for she was of the Phemorian royal line. Their psychic powers ran stronger than those belonging to any of the Sermetic royal houses, whose inherent psychic ability had been diluted in the ages since their banishment from Phemoria. How could Khalid have overpowered her? There was only one answer, which dawned upon her as she'd breathed her last — the son that her mother had grieved had somehow escaped his execution.

The thought of Khalid made her blood run cold, and seeing him today had been more disturbing than recollecting her death. In that moment she felt she had two options — kill him, or run and hide. As her son had refused her the only option that would bring her any true peace, she had been forced to pursue the remaining option. And if there was anything she knew how to do, it was hide.

It was dusk on the outskirts of the Phemorian capital of Tonissia, and the night mists were beginning to rise beneath a light drizzling of rain. Her cloak deflected all the moisture from her body but her face was already awash with tears and she barely registered the additional spray, only the cool sting of the night air. At present, Satomi felt this was the one place no one would think to look for her. Everyone avoided this landmark, as renowned for its ghosts as the crash site at Dead Man Downs. This was the playground of the Phemoray and as such was hallowed ground. The magnificent Cathedral of Trees that once stood here had withered long ago — the energy of this place was so spent it could no longer nurture life. Beyond the decrepit remains of the dead forest Satomi came to a large marble staircase leading up to the sacrificial platform. As she scaled the stairs she gazed down into the cavernous void known as the Pit of the Obstinate.

Into this void had been cast many a Phemorian woman who had displeased her husband — until Thurraya's revolution put an end to the practice. The last official blood sacrifices made here were all high-ranking male officials who joined the last king of Phemoria in death.

This pit of horrors past was at the root of all the curses that had overshadowed her life. A revolution was spawned here, and a curse that had so far lasted a thousand years had been unwittingly unleashed upon the Phemorian queens. But with the crown of Phemoria and its curse locked away somewhere, for Satomi this site was now little more than a remote place to process her situation.

Satomi stood on the sacrificial platform that overhung the abyss, staring into the chasm where skeletons were hidden by the darkness of night. Should she join them? The thought seemed an easy solution to her woes. Just a little lean forwards and all her harrowing thoughts and hurtful feelings would vanish. There was no one here to prevent her death this time.

It was a cruel twist of fate that had restored her to life, only for her to discover her family were once again keeping secrets from her, perhaps even plotting against her. Her beloved husband wasn't even aware that he was choosing their arch enemy over her. It was irrelevant why her son had freed, and was aiding, Khalid — it was not as if he was still blissfully unaware of his past. He knew Khalid had destroyed their family. Maiara had told him, and hence his recent actions could only be interpreted as a deliberate betrayal. Khalid could have been exerting some form of mind control over her kin, but in either case, the AMIE crew could not be trusted. It was a worry that her younger sister, the ruling Qusay, was now deeply indebted to AMIE for delivering her from her curse. Khalid could usurp the throne of the planet of his birth and exile, and there was no one to stop him.

'You are the true heir to the Phemorian crown, don't ever forget that.'

In a blinding flash, Satomi's mind was teleported back to the day that she had fled Phemoria. So all encompassing was the vision that she stepped back from the edge of the abyss and collapsed to the ground.

'You must survive,' her co-conspirator had told her. 'And when you feel powerful enough to crush the Phemoray, seek me out, for I will aid you to banish their curses. I have tried before and learned a good deal from my mistakes.'

In her vision Satomi noted her advisor toying with a ring upon her finger. The ring itself was made of metal, but to her etheric sight it was black as night. Yet around the dark energy a shield of golden light was containing it. 'That ring is cursed; did the Phemoray give it to you?' she had asked.

'No,' was the reply. 'But it takes a curse to fight a curse, and this tool was ultimately of their making.'

Satomi had never observed such a wonder. 'But how do you keep its negative force contained like that?'

'By my will, and my conviction in ensuring the glory of Phemoria.'

The vision turned hazy and plunged into darkness.

Again, Satomi confronted her old ally; she was older now, and addressing her directly.

'You are the true Qusay,' she told Satomi — but this was not a memory. 'You know what must be done to end these curses; you saw the vision with your own divine second sight!'

The face faded to a vision of herself standing before the throne of Phemoria. 'I am Qusay now,' she claimed, ahead of transforming into her sister the Qusay-Sabah Clarona.

'The crown of Phemoria was forged from jewellery found on the dead women in the Pit of the Obstinate. Their souls were drawn forth to the crown by the bloodletting of a man and the Phemoray were born.' In her mind Satomi heard a woman advise her, but it was not a voice she recognised. *'To reverse the curse, reverse the spell. Separate the crown into the original jewellery and return it to the pit. The Phemoray were attached to the crown when a male was sacrificed at the hands of women, they can only be cast out of the crown by a woman resurrected at the hands of a man.'*

Satomi turned about to find herself standing on the sacrificial platform before the Pit of the Obstinate once more. Her granddaughter was standing alongside her as the spirits of the Phemoray rose up from the abyss before them.

'You have betrayed us, Thurraya,' the spirits accused the young girl, as if she were her namesake.

'I have not betrayed you,' Thurraya answered. 'I am here to lead you home.' Her granddaughter manifested a blade in her hand, slit her own throat and dropped into the pit.

'NO!' Satomi awoke screaming.

It was daylight now, although the day was dark and overcast. 'I am the one to do this. I am a woman resurrected by a man!' Satomi was still embroiled in her vision, and stood to address the pit, from whence the skeletons of her wronged ancestors stared back at her. 'You shall not take my granddaughter.'

Satomi felt her will to live harden. Khalid may have had all of AMIE fooled, but she would not permit their blindness to place the next heir to the throne of Phemoria in danger. Alone and in exile this crusade would be near impossible, but if Satomi fulfilled the prophecy she'd just seen then she would have all the forces on Phemoria at her disposal.

She pulled a knife from thin air, and kneeling before the chasm she sliced her palm and allowed the blood to drop into the void as she swore an oath to her ancestors. 'I will end these curses, and I will destroy Khalid.' Why else would she have been awarded this glimpse of the future, if not so she could change the outcome?

Today's premonition had not only reminded Satomi of her inherent purpose, but of a very powerful ally. There was someone she could trust, who could advise her better than any in regard to these matters, and she quietly thanked her ancestors for sending her the insight to answer her own question.

She would not be joining them in the hereafter today; she had much to accomplish. This was why she had been brought back from the grave. Satomi stepped away from the void with a renewed sense of purpose. 'Before I was a wife, before I was a mother, I was committed to delivering Phemoria from the Phemoray. This is *my* calling and I shall see it done.'

Her inner turmoil ebbed and Satomi knew her resolve was sound as a clear course of action began to unfold in her mind.

PART 2

EMERGENCE

6

SHADOW BOXING

Mission Log — Day 5

Two days since my mother's dressing down and as none of my kindred or crew mates have shown up to spurn my course of action, I can only gather that Taren has consoled or subdued Princess Satomi somehow. Even though I did discourage Taren from allowing anyone to contact me, she would seek me out if my mother caused any damage that was beyond her control.

Hence I have forged ahead with my own agenda, and since I defended Khalid to my mother we have engaged in several fairly civil conversations, during which Khalid did not lose his temper once.

This has proven rather fortunate timing, as Telmo was forced to separate Khalid from the pacifying bite of the rainbow monkey because Karisha has started demonstrating PK ability from gorging herself on Khalid's blood. Telmo has begun teaching Khalid meditation techniques to calm himself instead, and although our patient is having difficulty taking the practice seriously, there has been a marked difference in his attitude.

The topic of our discussions has been the clean up of the lost souls at Dead Man Downs. I wasn't there the first and only time Khalid cleaned house at the shipwreck, and as that event has yet to happen in this timeline, Khalid can only offer theories as to how he would attempt the feat.

119

It is common knowledge that the last ill-fated voyage of the Inssurecto and its accompanying fleet began over a thousand years ago, at the conclusion of the sexual revolution on Phemoria. At that time the Qusay used psychic means to seize control of the planet from their menfolk and cast those men who survived the slaughter into exile on Sermetica. The Insurrecto was the last ship of male refugees to be launched from Phemoria. With their communications systems destroyed, the vessel was locked on a one-way journey they had neither the fuel nor the food supplies to complete. The fuel was expended by the time the Insurrecto entered Sermetica's atmosphere, and it was thought there had been no survivors from the crash at Dead Man Downs. The site had been deemed cursed, as everyone who had ever set out to gain access to the wrecked spacecraft had never been seen again — at least that's how the legends told it. But Khalid, having been virtually raised by the demons who frequent the site, had a rather different take on the tale.

The Qusay Thurraya had been the Phemorian queen who led the sexual revolution. She had assumed that she and her royal female kindred were the only ones dabbling in supernatural magic, but the man who came to captain the last flight of the Insurrecto was none other than the last true prince of Phemoria and Thurraya's own son — Chironjivi. The young prince had been spying on his mother and her female minions as they made a blood sacrifice of his father and his best men. The crown of Phemoria, along with the supernatural force now known as the Phemoray, was forged from the jewellery of murdered women cast into the Pit of the Obstinate during eons of male rulership. Chironjivi used this knowledge to create his own force of lost souls, and every man on board the Insurrecto gladly forfeited his life for the promise of revenge on their Phemorian womenfolk, and on all female-kind.

The Soul Keep was where all of the crew had taken their own lives, rather than die a slow, inevitable death. According to Khalid there were no skeletal remains in the chamber, only a large vat, which had been cargo bound for Sermetica on the ill-fated voyage and pilfered by the crew. Chironjivi vowed to seek revenge on behalf of the betrayed, banished and slaughtered male populous of Phemoria. To join the campaign, each crew member took his own life by throwing himself into the vat of molten metal that they had gathered from their ship, and the ignition key was used to launch them to their death. This smelter became known as the Soul Keep, and from the soul-filled metal within, the amulet Zeven extracted from Khalid had been forged. Chironjivi promised that the amulet would give Khalid psychic protection, which it had to a point, but I also suspect the evil trinket was dulling Khalid's true power. As Chironjivi never sacrificed himself for the cause, he'd not joined his spirit to those of his tormented crew, so we must dispose of his demon separately to ensure that Chironjivi never leads the ghost crew at Dead Man Downs again.

The unnatural earthly form of Chironjivi had been destroyed on the day Khalid was incarcerated with a psychic restraining device and Chironjivi's soul had been trapped in Khalid's body with him. This event severed their control of the ghost crew, all of whom raced back to Dead Man Downs, wanting to lay claim to the physical form that Chironjivi had temporarily vacated — to award Khalid a connection to his demon's remote viewing capability and command of the legion. In their fight to seize Chironjivi's form, the fragile mass of bone, flesh and blood was torn apart and destroyed. This was the last vision Khalid received from the ghost crew before he was cast into prison and five years of hell, sharing the mind space of the cursed prince who claimed to be his father.

As reluctant as I am to lead Khalid back to the source of his dark power and past, I shall rest easier when this force is safely contained and hidden elsewhere. For it could still be some time before the timing is right to return these souls to their true source where they can finally rest in peace.

Today, Telmo, Khalid and I shall run the mission to retrieve the Soul Keep, the outcome of which shall be very telling.

Dead Man Downs was located in a canyon deep in the desert wastelands of Sermetica, thousands of miles away from any of the planet's floating cities and mining colonies. Zeven chose the dusk hour to execute the mission as it was the most tepid time of the day on Sermetica — the night-time cool in the desert was not as unbearable as the daytime heat, but the ghosts of the *Insurrecto* became feistier after sundown. The trio stood on the canyon ridge above the crash site, observing the shipwreck before proceeding.

'So why are we wasting time gazing at this wreckage?' Khalid queried their landing spot. 'I'm not sentimental about this, you realise?'

'It seems awfully quiet down there,' Telmo commented on both his physical and supernatural perspective. 'The damned energy here is not a severe as I anticipated. In fact, the vibration I'm picking up is not so much evil as … sorrowful.'

'Then you're wrong, kid.' Khalid grinned sceptically. 'This crew don't have a conscience, and neither do I.'

Telmo raised both brows doubtfully.

'Where did Chironjivi leave his body? Captain's Lounge?' Zeven guessed, having memories of confronting Khalid at Dead Man Downs in other timelines — experiences that, for Khalid, had never happened.

'You've been here before,' Khalid deduced, wary but impressed.

'You could say that,' Zeven warranted. 'I might tell you about it sometime … we'll see how our first date goes.' He grinned in challenge.

'Well let's get on with it —' Khalid began as Zeven grabbed hold of his arm and shifted them to the Captain's Lounge of the *Insurrecto* before he'd even finished the sentence, '— then.'

With a thought from Zeven the lights came on — no active power cells required. 'Yep, this is pretty much how I remember it.' Zeven nodded in agreement with himself as they all eyed the skeletal remains scattered everywhere in the lounge.

'Home, sweet hell,' Khalid bantered.

Once, Zeven had believed all the bones here belonged to the crew of the *Insurrecto*, but if what Khalid claimed about the Soul Keep was true, then … 'Who do all these bones belong to?'

'These are all that remain of the women, girls … even babies —' Telmo motioned to some smaller remains, '— that were sacrificed to Chironjivi and his demon crew. I did a cleansing rite to release the tortured innocents from his place once, as I shall again today.'

'If the rite didn't work the first time, what makes you think it will work now?' Khalid scoffed.

'It did work the first time,' Telmo replied, having completed the rite in a past timeline.

Zeven looked to Khalid, horrified by what the discovery meant. 'They made you collect these women and deliver them to their death here?'

Khalid was disturbed by the query, and the still atmosphere in the lounge stirred as small cold draughts began to whip about. 'The curse kept Chironjivi alive, but the fresh blood of innocents strengthened the supernatural power of the crew,' he informed, as the disturbance in the room began kicking up dust and light debris. 'They never forced me to bring these females to them, I did it freely, to gain the favour of the spirits here and utilise their power.'

Telmo seemed a little wary of what was going on around them, and whatever etheric activity he was seeing he kept to himself. He had warned Zeven that this mission would be more confronting for Khalid than he realised, but it was an important step on his road to self discovery.

'You were compelled.' Zeven held up the coffer containing the amulet retrieved from Khalid's palm.

'You're wrong.' Khalid didn't want to accept that. 'I am *evil* ... in its purest form.' He began to tremble as glasses and bottles behind the bar began to rattle in their racks.

Was Khalid's own power breaking through its restraint? Were the ghost crew acting up? Or was the disturbance being caused by the souls of the betrayed women being agitated by the presence of their reaper?

'Because if I am not evil? Then I must sympathise with what I allowed to happen here.' Khalid shook his head to resist that compulsion — and although Zeven could not read minds, he was fairly sure Khalid was reliving some fairly horrendous memories.

'That's your conscience waking up, and that's a good thing. But the fact remains that if you had not been cursed, these women would not be dead!' Zeven wanted to allay his charge's rising panic, and relieve him of some of the guilt. 'Did you indulge in this bloodlust, did you enjoy it?'

'No! I see any dependence as a weakness,' Khalid spat back as his trembling intensified. 'It is *pathetic* to rely on others to sustain you.'

'So it is,' Zeven granted. 'But someone truly evil would not recognise that.'

'Stop trying to make me feel better!' Khalid insisted, as glasses and bottles began to burst. 'It's agonising!' He clenched his fists to endure his conflicting thoughts and emotions.

'Psychotic episode,' advised Telmo, who was telepathic. 'We may have to abort.'

'Is that him?' Zeven pointed to the shattering glasses behind the bar.

'No,' Telmo warned, but Zeven felt they had come too far to abort.

'I'm so sorry.' Zeven placed his free hand on Khalid's shoulder as the distressed man had backed up to sit on a stool. 'I know being here is a cathartic experience —'

'Is that what this is?' Khalid held his chest, having never felt remorse. 'It fucking hurts!'

'I know it does,' Zeven sympathised, 'but if you just tell me what we need to do, I'll get you out of here as fast as possible.'

The disturbance in the room died down as tears began leaking from Khalid's dark eyes, and he wiped them away, amazed and horrified at once. 'I didn't even think I *had* tear-ducts. What the fuck?'

'Just breathe,' Zeven encouraged, and Khalid was so freaked out that he actually complied, but he was sucking in air so deeply that he was starting to hyperventilate.

'Command Chironjivi's bones to rise from the ground,' Khalid muttered through his stress.

Zeven did as instructed, and a skeleton-worth of bones rose to float above all the others.

'Now incinerate the bastard. And sweep his ashes into that coffer with his amulet.'

At Zeven's mental command the bones turned to ash, which he caught up with a whirl of wind and directed into the coffer. Once the last speck was inside, he locked the lid closed. 'Done.' Zeven looked to Khalid, to find he'd calmed a little.

'Now for the rest of the crew.' Khalid got to his feet to lead the way through the *Insurrecto* to the one evil treasure that the crew of AMIE had never managed to lay their hands on — the Soul Keep.

As they moved down the corridors of the *Insurrecto*, Khalid seemed unnerved.

'Something wrong?' Telmo asked.

'The crew are not usually this quiet,' Khalid observed. 'Especially not when strangers wander into this part of the ship.' He picked up his pace as he spotted the door to the Soul Keep open. 'It's almost like —' He entered the room with Zeven and Telmo hot on his heels, to witness the Soul Keep vanishing, along with two cloaked women '— they're no longer here,' Khalid finished. 'Who the *fuck*? No one else knows about the Soul Keep.'

'I didn't get a good look at them.' Zeven turned to Telmo.

'One was brunette, one blonde.' Telmo inspected the image he'd captured in his mind and noted their long hair protruding from their hoods. 'Very tall — Phemorian most likely? *Very* powerful,' Telmo added.

'Because they have PK,' Zeven assumed.

'Because they have cast a shield in their wake,' Telmo advised. 'We can't follow them. Try it.'

Zeven did try, and did not move from where he stood. 'Shit!'

'Deep shit,' Khalid concurred. 'Those demons have no allegiance to anyone right now, they are open to a benefactor.'

'Surely they would not align themselves with Phemorians?' Telmo reasoned.

'Never,' Khalid agreed.

'Unless?' Zeven, who had started pacing, stopped still, thinking twice about assuming anything. 'They already have an allegiance to a Phemorian. Someone's had dealings at Dead Man Downs since before you were born. That person told Chironjivi about the royal breeding arrangement and snuck the rotting bastard into the Phemorian royal palace the night he possessed your father. This same person must have saved you as a baby and got you away from the Phemoray who would surely have demanded you be killed.'

'That's a pretty tall order,' Telmo warranted. 'Do we know of a Phemorian who is that brave and powerful?'

'Maybe Jalila Lamus? Although by my reckoning she's probably too young to have played a major role in these affairs. More snooping around on Phemoria is required,' Zeven decided. 'But our job here appears to be done.'

'I will stay behind and perform the clearing rite,' Telmo volunteered.

The energy of this site gave Zeven the creeps. 'You sure you want to do that on your own?'

'There is nothing left here for me to fear, I assure you.' Telmo waved the offer away. 'Better that you get Khalid clear of this place once and for all.'

'Right then.' Zeven went to grab Khalid's arm, but he stepped away.

'I should clean up my own mess,' he decided. 'I brought these women here, I should help them leave.'

'I said *I* have nothing left to fear here,' Telmo clarified. 'These souls harbour great resentment towards you. I can't guarantee your safety.'

'I'm not asking you to.'

'They *want* you to feel their pain,' Telmo accentuated.

'I want that also,' Khalid professed.

'What you experienced in the lounge before was just a warning,' Telmo cautioned, but Zeven could tell he was quietly impressed by Khalid's stand.

'Look, don't you think you've had enough bad experiences in your lifetime?' After five years trapped in a body with Chironjivi, Zeven didn't think any more punishment was necessary.

'But I didn't *feel* any of it!' Khalid became agitated. 'And until I deal with this fucking thing you call a conscience, I'll never be able to feel anything good.'

'I believe you are right about that,' Telmo awarded, appearing proud of their patient.

'Well, it's all part of the program, I suspect.' Khalid was not going to be led blindly along by anyone. 'So let's get on with this gutting, before I lose my nerve.'

'What if he has a psychotic break this time?' Zeven asked.

'He might,' Telmo granted. 'Everyone needs their dark night of the soul, Zeven, we've all had them. I understand you want to spare your friend the pain —'

'Friend? *Really?*' Khalid scoffed. 'Since when?'

'Since always,' Zeven mumbled, having a flashback to his time in the universe parallel when Wu Geng had made the same query. 'It's your curse I have a problem with.' Zeven smiled to himself, glad he knew their history.

'I realise this,' Khalid conceded. 'But as I have no wish to go back to being possessed, or to go insane, I'm going to have to face my demons. And this lot are only the beginning.'

'Then we shall face them together,' Zeven resolved.

'Help me and you shall be hated like I am,' Khalid sneered. 'And I might remind you that you are related to many of my misdeeds of horrors past. How is Mr Popular going to deal when team fabulous turns against him? Hmm?'

Zeven looked a little shocked by Khalid's knowledge.

'Don't think I don't know you've banded together a bunch of psychics on board that AMIE craft of yours, and that you lot were responsible for putting me in jail in the first place,' Khalid said.

Zeven shrugged off his conclusion. 'That only goes to show I owe you a few favours. Don't waste your breath,' Zeven shot down Khalid's argument, and looked to Telmo. 'Where do we start?'

Sorting bones into skeletons was not so tedious for two men with PK, but finding somewhere to lay them all out separately had forced them to move the exercise outside onto the desert canyon floor. Telmo had conjured up a few torches and staked them in the ground, and the chill of the air seemed amplified by the nature of their labours.

By the time all the skeletons lay in neat rows, the large orange Sermetic moon hovered directly overhead, adding an eerie red glow to the hellish scene.

'What now?' Zeven was eager to have this gruesome business completed.

'Now we remove Khalid's restraint and leave him here alone for a couple of hours,' Telmo instructed.

'He could pop off —' Zeven objected, knowing it would only take an hour for the effects of the restraint to wear off.

'Where is the trust now, buddy? And where would I go?' Khalid posed. 'I am wanted by the USS, and there is nowhere you couldn't find me anyway.'

'Unless you know how to do the shielding trick?' Zeven resisted the urge to trust him, even though Telmo obviously did.

'Seriously, have you not figured that out yet? It's *so* simple!' Khalid teased.

'But only if you have mastered how to shapeshift,' Telmo theorised.

'Which I haven't,' Khalid concluded his case.

'I don't know that.' Zeven sidestepped to get back to the other matter. 'So, what are you saying, if you change form as you teleport, that renders you untraceable?'

'Well, when pursuing someone via teleportation you picture that person,' Telmo expanded on his hypothesis. 'But if they have altered their entire genetic structure, they are no longer the person you have pictured.'

'But if I knew where they were going I could find them that way,' Zeven reasoned, of the mind to track down the Soul Keep.

'If you knew all their aliases, and could recognise them in a crowd,' Telmo granted.

Zeven considered he must make note of that in his mission log as Telmo continued, 'But we have to start trusting Khalid sometime, and if we don't remove his psychic restraining device then he'll miss gaining all he could from this experience.'

Zeven considered the request more seriously. 'Two hours,' he consented. 'I'll be watching from the canyon ridge.' He vanished to begin his vigil, and Khalid's restraint vanished with him.

*

It felt liberating to have one ankle that wasn't metal bound, and once he had his power back he could repair his busted ankle and lose the leg brace as well. Not that Khalid had any true healing capability that he was aware of, but he knew exactly how the ankle had felt and appeared before his little accident, and thus he could use his PK to restore it. Perhaps he'd been hanging out with the good vibe club a little too long, but with the psychic restraint removed, he felt its oppressive influence lift and vital energy flowing more easily through his being.

'So, boy wonder.' Khalid sought to waylay Telmo; his tone might have been sarcastic but for the first time in his life he felt a fearful emptiness in his gut. 'Am I signing my own death warrant here, do you think?'

'That depends on whether you can be baited,' Telmo replied.

'How do you mean?' He'd been watching this kid, who seemed to have an answer for everything and never lost his cool; Khalid quietly respected that.

'These souls will air their grievances to you, and as long as you remain humble, accepting and full of good will and remorse, you shall fare well,' he counselled. 'But turn angry or defensive … and the worst could happen.'

'Good to know.' He eyed the field of skeletons.

'You don't have to do this,' Telmo empathised.

Khalid looked back to his youthful advisor. 'I think we both know that I do.'

The kid appeared mournful. 'If our agendas align this will prove expedient to our cause. I've taught you how to meditate and still your mind —'

'You knew it would come to this.' Khalid had mocked the practice at the time, unable to see what purpose there could possibly be in attempting stillness and oneness with all there is.

'Some things are fated,' Telmo replied, graciously, neither confirming nor denying the supposition. 'I'll be back in two hours to see how you fare.'

He vanished, and Khalid was left alone for the first time since before his incarceration; this was a relief in itself — alone was his natural state of being. Yet as he wandered down the lines of dead women, he knew he was not really alone, and taking a seat in the middle of the graveyard, he suspected that soon his ghostly company would be making themselves all too apparent.

For the longest time Khalid sat trying to empty his mind of thought, focus on his breath, and find a happy place. His rescue from his father was more of a relief than a heart warming experience, but there was one event that made him tear up every time it came to mind: meeting Thurraya. It was hard to believe a six-year-old girl had had such a profound impact on his psyche; she'd cracked open his heart of ice and he felt it thaw a little every time he recalled the child defending him with her life.

'*Deceiver!*' A cold wind whipped past his body, and stung him with its bite.

'*Coward!*' Another kicked up gravel and dirt to graze his skin.

'*How could you do this to us?*' whispered another.

Then the sound of a baby screaming in terror chilled Khalid to the bone and his gut turned.

'I understand now,' he said out loud. All he had to do was imagine delivering Thurraya to Chironjivi for his pleasure, and Khalid keeled forwards and began to vomit.

'*You understand nothing!*'

This time the force of wind shot right into him, and Khalid began to relive each of his victims' horrifying memories of being raped, tortured and torn apart by the curse he'd once considered family. '*Forgive me,*' he repeated throughout, and when the suffering became too great and he felt he would rebel or flee, his will was stayed by the thought of young Thurraya telling him, '*People change. And no matter what others decide about you, only you know what your heart's intentions truly are.*'

But what were his intentions?

Before meeting Ray he'd been determined to escape this rehabilitation program at all costs and return to scheming political espionage. But this truth-seeking business was becoming even more fascinating and addictive than world domination — albeit painful and shocking — this was self domination, the one thing Khalid never dreamt possible. He'd been under the illusion that he drew all his power from the amulet in his hand and that he must remain bound to the curse or lose his supernatural gifts, hence there was no possibility of ever truly being independent. He had his captors to thank for waking him up to the truth of that matter, which was probably the single greatest gift anyone could have given him. It hurt to think he nearly killed the man who was now doing him this great service. It felt uncomfortable to be beholden, but as much as he hated to admit it, he couldn't think of anyone he'd rather be indebted to. These musings filled him with sentiment. He felt a void erupting in his chest where his heart was supposed to be and his throat ached like he'd swallowed a stone that had wedged in his gullet.

With each horrendous memory the ghosts shared with him, Khalid felt their anger lessen and his guilt ease accordingly. This was forgiveness — he was aware of the premise, but had never really experienced it first-hand. It was rather amazing that the ordeal was making him feel lighter, stronger, *euphoric* and very determined to ensure that the demon crew from Dead Man Downs never set up shop again.

'Calling all souls who would quit this place,' Telmo's voice rang through the night. 'A portal has opened to enable your escape.'

The assault on Khalid's senses abruptly ceased, as thankfully the ghosts were apparently more interested in liberation than revenge.

'Leave grievance and sorrow with your bones on the ground, for these will not serve, where you are bound.'

Khalid became conscious of being flat on his back, and in his delirium he saw what looked like blue fireflies ascending from the canyon into a vortex of light beyond.

'Forgive your trespasses, and leave love in your wake,' Telmo encouraged the souls who were straggling. 'And may that wisdom guide you always, compassion for goodness sake.'

The phenomenon was resonating the most harmonious sound that filled all Khalid's senses with a calm high, transcending even the monkey's bite. His heart had ceased to ache, but his head was throbbing and felt lead-weighted. Thus Khalid stayed watching the celestial event diminishing above until his self appointed saviour came to stand over him and block the view.

'So what's the verdict?' Zeven posed. 'Do I get another date?'

'If this is what love feels like …' A grin sucked the last modicum of energy Khalid had left him. 'I think it's over … ra—' His eyes and mind gave up trying to focus and he blacked out.

She had to be a little bit clever about this; her timing needed to be just right. If Ray got caught sneaking off again she was fairly sure she'd be getting kicked off the AMIE vessel, or at the very least confined to her room for the rest of her childhood.

During her debrief, Captain Gervaise had specifically told Thurraya that she was not to pop off and visit Daddy under any circumstances. Strictly speaking, it was not her father she was aiming to pop off and visit in this instance, but after being sworn to keep Khalid a secret — even from her own mother — being six years old did have its advantages when it came to claiming a lack of comprehension.

With her father away, Ray had been sleeping in with her mother, and last night she'd had a lucid vision that her father's secret friend was being viciously attacked by evil spirits. Normally Ray would have dismissed it as a nightmare, but as her mother's talent was remote viewing and the vision had been so vivid, Ray suspected that she'd witnessed an event that had really taken place overnight. What if nobody else knew and Khalid was in trouble?

The captain had told her not to speak of the man again. He warned her that Khalid had done many bad things to people, including her grandmother — which did explain why the Princess Satomi had threatened him with a knife. He was not to be trusted. Ray was also forbidden to speak to anyone else about the man, thus she felt she had no choice but to investigate herself; what if his life depended on her?

She waited just inside her door for her grandfather to pass her by on his way to breakfast; he had his head down, and was not looking in the best of moods.

'I'm so sorry I made Grandma mad at you, Grandpa.' She grabbed his attention with the remark, and then burst into tears. 'It's all my fault you're not happy any more!'

'Oh, sweetness.' Sidetracked, Mythric fell to one knee to hug her close. 'I don't know what upset your grandma, but I'm fairly sure you had nothing to do with it. It's your father who has a lot to answer for,' he concluded, under his breath.

Ray used that as an excuse to howl anew. 'Please don't be mad at Daddy … he didn't do anything wrong!'

'I'm not *mad* so much as frustrated.' Her grandfather attempted to diffuse her distress as she clung tightly to him.

'Shall we go get some breakfast?' he suggested, rising with her still in his arms.

'No!' Thurraya objected, letting him go to slide down his body, while still clinging on to what psychic charge she'd built up from their energy exchange. 'I have some homework I have to finish first. I'll catch you later.' She stepped back into her room, waving and forcing a smile.

'You okay?' Mythric double-checked before departing.

'Yeah, I'm good,' she assured, with a sweet smile. 'Thanks, Grandpa.'

Ray shut the door, and waited to hear him walk away. She clapped her hands to applaud her success and closing her eyes, she focused on finding her father's new friend.

It was the crack of dawn on Frujia when Khalid's eyelids parted. There was just a hint of light in the sky, as the sun had yet to peek its fiery body over the horizon.

Before this week, Khalid had lived his life by the time and alarms; he'd not imagined he had an internal body clock. But during his stay on Frujia he'd gone from being a night owl to a lark.

His captors were still fast asleep in their hammocks — Zeven had the canister containing the remains of Chironjivi in his possession and was cuddling it like a great treasure. The rainbow monkey was alert, however, and was all over Khalid the second he sat up.

'Shhh!' he urged her to stop squawking. As he swung his legs over the hammock to climb off he realised his leg brace was gone and his ankle was as good as new. *When did that happen?* He stood up and walked around, then suppressed a laugh of relief to be mended. 'Look at this,' he appealed to the monkey, who clapped excitedly for him. But truly the most thrilling thing was that his captors had not replaced his restraining device, and he felt sure that was not something they'd overlook. *They trust me*, he realised, and the notion was a little scary, as he wasn't sure he trusted himself.

Karisha squawked to get Khalid's attention and then manifested a piece of fruit in her hand and offered it to him.

'Oh, I see, you're too clever to go fetch fruit now, is that it?' Khalid accepted her offering. 'You'll turn into a big, fat, rainbow fur ball if you don't exercise.'

The monkey blew a raspberry, unimpressed by his advice.

Khalid bit into the sweet flesh of the stone fruit in his hand, and looked out towards the sunrise as he savoured the flavour. The cool, damp morning air was filled with the smells of nature, and he drew far more delight from the aroma than he had to date; this was the scent he was coming to associate with home. He'd always assumed that scheming and betrayal was what made life satisfying, and yet here he was doing absolutely nothing and he'd never felt so completely fulfilled by the moment. As usual, the whiz kid was right; last night's events had changed him, he felt renewed right to the core of his being — as if every single cell in his body had been scrubbed clean of all its heaviness. The jungle was starting to hum with the sounds of daytime animals and bugs that seemed to beckon him to explore with new eyes.

Intent on living in the moment, Khalid headed for the stairs that led to the bank, then paused to reconsider. *If they wake and find me gone they're going to think I've taken off.* He moved to write a note, and then called himself out on it. 'Idiot.' He conjured up a note and left it on the desk.

Khalid waited until he was on the bank and heading down the jungle track before he let loose a *yahoo!* His captors were right: his powers were his own. And with two good ankles he broke into a run to celebrate.

The entire world was more vivid today. Instead of repelling him, he sensed nature embracing him as the jungle parted and the track he was running along led onto the beach. He'd always avoided the sun, but the dawn rays — and the sight and sound of the surf crashing against the shore — felt so revitalising to him now that he had to wonder why he had deprived himself of these simple pleasures for so long. The answer was simple really, his demons had denied him. Up until this moment, despite how much control Khalid thought he'd had over his own choices, none of them had been his own.

'I like sun,' he decided. 'I like nature, and water, and animals! I *love* the elements.' He threw his arms wide to absorb the sunshine. '*I love!*' he cried out in victory, and fell to his knees in the sand as tears of relief overwhelmed him.

'I am alive,' he mumbled, 'I am *free.*' He wiped the tears from his face and breathed deeply to contain his overwhelming relief. 'Thank fuck for that.'

'Who is fuck?'

The little voice startled him and he looked aside to find Thurraya standing there, and immediately covered his own mouth in a fruitless bid to withdraw the statement. 'No, I didn't say that, I said … Frank, thank Frank.'

Thurraya was grinning at his discomfort.

'What are you doing here?' He looked about to see if she was accompanied.

'I had to see if you were all right after fighting those demons,' she replied.

The concern in her voice made him want to weep all over again. 'How do you know about that?'

'I dreamt about it.' She came to kneel beside him on the sand. 'How you kept asking for forgiveness but the demons wouldn't listen.' She threw her arms about him and gave him a hug.

Khalid's heart shot into his throat and his eyes and nose started running, he couldn't contain it. 'I needed to be punished,' he admitted. 'And I felt I might not endure it, but the thought of you saved me.'

'Really?' Ray pulled back to see if he was serious. Seeing how upset he was, she reached in her trousers and handed him her skull-patterned handkerchief. 'If you were thinking of me, maybe that's why I dreamt of you?' she theorised, then noting the design on the hanky she'd handed him, she grimaced. 'Oh … that seems a little in bad taste, but at least it's not too girly.'

'It will certainly do the job.' Khalid swiped his face, and then wasn't sure what to do with it.

'You should toss it to the breeze,' she advised. 'So that air elementals can learn from your experiences. They're not very good with emotions, like water spirits are, but they're good communicators, so it pays to have them onside.'

'Really?' Khalid was fascinated.

'Yep. And they're real good at finding parking spots too.'

Khalid laughed at this, not because he didn't believe her, but because he found her conversation so delightful. 'And how do you know this?'

Thurraya shrugged. 'Just do. But I know it's true, 'cause I even see them sometimes during the rare times I'm in nature, or Ringbalin's greenhouse.'

Khalid found her answer rather curious, but he didn't want to pry — the less he knew about his keeper's daughter the better. 'Well, that does sound like it would come in handy.' He held the tiny cloth up and let it go; they watched it tumble off down the beach.

'Now all your troubles have blown away on the breeze.' Thurraya clapped her hands, and Khalid wished that were so. 'Now what should we do?'

Khalid laughed out loud as the answer was very clear. 'As happy as your visit has made me, you need to pop back from whence you came. Your parents would have a *fit* if they knew you were alone with me.'

Thurraya stood up, appearing not entirely pleased with the suggestion. 'Show me some jungle first.' She grinned and bolted for the gap in the trees behind them.

'Here I am trying to be good —' he dragged himself up to his feet '— and you're encouraging me to be *bad*.'

She turned about and ran backwards, waving him after her with both hands. 'A walk in nature is *good*!'

'Your parents won't see it that way.' He used his PK to make her stop, but she only laughed as she broke free and kept running.

'What the?' He took off in pursuit.

'Come on, come on,' she called from down the track. 'There is a pool with fish!'

Khalid slowed his pace, quietly thanking goodness that she'd come to a halt and he could catch up with her.

'Come look at this.' Ray was kneeling near the pool, beckoning his approach, but as he got nearer he noted something grey moving around in the tree close by her.

The creature was eyeing Thurraya, but stilled and froze as it spotted Khalid. It was a monkey that rather resembled Karisha if she'd been dipped in grey soot. The monkey opened its mouth and there was something gleaming on its tongue. 'My amulet.' A pang of fear reverberated through his entire being as he realised the blood-sucking monkey had got its hands on the canister containing the evil spirit of Chironjivi.

'What is wrong?' Ray noted his horror and turned around to see the filthy monkey snarling at her.

As Ray let loose an ear-piercing scream, the world seemed to slip into slow motion and Khalid could hear his heartbeat thumping in his ears as the monkey leapt towards Thurraya. With a split second to consider his options, Khalid envisioned himself in Ray's place, and in the next moment he felt the monkey land upon him and sink its teeth into his flesh.

When Zeven woke he felt groggy, but as the sun was just rising he knew it was early, so he hadn't had much sleep. He moved to rise, but a stinging pain caused him to reach for his neck. The area was tender and it left blood on his fingertips. 'Ouch!' He rose to check his reflection in the mirror, and found a large bite on his neck that was already infected. 'That monkey has to go,' he mumbled, realising he was too stoned to be angry about it.

'Hold on ...' He wasn't holding the canister any more. Zeven staggered back over to check his hammock, but there was no sign of the item. His concern escalated as he noted Khalid's hammock empty, but he was too stoned to be truly panicked.

Telmo, still asleep, also had a nasty bite on his neck.

'Telmo!' Zeven roused the energy to stagger over and shake him. 'Wake up!'

'What's happened?' Telmo bleary-eyed, held his head.

'I think Khalid and the monkey are conspiring against us.' Zeven pointed to his neck. 'You have one too!'

Telmo's fingers made contact with the bleeding mark on his neck, and he sucked in air at the sting.

'The canister containing Chironjivi is missing, and so is Khalid.' Zeven concluded, 'I hate that I'm so calm about this.' He staggered to a seat at the table he used for a desk and found the note from their charge.

'What's that?' Telmo half fell out of bed and then crawled over to investigate.

'*Going for a walk, back soon, Khalid.*' Zeven looked to his advisor as he knelt and leaned on the side of his chair for support.

'If he was really out to betray us, why would he bother leaving a note?' Telmo reasoned. He sat back on his haunches and spotted something on the floor beneath the desk.

'I'm stunned Khalid left a note! That's like a sign of consideration ... whoa, progress,' Zeven said, watching Telmo mucking about under the desk. 'What are you doing?' Telmo popped up with the open coffer in his hand and shook it about to make it plain it was now empty.

'No, no, *no!*' Zeven was exhausted just thinking about taking action in his current state. 'I intended to conjure up some manner of bio-containment setup for it last night.' He held the top of his nose and squeezed it to relieve the stress. 'I must have passed out after returning Ahura to the other side of the island after he fixed Khalid's leg. Stupid!'

'I was passed out before you even returned!' Telmo shared responsibility for the mishap. 'You are pushing yourself too hard! You may have superhuman abilities, but you are *still* human.'

'I'm certainly feeling that this morning.' Zeven touched his wound and winced. 'How did this get infected so quick?'

'Give me a look at that.' Telmo inspected the wound. 'As I thought, this bite is laced with sub-etheric matter.' He stood to conclude, 'It's not Khalid who has the amulet, it's Karisha.'

A child's scream pierced through the morning hum of the jungle, sending the resident birds soaring into the sky in a great plume of commotion, and the sound struck fear into Zeven's heart.

'*Thurraya.*' With the thought of his daughter, Zeven desired to join her and his wish was immediately granted.

The relief of arriving to find Thurraya unharmed was overwhelming; she looked on as Khalid battled with the soot-covered monkey. Zeven grabbed hold of his daughter and pulled her further from the action.

'Daddy!' She panicked as she was hauled backward. 'You have to help!'

Every time Khalid got a good grip on the monkey it would vanish and attack from another angle. The only way to stop the animal was to kill it; yet killing went against everything Zeven believed in, and in this case the error was his, not the monkey's.

'Do something!' Khalid was a mass of bites and becoming too sedated to defend himself.

'Don't look, baby.' Zeven covered Ray's eyes, with the intention of snapping the creature's neck.

Closer to Khalid, Telmo appeared, and with a split-second evaluation of the situation, he manifested a psychic restraining device that clamped around the animal's neck.

Zeven gave quiet thanks for his comrade's quick thinking. The monkey attempted to flee but Telmo grabbed the critter.

'The amulet is in its mouth,' Khalid advised as he collapsed onto the ground.

Ray ran to him and hugged his bloody form. 'You saved me! This is my fault … I should have gone home when you told me to.'

Zeven was stunned and a little disturbed to see his daughter's open display of affection towards their past nemesis.

'I owed you one, kid,' Khalid mumbled, patting her head as he struggled to stay conscious.

'Open,' Telmo commanded the monkey, holding it firm in one hand as he put pressure on both sides of its jaw until it opened wide to expose the amulet on its tongue. 'Zeven, the coffer.'

The monkey struggled harder when it saw the container appear, and as Zeven directed the amulet back into containment, all the soot covering the monkey detached and flew into the coffer also. When Zeven slammed the lid closed and locked it, the monkey passed out and they all breathed a sigh of relief.

'Time for a new containment system, and a safer hiding spot,' Zeven remarked.

'No, no, stay awake.' Ray shook Khalid and then looked to her father, with tears rolling down her cheeks. 'I think he's dead.'

Telmo quickly moved to check for a pulse. 'No, he's still with us.' He smiled to reassure the girl, and then looked to her father. 'But I think he's so pumped full of monkey venom, he's having difficulty breathing.'

Zeven went down on his knees beside Ray. 'Are you all right?'

'Please don't make me leave,' she appealed. 'I have to make this right.'

Zeven realised he could not send Ray home in this state and expect her to act like nothing had happened. 'We need to have a little discussion before you go anywhere.' He let her know she was in trouble. 'You've got some explaining to do.'

But Ray was not fazed by the notion of a reprimand. 'Thank you!' She threw her arms around him and squeezed tight.

Zeven let Ray go and stood to request of Telmo, 'Take Khalid and Ray back to the hut.'

'I'll get him rigged up to a respirator, just in case,' Telmo advised.

Zeven nodded. 'I'll fetch Ahura, and join you presently.'

Ahura may have seemed a little odd, exhibiting a childlike wonder and enthusiasm for everything he observed on the island since he'd arrived, but according to Vadik he'd demonstrated just about every psychic talent known to the USS. If the Dropa Prince couldn't heal Khalid, no one could, for Ahura had proven more capable than Ringbalin, Zelimir, Kassa and Swithin put together. He claimed to see auras and had reportedly raised dead animals and healed them as good as new, no surgery required.

On a whim Zeven had chosen to join Vadik, and was so very grateful for that when he discovered where Ahura was currently.

Vadik was on the beach outside the hut where they had set up a temporary home, and he was gazing at the sea with his jaw gaping open.

'Vadik, where is Ahura?' Zeven announced his arrival.

The query startled the big man, but he appeared very relieved to see Zeven. 'Thank the elements you are here, I was just about to call. He's done some strange stuff in the past few days, but if this don't beat all.' He referred Zeven to the water.

The beach here was inside a calm little bay, but the surface this morning was churning with activity; there were fins and tails thrashing everywhere.

'He's in there?' Zeven nearly choked on the fear the thought invoked in him. 'Why did you let him walk into that?'

'It was perfectly calm before he entered!' Valik held his hands up in truce, not prepared to be liable. 'The man is some sort of nature guru! He keeps attracting this shit! I just control the elements, Mother Nature is not my bitch ... but she's certainly his.'

'So he's not being mauled?' Zeven couldn't see any blood in the water.

'From some of the shit I have seen him do, he'd probably survive it anyhow.' Vadik cast a questioning eye in Zeven's direction. 'If I didn't know better, I'd think he was immortal.'

Zeven's attention shifted to Vadik and he forced a laugh, about to deny that truth, when a cry of delight drew his attention back to the water.

Ahura had shot out of the water on the back of a huge ray shark, and it glided through the air with as much ease as it did through the water. Many of the large sea creatures followed suit, launching themselves into the sky to fall in behind Ahura like a great flock of birds.

Zeven was completely gobsmacked; he'd never seen a natural event like it.

'This —' Vadik motioned to the flock '— is not normal. For a start, those creatures can't breathe out of water and are deadly vicious.'

'It only proves he's likeable.' Zeven wandered closer to the water in the hope of waving Ahura down.

'Likeable!' Vadik ran to catch Zeven up. 'The only way anyone could get up the balls to walk in the water with this lot is if he knew he couldn't be killed. The man has no fear, because he has nothing to lose.'

'Or he's trying to carry out a death wish in a very extravagant manner.' Zeven held his neck, as the bite was starting to give him a headache.

'What is that?' Vadik took Zeven's hand away to inspect it. 'It looks gross.'

'That's what I need Ahura for,' Zeven advised. 'Khalid is covered in these things —'

'Ha ha, karmic justice.' Vadik was stoked.

'He got this way saving my daughter.' Zeven rebutted his delight. 'It could be her we were fighting to save right now.'

Vadik sobered. 'Sorry, Bob, I'll get him down.' Vadik went quiet and focused inward, whereupon the wind went from beneath the fins of the flying sharks and they glided back into the water.

Wondering why his game had come to an end, Ahura looked about to see his minders waving him down, and he suddenly appeared before them. He was dried, dressed and happy to see Zeven. 'My friend!' He bowed to Zeven. 'Back again so soo—' He noted the bite on Zeven's neck. 'This is very bad.'

Zeven stepped away to stop him fussing, even though he was feeling a little warmer than usual. 'It can wait. Your son fares *far* worse. Follow me.' He didn't wait for a response, but vanished to the treehouse.

7

GAMBLING WITH ABSOLUTES

There had been little rest for the acting prime minister of Phemoria since she had assumed head of state in their monarch's stead. She was just about to call in her assistant to give her leave in the wake of another twenty-hour day, when she entered the office of her own accord.

'General Prochazka is here, requesting to —'

'This is no request.' The general pushed the girl out of the way. 'Go home; you will not be needed again today.' She shoved the younger, less robust woman out the door, and then slapped her hand down on the wall-mounted closing mechanism. The door shut and they were alone. 'Acting Prime Minister Lamus.' Prochazka walked forwards to stand before Jalila's desk and gave the slightest nod of her head instead of bowing as she would before the Qusay.

'That seems such a mouthful, General; a simple "Prime Minister" will suffice.' Jalila did not rise, but forced a smile and offered the general a seat.

The muscle-bound warrioress was the only member of the Valoureans who did not wear the deep-red leather and metal uniform for which they were famed and by which they were easily recognisable as the queen's guard. Instead she wore a uniform of deep purple leather to set herself apart as their leader, and to ensure that there was no mistaking her. But with the authority she wielded in her voice and presence, there could be no mistake that Prochazka was commander and chief of the most feared fighting force in the whole of the United Star Systems.

'Why did you lead a man into our holy of holies?' she demanded, with obviously no intention of sitting down.

'I was on the Qusay's business,' Jalila replied calmly. 'So I suggest you ask her, when she is again granting audiences. Until then, you will have to take my word that there was a *very* good reason.'

Prochazka's eyes narrowed with contempt. 'And what of the prisoner you released from solitary? Do you not know that he was the one who damaged our last Qusay beyond repair?'

'There seems to be some debate about that,' Jalila commented, although in truth she wasn't sure she trusted all her informants yet — although the healer made her grin every time she thought of him.

'You stupid child!' the general barked. 'There is nothing to debate. *I* was there! I locked that rabid creature away myself! We must hunt him down at once!'

'You will do no such thing.' Jalila was as cool as the general was fiery. 'I am in charge at present and you will follow my orders to the letter, is that understood?'

Prochazka stopped seething. 'You, in charge?' She smiled most sincerely. 'There seems to be some debate about that.'

Jalila stood, losing her patience. 'You saw the Qusay-Sabah Clarona hand her ring of sovereignty to me.'

'But it seems the ring was not the Qusay-Sabah Clarona's to give.'

'Have you been drinking?' Jalila considered the general's argument completely ridiculous.

'Of course!' she admitted. 'But that will *never* affect my judgement.' Prochazka took a few steps backward, and a cloaked figure took form and manifested beside her.

'I could have you arrested for breaching security. Who is this? Show yourself.'

At first Jalila expected to see one of the new royals whose acquaintance she had made in recent days, as there were very few known psychics who could teleport.

When the person in question pulled back her hood, it took a moment for Jalila to put a name to the face, for she had been a girl when last she'd seen her. 'Princess Satomi,' she uttered, flabbergasted.

'That is correct,' the woman replied. 'And *I* am your rightful Qusay.'

Jalila shook her head slightly to disagree. 'You lost the right to rule when you abandoned Phemoria.'

'I have been kept prisoner all this time.' Satomi took a few steps closer. 'But now I am *free*, and here to claim my birthright as Qusay. And you will return my ring and kneel before me, or I shall kill you where you stand.'

Satomi's large grey-mauve eyes, indicative of the royal line of Phemoria, stared her down, and given little option, Jalila sank to one knee.

The princess held out her hand and allowed Jalila to take hold of it to replace the ring on her middle finger.

As the ring was then shoved in her face, Jalila kissed it and bowed her head. 'Welcome home, Majesty.'

'Your cooperation is greatly appreciated.'

Jalila's head shot up, and she saw the Princess Satomi's form transform into Jalila's own image. 'You can shapeshift?'

Satomi smiled broadly. 'And now I know all that you do.' The princess looked to the general. 'Time to deal with my sister.'

It seemed ironic to Jalila to see the general bow low before this false image of herself.

'Knock her out.' The princess glanced back to Jalila.

'With pleasure, Majesty.' Prochazka pulled out a metal baton, and slapping the bludgeoning end into her free palm she headed for Jalila.

Upon Zeven and Ahura's arrival at Vadik's hut, Telmo had Khalid on a respirator, but his many wounds were festering and Telmo didn't have to mention that their patient had a fever — that was plainly obvious.

'What caused this?' The Dropa Prince appeared deeply concerned, and Zeven wasn't surprised. Just one bite was making him feel weak and feverish, so Khalid must be feeling ten times worse!

When Zeven advised Ahura what had happened, the Dropa Prince was not happy.

'You said you had the curse contained.'

Zeven opened his mouth to apologise, but Ahura had already moved on.

'But we must work with what is.' He looked back to Khalid.

'Who is that man, Daddy?' Ray asked.

Zeven grabbed her hand to lead her downstairs. 'Ah … that's … Frank.' Zeven used the first easy-to-remember name that popped into his head.

'Oh, so *that's* Frank,' Ray replied, which perplexed her father.

'Never mind who he is.' Zeven sat her down in the kitchen. 'What are you doing here?'

'She remotely witnessed some of our patient's ordeal at Dead Man Downs.' Telmo had already queried her while they were waiting for Zeven to return.

'I had to see if he was all right,' Ray justified.

'No more sleeping with your mother when I am away,' Zeven suggested, feeling too depleted to serve up a harsh reprimand.

Ray nodded to confirm. 'Does your patient not have a name? No one seems to use it.'

'Never you mind what his name is.' Zeven found his zeal. 'He is top secret! You know what that means?'

Ray nodded. 'No one is supposed to know about him.'

'That's right. And you coming here the first time already caused a security breach when Grandma followed you.'

'And now Top Secret is sick because of me!' Ray concluded, ready to burst into tears. 'He told me I should go home, after I'd seen he was all right. I'm hopeless!'

'No, you're hope*ful*,' Telmo gave his view. 'But the work we do is dangerous, and has far-reaching ramifications.'

'Ram-a-fa-what?' Ray frowned.

'Affects a lot of people and planets,' Zeven simplified.

'Oh!'

'And that's why we do not make a move without the captain or our timekeeper's permission. You got that?' Zeven stared her down, trying desperately to hold his stern expression in the face of Ray's pout — she appeared to be taking the scolding very seriously.

'I will tell the captain in future.' She breathed a heavy sigh.

'Good. Now ...' Zeven looked her over and imagined her without all the dirt and blood splatter on her skin and clothes until the telling stains faded away. 'You should head back before anyone misses you, and tell no one where you have been.'

'But, Daddy, you're sick.' She wiped the sweat from his brow.

'I'll be fine. Frank is a healer.' Zeven kissed her forehead and stood. 'Off you go.'

'Bye, Telmo.' She waved, to delay her departure further. 'It was nice meeting you.'

'We shall meet again soon,' he assured her.

The girl's big dark eyes shifted back to her father. 'I love you, Daddy.' She vanished, leaving Zeven feeling like a complete heel.

'Aww.' Telmo was touched.

'If I cannot control her now, can you imagine what she'll be like as a teenager?' Zeven knew it was hopeless.

'She controls you just fine,' Telmo ribbed. 'She's a very old soul, that one.'

'I can do nothing!' Ahura walked down the stairs to join them. 'These wounds did not come from the natural world, and they do not respond to my intention.'

'I feared that might be the case.' Telmo looked to Zeven. 'We've had trouble dealing with such wounds before.'

Zeven bit his lip, recollecting those instances. 'Back in Zhou, Ji Fa's wounds never really healed,' he concurred. 'And when Rhun was wounded by the reptilians, the Dropa's "egg" cured him.'

'The Dropa's egg?' Ahura had no idea what Zeven was talking about.

'It radiated cosmic light —' Zeven began to explain but was struck by an idea. 'I need to try something. Back in a tic.'

Two minutes later Zeven returned, soaking wet, but his bite was healed.

'What did you do?' Ahura was amazed as he inspected the wound.

'Oceane.' Telmo guessed Zeven had gone to bathe in the celestial light of the being who was their soul source and was horrified by the paradox this posed — keeping Khalid ignorant to Oceane's existence was AMIE's number one priority.

'You must take my son there, immediately,' Ahura urged.

'It is not that simple, I'm afraid,' Zeven advised Ahura, but a glance to catch Telmo's doubtful expression did not raise his hopes of success. 'I must convince my superiors to give permission first, and that will not be an easy argument to win.'

'All you have to do is conquer a fear!' Ahura stressed, as if he knew all the details already. 'Which is a small price to pay to save a life, don't you think?'

'You are preaching to the converted here,' Zeven spoke for Telmo and himself. 'I will not allow Khalid to die.' Zeven approached Telmo. 'Put Khalid in stasis to buy us some time. Then take that cursed coffer, change the appearance of it, and hide it on Oceane somewhere no one will find it until we are ready to dispense with the curse properly.'

'I want to come with you to appeal my son's cause,' Ahura decided.

'I cannot allow you to do that,' said Zeven.

'I already know who your superiors are and what your ship looks like,' Ahura argued. 'Your minds are like open books to me.'

'I gotta get my Juju back,' Zeven decided, tired of everyone reading his mind.

'I doubt it would make any difference with this one,' said Telmo.

'Despite what you know, your presence would only distract from the true issue,' Zeven told Ahura, backing up a couple of steps to take his leave. 'Stay here and assist Telmo, I shall be back as soon as I can.'

*

'Taren? Taren … wake up.'

Her body shaking woke her with a start. 'What? What is it?' Her bleary gaze came to focus on Zeven, and her eyes opened wide; he was the last person she expected to see. 'You're here …' She sat up and Lucian stirred.

'We've got trouble,' both Zeven and Taren informed each other at once.

'Oh … *joy*,' Lucian whined and rolled over, clearly hoping to avoid getting involved.

'I need to speak with both of you ASAP.' Thankfully, Zeven allowed they would probably need a moment to gather their wits. 'I'll meet you in the captain's office when you are conscious.' He vanished.

'I don't know if I can take any more Zeven drama this week.' Lucian rolled on his back and rubbed sleep from his eyes.

'Maybe this is about Satomi?' Taren was still looking for a lead as to her whereabouts.

'We can only hope.' Lucian raised himself, kissed her head, and clambered out of bed to get dressed.

Taren had them both ready and the bed made with a thought.

'Excellent,' Lucian mumbled, when he realised the clothes he was looking for were on his body. 'Now we've time to get coffee.'

A coffee appeared in his hand, and by the time he'd looked to Taren she'd taken hold of him. Two seconds later they were in his office.

'Well then,' he muttered, still bleary. He wandered behind his desk and took a seat. 'Continue.'

Taren half sat on the front of the desk and folded her arms as they both looked to Zeven.

'Have you lost your mind?'

Both Lucian and Taren were wide-eyed and fully awake after Zeven outlined his request and the story behind it.

'We've spent years ensuring that Khalid will never find Oceane, and now you want to take him there!' Taren was, not surprisingly, very opposed.

'He saved Ray's life!' Zeven stressed. 'With no thought for his own mortality. Does one good turn not deserve another?'

'Not in this case, no!' Taren put her foot down. 'It could be a trick —'

'He's *dying*, cousin … there's no trick about it!'

'It would be all the better for us if he did die,' Taren concluded coolly.

Zeven was more than a little disturbed by her view. 'On Kila, after Khalid got dragged into our mission, I wanted to kill him! I was *so* ready, and you know what stopped me? *You.*'

Taren was a little stunned by his claim.

'You said, if we kill him, what makes us any different to the Orions? Or in this case the MSS,' Zeven explained. 'So we let him live, and he went on to become more spiritually advanced than we were!' Zeven became most impassioned as he realised. 'From the beginning he was right about the Dropa, and we were wrong! *We* were wrong, and *he* died because of it! Please don't repeat that error, *please.*'

'Look,' Taren said, 'if there was *anything else* I could do to help, I'd do it. But you're asking me to risk the fate of two universes *and* our oversoul! The stakes could not be any higher!'

'Isn't that the ultimate challenge of any spiritual warrior? To feel the fear and do it anyway, *because* it is the *right* thing to do.' Zeven knew that for once he held the moral high ground.

'Damnit!' Taren backed away to cuss, and looked to Lucian seated behind his desk, calmly sipping his coffee while they argued the fate of their existence. 'What is your view on this?'

'As far as I can see this mission does not have anything to do with AMIE, apart from countering our main objective,' Lucian replied. 'Moral paradoxes are your department.'

'Argh!' Taren threw her hands up and collapsed in a seat. 'Why must it always fall to me to decide? The *Zagriata* are supposed to be a unit.'

'Well you can go put it to the unit,' Lucian suggested, 'but I think you'll have a rebellion on your hands.'

Taren served her husband a look that implied he was being a smart arse.

'Speaking of rebellions,' Zeven thought to enquire about the Princess Satomi. 'How did you manage to pacify my mother after she discovered I am aiding Khalid?' The memory of her slap still stung.

'I didn't,' Taren sounded none too happy. 'That's the trouble I spoke of earlier. Satomi has vanished and has cast some shielding spell in her wake, so we've been unable to locate her.'

'A shielding spell.' Zeven's memory shot back to the theft of the Soul Keep from Dead Man Downs. 'That means she can shapeshift,' he advised.

'She's *changed form*, of course!' The realisation hit Taren like a brick in the face, the trick seemed so obvious now. 'That's how she does it.'

'Khalid figured it out at Dead Man Downs, when the smelter to which all the ghostly crew there are attached — the Soul Keep, he calls it — was stolen before our eyes.'

'By whom?' Taren was obviously stunned that anyone could know about the Soul Keep, when even they had only just discovered the form of the curse's source.

'Two women,' he relayed. 'Cloaked. We suspect they were Phemorian, as we were unable to psychically pursue them.'

'Holy shit!' Taren stood again and looked to Zeven. 'You think one of them was Satomi?'

'I sure hope not.' He found that premise hard to swallow. 'But if she can shapeshift who knows?'

'I'm not a big believer in coincidence,' Lucian finally weighed in on their woes, 'and this seems a *monumental* one.'

'Dear universe,' Taren drew a deep breath. 'I hate to imagine what she plans to do with that. But whatever it is, it's going to be directed at Khalid. If he dies, there will be nothing for Satomi to aim her anger at.'

Zeven was horrified by the reasoning, but was having difficulty gathering his argument.

'There is us,' Lucian pointed out. 'I do recall her saying you were worse than both your parents put together —'

'She said that?' Zeven was shocked.

'Which seems to imply —' Lucian summed up.

'An existing resentment towards my parents.' Taren saw his point. 'I informed my mother of Satomi's resurrection, but I implied that she seemed a little delusional in the wake of it and anything she said was not to be believed without question.'

'If she goes telling Phemorians that we freed and are abetting Khalid, everyone will turn against us, maybe even your father,' Zeven feared.

'So we have to get Khalid to somewhere, away from AMIE, where he cannot be found or located,' Lucian concluded calmly. 'The best place for him is Oceane.'

'But he is not of our soul-group,' Taren reasoned. 'The presence of Azazèl-mindos-coomra-dorchi may not be able to shield or heal him.'

'Well, if it cannot, we've risked nothing,' Zeven seconded Lucian's view. 'Khalid will be dead.'

Taren sank into a seat again, to re-examine the argument. 'I need tea in the morning before I'm asked to —'

Zeven was holding a cup in front of her before she had time to wish one up for herself.

'Many thanks.' She accepted it, and sipped it while she continued her silent musing.

'I've had Telmo hide the coffer containing the curse on Oceane also,' Zeven informed, but Taren looked to him wide-eyed and fit to freak. 'But not even I know where it is or what it looks like. Telmo is the only one who can locate it.'

'Good job,' Lucian awarded, and the captain's view calmed Taren a little.

'My heart and my head are so conflicted on this.' She placed her empty cup aside.

'Then leave them out of it,' Zeven suggested. 'What does your gut tell you? And the amulet on your arm? When you think about allowing a repentant man to die.'

Taren focused on this, holding her right hand over the armband that held the Juju stone pressed to the flesh of her left upper arm; her expression was pained.

'Now think about saving him.' Zeven watched as her torment turned to peace and he knew that the cosmos was with him on this.

'The Juju rules in your favour,' Taren admitted, feeling somewhat relieved to have had some guidance on the matter.

'Yes!' Zeven fisted the air. 'I'd like my Juju back now, as Khalid is healed enough to stand in its presence. And I need one for Telmo, too.'

'What are we to do about Satomi?' Taren asked, as she materialised the said items and handed them to Zeven.

'Well I dare say if you report to your mother and advise her that we suspect Satomi to have stolen away with the source of Khalid's curse,' Lucian suggested, 'that would seem to support your claim that she's gone a little loopy and is not to be trusted, which will raise the Qusay's guard at least.'

'The halfling of shadow they call him; I don't know that anyone on Phemoria has pegged that halfling as Khalid, at least not openly.' Taren had learned this from Zeven's conversation with Jalila Lamus. 'The acting prime minister should also be warned about Satomi.'

'Mother has an accomplice on Phemoria, so beware,' Zeven cautioned. 'Someone helped bring Khalid's curse about, and got Khalid out as a baby, so someone knows the truth of the matter.'

'Satomi herself escaped Phemoria as a young girl.' Taren considered the same person could have been aiding her now. 'But who?

'Whoever it was had no problem dealing with the curse at Dead Man Downs.' Zeven imagined such a woman must be formidable, and even more so with his mother as an ally. 'Those ghosts hate Phemorian women more than death itself, so she must have a means to keep them in line.'

'And there seems to be something else you are overlooking.' Lucian was loath to point it out. 'Satomi is the elder daughter of the Phemorian line and the rightful heir.'

'She abdicated,' Taren argued.

'Correct me if I am wrong,' Lucian winced, 'but your mother pardoned her the day we removed the cursed crown from her head — only at the time we all believed her dead and buried.'

'Oh shit!' Taren realised he was absolutely right. 'We must both move quickly.'

It had taken the Qusay-Sabah Clarona several days to recover her sensibilities following the ordeal that had seen the cursed crown of Phemoria finally lifted from her head, and she now felt ready to reassume her rightful place as head of state. As her daughter seemed most determined to end heretical rule on Phemoria, she considered it prudent that she work with the new acting prime minister to create a governing body worth abdicating for.

In removing the cursed crown from her head, her daughter had not only ended the curse but overthrown her in a shadow rebellion. Now that she had regained her health and sensibilities, Clarona could declare war on her daughter and Sermetica, in a bid to reclaim her throne. Still, considering what she had allowed to transpire under the guidance of the Phemoray, she realised that individuals were not infallible, and that they were subject to manipulation — both supernatural and earthly. The judgement of a governing body would be far more difficult to undermine, and Clarona considered that it might be time to pursue a new form of governance for Phemoria.

Funny that she felt not the slightest bit sentimental or defeated about the rule of the Phemorian royal line ending on her watch. On the contrary, she felt pride in the fact that all those daughters who would be born into her line in the future would never have to experience the curse of the Phemoray, or the pressure and loneliness of ruling as sole monarch.

The thought of Jabez Anselm filled her chest with a warmth that took her breath away — her heart had been as ice for so long that the glowing sensation was a wonder to her now. Pride in her daughter added joy to the mix, and her eyes overflowed with tears, as they had been for days.

'Not today.' She brought her surging emotions into check as she dabbed the tears from her eyes with a lace cloth. 'This is the first day of a new era for Phemoria, and not the occasion for tears, happy or sad.' She'd never had the chance play the good Qusay before;

Clarona wasn't sure she knew how. 'Just be yourself,' she counselled her image in the mirror of her dressing room, although it was so long since she had been herself that even Clarona had to wonder what she was really like.

She was about to find out, she supposed, as one of her dressers closed the clasp on her necklace and Clarona was ready to face her court.

As usual, her day started with a private council with General Prochazka and Jalila Lamas.

'General Prochazka. Prime Minister Lamas,' Clarona greeted them from her throne as they entered side by side. 'I trust all fares well with our affairs during my infirm.'

Both her subjects bowed to her, although the general bowed more deeply than Jalila — perhaps she felt her new appointment put her above royal homage?

'We do have one urgent matter to discuss.' General Prochazka came forward, with a couple of documents in hand, which Clarona expected needed to be signed.

But upon being presented with the first document, the Qusay realised it was one she'd penned herself and signed only days before. 'This is the pardon for the Princess Satomi. What of it?' she asked, even as it clicked in her mind that if Satomi was pardoned and again living and breathing, she was now a rightful claimant to the throne of Phemoria. Thankfully Clarona had not told anyone of Satomi's resurrection.

'Indulge me, Majesty.' The general handed her the second document.

Clarona opened it to find a summons for her own arrest. A metal device clamped around her ankle and before she could query it, the Qusay had been psychically restrained.

'You are under arrest,' Prochazka advised.

'What are the charges? And on whose authority —?'

'On my authority.' Jalila shifted form into that of Clarona's long-lost sister.

'Satomi,' Clarona gasped, having not seen her older sister since before their mother's death. She had barely aged at all.

'You are being arrested on the charge of conspiring with rebels who are harbouring our bastard brother!' Satomi seethed.

'No!' Clarona denied the charges, and looked to the general. 'Surely you do not believe this lie? My sister is not in her right mind.'

'No ... *you* are the one who is not in your right mind, little sister!' Satomi asserted. 'You have been tricked into believing your daughter and her father's good intentions, and I almost was myself, but the truth is our families are poisonous snakes!'

'How can you say that? You would not be *alive* but for their aid!' Clarona stood to confront the challenge head on. 'They are the *Zagriata*, appointed by creation itself! You shall be damned if you defy their efforts to unite the Star Systems and bring a lasting peace to all humanity.'

'The *Zagriata* are a bedtime story!' Satomi was angered by what she saw as ignorance. 'They have just used this fallacy to suck you and *everyone* into their scheme!'

'Their scheme?' Clarona was baffled.

'To rule the USS as a shadow government,' Satomi concluded.

'That's ridiculous!' Clarona objected. 'They could have taken Phemoria easily, but they did not. They only freed us from the curse that you ran from and left me to deal with! And I would have suffered that curse my whole life but for their compassion. They forgave me my trespasses of the past, which were not of my choosing, and I wish nothing more than to follow that example. I forgive you, Satomi, for skirting your responsibilities to Phemoria and leaving a girl to do a woman's job, but if you continue with this coup, forgiveness will not come so easily.'

'*Forgive our enemies*, I will *not*! I will hunt Khalid down and anyone who gets in my way will die with him. Then I will teach Sermetica a harsh lesson about what happens to those who bring traitors into our midst.'

'No!' Clarona's heart was breaking to think her rescue from the Phemoray was just a trick — but deep down she knew it had not been. 'My family came for me once, and they will again. They will not allow you to start another war!'

'It doesn't matter what you think.' Satomi approached to touch her sister's cheek and then assumed the appearance of the Qusay-Sabah Clarona. 'I am Qusay now.'

'Traitor!' Clarona had no idea her sister could shapeshift; no one would even know that she was missing.

'Send her to the celestial city,' Satomi instructed the general. 'Even the *Zagriata* will have quite a time trying to free her from there.'

'No!' Clarona begged as Prochazka led her from the room of court.

Without the Phemoray, or the curse being destroyed altogether, there was no way back to the Earth plane from the spirit city. 'I have just got my family back, please don't do this; banish me anywhere but there!'

'I'm not asking you to make any sacrifice that I am not prepared to make myself.' Satomi walked to the throne and took a seat. 'I will oppose my family to redeem Phemoria in the eyes of our foremothers and so shall you.'

'General Prochazka,' Clarona appealed once they were alone in the waiting room beyond the room of court. 'You have always been so faithful to me —'

'I am faithful to Phemoria.' The general turned to face her and placed Clarona's hands in cuffs to escort her through the palace. 'I serve the true Qusay of Phemoria, and the Qusay-Sabah Satomi is that true ruler — you made it so by your own hand. I don't make the laws, I just see them carried out.'

'Just promise me that you will never allow my sister, or *anyone*, to put the crown of the Phemoray on their head,' Clarona appealed, as a hood was pulled over her own head to mask her identity.

'I hate the Phemoray more than I hate Sermetic men,' Prochazka spat. 'You can rest assured that I shall see the crown of the Phemoray destroyed!'

'No, you must not.' Clarona panicked, having been advised by her daughter that that would be most unwise. 'Unless you know how to reverse the curse, you will only —'

The general grabbed her cuffs, and abruptly pulled her near. 'Do I have to gag you?'

'You'll just release Phemoray to —'

A muffling gag was crammed in her mouth and the outer adhesive grip stuck to her face.

'Now walk with me, quietly,' the general advised, 'or you shall be unconscious a whole lot sooner.' Prochazka grabbed her by the cuffs and led her to the holy of holies built by the Phemoray to protect Phemoria's most gifted psychics from being corrupted by earthly pleasures and desires.

At least that was the story the Phemoray spun. But in truth, these females were confined to a life in the celestial sphere to keep them under control and prevent them from rebelling against the Phemoray. The threat of their termination was also used by the Phemoray against the ruling Qusay; the notion of killing so many of her countrywomen ensured that the women through whom the Phemoray ruled always toed the line. The women in status in the vault beneath the royal palace spent their whole lives in spiritual service, isolation and celibacy, which was virtually how Clarona had spent her entire adult life to date. *A few days of true freedom is not enough.* She wept for the family life she had waited so long for, and for her sister who was making a grave mistake, but mostly her tears were for the inhabitants of the USS. For if the Phemoray were released there was no imagining the extent of their retribution that would no doubt begin with her own family.

8

KEY TO THE KINGDOM

Where could she be? Aurora was in a panic; she'd searched the ship from one end to the other, she'd even summoned her daughter to the captain's office over the ship intercom system, and still no sign of Ray. With little else for it she began her search over, and was greatly relieved to find Thurraya sitting on her bed.

'Baby, where have you been? Why didn't you answer my page?'

When Ray looked in her direction, tears were streaming down her face — Aurora had never seen her so upset.

'Ray … what's happened?' Aurora came to crouch before her as Ray attempted to brush the tears from her face with the long sleeves of her shirt.

'Nothing … that I can tell you about,' she replied.

'Does this have something to do with why Grandma was angry?' Aurora approached the situation indirectly.

Ray nodded to confirm this. 'I've done something really bad this time.'

'This time?' Aurora suppressed her urge to be angry, lest Ray clammed up again. 'You went to visit Daddy *again*, when the captain expressly forbid you to do so?'

'Not exactly,' Ray defended.

Aurora, frustrated, took a breath to try again. 'Sweetie, if something has upset you I need to know.' She raised herself to sit by her daughter on the bed, and put an arm around her in comfort.

160

'It's very bad.' Ray's tears welled anew.

'Maybe it isn't as bad as you think,' Aurora attempted to allay her daughter's rising panic. 'Please, tell Mummy what's happened.'

'A man is dying, and it should have been me, Mummy,' she confessed, and the tears started tumbling. 'He saved me from the cursed vampire monkey and now he is dying from his wounds.'

'Who is dying?' Her story sounded so outrageous that Aurora wondered if she'd just had a vivid nightmare.

'Daddy's friend, Top Secret,' Ray replied. 'I don't know his real name. Daddy and Telmo got bit by the monkey and now they are sick too!'

'Sick?' Aurora wondered if this was why no one was allowed to visit, perhaps they were in quarantine? With that thought she grabbed Ray to inspect her for any sign of sickness.

'I wasn't bitten, Mum.' Ray objected to being handled and pulled away. 'Top Secret saved me, and now he is suffering for it.'

'Thurraya!' Mythric walked in sounding relieved as he looked to Aurora. 'You found her, I see?' Then he noted the vibe in the room was not a happy one. 'Where did you get to?'

Ray merely looked to the floor in shame, tears still rolling down her cheeks.

'It seems she caught a ride on one of your cuddles to see her father again,' Aurora outlined.

'What the hell is Zeven doing that everyone who returns from seeing him is completely distraught?' Mythric's slow simmering beef rose to the fore. 'I'm getting a little tired of not being told what is going on in my own family, or even in my own world. I just found out on the news that Khalid escaped prison almost a week ago!'

'Oh, my stars! We must tell Taren.' Aurora rose.

'You think she doesn't know?' Mythric challenged. 'Her father is the chairman of the United Star Systems — she knows!'

'Then why has no one mentioned this news to us?' Aurora wondered. 'Why are we not running a mission to recapture him?'

'Precisely,' Mythric seethed. 'I have a good mind to quit this crew and go and find out what my son is really up to.'

'No, Mythric, not you too,' Aurora appealed. 'The captain and our timekeeper have never steered us wrong in the past, we must trust —'

'They have driven a wedge between my wife and my son. I have the right to know why! We have the right!' He included her in the equation, gripping the spot on his left arm where his Juju stone was located; it was obviously paining him, meaning his thinking was not in tune with cosmic law.

'Ray seems to think Zeven is unwell.' Aurora was more concerned about this fact than what he was up to — she trusted her husband would always do the right thing by AMIE.

'All the more reason,' Mythric lowered his voice, 'to sneak off and find out what is really going on.'

'No,' Ray insisted. 'You shouldn't break the rules. I did, and I've made an awful mess of things.'

Mythric was curious to hear her say so.

'Apparently Zeven is harbouring some top secret charge who has been badly injured saving Ray's life.' Aurora conveyed what she garnered from her daughter already.

'Really.' Mythric was intrigued to learn this, and came to crouch beside Ray. 'And this charge of his, was he the one who upset Grandma?'

Aurora gasped, as she realised Mythric was implying that Zeven might be harbouring Khalid — Zeven's disappearance and Khalid's jail-break would have happened around the same time.

Ray froze, afraid to answer. 'Grandma is wrong about him, he is good now! Grandpa?'

Mythric stood, incensed by the news. He was shaking his head, unable to believe his son would aid the man who had ruined all their lives.

'He's been fighting his demons,' Ray appealed, gripping Mythric's arm to make him listen, and ensure he didn't pop off anywhere.

'I'm sorry, Ray.' He pulled away from her. 'You're too young to understand —'

'Mythric!' Aurora moved to grab him and prevent him leaving, but he'd already vanished. 'Shit!' she freaked and then covered her mouth. 'We are in so much trouble.'

'Not if we fix this.' Ray grabbed hold of her mother's hand. 'Shall we?'

Aurora gasped, torn between wanting to know the truth, and reporting Mythric's AWOL to the captain.

'Quick, Mama, before I lose my charge,' Ray urged. 'Top Secret saved my life, I can't let Grandpa hurt him more!'

'Oh, what the heck.' Aurora resigned herself to the consequences. 'Let's go.'

'I'm sick of being left behind to babysit, while you all run missions without me!' Vadik was protesting, as Zeven readied everyone else to move camp from their idyllic hut on Frujia. 'I don't even have anyone to babysit any more, if nature-guru is going with you.'

'I told you, I don't have clearance to take you where we are going.' Zeven was frustrated; any amount of delay could cost them dearly.

'Then get it!' Vadik insisted.

'I *don't* have time!' Zeven stressed. 'Telmo!'

Telmo moved to approach Vadik. 'Now listen here —'

'No way!' Vadik backed away from the fair whizz-kid. 'Every time I talk to you I forget stuff.'

'Then be a good chap and forget stuff on your own.' Telmo clicked his fingers.

Vadik's face went blank and the big guy wandered off downstairs as Telmo moved to inspect the readouts on Khalid's stasis unit.

'Thank you.' Zeven approached, readying himself to transport the stasis unit with him. 'Are we good to go?'

Telmo glanced back to Zeven, but looking beyond him, the smile fell from his face. 'I think there will be a delay.' He referred Zeven to Mythric who had just appeared behind him.

'Where is he?' Mythric demanded to know, as Zeven and Telmo stood with their backs to the stasis unit, as if to hide it.

'You are not supposed to be here,' Zeven warned his father. 'You are in breach of your AMIE contract.'

The warning was wasted on Mythric, who pushed Zeven and Telmo out of the way to look inside the unit, and seeing Khalid, he slammed both fists down upon it. 'No wonder Satomi was furious! Why?' Mythric's wrath turned on Zeven. 'Why would you betray your family like this? Why is the timekeeper allowing you to?'

'That's a *long* story.' Zeven maintained his calm, just. 'But in short, in another universe, you and I made a vow to save Khalid from his curse in this one.'

'Bullshit!' Mythric shoved Zeven backwards. 'I have never wanted anything more than to kill him with my own bare hands!'

'In the universe parallel he saved *all our arses. Yours* most of all.' Zeven stood tall to defend his decision. 'And you don't have to kill him now, because he is *dying* ... from injuries he sustained saving *your* granddaughter!'

'It's true, Grandpa,' Ray announced her arrival. 'Please don't hurt Daddy.' She ran to Zeven's defence.

'Aurora!' Zeven was worried when he noted that Ray had brought her mother with her this time — was his wife about to turn against him too?

'Take Ray out of here,' Mythric ordered Aurora, who ignored him and wandered over to the stasis unit to gaze at the man in question who was covered in festering wounds.

'This could have been Thurraya,' Aurora uttered, with a deep sense of gratitude in her voice. 'Whatever Khalid has done in the past, I am thankful that I am not observing my daughter's cold body in here.'

Mythric's anger ebbed only a moment. 'It does not absolve him of what he did to your mother. If you don't let him die, I will kill him myself.'

'If my son dies, how shall he ever make amends for the crimes of our curse?' Ahura walked up the stairs into the main floor of the hut.

'Your son?' Mythric was baffled by the new arrival who appeared a taller, more comely version of Khalid. 'Who are you?'

'This is Kaveh Ahura Mazida, Khalid's true father and prince of the race we have come to know as the Old Ones,' Zeven did the introductions.

'The Old Ones?' Mythric had always thought them a myth dreamt up to explain how the inter-system gateways came into being. 'But Chironjivi —'

'Was the father of the curse, and that is all,' Zeven explained. 'If anyone has been wronged in this situation it is Khalid and his father, who have both suffered due to that curse for fifty *long* years!' Zeven concluded his case. 'It is the curse you have a beef with, not Khalid.'

'And where is the curse now?' Mythric wondered.

'The amulet I removed from Khalid's hand, to which Chironjivi is attached, has been hidden by Telmo.' Zeven pointed him out to Mythric, for they had never met in this timeline. 'But the "Soul Keep", to which the rest of the ghostly crew at Dead Man Downs is attached, has been stolen by a couple of Phemorians, and I strongly suspect one of them was Mother.'

Aurora and Mythric both gasped at the accusation.

'How would she even know about the curse?' Mythric defended. 'I didn't.'

'I bet you didn't know she could shapeshift either?' Zeven posed. Again his father was stunned. 'That's how she covers her psychic tracks,' Zeven explained.

Clearly this was news to Mythric, who shook his head in disbelief. 'She would have told me.'

Zeven shrugged. 'You may have been married for thirty-odd years, but you really only knew Satomi for one of them … I'm sure there are many things she did not tell you.'

'If that is true,' Mythric didn't like the implication, 'it is only because her life was cut short by —'

'The curse!' Zeven stated before his father laid blame in Khalid's quarter again. 'The curse that Mother has now stolen half of!'

'To what end?' Mythric supposed. 'Perhaps she intends to destroy it?'

'Maybe?' Zeven wanted to give her the benefit of the doubt. 'But more likely she intends to use it to extract some sort of revenge on Khalid, and AMIE. Which is why I have to leave here, and quickly!'

'And go where?' Mythric posed. 'Where in the universe do you think you can hide where Satomi —' He gasped as he realised there was only one answer. 'Oceane! The timekeeper gave you permission to counter our one main objective.'

'Ironically,' Zeven admitted, 'it is our only option.'

'Then you should get on with it,' Aurora resolved first, and approached to kiss her husband. 'I trust you have the best interests of all in hand.'

When their lips parted, they both looked to Mythric and Ray ran to join them in their stand.

'If I were to tell the rest of the crew what you are up to, AMIE would be no more.' Mythric obviously still felt this was an act of betrayal.

'Well, you must do as your heart compels you,' Zeven replied, as he lifted his daughter up, kissed her farewell and set her down again. 'As I must.' He looked to Telmo and Ahura waiting alongside the stasis unit containing Khalid's body. 'Let's go.'

'I want to come,' Mythric waylaid his son, who shook his head.

'That's a very bad idea. I'm not healing Khalid so that you can beat him up again. The whole reason I brought him to Frujia was to try and give this man some good life experiences, because basically he's had jack-shit! I don't think you beating the crap out of him is really going to teach him what compassion is, do you?'

Mythric was a little stunned by his son's sound psychological reasoning. 'When did you get so bloody wise and forgiving?'

'After I ran a mission in the future, and came back here to prevent the disaster that led to that mission from ever happening.' Zeven felt he may as well confess everything.

'The timekeeper sent you back here.' Mythric's eyes narrowed, looking to place blame for his wife's hostility in another quarter.

'No.' Zeven again shocked Mythric with his denial. 'Telmo and I ran this mission of our own accord. Taren knew nothing about it until a week ago, and even then I didn't tell her I intended to aid Khalid. But from the previous timeline I knew he was about to break out of prison anyway and cause us all manner of grief. Now, he is saving our lives.' Zeven motioned to the stasis unit. 'Did I make the right choice? You tell me.'

Mythric was absolutely speechless — it was all too much to process.

'A week ago,' Ahura offered his view, 'I thought I was a *monster*. But it turns out I'm not. The truth of what really happened lifted a veil from my eyes and now I see the path ahead far more clearly.'

'Mother never gave me a chance to explain,' Zeven told Mythric. 'Does she really think I would do something like this just to spite her? I'm doing this in the hope that, once we shovel away all the lies and bullshit of the past, we'll discover that we have all been deceived by our selfish, power-hungry forefathers and mothers, and we don't need to repeat their horrendous mistakes, or bend to the will of the curses they created for themselves. I'd like to think that humanity has evolved in the last thousand years.'

'I get it,' Mythric conceded, his anger waning. 'And I still want to come.'

Zeven was still reluctant.

'If your mother shows up to exact her vengeance, I may be your only hope of getting her to see reason.' Mythric made a good case.

Zeven cocked an eye. 'Welcome to the AWOL club.' They shook hands on the decision. 'Damn fine to have you aboard.'

'Come here, pumpkin,' Mythric waved his granddaughter forwards for a hug. 'Charge up and take your mum back home.'

Ray was happy to oblige. 'You won't hurt Top Secret? Or be mad at Daddy?'

'No, baby.' Mythric hugged her close. 'You were right. Daddy knows what he's doing, so the least I can do is be helpful, right?'

Thurraya nodded to confirm, a smile on her face that only lasted a moment as she turned back to her father. 'What about the monkey, is Karisha all right?'

'She's perfectly fine,' Zeven assured. 'Telmo just had to wipe out her memory of us, and she's now back in the jungle where she belongs.'

With a satisfied smile, Ray returned to her mother and took hold of her hand. 'I guess we fixed it, huh?'

'You bet we did.' Aurora served her a wink, and looked back to Zeven. 'What shall I tell the captain and Taren?'

Zeven grinned. 'I think we could venture so far as to tell them the truth.'

His team all nodded in accord.

'So proud of you.' Aurora blew Zeven a kiss, as did Thurraya, before they vanished.

'You have a very beautiful family,' Ahura told Zeven and Mythric.

'Yep,' Zeven grinned, 'for a philanderer who was the son of a shameless flirt, I think I did good.'

Mythric finally cracked a smile as well. 'Now if we can just get your mother past the past, we'll be home free.'

'But first things first.' Zeven looked back to Ahura. 'Let's see about mending your family. Shall we, gentlemen?'

They all laid hands on the stasis module and focused their intention on being on Oceane.

To request an audience with the Qusay-Sabah Clarona, Taren materialised in the waiting room beyond her mother's room of council, as there was a court official at the desk therein who saw to the Qusay's appointments. Her mother had told her at their previous meeting that she intended to reassume her official duties, and that Taren could not just pop in and out at will, she needed to take the proper channels.

Usually this room was rather full with people, and she would have appeared unnoticed, but the chamber was entirely empty, all bar one occupant — a Valourean clad in purple leather, who she assumed must be a high-ranking member of the order of the Qusay's guard.

The warrioress rose immediately from behind the desk to confront Taren — not the least bit fazed or surprised by her mysterious appearance. 'State your name and business,' she requested in a very intimidating fashion.

'My name is unimportant,' Taren informed. 'I am here on behalf of President Anselm of Sermetica.'

'Really?' The burly woman backed up a few paces, looked Taren up and down, and then smiled. 'So you are one of Anselm's new psychic army?'

'That is correct,' Taren replied.

'You are very small of frame for a warrior,' she scoffed, sounding pleased about that.

'But just the right size for a peacemaker.' Taren didn't take offence.

'Peace! Peace is not something a general gets to talk about very often.'

So this must be the infamous General Prochazka. She was something of a legend on Phemoria, as she had been head of the Qusay's guard for over seventy years and a Valourean for over two hundred! Clearly she was a woman in her prime; her stern countenance only added to her formidable beauty. Prochazka may have been a soldier, but everything about her screamed *untamed* — from her thick locks of long, unruly chestnut hair to the stormy green-blue of her eyes. The question for Taren was — what was she doing sitting in as the Qusay's secretary?

'And it is not often one sees a legend doing a cleric's job, General Prochazka.'

The flattery brought a forced smile to her face. 'I am just seeing to it that our Qusay's first day back in office all runs smoothly, Doctor Gervaise, or should I say, *Princess*?' She bowed, but her sights did not leave Taren, nor did the grin leave her face.

Perhaps the family resemblance was strong, or the Qusay had confided in the general about her? Perhaps the very fact that she had exhibited PK gave her away? 'Well, now it is clear that we are both aware who we are dealing with, may I please have an audience with my mother?'

'But of course!' the general announced in a tone that seemed overly accommodating. 'I feel very sure my Qusay will want to see you. One moment.' The general bade Taren to stay put as she strode over to the court doors and entered, closing the door in her wake.

Something felt odd to Taren, and the Juju stone on her arm had begun to ache, which meant something certainly wasn't right. Her gut instinct was to leave immediately, but her head told her she needed to find out the cause of this premonition, because if something was off here, she must ensure her mother was protected.

It took far too long for the general to re-emerge from the courtroom, and when she did she was followed by a whole battalion of Valoureans, who marched in a two-by-two formation through the large waiting area and out the doors at the opposite end of the room, without a sideways glance in her direction.

They look like they are on a mission.

'My Qusay will see you now, *Highness*.' Prochazka did not do the honour of showing Taren into the courtroom, but did a sweeping bow that flowed into an about-face, whereupon she fell in behind her troops and left the room.

What was that all about? Taren could feel the cynicism just oozing from the general. Either she didn't approve of Phemoria's plan to form a governing body, or she had some other beef with her.

At this point the cleric emerged from the courtroom. 'The Qusay-Sabah Clarona will see you now,' she announced, holding open the door of the court.

So Prochazka was awaiting her troops. Taren roused half a grin, realising the general had been toying with her to a degree. But why — if she realised she was the heir to the throne — would she show such disrespect? Perhaps the general didn't believe her claim, or thought her too young to bother about? Or was there another reason? If Satomi had pulled a coup already then Taren was no longer the heir to the throne — Zeven's young daughter, Thurraya, would be! That realisation was something of a shock, but there was little point speculating. Taren would know the truth soon enough, and it wasn't as if she was blindly walking into a trap; she'd had her suspicions before she'd come.

Upon entering the room of court, Taren couldn't help but notice the large armed force of Valoureans standing at attention around the interior walls, but this was not unusual.

'Qusay,' Taren bowed before the woman who appeared to be her mother.

'You have word from President Anselm?' The Qusay's tone was very formal, and there was not so much as a hint of a smile on her face.

'We have obtained some information regarding the Princess Satomi's movements, which the president felt should be brought to your attention,' Taren advised.

'Oh really?' the Qusay asked, intrigued. 'I have been concerned about my dear sister. What have you learned?'

'We have reason to believe that the Princess Satomi may have been involved in the theft of a very ancient, very *evil* artefact, that is a component of a curse we are attempting to counter.'

'You think that my sister might try and use this evil implement to steal my throne?' the Qusay supposed with concern.

This was not her mother, Taren felt sure of it. The true Qusay had been very emotional the last time Taren had seen her — feeling for the first time in her entire thirty-odd year reign was overwhelming — and even with a queen's countenance, she could not have cooled so much in a few days.

'We do not presume to know the Princess Satomi's intentions; our concern is for your safety. Which is why I have brought you this.' Taren pulled out a piece of stone from her pocket and walked forwards to present it to the Qusay.

This was not a Juju stone, but Satomi would be none the wiser as Taren made the pretty blue stone glow for effect, so it would look unique to anything seen before.

'It is beautiful.' The queen eyed it over, not keen to touch the illuminated stone. 'Is it an amulet of some description?'

'It certainly is,' Taren said with a sincere smile. 'It will protect your Majesty from sub-etheric evil.'

'How wonderful!' The Qusay reached for it.

'It will also aid you to tread the path of the righteous.' Taren stared the Qusay in the eye, and her fingers paused before they touched the stone. 'What's the matter?' Taren whispered, 'has Satomi got your tongue?'

The Qusay stood and Taren backed up a few steps. 'Think you are so clever, don't you?' said the queen, and with a wave of her hand, a psychic restraining device appeared and clamped around Taren's ankle. The device was cast off before Taren even noticed it and rolled across the floor — her Juju had repelled it.

'Two can play that game.' Taren directed the device towards the Qusay, who turned to smoke and vanished before the item reached her, whereupon the mental restraint fell defunct on the floor once again.

'The true Qusay has many talents but shapeshifting is not one of them. What have you done with the Qusay-Sabah Clarona?' Taren demanded to know, as she watched the smoke thicken into a form once again.

'She is somewhere you shall never retrieve her.' The Qusay returned to a physical form but still appeared as the Qusay-Sabah Clarona.

'You sent her to the celestial city!' Taren knew there was little to no chance of getting her out of there.

The Qusay came striding towards Taren, and a sword appeared in her hand, which she pointed at Taren in threat. 'What have you done with the halfling of shadow?'

Satomi must have decided that if she couldn't best Taren with psychic force, she'd resort to good old physical threats — but it would serve her no better. Taren teleported herself to the other side of the room.

'He is where *you* will never find him.' Taren rested easy in knowing Satomi had not been on board their vessel long enough to learn anything of AMIE's true mission.

'Oh, the Valoureans will find him, and his allies, and they will kill *on sight*,' the Qusay assured, vanishing and reappearing behind Taren with the sword at her throat. 'Our foremothers were right, all men are perfidious snakes,' the Qusay hissed into her ear.

'Zeven has not one ounce of treachery in him! His intentions are pure —' Taren elbowed her assailant in the ribs, whilst batting the hand holding the weapon away from her throat. As she turned about she smacked the same elbow into the impostor's face, and the Qusay fell to the floor unconscious.

Taren was rather surprised by her own strength, she hadn't had to use her secret service combat skills in some time, but she was even more shocked when the body of her mother, lying on the ground, transformed into a Valourean and not Satomi. That would explain how she could lift a hand to the Qusay and her guard did not attack; clearly her aunt was as slippery as a snake. 'You can hide from me,' Taren challenged, 'but I will flush you out eventually.'

All the Valoureans around the walls remained stone-faced. 'You will not get away with this.'

'With what?' One of the guards took Satomi's form. 'Taking what is rightfully mine?'

'No.' Taren approached her. 'Destroying the peace we've worked so hard to establish —'

'Ha!' Another Valourean assumed Satomi's appearance. 'There can be no peace while the halfling of shadow lives!'

Taren backed up a few paces, back towards the throne, realising that any one of the fifty-strong force of Valoureans could be Satomi — how were they doing this?

'So you run and tell your father what I have done.' Yet another Valourean assumed Satomi's form. 'And save us the trouble of declaring *war*.'

'This is insane!' Taren could hardly believe how quickly six years of planning had come undone, and she couldn't blame Zeven for it as she believed in his agenda. 'Satomi, if you would only allow us to explain —'

All the Valoureans present took Satomi's form to order at once, 'Kill her!'

As Valoureans reached for their weapons and came rushing in her direction, Taren could have frozen them all and continued the argument. But the chances were that Satomi was not even present in the room, and there was little point in trying to reason with Valoureans following their Qusay's orders.

Taren had learned all she needed to, and so chose to vanish back to AMIE.

*

173

When Taren appeared in Lucian's office she was cursing and swearing.

'Not good news, I take it?' The captain stood and came out from behind his desk to see if he could calm her down.

'Satomi has deposed my mother as Qusay and sent her to the celestial city where we cannot reach her ... not without reversing the curse of the Phemoray first.' Taren began to list their woes. 'She has served her Valoureans a *death* warrant on Khalid *and Zeven* —'

'Stop!' Lucian grabbed hold of his wife, hoping to prevent her from free-falling into a total meltdown. 'No one can find our crew on Oceane ... no one close to Satomi even knows it exists, and we are all protected by the Juju.'

'Satomi's ghost has been following Mythric around for as long as she has been dead!' Taren reminded him. 'She's probably been to Oceane.'

'Even if she were to teleport there, she is one of our soul-group and being in the presence of her soul source would fill her full of compassion,' Lucian countered. 'It is probably the best thing that could happen.'

'And she probably knows that too,' Taren reasoned, 'and will avoid going there, but there's nothing to stop her sending her troops there. All she needs is a good telepath to pass on a visual image to someone with PK and —'

'Besides Satomi, everyone in existence known to have PK is on our side,' Lucian pointed out. 'It will take the Valoureans *years* to reach here with the inter-system gateway to this system out of order.'

'I can see now why Zeven told me to get a big chunk of Juju and place it in the heart of this ship.' Taren had done as advised. 'I thought it was to protect us from Khalid! Ha!' It was amazing how fast causality had spun around.

'But we are safe.' Lucian brought home the point he was trying to make. 'And your mother, although unreachable at present, is not beyond salvation and is perfectly safe.' He felt all the tension rush from her body. 'The first thing we need to do, the way I see it ...' He let his grip loosen and rubbed her arms in comfort. '... is warn your father, so that he is not deceived by Satomi's disguise.'

'If we tell Father he'll declare war on Phemoria in defence of my mother.' Taren was stressing again. 'That's exactly what Satomi wants!'

'Then talk him out of it. Anselm has trusted us to handle situations like this before, and will again if you request his cooperation,' Lucian warranted.

'I don't know how we'll fix this.' Taren was overwhelmed.

'Only because you haven't given yourself any time to muse the possibilities.'

'So much for the psychic bill of rights being passed by the USS!' Taren broke free from Lucian to pace. 'Or dealing with the MSS persecution —'

'Wait.' She stopped still. 'Zeven mentioned that Kalayna held the key to that solution. But then —' Taren gasped.

'What now?' Lucian queried.

'The crown of Phemoria.' Taren pointed to the captain's desk.

Lucian assumed she'd sent forth a desire for it to manifest there, but it did not. 'The vault on Phemoria must be psychic-proof, like the prison cells used to contain criminals with Powers ... you could get in, but won't get out until the vault is opened.'

'Indeed.' She saw his point. 'I could die waiting! But I must get my hands on that crown somehow, because if they try to destroy it without reversing the curse they'll set the Phemoray free to do as they please.'

'That would not be good news for anyone in the USS.' Lucian shared her urgency on that count.

'I have no idea where such a vault would be located, either.' Taren crossed off being able to find it with her PK. 'Or what it looks like. *But ...*' Her expression lightened. 'Jalila Lamus would certainly know.'

'The acting prime minister is either in on Satomi's coup,' Lucian figured, 'or she's been sent to the celestial city along with your mother.'

The fact didn't seem to faze Taren at all. 'I believe I have a very good idea who has been aiding Satomi, and perhaps Chironjivi in the past.' She outlined how another piece of Zeven's puzzle was falling into place. 'I met General Prochazka of the Valoureans today. She is certainly old enough and powerful enough to fit the profile of Zeven's mystery woman. She'll know where the Soul Keep *and* the crown of the Phemoray are hidden, I'll warrant.'

'I wonder what your father knows of her?' Lucian posed.

'A very good question,' Taren agreed. 'I do know of a means to communicate with the Phemorians in the celestial city, so I can check Satomi's story in regards to Mother, and she may also know where the crown is hidden. I just need the aid of a good telepath.'

'How fortunate that we have a couple.' He served her an encouraging smile, and was appeased to receive one in return.

Lucian's intercom buzzed and he pressed the touch pad on his desk to respond to the page that was coming from Aurora's desk. 'What's up, Aurora?'

'Can I come in? I have a fairly urgent mission update from Zeven.'

'One moment,' he waylaid her and looked to Taren.

'I guess there is just no controlling this lot.' Taren realised that there must have been another breach for Aurora to know anything of what her husband was doing. But she gave a nod. 'I need to speak with her about Thurraya in any case. As Satomi has now taken the throne of Phemoria —'

'— Thurraya is the heir apparent.' The fact was startling to Lucian, as the girl would be a sought after commodity now. 'Permission granted,' the captain responded to Aurora's request. 'Is Ray with you?'

'Yes, Captain, she's right here.'

Lucian breathed a sigh of relief on that count. 'Bring her in, I need to speak with the both of you.'

Once, many years ago, when Zeven lost his powers, his father delivered them both to Oceane to keep him safe from psychic detection. On this stormy planet that was ninety per cent ocean, Mythric had dreamt up a dwelling for them to inhabit. That stilted hut still stood high above the water level which, on the highest flatlands of the small landmass of Oceane, was still knee-deep. Inside this dwelling was where they chose to land.

'Good to see the old place still standing.' Zeven left the stasis unit and wandered over to pull up a grass blind that opened the interior to the balcony, to let in light and air. It came as no surprise that it was teeming rain outside as this was always the case here.

'This place is deeply stirring to my blood.' Ahura followed Zeven out onto the open, covered verandah and breathed deep the atmosphere.

Huge unfurling reeds sprung out of the wetlands all round, and the only ground to be found above the water level were large mounds of rock, some the size of mountains. But the constant storm that raged here was a multi-coloured spectacular.

'I'm glad you like it.' Zeven grinned, figuring Ahura was picking up on the high resonance of the celestial architect who was cultivating this little landmass. The timekeepers knew this being as Azazèl-mindos-coomra-dorchi — the entity that all of the timekeepers would some day, on some higher level of existence, merge to become. 'It's going to be home for a while.'

'The atmosphere here is saturated with an ethereal yet propagative energy.' Ahura descended the stairs to stand in the warm rain.

'Yep, it's spring on steroids!' Zeven agreed, as a memory of crash-landing here with Taren Lennox not long after they'd first met flashed through his mind and made him grin.

'It is more than that,' Ahura insisted, basking in the different coloured light bursts exploding inside the storm clouds above. 'It's pure spirit!' He held his arm up towards the sky as if to draw the energy into himself.

'And hopefully that spirit can shield us all from being found.' Zeven looked to Mythric and Telmo as they stepped out under the protective awning, where they all observed Ahura rejoicing.

'We *are* found,' Ahura laughed like a man possessed. 'You don't get any closer to found than this!' He dived off the stairs and into the water.

'Has he forgotten why we are here?' Mythric thought he'd want to see to Khalid's safety and wellbeing.

'Ahura is a very live-in-the-moment kind of guy, and a *little* eccentric,' Zeven advised. 'But after fifty years in a Phemorian prison that is to be expected.'

'And Khalid is in a perfect state of stasis at present.' Telmo had a good look around their new home. 'So there is no rush. I have a feeling we are going to be here quite some time.'

'Were you telling the truth before, when you spoke of visiting another universe in the future?' Mythric was finding that part of the tale hard to swallow.

'Of course. I've told you about similar missions I've run in the past,' Zeven pointed out. 'But with any luck we are done traversing universes and can now focus all our efforts on saving this one from its past.'

'And I went with you, to this other universe?' Mythric was intrigued.

'No.' Zeven thought it best not to mention that Khalid had killed Mythric before departure and prevented that. 'But you have a past life incarnation there, who is, of course, an old friend of mine.'

'Of course …' Mythric emphasised with scepticism, to conclude flatly, '… You're shitting me.'

'I shit you not,' Zeven insisted. 'Rhun Gwynedd, Governor of Kila. I'm going to run a mission with him here in a few years' time —' Zeven clammed up, as he realised he'd said too much, which of course piqued his father's curiosity.

'Idiot!' Telmo did not miss the opportunity to swipe Zeven across the back of the head.

'No, go on.' Mythric shoved Telmo out of the way.

'But you won't get to meet him then, as the captain and the timekeeper do a good job of keeping that episode under wraps.' Zeven was apologetic.

'But you speak as though you've already done the mission?' Mythric was perplexed.

'Well, of course I have,' Zeven laughed. 'Or otherwise how would I know it was going to happen?'

Mythric, having never time-jumped, was frowning as he tried to wrap his head around the paradox.

Telmo was also frowning, but for an entirely different reason. 'In case it was unclear, *idiot* means shut up. You're showing off, and things never bode well for you when you do.'

'Thank you, *Mother*,' Zeven heeded the caution, however ungraciously.

'Daddy!'

The sound of his daughter's voice sent a shockwave through his system for a moment, and Zeven was stunned to see Aurora with her, and a suitcase.

'I thought I was clear that you girls were not —'

'Taren sent us.' Aurora appeared to be putting on a brave face.

Thurraya, on the other hand, was genuinely thrilled. 'Captain's orders!' Ray ran to him for a hug.

'But you guys just left us. What's happened?' Zeven queried, and Mythric and Telmo were also keen to hear.

Aurora's sights turned to Mythric, and she had tears in her eyes. 'Satomi has seized the throne of Phemoria and declared herself Qusay.'

'What?' Mythric was winded by the news. 'I don't believe it,' he uttered in a tone that was completely contrary to the statement.

'Thurraya is now the heir apparent.' Aurora breathed deeply in order to keep calm.

Oh shit! Zeven considered Taren's life to date and had no desire to see his daughter face such trials and deceits.

'Do you think I will make a good Qusay one day?' Ray asked. 'I'm a *princess* now.'

'You always were.' Zeven forced a smile, kissed her forehead, and set her down lest she notice how his heart was thumping in his chest. He looked into Aurora's weeping eyes and saw the same concerns there; he did not have to say a word.

'If Thurraya needs guardians,' Aurora struggled to deliver the ruling, 'then you are all the men I want on the job.' She glanced back to include Khalid in the equation. 'Fortunately the captain, our timekeeper and I, are in agreement on —'

'Ha ha ha!' Ahura's cries of joy drew everyone's attention, as he shot out of the water, did a flip and landed back in the water again.

'Who is that?' Aurora was rethinking her statement.

'That's Frank,' Ray told her mother. 'He's a healer.'

'Oh,' Aurora was stunned by how well informed her daughter was. 'That's not the first definition that immediately springs to mind.'

'He is one of the Old Ones,' Zeven advised, hoping to set his wife's mind at ease.

'He's an ex-con, who's been in prison for fifty years.' Mythric was more cautious, still reeling from the news of his wife's coup.

'Zeven?' Aurora was immediately alarmed.

'He was under the influence of a curse that time, and that is not the case any longer,' Zeven set the record straight, and served his father a look that implied he did not appreciate him scaring the women.

'I have to go to her,' Mythric concluded.

'Don't!' Aurora was quick to grab his arm. 'The Qusay has issued a death warrant on Khalid, and all those aiding him.'

'Who is Khalid?' Ray wasn't following, but everyone else was.

'No one we know,' Zeven sidestepped the query.

'It's Top Secret, isn't it?' Ray posed and everyone fell quiet.

'Well the good news is no one has any chance of getting here inside three years from now,' Telmo announced with cheer, and tapped Ray's nose to dispel her fearful expression. 'So we have a little time to form a plan. Meantime, let's go check out the mad man, he's pretty funny.' Telmo led her away from the pending confrontation.

'The only thing that has been stopping me from pursuing my wife was not knowing where she was.' Mythric swept off Aurora's grasp. 'What must she think of us?' Mythric was shedding tears of frustration. 'She stood by me for thirty years, for many of which I was completely wasted, and the second I get a chance to repay that loyalty, I'm helping to resurrect her enemy?'

'I know it makes no rational sense,' Zeven appealed, 'but it makes sound spiritual sense. Stop seeing this through Mother's narrow sights and try to see the broader view.'

'We are of the House of Vidor,' Mythric protested. 'We are warriors! Not psychoanalysts! Zaman Vidor, *time warrior*, that is what your name means!'

'Spyridon Vidor, *spirit warrior*, that's what your name means!' Zeven countered. 'I've lived up to my name, isn't it time you lived up to yours?'

Normally, this argument would have ended in a punch up, or with one of them storming off to do exactly what he wanted anyway, but there was no true anger behind their words to one another — here on Oceane, they could only speak the truth and think the best of one another.

'Then what do you suggest, all-knowing one?' Mythric calmed down and opened himself to being advised.

'Just stay put, see us through this.' Zeven motioned to the unit containing Khalid. 'You are going to have to convince *yourself* that my path is righteous before you'll have any chance of getting Mother to see it that way.'

'Well said,' Aurora awarded in support. 'She's already attempted to restrain and kill Taren. I know Satomi is more fond of you,' she was quick to add. 'But Satomi has not had to live, or be dead, without you for a very long time … making yourself absent for a bit might aid Satomi to realise where her heart and priorities truly lie. This is not good versus evil here, this is love versus fear.'

'I fear her love for me will prove no match for her love of her home planet.' Mythric was disillusioned by their resolve.

'I am quite sure she had more wonderful experiences with you in one year than she had in her entire life on Phemoria, which is why she was prepared to leave it all behind for you once,' Aurora disagreed.

'No, that was because she was fleeing from a curse and being hunted by Valoureans,' Mythric was cynical. 'But it was neither of those threats that got her in the end.' His hallowed sights rested on the stasis unit containing Khalid's body.

'As far as Satomi knows, you know nothing about what Zeven is up to,' Aurora stated. 'Which might get you closer to her and back in her favour, once the shock of all that's happened has worn off.'

'That's dishonest.' Mythric grinned. 'Aren't the righteous supposed to be truthful?'

'Honesty is not about what you say.' Zeven gave his view on the matter. 'It is about what you intend. If your intentions are for the greater good then there can be no regret, for whether you are evil or righteous is, in the end, only judged by yourself.'

'No.' Mythric appreciated their advice. 'I cannot let Satomi go on thinking we are all against her … that *I* am against her.' Mythric reached for the armband containing his Juju stone to remove it, but Zeven gripped his father's wrist to prevent him.

'She won't trust you, she'll just torture you to find out what you know.' He released him.

'Well you know, a bit of S&M with the Valoureans might not be entirely undesirable,' Mythric made light of it.

'I'm serious!' Zeven would have thumped his father, if he wasn't full of so much good will. 'And if Mother does let you in … then you shall be my nemesis, and she'll have someone else under her command who has PK! Then Ray will not be safe anywhere! In fact that will be the first assignment she hands you, to test your loyalty.'

Mythric resented that. 'I would die before I would endanger Ray, and if she is wearing a Juju and I am not, then I cannot reach her.'

'You don't know what Satomi is capable of!' Zeven was impassioned, but not angry. 'You've already been surprised by her several times today.'

'You're right,' Mythric freely admitted it. 'But it is all beside the point.'

Zeven raised his brows, eager to be enlightened.

'If it was Aurora, what would you do?'

It was a loaded question, and both men knew Mythric had won the argument — right or not.

'I will betray no one,' Mythric resolved, as he pulled the armband containing the Juju off his person. 'Not you, not AMIE, not Thurraya, and *not* your mother.'

'You can't be on everyone's side,' Zeven rationalised, as Mythric placed the item in Zeven's hands.

'Watch me.' Mythric's resolve hardened.

'There is an old proverb that advises ...' Telmo returned to the debate, 'that the person who says it cannot be done, should not disturb the person doing it.'

'So you agree with him?' Zeven was surprised by this as Telmo was always so logical.

'Is there any point in arguing?' Telmo submitted. 'We must all do as our hearts compel us. What you have achieved with Khalid most would consider impossible ... should we not give Mythric the opportunity to achieve the same with your mother?'

'He's right.' Mythric was given renewed hope and slapped his new associate on the back for it — Telmo tried to look flattered, although he wasn't the boisterous type himself. 'You've managed to play both sides and stay true to both,' Mythric put it to Zeven. 'Why can't I? Would that not be advantageous to me living up to my birth name?'

'Um ... Mother hates me? And you're next.' Zeven didn't want to accept he was about to let his father deliver himself to the Phemorians for torture. 'But go, be tortured, see if I care!' Zeven lost his temper for only a second. 'No, actually I *do* care,' he admitted in a complete emotional turnaround. 'That's why I'm pissed!' He hugged his father with force, and Mythric returned the gesture.

'I know,' Mythric assured him, and with a slap they released each other. 'But this is me versus a planet of women.' His mood took an upswing. 'I think the odds are in my favour.' With a wink, Mythric vanished, and Zeven was left rattled.

'It was all going so right.' He was frustrated by where the course of his actions was now leading. 'My main objective in kidnapping Khalid was to avoid a war between Sermetica and Phemoria so that the psychic bill of rights could be passed, and I achieved exactly the opposite!'

'Which only shows us that if, by taking Khalid out of the equation, the result is still the same, then we have still not addressed the root of the problem,' Telmo deduced. 'But we can continue to chip away at it, by dealing with what we know we can do right now.' He moved to bring Khalid out of stasis.

'Are you staying with us then?' Zeven queried his wife, hoping her things were also in the suitcase she had brought with her.

Aurora looked around at the shack and the boys club that would be occupying it. 'What would I do here?'

'You could help me with Khalid,' Zeven proffered. 'Teach him how to act around a lady.'

'Ha,' she scoffed. 'I'm yet to teach you!'

'Harsh.' Zeven held his heart, faking hurt.

'I'd just end up playing house maid to you all … I think I'll pass.' Aurora screwed up her nose, sorry to disappoint. 'But Taren assures me that she'll bring me to visit Ray whenever I wish. And I can look in and see what's happening with you all at any time.' She pointed to her head — referring to her power for remote viewing.

'Just like when Ray was a baby, and you'd leave her with me on Frujia whilst running missions for the triple S.' Zeven pointed out that this wasn't the first time the family had been split apart, and Ray adapted to the situation far better than her parents did.

'Uh, the good old days.' Aurora sighed at their current woes. 'I'm going to miss you guys.'

Zeven gave her a kiss and a hug, seeking reassurance for them both. 'Will you stay here in the hut with Ray while we resurrect Khalid?' he requested. 'Just in case it doesn't work, I don't want Ray to witness him dying on us.'

Aurora nodded to agree. 'In any case, I'd like to thank him personally for protecting our daughter.'

'That will mean a lot to him, I'm sure.'

'How do you want to do this?' Telmo requested, as the compression seal on the stasis unit disengaged with a hiss of cold air around the rim of the lid, whereupon it slowly opened.

Zeven turned his attention to dealing with Telmo's query. 'I'll just teleport him out to that big flat rock out yonder.'

'Which rock?' Telmo moved closer to the balcony so he could view the location for himself.

'It must have dropped from out of the mountains since last I was here, but it's perfect for what we need.' Zeven looked to Telmo who was frowning. 'Is there a problem?'

'No problem,' Telmo assured. 'You are right, it does suit our need perfectly.'

'You are going to make him better?' Ray came back into the dwelling, and took hold of her mother's hand.

'We hope so, sweetness.' Zeven winked at her as he and Telmo laid their hands upon Khalid.

'We'll watch from here, okay?' Aurora drew Ray close to her as Zeven and Telmo teleported Khalid's diseased body out into the wild weather of Oceane.

Upon landing they were all instantly soaked by the torrential rain as they lowered the patient's body down to lay comfortably on the rock, and there was still room for Zeven and Telmo to crouch either side of him.

'Is it working?' Ahura jumped out of the water and landed firmly on his feet upon the block also.

'As with us, the wounds are washing away,' Telmo called over the weather, 'but —'

As the blood and flesh of the wounds were washed from Khalid's body, the debris turned into a glowing blue liquid that flowed down from Khalid over the rock and into the surrounding water, which had also begun to glow.

'Liquid light,' Telmo posed, inspecting his own wound to find it had merely washed away as Zeven's had.

Zeven was exulted by the spectacle, and bemused by it. 'How is that even possible?'

There was a rumble deep within the earth that unnerved them all.

'Earthquake?' Zeven feared.

Telmo shared his apprehension. 'Etheric quake.'

'Pardon?' Zeven began to panic as the rumbling of the earth increased in measure with the spread of the glow outwards through the water of the wetland — a storm of light more intense than the tempest above.

'My girls!' Zeven noticed the event had reached the water below the hut, and was of the mind to teleport to them as the landscape shook violently and he was forced to kneel to keep his balance. He looked to the rocky mounds around them, to observe that they were not so much crumbling, but transforming — as if another landscape was punching its way up through the existing one.

'What's happening?' Zeven looked to Telmo who was holding Khalid in place.

'I think we may have located the Dropa city,' he replied, his voice reverberating with the trembling of the earth.

'His blood is a key!' Ahura laughed with insane delight.

Khalid suddenly gasped into life. 'I remember!' he cried, in rapture. '*Karmandi!*' His entire body began exuding the same blue-white light.

'Whoa!' Zeven exclaimed.

Telmo struggled to stand and looked to Ahura. 'Home.' He smiled, his arms flung wide to embrace the experience.

'What's that pretty light mean, Mummy?' Thurraya and Aurora gazed on in amazement as the bright liquid light began to illuminate the site where Khalid was being healed.

'I have no idea, baby.' Aurora was enchanted by the pretty phenomenon as it spread through the water beneath the hut they were in.

'I think everything is going to be just fine,' Ray deduced with a clap of her hands, but as the ground beneath them began to tremble, their mystified expressions turned to frowns. 'Or maybe not.'

As the rumbling intensified Aurora was momentarily confused as to whether to lead her child back into the swaying dwelling, or into the glowing, churning waters below. 'Ray.' She crouched down where they were. 'Do you have any charge left from Daddy? Can you get us back to AMIE?'

'I'll try.' Thurraya held her mother, and closed her eyes tight a moment. Then opening them again she shook her head. 'It's not working!'

'Never mind.' Aurora grabbed Ray up into her arms as the stilted supports of the hut were heard to creak and crack with stress. 'It's going to be okay.' She headed down the stairs to take her chances in the water, and once clear of the dwelling, she stood thigh-deep in the water, clutching her daughter close.

'Look, Mummy!' Ray pointed back to where they had just come from.

Aurora swung about to observe the hut fading from existence, and she backed up slowly and carefully, stunned beyond rational thought, as a huge temple manifested in its place.

9

VOID OF FEELING

Aware now that Satomi could shapeshift, and her image no longer served as a reliable psychic marker, Mythric teleported himself to the Qusay's private audience chamber on Phemoria, which was located behind the throne room proper in the royal palace. Fortunately for Mythric, he'd been invited into this chamber — that no man had been inside for eons — by the Qusay-Sabah Clarona the day the timekeepers had removed the cursed crown from her head. In that instance the Qusay had requested that he fetch her sister's remains from the crypt beneath the House of Vidor on Sermetica, and return her to Phemoria, where she could rest in the peace. Naturally he had been beyond overjoyed to find his only love had been placed in stasis at the time of her death, and pooling the talents of fellow timekeepers, Dr Kassa Madri, Swithin Gervaise and Ringbalin Malachi, they had been able to bring Satomi back to life and heal her of her death wounds. It was hard to believe that all that good will and intention had led here — to the brink of war.

The chamber was empty at present, but as the Qusay usually took her meals herein, she was bound to enter several times during her working day. He needed to get his wife alone if he was to have any hope of getting her to hear him out.

This room was lavishly adorned with furnishings and decorations, so it wasn't difficult to find somewhere to hide. When one of the several side-doors to the royal chamber opened, Mythric concealed himself behind a bulky, floor-length curtain.

A house servant entered with a tray and placed it upon a small dining table, then turned about and, to Mythric's shock, headed in his direction. He was not so intimate with what behind the lounge looked like to envision himself there; he could have shifted to behind another curtain, but she was bound to open them all. As she neared, he was quick to step towards the side of the window and hold his breath as the maid drew the heavy curtain aside. She reached under the curtain for the tasselled end of the silk rope, which he was quick to direct into her hand and when she hooked the rope back on to its heavy metal fastener on the wall, Mythric found himself tied up inside the curtain. Still, he breathed a sigh of relief when she moved on to the next one. It was moments like this that he wished he'd learned Zeven's invisibility trick.

Mythric, like many people who had the Powers, had spent much of his life denying he had any and doing his best to drown them out with alcohol. If a task could be completed without using any supernatural force, it was his natural instinct to use the mortal means.

Like wriggling out of this curtain. He could have teleported out of the situation, but in this instance he would have betrayed himself as when he was halfway through shimmying out of the bind, another door opened — this time it was the double doors that led into the courtroom. At the sound of several heavy-footed people entering — he guessed Valoureans — Mythric stayed put and listened while they did a lap of the room, including checking behind the curtains; if Mythric had not been bound inside of one, he would have been found.

'All clear, Majesty. There are guards posted outside every door.'

'Thank you, Captain, that will be all.'

Mythric was surprised to hear not Satomi's voice, but that of the Qusay-Sabah Clarona. Was the timekeeper's intel wrong? Had Satomi been deposed already? Or had his wife just shifted form to assume the appearance of her sister?

He waited for the Qusay to be seated and eating her lunch before he teleported himself into the middle of the room. 'Hello, my love.'

As the Qusay spotted him, she smiled and placed her eating utensils aside. 'Spyridon Vidor. I suspected she might send you next. If you are here to try and romance me into giving up my birthright, I'm afraid you will be sadly disappointed.'

'I came of my own accord, and I would never ask you to give up what is rightly yours,' Mythric posed. 'But as the crown of Phemoria is rightfully yours, why are you wearing the guise of your sister?'

'It was easier than trying to explain that I'd been resurrected from the dead after thirty years.' She took a sip of her wine. 'I guess you regret that now. My sister certainly does.'

'To see you living and breathing … I have thought of little else for thirty years.' It was off-putting trying to pour his heart out to the Qusay when her appearance was of a woman he barely knew. 'My only regret is that you believe that your family have somehow betrayed you.'

The Qusay was angered by that statement, and stood. 'Have you discovered what our son is up to?'

Mythric nodded, solemn. 'He is healing a man I wanted to kill.'

'Past tense?' she noted.

'Khalid is dying, Satomi, from wounds he sustained saving our granddaughter's life.'

'What?' She was shocked to a smile, which departed very quickly as her anger returned. 'And our son is trying to save him?'

'He saved Thurraya's life!' Mythric repeated, as she seemed to be ignoring that point.

'And took mine!' Satomi defended her right to feel betrayed.

'Yet, here you are,' Mythric pointed out.

She shot a killer glare in his direction. 'So, no harm done then, is that what you think?' Her voice was harsh with disdain. 'I watched from my grave as Khalid destroyed you! My son grew up with the impression his parents *abandoned* him, and my granddaughter is now defending the very man responsible for all of this!'

'Our son is trying to prevent any more harm being done in the name of the damn curses that have destroyed all our lives!' Mythric took a few steps towards her and felt a psychic restraining device clamp around his ankle; the event brought him to a standstill.

'You gave up your amulet to come here.' Satomi was surprised to get a restraining device on him after failing to do so on Taren. 'Not a very smart move.'

'This is no game. I came here to be with you! That's all I ever wanted … you don't need to restrain me.'

'You are taking my side?' She raised both brows and laughed. 'Then bring me Khalid and my granddaughter!'

'I cannot find them without my amulet,' Mythric informed her, looking to his ankle. 'And now I am restrained that is doubly impossible.'

The Qusay summoned up a pretty blue glowing rock. 'Is this what your amulet looks like?'

Mythric looked it over. 'No.'

Her eyes narrowed, as the stone again vanished. 'Then I'll take your restraint off, you can conjure forth the true amulet, and then do as I bid.'

'I cannot,' Mythric proffered, 'only the timekeeper can manifest a Juju stone at will.'

'How convenient.' She doubted his story. 'If that is the case then you are of no use to me for anything but information.'

'Use?' he queried indignantly. 'You stood by me all that time, your feelings could not have just *vanished* —'

'You are quite wrong about that,' she said coolly. 'I knew you were going to try and play the love card, so I had all my feelings for you, our son and my sister, stricken from my memory. I didn't even need a psychic to do it, just a good hypnotherapist.'

The fact thrust an emotional blade deep into his heart, and Mythric could barely breathe for the aftershocks pulsing through his being. 'Zeven was right, I did not have a clue what you are capable of. I never recovered from your death, but you have cast me aside in an instant.'

'If my death was so devastating to you, then you should want to aid me to avenge it,' Satomi shot back.

'Yes, I want to aid you,' Mythric insisted. 'But killing Khalid is not the solution! Someone orchestrated his conception, his escape and his curse! That's who we need to *find* ... *they* are responsible! And I'm guessing it was whoever aided you to steal the Soul Keep from Dead Man Downs.'

'Guards!' Satomi summoned them into the room, and they entered through all doors — a swarm of red leather, metal spikes, boots, make-up and hair product. 'Seize him!'

'You know I'm right.' Mythric didn't resist arrest, as there was little point.

'You are *nothing* but my prisoner,' Satomi snapped. 'Interrogate him, but don't kill him. Pain enhancing drugs might aid him to divulge some information that is actually useful to our cause.'

'I'm not giving up on you, Satomi,' Mythric yelled back as he was led away. 'It doesn't matter how much you torture me —'

An elbow to the face from the closest Valourean cut his confession short. His face went numb and warm blood oozed from his nose and down his throat; even without pain-enhancing drugs, it hurt like hell.

'Have him thrown in psychic containment,' he heard Satomi add, despite the ringing in his ears. 'Someone is bound to come looking for him.'

Mythric was not as confident of swinging his wife around to see reason if their emotional bond had been severed, and by all appearances it had. Fortunately, Zeven and the others knew of the risk he'd taken. If they didn't get word from him, sooner or later they would assume the worst and come to fetch him — he could only hope he was still breathing by then. He wanted, more than anything, to stand by Satomi, but after her Valoureans finished with him, Mythric doubted he'd be able to stand by anyone for quite some time.

In the lounge of President Anselm's private high-rise apartment on Sermetica, Taren was in the midst of explaining the whole sordid truth behind the silent coup Satomi had orchestrated on

Phemoria. She had made her father vow to say nothing until she'd finished her brief, which began with Zeven calling her to the pod bay control room about a little over a week back and ended with her confronting Satomi in the throne room of Phemoria only hours ago. She couldn't remember the last time she had seen her father truly furious, and for a moment he couldn't even speak.

'It was Zeven who broke Khalid out of prison,' he stated through gritted teeth.

Taren understood her father had spent money and resources trying to discover the truth about that escape, so his anger was not entirely unexpected. 'Unlike the rest of us, Zeven separated the man from the curse, to realise Khalid has been wronged more than any of us, his true father also … have you not been listening?'

Anselm had to stand and pace out his frustration. 'We can kiss the psychic bill of rights goodbye, and prepare for war instead.'

'Satomi is just begging for an excuse to pit her psychic army against your new task force …' Taren stood also. 'Please don't give her one.'

'I only just won your mother back!' The true source of his anger surfaced. 'Am I to just allow her to spend the rest of her days in a coma state?'

'You know I will not let that happen,' Taren approached to reason with him more intimately. 'We have to find the Soul Keep Satomi is hiding and bring it together with the canister containing Chironjivi's evil spirit, and the crown of the Phemoray. Then the curses can be reversed, and all the women of the celestial city will return to consciousness safely.'

'And if we just shut the complex down?'

'We kill them all.'

Clearly, Anselm just wanted to kill something, but headed to his bar to pour a drink instead. 'Before we've even had the chance to announce Sermetica's reconciliation with Phemoria, it's been bloody destroyed, *by Khalid*, surprise, surprise! Even defunct he's a pain in the arse!' Anselm drank down his shot.

'What has happened is no person's fault —'

'Bullshit!' Anselm strongly disagreed. 'It's Zeven's fault for messing with timelines without your consent! I have a good mind to issue a warrant for his —'

'Please don't. I happen to believe he is doing the right thing.' Taren wasn't appreciating the dramatics. 'What do you know of General Prochazka?'

Anselm calmed as he considered the query that seemed to come right out of left field. 'As she is the head of the queen's guard, rather than the armies of Phemoria, no one on Sermetica has had much to do with her; she is renowned for her hatred of Sermetic men.'

'Have you met her?' Taren felt he was holding something back.

'Just once.' He seemed distracted, perhaps by a pleasant memory. 'The night your mother and I —' He snapped out of his daze, and forced a grin.

'Gotcha,' Taren confirmed, to avoid the awkward moment.

'Prochazka briefed me before that liaison, led me to the would-be-Qusay's chamber and guarded the door until I emerged again.' Anselm poured another shot.

'Interesting.' Taren considered. 'I wonder if she has performed this service for all the queens of Phemoria.'

'I would think so,' Anselm concurred. 'She wouldn't entrust that responsibility to anyone else after what happened with the previous queen.'

'That puts her on door duty the night Khalid was conceived.' That only confirmed what Taren already suspected.

'You think she let that curse loose on her queen?' Anselm scoffed. 'No Valourean would betray her queen, least of all her general!'

That part didn't make sense, it was true. 'But she must know what happened that night.' Taren knew what the general looked like, and could teleport to her at any time. Still, her instinct told her to be cautious when dealing with this woman. For if she was the one Zeven was looking for, she had been dealing with the curse at Dead Man Downs for some time, which made her incredibly resourceful and dangerous.

'Do not go after Prochazka,' her father warned.

Taren shook her head to assure him. 'Not at this point. If I am not mistaken she has left Phemoria on a mission to reach the AMIE craft, which is going to take her at least three years in transit from the Maladaan system, since the inter-system gateway in the Oceane system is still out of order, and all the people with PK are on our team. So we have a little time to get our hands on those curses.'

'And what am I to do in the meantime?' Anselm queried, completely baffled.

'Carry on drafting the bill of rights, and don't give Phemoria any reason to go to war,' Taren advised.

'This is a very dangerous game you're playing, my little timekeeper.' Anselm seemed to be losing his faith in her.

'It always was.' She reminded him of all the successes they'd had in the past. 'This is just a minor delay in the proceedings.'

'Fix it,' the president sternly advised. 'Maladaan has already imposed sanctions on us for instigating this bill, and if I lose the support of Phemoria, Frujia will waver — and without that export trade Sermetica will plummet into a food crisis! Then I am not going to be very popular with anyone.'

'I am on it,' Taren gave him her heartfelt assurance as she gripped his forearm that was rested on the bar. 'And thank you, for the trust.' She squeezed his arm and turned to leave.

'What? Not even a kiss for my patience?'

Taren turned back, and happily obliged him with a kiss on the cheek. 'I wasn't sure I dared.'

'Be careful out there.' He was solemn and disenchanted, and Taren couldn't blame him, she was feeling a little like that herself.

'Ditto,' she forced a grin.

'Keep me informed,' he added as she backed away.

'Roger that.' She vanished back to AMIE.

As AMIE's pilot was AWOL, Lucian and their co-pilot Leal Polson were doing a routine systems check, whilst awaiting Taren's return from her meeting with Anselm.

'Oxygen tanks?' Lucian ran down the check list.

Leal ran the system analysis. 'Eighty per cent.'

'Fuel?'

'Five out of six cells remaining,' Leal reported, and Lucian nodded, pleased.

'Water?'

'Look, Captain,' Leal diverted. 'I know it's none of my business, but the crew are getting a little uneasy about what is going on between Zeven and his parents. There's even a rumour going around that he might have had something to do with Khalid Mansur's escape from prison?'

'Who started that rumour?' Lucian faked a cynical stance.

'Mythric,' Leal replied and the captain rolled his eyes.

'Well, Mythric has joined Zeven's quest now, so I guess he is no longer opposed.'

There was a bleep from a monitoring desk behind Lucian.

'The radar?' Leal recognised the sound; he'd not heard anything from that desk since they'd parked in the Oceane system.

They both moved to take a look.

'Holy shit!' Leal was astonished by the readout. 'There is a Phemorian ship right on our arse. They are lining up to dock with Module D.'

There was a crashing sound and the ship shook as it made contact with the other.

'Steady on!' Leal grumbled. 'I could dock better than that with my eyes closed! They are overriding the lock codes.' His anger turned to panic. 'How is that even possible?'

'It reeks of PK.' Lucian got on the intercom. 'Captain to all crew, AMIE is being breached by a Phemorian vessel. I suspect Valoureans, so *do not* engage, hide yourselves, or escape by any means necessary! This is not a drill!'

'They're in.' Leal threw his hands up, bewildered.

As the ship's deafening alert alarm began sounding, Lucian's communicator chimed. He pulled out the palm device to find a voice message from Swithin.

'*It's fucking Valoureans —*' That was it, the message ended with a thump.

'Shit!' Leal jumped from his seat to follow the captain, who was already sprinting towards the launch bay.

'They are after Thurraya,' Lucian advised as they ran.

Neither of them had PK, but he needed to get word to Zeven on Oceane.

'Where is she?' Leal panicked.

'With Zeven.'

'Send Zeven a message?' Leal suggested, having no idea where Zeven was.

'No communicator will work where he is.' They entered into the launch bay and Lucian locked off the doors through from the main flight deck. 'Quick, lock the stairwell door in maintenance.'

As Leal ran across the launch bay crammed full of exploration craft to fulfil the request, Lucian climbed the stairs to the control deck to start priming a pod for launch and to set its co-ordinates.

'What's the plan?' Leal scaled the stairs to join him in the control tower.

Lucian would have preferred to launch Leal down to Oceane, and stay put here to defend his crew. But Leal didn't know the planet at all, and there was no time to explain. Right now AMIE's prime objective was to prevent Thurraya and Khalid from falling into the hands of Phemoria. 'We launch me in a pod down onto Oceane,' Lucian advised, and Leal was baffled.

'Why? There's nothing there,' Leal stressed.

'That's exactly right. But Taren will find me there, never fear,' Lucian assured him, relinquishing the control chair and pushing Leal into it. 'I need you to make it look like a misfire. Can you do that?'

Leal nodded to confirm that he could, and Lucian slapped his shoulder. 'What shall I tell the Valoureans?'

'Tell them I am with Taren.' The captain headed from the room. 'I'm strapping in.'

'What about your suit?' Leal reminded him.

'I won't be in space long enough to need it,' Lucian said on his way out. 'And the misfire tale will be easier to sell if all the suits can be accounted for.'

Lucian fastened himself into the primed pod, and switched on his com-link. 'I'm good to go.'

'*Initiating launch sequence*,' Leal advised via Lucian's headset, as the pod's cradle aligned with the launch tube. '*In five, four, three, two —*'

The power died, and the pod went completely dark. Even out through the small window, all Lucian could see was darkness. Even if the ship had lost power, this pod was independent of it and should have still been functioning.

'Shit! Leal?' There was no response, and without power his pod would not open.

It was only when the backup generator kicked in and minimal light was restored to the hangar beyond, that Lucian realised he was holding his breath, and sucked air into his lungs. The pod was still completely defunct, however.

'*Captain?*'

'Leal!' He gave a huge exhale of relief. 'Get me out of here. Nothing is working including my oxygen.'

'*I don't understand why you don't have power —*'

A huge blast was followed by the sound of metal crashing.

'What was that?'

'*That was the door to the flight deck getting blown out of the wall.*'

Lucian clenched his fists to control his urge to punch something.

'*You! Get away from there.*'

It was a female voice. Leal must have left the intercom open his end, which meant Lucian's transmission was blocked. 'Shit, Leal!'

'*What were you doing?*' she demanded to know.

'*Running a system check,*' Leal replied, '*we've had trouble with pods misfiring —*'

A crack brought his explanation to an end. '*Is there anyone in there?*'

'*No.*' Leal spat — blood Lucian imagined, and resentment churned in his gut.

Another crack, this time followed by a moan.

'Damn it!' Lucian began thumping the ceiling of the pod to give himself away — if he wasn't going to be able to warn Zeven, then he wanted to stand by his crew. He had no hope of getting this pod — built to endure the rigours of space and the toughest landing — to open with his own brute strength.

'*Where is the heir of Phemoria?*'

'*Not here,*' Leal mumbled.

'*Then where?*' She demanded an answer — conjuring in Lucian's mind an image of his co-pilot's tormentor, weapon raised in threat and ready to serve Leal another blow if his answer was not to her liking.

'Stop!' Lucian thumped harder — his exerted effort doing nothing for his air supply situation.

'*General,*' another Valourean interrupted the interrogation. '*There is someone in the pod.*'

'*Liar!*'

One final crack and Lucian heard Leal hit the floor with a thud.

'Son-of-a-bitch!' Lucian thumped his dashboard so hard his fist bled, and he cussed under his breath as the pod was lowered back onto the launch bay floor, and released from its cradle.

A purple-clad Valourean came to stand over the pod and looking in at him, she laughed with delight — from Taren's description, this had to be Prochazka. 'Well, Captain, it seems you are stuck in there.'

'How inconvenient for you,' Lucian replied, 'as I am the only one on board who knows anything pertaining to your quest.'

'My quest is to do the AMIE project as much damage as possible.' She forced a grin that was full of disdain. 'All I need do is check where this pod was headed and I warrant that I shall find what I am looking for. It is fitting really, a captain should go down with his ship, or in this case *up.*'

Lucian's first impulse was to be angry, but then he noted that the general had some very dark spirits hanging around her. 'You have been cursed.' He was shocked to a passive state as he watched a flash of dismay cross her face. 'You won't escape it, you know. Not on your own.'

'I didn't ask for my fortune, Captain.' Prochazka's expression hardened again. 'If the heir of Phemoria is on this ship you had better tell me, or she dies with you this day, along with anyone else who does not disembark in my custody.'

The implication was that they intended to blow up the AMIE vessel, which Lucian resented more than the death threat. 'We only have a skeleton crew, and most of them are not on board at present, including Thurraya. She is with her parents — you won't find them here either.'

'How many crew *do* you have on board at present?' Prochazka grinned, realising the query posed a moral quandary for him. 'Tell me, or the one in the control room up there dies … if he's not dead already,' she allowed, indifferent to the outcome.

Was it better to tell her the numbers to ensure his crew got off the vessel with their lives, or should he conceal their number in the hope Taren returned in time to salvage the situation? 'What do you intend to do with my people?'

She raised both brows to consider. 'Well, the men among you are of good psychic stock and will make for good breeding.'

'What?' Lucian was momentarily stunned and repulsed by the claim.

'And the women, well …' She served him a broad smile. 'Gotta feed those demons.'

'Go fuck yourself.' Lucian decided his crew were better left to fend for themselves.

'Why would I bother, when your crew are all so attractive?' Prochazka was suddenly cracked over the head with a wrench, which didn't knock her out, but really pissed her off. Looking down at her feet, she was enraged. 'You dare slap a restraining device on me, you treacherous man-loving whore!'

'What of it?' Jazmay Cardea's voice replied.

'No, Jaz,' Lucian uttered under his breath. 'You should have run.' She was the only one of them left on board who had PK.

Everything went silent for a moment and Lucian struggled to see what was going on.

'*Holy fucking shit.*' Jazmay was thrown face-down on top of his pod.

'Jazmay, what is going on?' In his mind he wanted to scold her for giving up her chance to get her family away to safety.

'They're all shifters! Satomi must have passed her talents on to them! They *all* have PK!' she managed to advise before she was raised up and slapped aside, out of his view.

That was how Jazmay had acquired her PK talent — from stealing and emulating Taren's DNA, she gained access to her memories and talents; this was something any shifter could do, with a touch.

The fact sent shockwaves through Lucian's system; Satomi's play was audaciously risky but brutally effective. Her Valoureans would be unstoppable now. 'That's how you got here so quickly,' Lucian concluded as Prochazka took hold of the restraint that one of her guards had removed from her person and cast it aside.

'Resourceful, yes?' She grinned. 'Have a nice life, Captain, however many minutes of it you have remaining.'

Lucian was left completely winded, and that was partially because he was running out of air. He had to wonder what would come sooner: asphyxiation, or the annihilation of his ship.

Minutes ticked away as he considered what the future held in store for his crew, and he gave up hope of Taren arriving to save the day. In fact he was dreading that she would arrive in time and perish with the ship, trying to get him out. His thoughts lingered on his wife in their more intimate moments, as his breathing shallowed and he began to feel dizzy — it wouldn't be long now.

When Taren returned to AMIE, of the mind to join her husband, she'd expected to land in the captain's office, and was bemused to find herself in the launch bay. The first thing that caught her attention was the fact they were running on reserve power and that there was a big hole in the wall through to the flight deck, where the door had been blown out of its facings and was now lying on floor. 'What the hell happened here?' she uttered quietly, but the more relevant question was, was it still happening?

Scanning the area, which she knew like the back of her hand, Taren noted a pod had been lowered from its hangar and so she cautiously moved to take a look inside.

'*Lucian?*' she gasped, shocked to see him unconscious within, and she used her PK to crack the defunct pod open. '*He's not breathing,*' she wheezed, her heart pounding in panic as she checked for a pulse. 'Fuck!' Unable to find one, she grabbed his upper body and teleported them both down to Kassa's medical lab.

The room was also in near darkness, but with a thought she fired up all the equipment therein. 'Don't be dead.' She laid him on the surgical table. 'Electrocardiogram.' She got a grip on what she needed to do, but hooking him up to the monitor brought tears to her eyes — he was flatlining, and she had no idea how long he'd been clinically dead for. 'Where is everyone?' She ripped his shirt open and manifested a solid gel sheet to place on his chest.

She primed the defibrillator and the workstation within Kassa's lab, switching the latter to voice command. 'AMIE, run security cam footage of the launch bay over the last hour.' She grabbed up the electrode paddles as the unit charged, and as soon as it had, Taren planted the pads on Lucian and delivered their charge into his chest. His body rebounded with the force of the shock, but from his heart there was no response; the monitor continued to flatline. After repeating this procedure several times, Taren began to despair.

'This is not how this ends for you.' Taren's emotions welled — fury, sorrow, remorse, despair — but a glance at the monitor brought her shattered sensibilities sharply into focus. 'Prochazka.' The name left a bitter taste in her mouth, as she viewed footage of the general leering over the defunct pod she had found her husband in.

Taren was drawn to the screen, as Jazmay appeared in a heroic attempt to save Lucian and what happened next shocked Taren to the core. 'Holy shit … Satomi gave them all her PK —' It took a moment for the ramifications of that act to sink in — the Valoureans were now an extremely powerful force to be reckoned with.

'Show me the past hour of footage from the entry hatch camera, Module D.'

The footage began with Valoureans already in the ship, guarding the hatch door.

'Fast forward.'

When the image reached the point where Valoureans started exiting, Taren ordered AMIE to stop the footage and play it.

One by one she watched her crew escorted off their ship — Kassa, Kalayna, Fari, Zelimir, Amie and Ayliscia. The rest of the crew were dragged out unconscious — Leal, Swithin, Jazmay and Yasper. It seemed they had caught them all, but then something urged her to recount.

'Ringbalin.' Taren's already exhausted heart began pounding in her chest anew, hoping he hadn't been killed during the incident and left to die as Lucian had been. 'AMIE, scan the ship for life forms.'

Apart from hers, the only other life-form readings were coming from the greenhouse in Module C, which was naturally a mass reading; whether Ringbalin was among that mass remained to be seen. 'I'll have to go down there,' she said aloud as if her husband needed advising. Even if Lucian was dead, his spirit would be close at hand and no doubt yelling at her to get her arse into gear and go find Ringbalin. 'I'll be back.'

'Full power,' she demanded as she landed in the darkened greenhouse, where the only sounds to be heard were filters, pumps and sprinklers. The night sky returned to grace the ceiling overhead. 'My luck, night mode.' She didn't want to demand a switch to day mode, as Ringbalin was religious about his greenhouse — only heaven knew what damage a sudden shift in time would do to this sensitive environment.

The pathways were dimly lit, so she could see her way well enough. Still, if the Valoureans had left behind any assassins, this would be the perfect place to lay in wait. To risk teleporting to Ringbalin could land her in the midst of the enemy, if he had been captured. As she did have to search on foot, however, she decided not to pussyfoot around a confrontation — best to find those Valoureans or Ringbalin as soon as possible. 'Ringbalin! Are you in here?' she called as she ran the winding pathways, half expecting to find a body around every bend, or have someone jump out and attack her. 'It's Taren. Come out, if you're alive. Please!'

She completed the circuit, and came to a stop beneath the weather control tower, of the mind to head up the stairs, when she felt something grip her foot. 'ARGH!' She looked down to see a hand protruding from a fresh-turned bed of soil, and the rest of the buried body followed. 'Ringbalin?' It was hard to tell under all the dirt.

He stood, shook off and then spat the straw from his mouth. 'The captain said to hide. What happened? I was expecting to be star dust by now.'

'Why is that?' Upon consideration, Taren realised that was a stupid question.

'Because they are going to blow up the ship,' they both concluded at once.

'Of course they are.' Taren grabbed Ringbalin, and returned to where she'd left Lucian.

'What happened to the captain?' Ringbalin was devastated to see Lucian's lifeless form, still hooked up to the flatlining electrocardiogram.

Taren longed to have the luxury to grieve, but that could be conceding defeat and she was not about to do that.

'No time,' Taren held up a finger to beg that he allow her to think.

She needed Swithin to bring Lucian back from the dead, but he was unconscious and under Valourean guard, so she needed to keep Lucian's body as fresh as possible.

'I have it.' Taren grabbed both her husband's corpse and Ringbalin.

'Can't we stop them?' Ringbalin was bemused, as the ship began to rattle and shake. 'They're going to destroy all our work!'

No one had worked harder than Ringbalin, except for maybe Taren and the captain himself.

'The quantum will is not weighing in our favour.' Taren knew she couldn't win against an entire legion of Valoureans each as strong as she.

Ringbalin hugged close as the rumbling of the ship intensified, and Taren envisioned the grand hallway of the House of Vidor on Sermetica.

The huge, grand old manor, located on the outskirts of the government sector of the floating capital of Heavensgate on Sermetica, had been closed up since the death of the Duchess Maiara Vidor, and only kept minimal staff.

'This is the House of Vidor!' Ringbalin hissed quietly. Very surprised to find himself there, he seemed very conscious of being filthy in the midst of the spotless manor.

Ringbalin had been one of many psychic children who had been secretly fostered here for a time by Maiara Vidor. 'Why are we trespassing in one of Sermetica's greatest heritage mansions?' He watched as Taren floated her husband's body into the air and it began to trail her down the hall.

'This is the only part of the house I am familiar with,' Taren explained, 'but I need the crypt. Do you know where that is?'

'It's this way.' Ringbalin motioned behind him and Taren did a quick about-face.

'Lead on,' she invited, as the floating body swung around to trail them.

It was a little eerie moving through the dark, empty mansion; fortunately for them, it was the wee hours in the morning here in Heavensgate, so absolutely no one was around.

'Whoa,' Ringbalin held his head as they entered the huge kitchen area, 'this is such a flashback.'

'Nice memories?' Taren queried.

Ringbalin nodded as he led through to the rooms beyond. 'I can still smell the bread baking —'

'Can I help you?'

They both came to a halt and turned around to find a young male in his pyjamas holding a laser pistol. He was slight in build, like Ringbalin, and appeared slightly older, but that could have been his neat, dark moustache and beard making him appear older than he was.

'Just where do you think you are taking this … *thing*,' he referred to Ringbalin's filthy person in a snooty manner, before his eyes turned to the floating body. 'Oh damn —'

Taren willed his weapon into her possession, before he'd finished the sentence.

'You have PK,' he concluded, raising his hands to surrender.

'Correct,' Taren conceded, sticking the weapon through her belt. 'What's your name?'

'I am known as Ducer,' he advised. 'I'm the curator here.'

'Trance?' Ringbalin moved closer to view the man in question. 'It's me, Quanah.'

Quanah was the name given to Ringbalin by Maiara, which meant 'fragrant', referring to his talent to make flowers bloom wherever he went.

'Flower power?' the curator responded, amazed. 'You grew up!'

'Yes!' Ringbalin confirmed as they embraced — laughing with joy to make each other's acquaintance again. 'So did you!'

'You look like you've been buried.' Trance dusted dirt off himself and Ringbalin.

'I have been,' Ringbalin admitted, which intrigued his old friend. 'I always thought you'd become a spy or something? And yet here you are a respectable curator!' He chuckled at the notion.

'Happened by default really.' Trance shrugged. 'Never found a home other than here, and after her grace died, someone had to see to running the estate.'

'Ah, guys?' Taren motioned to the floating body. 'The crypt, *pronto.*'

'The crypt? Is this man a Vidor?' Trance was concerned.

'Crypt first.' Taren moved off after Ringbalin. 'Questions later.'

Through the extensive family cellars, where huge barrels sat ageing their contents, they came to the door of the family crypt.

'Are you okay?' Taren noted Trance was looking a little freaked out, and as he nodded to affirm, Taren overrode the security pad with a wave of her hand over the key-plate. The door slid aside and they entered the darkened crypt.

As it was night, sensors triggered the internal lighting and the chamber was not at all what Taren had been expecting; it wasn't old, dim and dusty at all. The majestic, hexagon shaped room housed many ornate sarcophagi and was completely white and spotless.

'Now which one of these was Satomi placed in?' Taren moved down the aisle reading inscriptions as she went.

'The one in the middle,' Trance replied, leading on towards the centre of the hexagon where a large skylight in the ceiling provided a window to the stars. Upon clearing some taller monuments, they entered the open central area, where stairs led up to one beautiful white coffin, and Trance was horrified to see the transparent lid open.

'What the?' He ran up the stairs to find the sarcophagi empty, and all the flowers that had been buried with the princess, dead and crumbling inside and all around the tomb. 'Satomi has risen from the grave!'

'Yes, we know that.' Taren waved her hand over the interior of the unit and the dead flowers blew away, before she laid Lucian's body within.

'You know that?' Trance emphasised, going into shock. 'Who are you?'

'You don't get to know.' She re-programmed the unit and was about to close the lid when Ringbalin waylaid the proceedings.

'Wait!' He picked up a few of the dead flowers and restored them to perfect health, before laying them in the capsule with his captain. 'See you soon, Captain.'

Taren closed the unit and reactivated the stasis function. As she observed her husband's dead body being put on ice her self control crumbled and she collapsed into tears, trembling with the aftershock.

'You did good.' Ringbalin touched a hand to her shoulder, and she calmed right down.

'But I have no idea what to do next?' she confessed. 'I'm so damn tired, I can't think straight.'

'No. No, no, no, no, *no* … don't!' Trance held high a finger in warning, backing away from something only he could see. His body went rigid and then into spasm, before he fell on the ground.

'Trance has a Power,' Taren assumed.

'Yep.' Ringbalin watched as the curator's body rose straight back up to standing.

'He's a medium,' they both concluded at once.

'You need to warn Zeven that the Valoureans are looking for Thurraya,' Trance advised in Lucian's voice.

'Lucian?' Taren's sensibilities went into overload. 'I'm sorry I didn't get back —'

'It's all right,' he insisted. 'I'm perfectly fine with being dead for now, it may even serve us? Forget me, and get to Zeven.' Trance went into spasm once more and collapsed unconscious on the floor.

Just that short message did wonders for Taren's moral; she drew a deep breath of relief to know Lucian was right by her and regained her focus. 'Well then, we need to move.' She walked over to where her new best friend had collapsed onto the floor.

'You are taking Trance with us?' Ringbalin followed her.

'As my only link with Lucian, he is a necessary risk.' She took hold of Trance's arm and reached out her free hand to Ringbalin.

'So where is Zeven exactly?' He took hold, bound to go with her regardless of the answer.

'Classified.' Taren smiled, knowing Ringbalin would be thrilled by the destination; in past timelines he'd studied biology samples from there, but had never been awarded the opportunity to visit the virgin planet.

'Oh my organic ancestors!' Ringbalin stood amid the towering plants that appeared to reach to the heavens, being washed clean of dirt by the warm pouring rain that was a constant on Oceane. 'These are tundrells!' He gazed up at the unfurling plants, thrilled beyond belief. 'They're like the prehistoric legends of the plant world!'

In another timeline Ringbalin had cultivated some of these plants, so Ringbalin had already told Taren all there was to know about them. 'Yes, it's thrilling, I'm sure.' She rose to walk on the water's surface and dragged Trance to a rocky mound where he wouldn't drown.

'It is!' Ringbalin emphasised, as he waded waist-deep in water after her. 'You have no idea! Where are we?'

'This, my friend, is Oceane.' She laid Trance on his side out of the water, and looked further up the tall rock face.

'As in the unexplored planet AMIE is hovering over?' Ringbalin was uneasy, yet intrigued.

'It's been explored,' Taren assured him, 'just not in this timeline.'

'Oh,' Ringbalin rethought his response. 'Huh?'

But Taren had teleported herself to a higher point on the rock formation, where she could see over the tundrells. From this vantage point the view was so devastating she had to sit down.

'What is it?' Ringbalin called, and when she could not respond straight away, he started climbing up the rock face to see for himself.

The rainbow coloured electrical storm that always raged here was raining fiery debris down all over the pristine planet.

'Is that AMIE?' Ringbalin begged her opinion, now that he'd climbed high enough to witness the spectacle.

'I'm afraid so.' She clenched her jaw, as she gazed at the place where Zeven and Mythric's hut had once been, that was now crushed under what was left of the marine module.

'Is that a hut?' Ringbalin queried about the spot holding Taren's interest. 'No, please don't say that's where —' He choked up, as she nodded.

'Perhaps the Valoureans found them before they brought the ship down?' Taren didn't know what scenario was more terrible.

'What are we going to do?' It took a lot to drive Ringbalin to despair, but he was just about there.

'We investigate,' Taren said coolly and holding an image of their vessel in her mind she willed it to reform and repair.

All the wreckage ceased to fall and instead rose from the ground twice as swiftly as it had descended, and disappeared up beyond the spectacular storm.

'Holy shit, boss!' Ringbalin's sorrow turned to excitement, as he watched the trashed hut restore itself to its former glory. 'Did you just reconstruct our entire ship?'

'I hope so.' Taren teleported herself down to his ledge, then grabbing him, she returned them to the base, where they found Trance stirring from his snooze.

'You can turn off the shower, I'm awake,' he mumbled.

'Wish granted.' Taren teleported them all to inside the hut.

'Well,' Ringbalin wiped the water from his face and looked around the place. 'No dead bodies, that's a good sign.'

'Dead bodies?' Trance rousted himself off the floor, where he'd landed. 'What is it with you two and dead people?' He looked around, then got to his feet, and wandered outside onto the porch. 'Where are we?' He stood in awe of the pouring rain — never seen on Sermetica. 'We are on *another* planet?' He processed his situation. 'This is nuts!' He turned back to them. 'But in a good way,' he said as Taren moved to search the other rooms. 'Wow! Your girlfriend is pretty amazing.'

'She is my boss,' Ringbalin advised. 'Her husband is the man we left back in the crypt.'

'How interesting,' he said, with a grin, before he was startled by something Ringbalin failed to see. 'Ah! Not you again! Go away!' He backed down the porch. 'You can't have my body.'

'Is the captain here?' Ringbalin guessed Lucian would be the jealous type, even when dead.

'Just tell me what you want to say, I'm happy to pass it on,' Trance stressed, having skirted around the end of the porch, before running up to hide behind Ringbalin.

'What's he saying?' Taren joined them near the balcony exit.

'Shush up and I'll tell you.' Trance focused on a spot by Taren, frowning as he listened.

'Well I don't know,' Trance replied to Lucian's ghost, 'I've never actually tried — Well, yes I'm a medium,' he defended, 'but I've not had much cause to develop my talents until recently, when they were *decriminalised* on Sermetica.'

'What is the captain saying?' Taren grew impatient listening to Trance debate the issue.

'He wants me to try and tap into the atomic memory of this place, and see if I can pick up on what transpired here.' Trance seemed willing to give it a shot.

'Sounds good.' Taren was a little surprised that Lucian had come up with that solution. 'You are full of surprises, my love.'

'Thank you,' Trance accepted the compliment. 'Oh sorry,' he ducked to defend himself as he withdrew his acceptance. 'Ah, the captain would like to say he has been doing some research into his Powers, and that he shall also see what he can pick up psychometrically.'

Taren grinned in approval. 'Any leads at this point would be most appreciated.'

'Right then.' Trance slapped his hands together and rubbed them vigorously. 'Let's see what we can see.' He closed his eyes, held his hands out and, fingers splayed, he used them as detectors in a search for residual thought forms strong enough to have left an impression on the atomic memory of this place.

'Wow!' He stopped still, facing outwards in the doorway of the porch. 'Do you see that?'

'What?' Taren looked out and saw nothing but the rain.

'Shush,' Trance insisted, 'I'm talking to the captain!'

'My bad,' Taren stepped back, 'but what do y—'

'What part of *shush* do you not understand?' Trance relaxed once more, and continued to focus out front with his eyes closed. 'What is that phosphorescent blue stuff?'

Taren had to bite her tongue; how she wished for second sight right now, or even telepathy, so that she could see what he was seeing.

'It's like liquid light pouring out of that guy? Is he dead?' Trance continued to confabulate with the captain. 'Whoa!' He wavered on his feet and fell down onto one knee. 'Feels like an earthquake? Have to get out.' He staggered up, and crossing the porch, he hurried down the steps and into the water.

Taren and Ringbalin followed him out and stopped on the stairs to observe Trance turn about to face them.

Eyes still closed, his expression filled with wonder as he slowly looked up. 'Fuck me,' he uttered in awe, before snapping out of his daze and opening his eyes.

Taren was about to question him when Trance looked aside, and she realised he was still consulting with Lucian.

'What do you mean I'm looking the wrong way?' the medium posed to his invisible cohort. 'What epicentre?' Trance's attention turned to a large flat rock. 'I can't see any portal!' he emphasised. 'It could be a door to the afterlife; if you go through it then there may be no coming back?'

'Wait a second!' Taren couldn't refrain any more, and headed down-stairs to walk across the water's surface to crouch before the medium and draw his attention. 'What's going on?'

Trance held out a hand to stall her interruption. 'Well, maybe your friends are dead too?' He paused to hear an argument, still holding Taren at bay. 'I haven't seen what death looks like, so I couldn't say for sure —' He rolled his eyes, and placed hands on hips to consider whatever he was being told. 'What *the fuck* is an etheric quake?'

'Hello?' Taren couldn't wait any longer to be briefed.

'The captain believes there's been an etheric quake here, whatever in the name of science, that is. He says the rift between the worlds is still open, and he intends to go through the portal and investigate.'

'*No* way!' Taren objected.

'He's fairly certain,' Trance continued, one ear listening to the information being fed to him, 'that your missing team members have all been drawn into another world, that he believes is ...' He paused at the punchline, seemingly finding it unbelievable.

'*Trance?*' Taren strongly urged him to continue.

A little fazed by the news, the young man's sights met hers. 'The captain believes it is the lost world of the Old Ones.'

Taren's jaw dropped. 'We found it ... by facing our greatest fear.' In cosmic terms, it made perfect sense.

'He says he *has* to go through.' Trance passed on Lucian's resolve, and before she could object he added, 'Were the situation reversed, what would you do?'

Every argument Taren could think was rendered redundant, and she wasn't happy about it. 'What if the portal closes and you are trapped there? What if it's not what you think?'

'Oh no.' Trance began backing away, and going stiff as a board, his body spasmed and disappeared underwater.

'Trance?' Taren went after him and pulled him up out of the water.

'I'm right about this,' he said in Lucian's voice, completely unaffected by the water. 'Lose your fear, and then tell me what I should do?'

It was odd seeing Lucian's countenance being worn by another, but she knew that expression all too well; he was not taking no for an answer. 'You should go,' she resolved, knowing if the situation were reversed he would not be able to stop her. 'Exploring new worlds was originally AMIE's primary objective.'

Taren was a little affronted when Trance unexpectedly kissed her, and she near slapped him for it.

'Sorry, I forgot I'm not myself.' He stepped back, hands raised in truce. 'I'll go after Zeven and co, you focus on retrieving the rest of the crew.'

'So you are sure the Valoureans didn't get Thurraya?' Taren was relieved when Trance nodded.

'They're still right here, I suspect, in a city that exists on a higher vibratory level.'

'Like Phemoria's celestial city.' Taren knew the parallel in this case was significant. 'Maybe Zeven was right about Khalid?'

'There is only one way to find out.' He grinned in conclusion.

'Go then,' she said with a tinge of jealousy, and yet managed to roust a smile.

He moved in closer to her once again.

'If you kiss me,' Taren warned.

'Nah.' He waved off the premise as if thinking nothing of the sort. 'I just need you to hold this body so it doesn't drown as I vacate.' He grinned, and with a finger beckoned her closer.

'Urgh,' Taren grumbled as Trance hugged her, but she felt Lucian's familiar aura, which was a welcome comfort at the close of his endless day of woe.

'See you on the flip side.' He kissed her cheek, and Trance's form became a dead weight in her arms.

'You come on back.' Taren swung around to face the large rock that had been pinpointed as the epicentre of the tear between worlds, but there was nothing to see or hear but the pouring rain. 'Well, at least this one has stopped freaking out.' She looked back to Trance, sleeping like a baby in her arms.

'So I guess it's just us now, huh?' Ringbalin came down the stairs to give her a hand to drag Trance out of the water.

'Looks that way,' she conceded, as Ringbalin grabbed up half the weight she was carrying.

'Where to from here?' he wondered.

'Let's go see what kind of a job I did putting AMIE back together, shall we?'

Ringbalin gave that idea the big nod.

'I don't know how anything living will have survived the demolition,' she forewarned.

Ringbalin forced a smile, probably grateful for anything they could salvage from the day's devastating events — as she was. 'I'd be happy just to see my bed.'

Taren let loose an exhausted laugh, in total accord with his reasoning. 'Hear, hear.'

The only word to describe the atmosphere inside the restored AMIE vessel was sterile. The ship's interior was more perfectly clean than it had been the minute it had been completed — for it had always had an element of feeling lived in, even when it was under construction. All the fixtures, fittings and systems were repaired and in perfect working order, but nothing organic survived. All the paper, bedding, pictures, and little knick-knacks were missing, and as Taren passed through she manifested the things she noted absent, but still, it was all as-new. Only now that they were missing did Taren realise that she'd never really noticed the decorations, and so could not accurately replace them. She was really only concerned with replacing things that were essential to

214

their survival, as this place would never feel like home until all their crew were safely back on board.

'I don't hold high hopes for the greenhouse,' Ringbalin proffered, as he accompanied Taren from the medical labs in Module A, where they had left Trance sleeping.

Via the quickest route, through Module B, they were on their way through to check on the situation in Module C — as the greenhouse was vital to AMIE's long-term independence and survival.

'Oh damn.' Ringbalin passed through the double glass sliding door to observe the barren bio-module that pretty much appeared the way it had when he'd first walked into it. 'Years of tending, reduced to space dust.'

'Now before you get angry and I implode ...' Taren humoured him; and although the joke did not rouse a smile, he calmed to hear her out. 'I've spent so much time wandering around this module with you ... allow me to have a stab at recreating it.'

Ringbalin dared to crack a smile. 'Do you think that's possible?'

Taren raised both brows in question and closing her eyes to consult her memory, she began to move through the module.

'Holy microbes, Taren, you're doing it!' He trailed her, grinning with delight as his garden began to reappear all around him.

'I can't really do much about your seedling rooms,' she regretted to say as they reached the far end of the module where his nursery was located, beneath the weather control tower. 'I don't know what you were growing in there.'

Ringbalin waved it off as a minor inconvenience, distracted by some of the plants she had manifested from memory. 'Goodness!' Upon closer inspection he was intrigued. 'I think you might have created a few new species here. I've never seen a blood orchid flower blue before.'

'Blue-blood,' Taren joked. 'PK is not an exact science; shall I change it?'

'No!' Ringbalin stressed, and then smiled. 'Or anything else. Gosh knows what else you've conjured up, but I can't wait to find out.' His expression turned mournful. 'Once I get the chance to get back to cultivating, that is.'

Taren backed up and took a seat on the stairs leading up to the weather control tower, where Ringbalin had also set up house — he had crew quarters but never used them. 'Yah ... we have a *whole* lot to achieve before then.' The magnitude of the chore made her head ache.

'When was the last time you slept?' He came to sit beside her.

'I've been on so many different planets today, it's a bit difficult to keep track of the time.' She yawned and rested her heavy head on his shoulder, then she made the fatal mistake of closing her eyes.

'Well, I think it's time ...' Ringbalin's suggestion was the last thing Taren's brain registered before it shut down.

PART 3

TRANSCENDENCE

10

WARP SPEED

Mission Log — Day (only the universe knows?)

It appears time itself has gone AWOL, as according to my calculations it should be about nine days since I returned to AMIE from the universe parallel. Yet as I have been drawn into another world where time functions differently I am told that months, or even years, may have expired at home in the short time we have been here in Karmandi — the city of the Dropa.

This is a worry, as about three years from when I arrived back on AMIE — the day after my daughter Ray's ninth birthday — I must be on AMIE to run a mission that I have already quantum-jumped to execute during my last mission in the universe parallel. Telmo's involvement is required also. I have no idea what kind of effect not making that appointment will have on this universe or the last. But trying to explain the concept of an urgent appointment to beings with no concept of time is something of a farce.

These Dropa appear not at all like the beings of the same name that I met during my stint as Ji Song in ancient China. But then Dorje Pema had explained that those Dropa had altered their genetic structure to adapt to the conditions of planet Earth. Rather than tiny childlike beings — as the Dropa of Earth had been — these entities appear far more human. They are more subtle in form than we are — they waft around in a colourful vaporous haze, and assume a spirit form only to converse and mingle with us. The same could be said of their entire city, which appears solid and present to us visitors, but apparently it is not the solid construct that we perceive it to be. The one thing these Dropa do have in common with the Dropa of ancient Earth is that their psychic aptitude is beyond compare. They know everything about us, in fact they know more about us than we do.

As for Khalid's connection to these Old Ones — I could not have imagined the full extent of it. It has also become apparent that not only was my gut instinct to run this mission correct, but that every move I have made was completely pre-determined.

Once the intense etheric light of their passage ebbed and the ground ceased to tremble, the wilds of Oceane had been replaced by a spacious futuristic shrine and the clean aesthetic inspired calm in the wake of their dimension shift.

The basic peripheral construct was an elongated circle that was open to the sky in the centre; thus, the first thing that was immediately noticeable was the deep indigo-coloured atmosphere beyond, completely clear of cloud. Fashioned from smooth white stone, the monument appeared so brilliant it glowed. In the moulded, wavelike architecture there were no joins — every surface opening and inset appeared to have been sculpted out of the one piece of enormous rock. The purpose of the beautiful edifice was not immediately clear as there were no idols, symbols or other motifs to implicate a place of worship. The dwelling seemed just a tranquil space from which to observe the idyllic countryside and ocean beyond.

Zeven and the rest of his men had landed on a circular platform located beneath the open centre of the arching ceiling, and this island was separated from the outer temple by a channel of clear water. The only object that appeared to have been dragged through into this world with them was the large block that they had laid Khalid upon.

'Why do you think this came with us?' Zeven queried Telmo, as they and Ahura jumped off the slab and onto the central platform — Khalid was still passed out.

'Probably because we were all hugging it so tight during the quake,' Telmo replied, observing the rock in question with a frown.

'I am home!' Ahura approached the canal, whereupon a walkway of the same white stone appeared and he crossed over onto the outer island. 'Come and see!'

'If we are where he says we are …' Telmo paused to watch Ahura go bounding off towards one of the exit portals that appeared to lead out into nature, but the Dropa prince just vanished into the scenery. 'This is *not* good.'

'Agreed,' Zeven concurred — they'd just arrived and had already lost a team member.

'No, I mean this!'

Zeven swung around to see that Telmo was referring to the rock that Khalid was laid out on.

Telmo leaned in closer to whisper his concern. 'This is the rock I hid the curse in.'

'Why didn't you tell me when I asked if there was a problem with using it?' Zeven hissed back quietly, as he noted his family appear across the canal from them.

'I didn't know we were going to open a portal to a higher dimension, now did I?' Telmo defended the call. 'The objective was not to let anyone know. If I'd mentioned it, then you would have known.'

'So why are you telling me now?' Zeven uttered aside to his cohort, as he waved to his wife and daughter, and they headed towards the bridge Ahura had left in his wake.

'Because you are leading this mission, and I am required to advise you of any threat.'

'Well, now you've doubled the threat,' Zeven chided.

'Zeven?' Telmo called for his full attention, and when he looked Telmo in the eye, he instructed, 'Forget I mentioned a threat.'

It took Zeven a moment to realise that he'd completely forgotten what they were talking about. 'Sorry, I drifted off, what were you saying?'

'Absolutely nothing,' Telmo grinned.

'You just mind-zapped me about something, didn't you?' Zeven didn't vague out like that often, and then only when he was with Telmo.

'That would be against my AMIE contract,' he defended.

'Which you haven't signed in this timeline yet,' Zeven called his bluff.

'A minor technicality,' he insisted.

Thurraya finally reached Zeven and crash-hugged his waist. 'That was fully *sick*, Dad!' she beamed, exhilarated.

'What just happened?' Aurora was too filled with wonder to be angered by the fright of their passage.

'I believe we just found a place where no one can find us.' Zeven grinned in a cocky fashion. He was unsure if there was a way back, but he felt a positive spin was best.

'Are we going to follow Frank?' Ray was very curious about his vanishing act, but looking to Khalid she was distracted. 'Top Secret is healed! You did it, Dad!' She slapped her father's hand with her own for a job well done and moved to observe Khalid more closely. 'Time to wake up, sleepy head, you're all better.' She nudged him a little and Khalid's eyelids flickered open.

As he came to focus on Ray, he was less grouchy than usual. 'What's happening, kid?'

'You saved me from the possessed vampire monkey, but then you got *real* sick,' she recounted. 'So Dad brought you to a secret planet where you could heal, but when your wounds mingled with the atmosphere ... it created a cosmic eruption that opened a portal to another world! That's where we are. Oh, and you're all fixed.'

'Sounds like I missed all the fun.' He propped himself up onto his elbows, and took a look around, bemused. 'Where the f—'

'Ah!' Zeven cautioned.

'Frank,' Khalid recanted, 'are we, exactly?' He looked to Zeven for answers as he sat up and had a proper look around.

'Your home planet, according to your father,' Zeven clued him in.

'Rubbish!' Khalid insisted, observing beauty around him. 'I was born on Phemoria.'

'Funny that you yelled the name of this city just before we were all transported here then,' Telmo said. 'And that your blood created the portal here.'

'Get the f— out of here!' Khalid stood. 'You weren't bullshitting about the Old Ones?'

'No, I wasn't.' Zeven frowned at Khalid's inability to control his cussing.

Ray chuckled at the error. 'He's hopeless.'

'So you really have been out to aid me, this whole time?' Khalid realised.

'What, breaking you out of prison and freeing you from that curse wasn't proof enough?' Zeven grinned at Khalid's quiet elation.

'No,' Khalid reasoned. 'I figured you were either delaying killing me, or handing me over to someone else who wants that pleasure, and there's a long list.'

'Daddy could have let you die,' Ray told him in no uncertain terms.

'Actually,' Telmo expanded on that premise, 'Zeven had to fight many people he holds dear in order to even gain permission to save your life.'

Khalid looked to Zeven completely dumbfounded. '*Why?*'

'Because I made you a promise —' Zeven began and Khalid finished the sentence.

'Once upon another universe, I know,' he emphasised, obviously still not believing that claim.

Aurora folded her arms and looked to her husband. 'When were you in another universe?'

'In the future,' Zeven stated, 'but not this future, another one.'

Aurora frowned in disbelief also.

'I know he sounds insane,' Telmo reassured both Aurora and Khalid. 'But I can confirm his account is quite true.'

Zeven raised both brows to appeal to Khalid. 'Is another universe any more nuts than another dimension? Yet, here we are.' He motioned around him.

'Come!' Ahura suddenly emerged from the scenery beyond the exit door. 'Everyone is waiting,' he announced, smiling broadly.

'Who is this?' Khalid queried, half-expecting what the answer would be.

'Um,' Zeven had planned for this to be a more private affair, 'this is your father, the Kaveh Ahura Mazida of the Dropa.'

'The Dropa,' Khalid uttered.

'That name is familiar to you?' Zeven was surprised that it would be.

'No more than the man in front of me, really.' Khalid appeared dazed.

'Father!' Ahura directed the greeting at Khalid.

'What?' everyone replied, equally confused.

'I thought you said *he* was *my* father?' Khalid looked to Zeven who was just as perplexed.

'Ahura?' He tossed the query back to the only man who knew the answer.

'On the physical plane of demonstration you were my son, *yes*.' Ahura was unable to suppress his elation and sounded a little crazed. 'But on this semi-etheric plane of expression *you* are *my* father, the Sharrujahan of Karmandi.' He bowed to Khalid, and everyone's jaws dropped.

'You've got to be f-freaking kidding me?' Khalid was utterly horrified. 'I'm not fit to rule my own body let alone a kingdom!'

'Well, hasn't your tune changed?' Zeven grinned, very pleased by the result of his efforts.

'Yes, it has!' Khalid stressed. 'I've just discovered the beauty of nature and the joy of a quiet life, and now you want to make me a ruler!'

'We are not thrusting anything upon you, Father, you *are* the Sharrujahan,' Ahura reasoned.

'Stop saying that,' Khalid insisted, 'and stop calling me Father! I think this is another one of your tests.' He looked to Zeven, with hope in his eyes.

'How did you know what Sharrujahan meant?' Zeven queried him back.

'Did I?' Khalid was horrified to admit. 'I've no clue.'

'Me either,' Zeven concluded. 'So let's hear Ahura out and find out, shall we?'

They all looked to Ahura who suddenly shook off his physical form like water, and assumed a spirit form that appeared like a colourful, vaporous mass that was primarily mauve and blue in colour.

'Did you kill us, Vidor?' Khalid queried aside to Zeven, his eyes transfixed on the anomaly.

'I'm not entirely sure.' Zeven could not look away from the spirit form either, as an impression of Ahura's physical face, torso and arms emerged to speak with them.

'*Majesty,*' Ahura began his address, without moving his lips, his thoughts echoed out loud. '*Your Qusay, and your subjects, are waiting to welcome you home.*'

'I have a wife!' Khalid was shocked and intrigued.

'*Well yes, Majesty, that's how I got here,*' Ahura joked. '*Won't you please accompany me to your court?*'

'I need a moment …' Khalid sat back down on the slab of rock.

'It's a lot to digest,' Zeven advised Ahura; even he was having trouble keeping up.

'*I shall inform the court that you are still recovering from your reality shift.*' Ahura reduced into a vapour, which flew back out the door.

'Wow!' Ray slapped her hands together, delighted. 'Frank is so pretty! Can I go with him?'

Zeven clamped a hand down on his daughter's head before she had a chance to run off. 'I think we should all hang together until we learn the lay of the land here.'

'Not only am I married, but I'm not even human, is that what you're telling me?' Khalid was bemused.

'You are a splendid being,' Telmo replied, with a grin of acknowledgement. 'It takes a superior kind of intelligence to survive what you did and still not be beyond redemption,' Telmo addressed his cynicism very seriously. 'For as the history of any universe will tell you, those souls become luminary to all who follow.'

'Look, after the things I've done and seen, I doubt I even have a soul worth speaking of, so forgive me if I am a little sceptical.' Khalid gripped his head.

'Well, the way I see it,' Zeven slapped a hand on his shoulder, 'the life you left behind was less than ideal, so what have you got to lose by investigating this one?'

'I have a wife!' Khalid stressed. 'All I know about women is how to torture one!'

Zeven looked to Aurora who frowned upon hearing this. 'That was the curse,' Zeven assured them all, and then crouched before Khalid to give him a pep talk. 'But back in that other universe, the ladies found you rather charming, and Wu Geng is in you somewhere —'

'Who?' Khalid frowned in disbelief.

'Here, allow me.' Telmo approached Khalid, intending to place a palm over his forehead, but Khalid deflected his hand before it could make contact.

'Allow you to what?'

'Help you to remember,' Telmo enlightened.

'Wait!' Zeven cut in. 'You could have made him remember Wu Geng at any time? Why didn't you mention that earlier?'

'It would have only confused his discovery of who he is in this life,' Telmo defended. 'But at this point in that journey, some of Wu Geng's tact would not go astray.'

'Yes,' Khalid agreed. 'Make me charming, or at least not as obnoxious.'

'You are charming.' Ray took hold of his hand. 'You saved my life; you're a hero!'

Khalid grinned at her sentiment. 'I wish I had your view of me.' He shifted his attention back to Telmo. 'Hit me, boy wonder.'

As Telmo held a hand over his subject's forehead, Zeven waylaid the process.

'I want him to have my memories of Wu Geng, as I spent more time with him than you did.'

'Well, I'm not really giving him any one person's memory,' Telmo explained, 'but merely opening the door to the Akashic memory of those events.'

'So he'll remember everything,' Zeven clarified. 'As though he'd never —' He stopped short of mentioning Wu Geng's death.

'Never what?' Khalid encouraged him to finish.

'Forgotten,' Zeven filled in the blank neatly.

'Shall we proceed?' Telmo proffered, to ensure they'd all said their piece on the matter.

Khalid appeared a little wary, but gave the nod.

As soon as Telmo made contact with Khalid's forehead the subject closed his eyes and his eyelids began flickering rapidly, whilst Telmo acted as a conduit for Khalid to access recollections of their time in the universe parallel.

Shortly after, Telmo retracted his hand and then gripped Khalid by both shoulders, to steady him as he processed information and recovered from their interface.

Zeven observed with bated breath as Khalid's eyelids parted and he looked about, his focus coming to rest upon him. 'You left me for dead!' Khalid broke free of Telmo's grip and rose to confront Zeven.

'I had no choice,' Zeven defended — he'd suspected that might be a sore point.

Khalid slapped Zeven's shoulder and burst into a smile. 'But you saved my arse in this universe, so I forgive you.' He embraced his old friend. 'The day I died I thought my mastery and cause were lost ... it blows my mind that they were not.'

'Well the insight seems to have perked up your spirits somewhat,' Zeven awarded, and with a mutual slap on the back they parted.

'As Khalid, I had a very narrow world view,' he explained with renewed confidence. 'But now that I remember Wu Geng ... being in another universe, on alien planets, becoming a timekeeper ... I'm not so afraid of venturing into another world.'

'A timekeeper?' Aurora queried. 'Like Taren?'

He turned to Aurora and grinned. 'Hello, cousin, I haven't seen you since Ji Fa's rebellious brothers left me at Yin to face this one's wrath.' He referred to Zeven and then looked to him. 'Ji Song found Hui Ru again. Of course she turned out to be the girl in the cafe.'

'The bitchin' blonde,' Zeven quoted with pride, Khalid's previous description of her.

'We were together in this other universe?' Aurora approached Zeven, grinning with delight.

'He spared my life as a wedding gift to you,' Khalid recalled. 'But I do believe he would have given you anything you asked for.'

'Really?' Aurora shimmied up beside her husband, savouring the news with deep gratification. 'That's very good to know.'

'You know I'd give you your own planet if you wanted it.' Zeven, who would normally have been discomforted by the exposure, returned her adoration.

'Another dimension isn't a bad conciliation.' Aurora gazed up at him, sentimental tears rimming her baby blues, as she smiled broadly.

'I wonder if this place has private rooms.' His wife's lips beckoned a kiss and as he leaned in to oblige, Khalid turned to Telmo. 'That reminds me, whatever became of Ansel when all the timelines changed?'

Zeven burst into a smile and the kiss went unaddressed. 'I knew it!' He left Aurora to join the conversation. 'Ansel was seducing you the night she passed out.'

'I guess you were right about me and the ladies.' Khalid grinned.

'Who was Ansel?' Aurora sounded a little annoyed.

'She was a shapeshifting reptilian that we met in our travels, who had a bit of a thing for Wu Geng,' Zeven informed her. He couldn't fail to notice that her expression appeared even more perplexed than it had before.

'So what happened to her?' Khalid prompted them to spill. 'Last time I saw her she was bleeding out on the floor beside me, after we were both slain by her ex, Vugar.'

'As we stopped the mind-eater virus from ever entering that universe, Ansel remained happily married to Vugar,' Telmo recounted in a clinical fashion, and Zeven considered that he might have been a little more tactful with the delivery. 'The Dracon became allied to Kila, and they aided the clean up of the rogue reptilian element on Earth.'

'That's fantastic,' Khalid was underwhelmed. 'Good for her.'

'Good grief! This sounds like some mission you went on,' Aurora had to say.

'It took approximately, what? Sixty — seventy years to complete?' Telmo was taking into account all the sidetracking — incarnation shifting, quantum jumps — they'd done, and Zeven nodded to concur that was about right.

'And I never even noticed you missing …' Aurora was completely mind-blown.

'And Dorje Pema?' Khalid's spirits lifted with the thought of his spiritual mentor. 'We've found the Dropa here, but what became of them when you changed the timelines?'

'We don't really know,' Telmo gave the short answer, but Khalid wasn't satisfied, for he raised his brows, eager to hear more. 'The Dropa never crashed on Earth the second time around. What became of them instead, we don't know. But they might?' Telmo motioned to the exit portal through which Ahura had disappeared.

'Then let's go!' Ray was already halfway across the bridge.

'You ready?' Zeven looked to Khalid, who raised both brows to consider.

'How do I look?' He glanced to Aurora for her opinion.

'Good,' she allowed, 'in a roguish kind of way.'

Khalid suddenly transformed his appearance to be more akin to Wu Geng's — clean shaven, hair short and slicked back off his face; this gave him a more noble and handsome appearance.

'Much better!' Aurora emphasised her delight. 'Wow!'

'Let's not get too excited.' Zeven grabbed his wife's hand to lead her off in pursuit of their daughter.

'Who knew he was *that* attractive under all that hair?' she commented aside to Zeven, who decided to ignore her doting tease. 'Sorry, you were saying something about a private room?' She invited him to resume a topic he might find more pleasing, and Zeven was more than happy to return to their thwarted kiss.

'Can I go through?' Ray snatched her parents' attention from each other, reaching into the imagery through the exit doorway and watching her hands disappear and then pulling them back out to make them visible again.

'No, Ray,' Zeven called to waylay her. 'Wait for us.'

'It's okay, Dad —' The girl vanished into the portal, which set everyone to running after her.

'Here goes!' Zeven charged on into the portal after Ray.

In this spectral state, suspended between the dominion of the living and the realm of the dead, Lucian felt like he was still present in the physical world, yet no one perceived him, nothing of the world responded to his touch. Much like being in a constant lucid dream, he'd been reduced to an observer. He could now sympathise with all the spectres he was used to seeing flitting about, and how frustrated the Grigori must be watching over their charges, with only intuition to guide them. It had been harrowing watching his wife trying to save his life, knowing the ship would be destroyed at any moment. He was still very connected to his emotions, and at that time he'd feared losing Taren more than the ship, which, given he was already deceased himself, seemed a touch moronic. Unfortunately, no one else on his crew saw ghosts, so it was a good thing Trance had happened along when he had, as now Lucian had the means to communicate with his wife from beyond the grave.

Death itself had been quite an education. Lucian's life to date had flashed through his mind's eye as he'd departed his body, and he was intrigued to view memories of an entire timeline, involving several missions, that he did not consciously recall living through prior to his demise. This must have been the second mission in the universe parallel that Zeven was claiming they had completed. The reason Lucian did not, and could not have remembered this mission during his lifetime, was because Lucian's host body in that other universe had been killed during the mission.

Despite a gift for tapping into the Akashic memory, Lucian's searches were still limited by his own knowledge — he couldn't reference an instance he didn't know existed. During this future mission he had learned he was capable of not only time-jumping backwards, as Taren had done before to save the AMIE project, but that they could quantum jump their consciousness into the body of any of their past life incarnations, but not without losing all conscious memory of the fact that they were on a mission in the first place. So they'd had agents working inside and outside of time, to ensure the entire team were awoken to their true purpose for being in that particular time and body, and not lost in the timelines.

But even with these precautions, Lucian wasn't the only crew member who'd lost their life in the universe parallel and subsequently forgotten the sidetrack. Ringbalin's memory of the event would never return either, for he had also been murdered before he could abort the mission and return his consciousness to his original body, residing on AMIE. Lucian had seen other allies die in this cross-universal expedition also, but no death pained him so much as learning that Taren's host body during the assignment in question had conceived his child. The one known constant of their timekeeping activities was that when they jumped their consciousness from one body to another, their consciousness was all they took with them. It saddened Lucian that their child must have been lost between universes and timelines somewhere, and what was sadder, he could not even discuss this with Taren as — according to Zeven — her memories of these events would not return for another four years.

When he considered all that was going on in Taren's world at present, her absent memory was probably a blessing. The last thing he'd wanted was to leave her to contend with a rebellion on Phemoria and freeing their crew, but someone needed to find out where Zeven and company had disappeared to, and as he was the only one who could see the portal that had engulfed their team members, he was the only sentient for the job.

Beyond the light barrier between worlds, Lucian entered an entirely white sanctuary, just in time to see the last of his crew pass through the portal at the end of the elongated circular structure. The advantage to being a spirit was the swiftness of motion; no need to coordinate a bunch of limbs to get you there — just set your intention and you arrived where desired. He was hoping this little trick would get him back to Taren's side when needed, but he hesitated to test the theory before he'd gathered the intel that he'd come for.

Beyond the portal was a corridor, of the same smooth, white, curved, light-filled design, and Thurraya was up ahead, skipping towards another portal at the far end. Behind Zeven was the portal he'd just come through and beyond there appeared to be nothing but countryside. 'Whoa.'

'It's like the building just appears as you need it, and responds to your wishes,' Ray advised him, as he admired the views out the long oblong shaped windows to either side of him. 'Watch this. Blue.' His daughter pointed to the walls and they immediately changed colour.

'Goodness,' Aurora entered to catch the trick.

Thurraya turned to face the side wall and pointed. 'Door.' She walked towards the wall and a doorway appeared to grant her access to outside.

'Ray, wait right there,' Zeven called to her through the opening and she stopped still as he headed through the doorway and into the countryside to catch her up.

In the field of assorted flowers, Thurraya stood with her hands palm upward, fascinated by the millions of tiny orbs of light that were swarming all over the field like millions of tiny bugs. 'How amazing and beautiful is this?' she said. 'They're elementals, Dad … I've never seen so many!'

'I didn't know that you saw them at all.' Zeven finally reached her.

'Well, not in space obviously, but when I am in nature, I have seen them.' One finally landed on her hand, and turning to show him Ray glanced back to whence they'd come, and her excitement waned. 'Oops.'

Zeven looked back to see nothing but nature. 'Oh shoot, Ray.'

'Sorry,' she winced, as he took hold of her hand and headed back in the direction they'd come.

An opening erupted out of thin air, and Telmo stood in the orifice shaking his head. 'Come along, children, let's not get lost.'

Zeven forced a grin as they returned to join the rest of the crew. 'Now, stay close.' He let Ray's hand go.

'I will,' she assured.

Zeven, satisfied Ray had learned her lesson, led off towards the portal at the far end.

'Kitten.'

Ray's request brought him to a halt and looking back he found Thurraya holding the said animal and cooing over it.

'*Smaller*,' she instructed and the animal in her hand shrunk to palm-size. 'Aqua.' The kitten changed colour. 'Aww … how *adorable*! Can I keep her?'

Zeven was a little wary of how quickly his daughter was adapting to her new environment; perhaps she'd learned her lesson a little too well? 'If it will keep you out of trouble. But no more creative animal making,' he thought to add.

'I promise.' Ray's full attention reverted to the miniature aqua kitten in her palm.

'What do you make of all this?' Zeven consulted Telmo.

'Semi-causal plane, semi-causal beings, semi-causal construct,' he concluded.

'Well, that clears things right up.' Aurora had not a clue what he was talking about, but Zeven did.

'So this is part of the Otherworld?' Zeven theorised. 'Or is this the realm of the Grigori?'

'No,' Telmo clarified. 'They function in a realm that is purely causal, but here in the etheric world they can manifest a form, much as the Dropa do. You could say that this place is akin to the Otherworld, as it is somewhere between the physical and the spirit realm, or otherwise we would have had to leave our physical bodies to enter this place.'

The celestial city of the Phemoray could be accessed from here, Zeven deduced on the quiet. Jalila Lamus had claimed the women whose souls dwelt there were the best psychics that Phemoria had to offer — powerful allies, if they did not approve of his mother's rebellion.

Upon confronting the portal at the end of the corridor, which also appeared to lead into the countryside beyond, Zeven took hold of his daughter's hand. 'Let's do this one together.'

'Good call.' Ray pocketed her kitten to take hold of Khalid's hand and he was surprised when her mother took up his other hand.

'A bit of moral support.' She smiled, also linking hands with Telmo.

The corridor in which they stood and the portal entrance before them immediately widened, to permit them all to stand side by side and enter together.

'Ready?' Zeven queried down the line, but Khalid knew the question was mostly for his benefit. Everyone else nodded.

'How does that matter?' Khalid replied. 'As far as I can tell this is our only way forward.'

'Put that way,' Zeven warranted, 'I should probably just have said, suck it up and good luck.'

Khalid was amused. 'That sounds more like you.'

Khalid found it extraordinary to suddenly remember knowing Zeven and many of the other timekeepers in other lives and situations. It had taken a long time to earn Zeven's friendship and trust, but he was like a fierce canine, and once that bond had been established there was clearly no breaking it — it had transcended universes and the sad circumstances of their history in this timeline. What was truly amazing to Khalid was that, with all his political plotting to secure his position in the world, in the end it was one true friend who had saved him from the hell that was his everyday reality in this life.

Time to discover who I truly am. He stepped into the portal along with his company, feeling truly supported for the first time since he'd been in Wu Geng's skin.

The passage through this portal felt different to the first. Like plunging into water but without the associated moisture and airlessness, the atmosphere of the huge space beyond was darker and more buoyant — to both the body and the soul. The weightlessness lifted their party up as they emerged from the passage and they floated into a huge expansive arena, hands still linked and mute with awed anticipation.

A huge reflective bowl-shaped floor mirrored an equally huge reflective bowl-shaped ceiling, but the construct was barely perceivable as the outer arena fell into shadow, and gave the optical effect of an infinite space.

All eyes were glued to the centre where masses of colourful, light-filled vapour performed a resplendent dance and sung in a chorale, the sound of which filled the body with a vibration of pure exhilaration and joy.

The vapours intertwined to form different geometric shapes, simple at first, like a sphere that linked to another sphere, then in between formed an equilateral triangle. From within this formation a pentagon emerged, within it a pentagram. But then bursting apart into spheres, the formations became more complex.

'The seed of life … the tree … the egg … the fruit …'

Khalid noted Telmo uttering to one side of him.

'The flower of life. Metatron's cube.'

'You know these formations?' Aurora queried Telmo first as she was closest to him.

'It is the sacred geometry on which all of creation is based.'

'Whoa, really?' Aurora looked back to the spectacle.

Khalid recalled that this teaching had been among the first of a plethora of knowledge that had been imparted to Wu Geng by his spiritual mentor, Dorje Pema — the sole survivor of the Dropa people, whom the timekeepers had encountered in the ancient world, of another planet in the universe parallel. Was this coincidence, or a message?

Your survival is far more important than you, or any of your team mates, realise.

Dorje Pema's final words to Wu Geng sprang to mind, and they made his dormant heart break; yet it was hope and excitement that poured from the old wound, not sorrow.

Your soul source may be different to theirs, but it is just as splendid. You are no more alone in your plight than we are. Make it home and you shall know we have not led you ill.

'Pema?' He only whispered the query, and the formation of vapour contorted to form the image of a closed flower, which opened into a lotus.

The sight brought tears to Khalid's eyes, for Dorje Pema meant 'indestructible lotus'. From the centre of the formation a vaporous form rose up, shimmering silver and purple tones, and wound its way towards them. The entity came to hover before Khalid and from it emerged the upper body of the childlike Dropa master that he, Zeven and Telmo had known.

'Is it really you?' Khalid let go of Aurora and floated closer, finding it difficult to believe it could truly be his beloved mentor.

'*It is us …*' she replied, using thought projection as Ahura had, once liberated from his physical form. '*Although this is no more our true appearance than the body you are wearing is yours.*' Dorje had always referred to herself in the plural, as even with all her fellow Dropa deceased she remained telepathically linked to them.

'But how did you end up here? In this universe?' Zeven asked.

'*The Eternity Gate,*' they both concluded at once.

'Ansel claimed it was a myth!' Khalid was intrigued, as he'd not lived to see the resolution of their mission.

'It exists,' Zeven assured. 'But very few craft ever successfully entered it and none ever returned to the universe from which they'd come.'

'*The Grigori made the passage,*' she stated, attention on Zeven, and Khalid was again baffled, having no idea what Grigori meant.

'We were invited to make the passage and advised to take no weapons,' Zeven answered. 'The Dropa were too,' Zeven assumed in conclusion. 'That's where you were headed when you got stranded on Earth. But how do you remember that timeline?'

'Akasha,' Telmo answered on her behalf. 'Nothing happens in any timeline that is not recorded there.'

'*So you see we have been in this universe far longer than you,*' Pema enlightened. '*We built the inter-system gateways, and have been working in cooperation with the Grigori to pave the way for human development in this universe, just as we did in the last. Many souls, both Grigori and Dropa, have incarnated into the royal houses of Phemoria* and Sermetica, in the hope of ending the war and the curses that the progeny of our cross-breeding with Phemoria instigated. Until finally our beloved Sharrujahan insisted on incarnating into the human race to redress the balance himself, and our son volunteered to assume human form in order that this divine person might be conceived.'

Khalid felt a trembling deep within his being that caused his entire body to quiver.

'When Ahura did not return, and you were born a male instead of female, the relations between us and the Phemorians of the celestial city became too strained to continue. But we were all betrayed, by one soul who should have returned to us long ago.'

'Chironjivi,' announced Ray, who'd been silent to this point. 'I remember now, why I came.'

'What could these events have to do with you?' Aurora gasped, as Zeven noted his daughter was trembling.

'Thurraya?' He took her in his arms to comfort her.

'Calm yourself,' Pema coaxed Ray with her soothing presence. 'There are many reasons why you returned to a physical state of demonstration.'

The child calmed and smiled, forgetting whatever disturbing thought had upset her.

'Is Ray's soul one of yours?' Zeven queried the spectre.

'We could not have retrieved our Sharrujahan without her assistance,' Pema advised.

'That explains why she is so protective of Khalid,' Zeven considered.

Khalid couldn't contain his inner quake any longer, and his body quivering drew the attention of everyone. 'What is happening to me?'

'Your true self wants to break through the consciousness barrier that encapsulated you when you were born into that physical form,' Pema advised. 'You must shed it, in order to comprehend all that you truly are.'

'Can I return to this form?' Khalid battled against his urge to shed the heaviness of his physical existence.

'We can assume a human form, as Ahura did in order to seed you, but we cannot be truly human unless reborn into that race.'

'Is there a difference?' Khalid stammered.

'*Of course,*' Pema emphasised. '*You shall regain your causal perspective, and shed all the pain and suffering of your past.*'

'So I won't remember my life as Khalid?'

'I believe what Pema is trying to say,' Telmo bridged the comprehension gap, 'is that you will remember Khalid, but in a causal state of being, you will no longer be emotionally connected to that life and detach from the outcome.'

'No,' Khalid rejected that notion very strongly and ceasing to desire to know who he really was, his trembling lessened. 'I'll lose my motivation. I have to go back.'

'*We barely managed to retrieve you, and had you died in human form, you would have been trapped by the same curse that binds Chironjivi to the physical plane of awareness.*' Pema outlined the risk of following his desire. '*Clearly, we are not equipped to withstand the stresses, vices and seductions of the physical world any longer. We must allow the Grigori to resolve the situation.*'

'I have been dealing with Chironjivi's curse longer than any soul living; I am better equipped than any to end this suffering,' Khalid explained his reasons. 'You were the one who told me I must endure and right all that had been wronged by Khalid's actions.'

'*All Khalid's wrongs have been undone. The family you sought to slay, lives.*' Pema motioned to Zeven. '*The curse that had hold of you, has been contained and parted from its minions.*'

'I had no part in that recompense. And even if I did return, deal with the curses and restore peace to the united systems, that would still not come *close* to balancing the karmic debt Khalid racked up in the universe of his birth,' he concluded, a little shocked by his own resolve and conviction.

Pema was smiling. '*After all you have been put through, you invite yet more suffering upon yourself?*'

The query brought tears to Khalid's eyes, for the answer was a revelation to him. 'I find no peace in the prospect of leaving good souls to deal with the horrors with which I have been intimate. I know for a fact that suffering for a good cause brings me more joy and peace than freedom from caring does.'

'Amen.' Telmo backed his reasoning, and the smiles of all present seemed to show their unanimous support.

'Then the Grigori have done their job well, and you are now ready to embark on the quest you took form to accomplish,' Pema allowed, shocking Zeven and Telmo a little.

'You arranged our intervention with the Grigori?' Zeven now realised why he had been so compelled.

Pema smiled. 'But it is only through your individual self mastery that their guidance could be heeded,' she allowed. 'So gratitude to you, Sammael.' She referred to Zeven and Aurora, who looked to her husband, amazed and intrigued, as Pema's gaze turned to Telmo. 'To you, Araqiel … and also to you, Azazèl.' Pema rose up to look beyond their group, whereupon the rest of them turned about to find the free-floating spirit form of Lucian Gervaise behind them.

'Captain …' Zeven was clearly panicked by his superior's form, or lack thereof. 'Have you learned a new trick?' He assumed the best.

'No,' their captain replied, calmly. 'I've performed this trick quite a few times already.'

11

TOUGH ENOUGH

When Taren awoke, she was disorientated; it took her a moment to figure out that she was in the weather control centre of Module C. The bed she was on belonged to Ringbalin and when she rolled over she found the biologist sound asleep beside her.

How long have I been out? She sat upright carefully so as not to disturb her colleague, and tried to gather her wits.

The day before was a traumatising recollection. It was tempting to go back to sleep, wake up the day before and see if she could alter the outcome. But too much had transpired in just that one day for her to cover it all, and causality would surely penalise her with some other unforeseen disaster she had yet to even contemplate. Lucian was dead, and her crew imprisoned — how much worse could it really be? Her circumstance caused a brief cascade of tears to drain from her eyes, but she brushed them aside, knowing grief was a waste of time. She had led them all into this, and it fell to her to get them out — it was that simple. And as long as there was a way, she would not collapse into despair.

'Hello? Anybody home!'

The call got Taren to her feet in a hurry, but once she spotted the source wandering through the greenhouse, eating a piece of fruit, she realised that she'd left their new associate, Trance, in the medical lab and he must have recovered from yesterday's events faster than they had.

'Oh damn, I fell asleep.' Ringbalin raised himself. 'I meant to go check on the patient and see if he needed anything, but?' He threw his hands up in conclusion.

'Well, you outlasted me.' She was a little embarrassed about that. 'Sorry, you had to carry me up here.'

'My day wasn't quite so long as yours,' he conceded graciously. 'I caught a brief nap whilst I was buried.'

Taren was amused by his tale.

'It was strangely comforting being buried like a seedling,' he added. 'A good lesson in empathy for me.' He reached for his glasses, and cleaned them with his grubby T-shirt before he put them on. 'Still, if you hadn't come along, you might not have had as much luck replicating me back into existence.'

'And heaven knows what details about you I might have overlooked, and would have to improvise on?' Taren joked.

'You saved my life,' he concluded in all seriousness and with gratitude.

'I was also the reason you, and all of the crew, were at risk in the first place.' She was not about to overlook that.

'*Life* ... especially of revolutionary nature, is fraught with danger,' Ringbalin stated. 'We all knew that when we signed up for AMIE.'

'I don't know if that would be your reasoning if you were being tortured by Valoureans right now.' Taren near suffocated on the guilt that thought invoked. 'Or dead —'

'We can fix the captain, we can free the crew, all we need is some fuel and an hour to get our priorities sorted.' Ringbalin tied his shoes, sounding so sure and determined that Taren felt quite the idiot for being so contrary.

'This is your handiwork, flower boy! I know you are around here somewhere!' Trance yelled as Ringbalin stood.

'We could just activate the rain function?' Taren suggested.

'He's probably had enough rain after our short stint on Oceane.' Ringbalin gathered back his hair and strapped it in a ponytail, which still didn't stop the long fair strands of his fringe escaping. 'I know Trance seems a little full of himself, but he's an okay guy, really.'

'I'll take your word on that.' Taren followed Ringbalin out the door. The impression she got of Trance was that he had a rather high opinion of himself, despite being self serving, moody, not too courageous and a bit of a snob.

'All that empty crew accommodation and I find you two together?' Trance commented upon sighting them descending the stairs. 'How curious.'

'Presumptuous pervert,' Taren commented aside to Ringbalin, in answer to his good guy assertion.

'He's just trying to establish if there is anything going on between us, in order to assess if he can make a move on you,' Ringbalin bantered.

'I … I.' Trance attempted to hide his guilty grin.

'Best tell him not to test a woman with PK,' Taren suggested, holding Trance firmly in her sights.

'I wouldn't dream of it.' He took offence. 'I just want your supreme commander-ness to take me home.'

'I'm afraid I can't do that,' Taren replied. 'I need you.'

Trance forced a laugh. 'Yeah, tell someone who cares.'

'Like the President of Sermetica perhaps, for whom I am working at present?' Taren suggested, and Trance seemed to have a revelation.

'You're the ones,' he uttered. 'The psychic task force that brought Khalid to justice.'

'We *were*,' Taren replied, a bitter taste in her mouth. 'Before Valoureans took my crew captive, destroyed this vessel, and killed my husband! Now you and Ringbalin are all the crew I have to help right this situation.'

'You want me to help you jailbreak your crew from Phemorian prison!' Trance backed up several paces. 'Have you lost your *fucking* mind?'

'Long time ago.' Taren really wasn't in the mood for dramatics.

'Half your crew has been captured by Valoureans,' Trance pointed out, 'and the other half have been sucked into another dimension! Forgive me if I really don't want to get involved in your shit.'

'You are involved!' Taren stated matter-of-factly. 'Tell me, as a psychic, that you are not sick to death of having that held against you, and being forced to repress your true potential!'

'Psychics are criminals on Sermetica no longer,' Trance argued.

'That's right,' Taren concurred. 'But if President Anselm doesn't get the psychic rights bill passed through the USS, Sermetica may be forced to fight to defend that right against every other planet in the USS.'

'But Phemoria harbours psychics —'

'Only women, and they don't want men having that same privilege at present, believe me,' Taren emphasised.

'You are not going to convince me that signing up with you is in my favour.' Trance folded his arms and took a stubborn stance.

'There is a war going on, Mr Ducer. Go back to your little hidey-hole and wait for it to come for you if you wish … but it will come if we don't stop it. So … wish us luck.' Taren didn't have the time or energy to spare arguing — it was easier to work alone than with someone uncooperative — and so headed for the main exit door.

'I remember you having more balls,' Ringbalin commented as he moved to follow Taren.

'I remember you having less,' Trance bickered. 'You are insane to follow her.'

'Yep, I accept that.' Ringbalin nodded. 'But at least I won't die for no good reason.'

'So, can I go home now?' Trance called after them both.

'Sure,' Taren yelled back as the automatic glass sliding doors parted in front of her. 'Feel free to make your own way.'

'Argh!' Trance was frustrated by his predicament. 'How am I supposed to do that, when I don't even know where I am?'

'That's a very good question,' Taren awarded. 'I sincerely hope you find an answer. But, if you're really stuck, we have deep space pods in the launch bay.'

'Stay safe,' Ringbalin suggested to Trance, and caught Taren up to accompany her to the mess to grab some sustenance.

It didn't take the Valoureans long to get back to Phemoria; the passage was virtually instantaneous. Still, General Prochazka managed to cram a maximum amount of terror into the short time that elapsed between taking them captive and reporting to her queen.

Before departing the Oceane system the Valoureans assembled the AMIE crew in the control centre of the Phemorian vessel and stripped them of their Juju stones — including Swithin, who was still unconscious. The Valoureans took pains not to touch the bare stones and cast them all into a coffer. Out through the front shield window, the AMIE craft could be seen and the distance between the two vessels was widening.

'Does anyone want to tell me where I will find Zaman Vidor and his daughter?'

There were few among them who knew who that was, but Leal knew and so did Kassa. They had been made privy to the information during their first tour of Module C, when Zeven and Mythric had discovered that Ringbalin had been the child who had saved Zeven's life when Khalid had attempted to murder him as a babe.

'There is no one by that name on our crew,' Leal spoke up to explain the crew's silence.

'Zeven Gudrun, Kale Tane, Starman, Bob, am I ringing any bells yet?' the general persisted, now focusing her ire on Leal, which was a worry, as she'd already knocked him senseless once today.

'We don't know where he is.' Leal knew the answer would not be received well. 'He's been on a mission since before we liberated *your* Qusay from her curse.'

The general smiled at his reminder. 'That didn't quite work as much to your favour as you'd hoped, did it?'

'Well, we didn't expect medals or anything, but flowers would have been nice.' He smiled, inviting the back-handed slap to the face which Prochazka was more than happy to provide.

'If someone does not tell me the whereabouts of the man I am seeking, your ship and anyone still alive on board her is going to be blown to bits! You have ten seconds to stop me.' She closed her eyes to count.

Leal looked to his crew mates, who all knew there were still at least two crew members on board. Ayliscia Portus, one of the Phemorians on their crew, who never showed emotion, was quietly choking with grief, as Ringbalin had not been captured. But as close as she was to the biologist, she still shook her head ever so slightly to advise Leal to tell them nothing.

'Time's up,' Prochazka announced, as through the front shield windows behind her the Astro Marine Institute Explorer could be seen as it exploded and began raining debris down onto the virgin planet of Oceane below.

The destruction of their ship and captain was devastating. Worse, the crew were restrained and separated, men from the women, leaving only seven-year-old Fari in the company of his mother.

'I want to go with the men,' the boy had cried.

'You will do as you are told!' General Prochazka insisted as she dragged Fari's grandfather from where he'd been herded with the men. 'Chief Ronan, how wonderful to see you are still living. Now I have the pleasure of avenging all the Phemorian agents you tortured and murdered during your time with the MSS.' She pulled him up by the neck of his shirt, but his focus was not on her ireful gaze, but on the ring she was wearing on her finger, that was right under his nose at present.

'That's a very interesting ring you are wearing,' Zelimir commented, then looked her in the eye. 'Where in wretchedness did you get it?'

The query utterly infuriated the general, whereupon she pulled her pulse laser and shot Zelimir Ronan, point blank, through the head.

'You fucking bitch!' Yasper, Zelimir's son, went berserk, but was quickly battered back into submission by Valoureans and dragged away with Leal and Swithin.

Jazmay was truly battling to say silent at this point, but for the sake of her young son and husband, she did.

The general dropped the ex-chief of the MSS, and noticing his blood on her purple suit, she frowned and conjured up a cloth to wipe it off. 'Still want to argue, little boy?' She looked back to young Fari. 'I'll happily kill them all.'

Fari only stared at her, a defiant expression on his face.

'You want to kill me … *get in line.*' She signalled her guards to take them away.

'You are already dead,' Fari replied as he was dragged from the command centre with the others.

For the most part of the short time they were incarcerated on board the Phemorian craft, Yasper was completely ropable, and Swithin remained blissfully unaware of their circumstance. But just before they were hauled out of the Phemorian craft, Yasper exhausted his cussing and anger and took a seat on the floor of the empty cell, between Leal and Swithin's slumbering form. Yasper had tried to stir Swithin, hoping to somehow resurrect his father before it was too late, but their project manager snoozed on.

'It doesn't matter anyway, we're all restrained and without Ringbalin your father would only bleed out all over again.' Leal hated to be the voice of reason.

'Where the fuck is Taren?' Yasper kicked out with the leg that had the restraining device on it, but was subdued by a sad thought. 'I sure hope she wasn't on AMIE when she blew.'

'I'm sure she wasn't.' Leal swallowed hard, knowing that the captain had not been so fortunate.

'Do you think she got the captain out, and Balin?' Yasper gently probed his facial injuries, and winced as he assessed how sore they were.

'We can only hope.' Leal was sorry he couldn't roust more confidence in his response.

'Why in the world are we in trouble with Phemoria?' Yasper couldn't imagine. 'We just saved their queen from a curse; you'd think they'd be a bit grateful?'

'I think it might have something to do with Zeven's family feud.' Swithin rolled onto his back and groaned, holding his head.

'It's about time you showed up,' Yasper grumbled.

'Oh, please don't start with the "Zeven helped Khalid escape from prison" theory.' Leal waved off Swithin's suggestion. 'I put it to the captain and he found the notion laughable.'

'What else could explain the sudden divide in their family?' Swithin proffered.

'How does that relate to this?' Leal posed.

'I don't know.' Swithin held his head, which clearly pained him. 'Perhaps Satomi told her sister Zeven helped Khalid, the man who *murdered* her, and persuaded her sister to seek retribution?'

'Against their own children? And why would Zeven help a man who betrayed his family?' Yasper argued. 'It all seems very unlikely, when the Qusay was so very thankful for our assistance with her curse.'

'Well, I thought Satomi would be a bit more fucking grateful I brought her back from the dead,' Swithin countered. 'But that doesn't seem to be the case now, does it?'

'I think our time might be better spent speculating why a comment about a piece of jewellery got Zelimir killed?' Leal proffered.

'It wasn't the comment,' Yasper admitted. 'The MSS did kill Phemorian spies.'

'But the way Zelimir phrased the question, "where in *wretchedness*, did you find it?"' Leal quoted. 'That's an interesting comment from someone who sees auras and energy fields, as Zelimir did.'

'You think he was implying it was cursed?' Yasper followed.

Leal shrugged and nodded to indicate it was worth further consideration.

'What else did I miss?' Swithin sat up, and was alarmed when neither of his companions seemed very chatty any longer.

Pangs of shock pulsed through Leal's being as he realised Swithin had no idea his brother had been killed.

'Where is Lucian?' Swithin noted who was missing. 'And Mythric and Ringbalin?'

'We don't know,' Leal gave the easy answer.

'Perhaps they got away?' Swithin was more hopeful of a rescue.

'Leal?' Yasper knew he wasn't telling the whole truth.

'Okay, what else?' Swithin urged to be enlightened.

'They blew up the ship.' Yasper hated saying it, almost as much as Swithin hated hearing it.

'Was anyone still on board?' Swithin sat up, his anger finally overcoming his pain. 'Like my brother? Your captain!'

'Leal was knocked out when apprehended, and the only reason I wasn't was so that they could use me to keep Jaz in line,' Yasper said. 'I didn't know who the Phemorians had captured and who they'd missed, until we were all assembled to watch the ship destroyed and my father shot in the head before my eyes!'

'Fuck!' Swithin backed off. 'Zelimir, shit! Sorry.' He took a moment to absorb the tragedy. 'So no one knows if those missing made it out or not.'

Yasper looked to Leal, who'd already confessed to him the sorry state he'd last seen the captain in.

'Last I saw the captain, he was slowly suffocating in a defunct space pod, in the launch bay,' Leal was distressed to admit. 'I do believe Prochazka left him there.'

Swithin's jaw clenched tight as he processed the news. 'And Taren?'

Both men shook their heads, uncertain.

'I don't think she was on board,' Leal ventured to say. 'The captain was waiting for her to return from a meeting with Anselm when the Phemorians showed up.'

'Well, that's something.' Swithin found a silver lining, which was so very unlike him. 'Before this thing is over, I predict there's going to be one hell of a bitch fight.'

The notion brought some cheer to their otherwise abysmal circumstance. 'If my wife has anything to do with it, there sure will be,' Yasper warranted.

'I just hope we are all still around to see it.' Leal joined them in their happy place for a second, as the thought of watching anyone smack down Prochazka was a very pleasing one at present.

The door to their cell opened and half a dozen Valoureans entered and dragged the men to their feet.

'Speaking of bitches ...' Swithin's snide remark got him elbowed in the gut.

'Easy on the merchandise.' The Valourean in charge grabbed Swithin by the chin. 'This one is almost too ugly to stud as it is, best not to compound the issue.'

'Did she say stud?' Yasper queried aside to Leal.

'You, on the other hand.' Her eyes turned to Yasper. 'You are *quite* the stallion. I predict you are going to be a *very busy* boy.'

The women of the AMIE crew were led from the Phemorian craft straight into a cell block and separated into three cells. Jazmay was imprisoned with Fari; Kassa and Amie were thrown in together; and Kalayna and Ayliscia were shoved towards the third cell.

'I don't see why I am restrained,' Kalayna grumbled as she was shoved through the door of her prison. 'I don't have a Power!'

'Then you wouldn't be on this crew.' The Valourean closed the cell door between them, but Kalayna continued to plead her case through the small barred window in the door.

'I'm not on the crew!' she stressed. 'I was kidnapped!'

'Irrelevant,' the Valourean assured.

'What are you going to do with us?' Kalayna jumped at the opportunity to ask.

The Valourean backed up. 'That is for General Prochazka to decide, but I feel sure it involves pain and *death*.' She grinned and returned to the cell block exit with the rest of her battalion.

'No way! You gotta let me talk to someone! I'm just an innocent bystander! Please!' When the exit door closed behind the guards, Kalayna turned back to see the displeased look on Ayliscia's face. 'Not to worry.' She crept over to whisper, 'You used to work for their SS, didn't you? Do you know the specifics of this cell?'

Ayliscia frowned, confused by Kalayna's sudden swing in mood from completely distressed to total control.

'Panicked and disloyal means less of a threat,' Kalayna quietly explained the scene she'd just made.

She didn't know Ayliscia at all; they'd really had nothing to do with each other before this moment, but if there was one thing

Phemorian women admired was strength and willpower in other women.

Her beautiful stern expression melted to indifference. 'This is a psychic containment cell,' she advised in an equally hushed whisper. 'The entire block cannot be exited via psychic means.'

'Surveillance? Visual, audio?' Kalayna looked about the sparse room that was entirely white and padded.

Ayliscia ticked her head towards the back corner. 'To focus on the cell doors, the blind spot is in the corner beneath.'

Kalayna immediately moved to said position, where the toilet was located and as Ayliscia nodded, she took a seat.

'If you want to cry about your situation, go ahead!' Ayliscia told her plainly. 'They will be listening to everything we say.'

'This is all your fucking boss's fault!' Kalayna took that under advisement and changed the topic, as she began digging into the padded waistband of her trousers. 'I didn't ask to be rescued from the space corps, you know?' Kalayna began pulling tiny tools out and laying them on the toilet cistern behind her.

'You ingrate, good-for-nothing.' Ayliscia approached Kalayna and leaned in towards her, slapping her own hand to make it look like she'd hit Kalayna. 'Shut up, sit here, and do nothing!'

The two women grinned at each other briefly, and Ayliscia's expression soured as she withdrew to the bed to brood and observe the object of her supposed disdain.

Kalayna rested her left foot on her knee to inspect the device on her leg. She looked at the hinge that allowed the device to open and clamp around the ankle, then selected a screwdriver and got to work.

Prochazka entered the throne room, carrying the coffer containing the Juju stones retrieved from their prisoners, and she bowed before the throne.

'Did you find my granddaughter?' Satomi stood, wearing the embodiment of her sister.

'I found the next best thing.' Prochazka held out the coffer. 'Their Juju stones.'

Satomi was mildly appeased. 'So Thurraya was not on board AMIE?'

'Nor were her parents,' Prochazka advised. 'They must be in hiding together. Perhaps on the ocean planet itself, but there were no vehicles missing from their manifest.'

'My son doesn't need vehicles to get about,' Satomi pointed out. 'What has become of the AMIE vessel?'

'Destroyed,' Prochazka stated with great satisfaction. 'And I ensured the captain went down with his ship.'

Satomi quietly gasped on the news, for the captain had led the mission to resurrect her to life. If not for him, no one would have been aware that her ghost was caught in limbo between worlds. During her time in the spirit world she'd witnessed the AMIE crew perform many good deeds and they had seemed to be on the right track to liberating the psychics of the USS. It was still unclear to her what had happened during the short time that she had been transitioning from her spiritual form back into a physical body, but something had possessed the crew of AMIE overnight to become involved with their mutual arch nemesis, and the friends of her enemy were her enemies also. 'That will teach my upstart of a niece to aid the scourge of Phemoria.'

'Do you want to reconsider allowing me to search the ocean planet?' Prochazka suggested.

'That depends on how you react to being in contact with the stones in the coffer in your hand,' Satomi advised. 'If you cannot abide them, the atmosphere on that planet will kill you.'

Prochazka immediately began unscrewing the coffer.

'There is also the risk if you *can* stand the energy of the stones, that you will be swayed towards their cause,' Satomi added, whereupon the general paused.

'The stones are enchanted?' the general assumed.

'All I know is that those stones have a connection to Oceane and are fortifying to the psychics my niece chooses to award them to. That is why I instructed you to avoid contact with them.'

'I shall take my own life before I betray Phemoria.' The general turned the coffer on its end, opened the lid and reached inside, before abruptly hurling the coffer away as if she'd been bitten by it. The hardened warrior near lost her stomach but managed to regain her equilibrium and back away as the stones and armbands scattered all over the floor.

'As I suspected,' Satomi released a heavy sigh. 'You cannot stand in the presence of cosmic light whilst playing warden to the curse of shadows.'

'I deeply regret that I can be of no further aid in your search.' Prochazka went down on one knee to beg forgiveness.

'There is no one else I would trust to carry such a heavy burden, General.' Satomi motioned her to rise. 'For while you control the demon crew from Dead Man Downs, I can rest assured that no one else can use them against us, including Khalid.'

'But what shall you do about your missing heir?' Prochazka probed. 'According to your vision she is the key to be rid of these curses.'

Satomi eyed the stones on the floor. 'We have just the man for the job.'

'Even with the pain enhancing drugs, Spyridon Vidor has not disclosed any information of use to us,' Prochazka countered. 'We may have to brainwash him in order to get him to cooperate.'

Satomi smiled at this. 'Time to try a more subtle approach. Get him cleaned up and brought to me.'

Prochazka nodded to confirm the order. 'What do you wish me to do with the rest of the crew?'

'Begin the interrogations, but leave them alive for now,' Satomi gave her directive. 'Their lives shall ultimately depend upon how cooperative Spyridon Vidor is prepared to be.'

'Very subtle, Majesty.' Prochazka grinned. 'But in the end they all must die. Proof of this coup must never be allowed to be substantiated before the USS council.'

'Of course.' As Satomi replied, she felt a pang of guilt. 'There is far more at stake here than any one life.'

Swithin, Yasper and Leal had been hauled off the Phemorian vessel, stripped naked, hosed down and scrubbed, as if, as men, they carried some sort of disease that could be cleansed away. This process was much to the amusement of their Valourean captors, who clearly regarded them as little more than livestock. Swithin was drawing the brunt of the Valoureans' violence as he cussed and lashed out at their aggressors with the most passion.

'He may not be much of a looker, but he's quite feisty!' commented the Valourean holding the hose that was pelting water at Swithin. The spray was so hard he'd lost his footing and was choking on the floor as he refused to cease cussing her.

Yasper was trying the reasonable and charming route, which wasn't doing him any favours, either.

'Shut the fuck up!'

He was slammed in the jaw for mentioning saving their Qusay recently.

'I don't care who you were or what you've done.' His aggressor grabbed him by the hair and dragged him up from the floor. 'From now on you are nothing but a cock with an annoying life support system attached. You got that, pretty boy?' She forced his head to nod and let him go. Her sights then turned to Leal, who had decided to take the *shut up and do what they tell you* approach.

'*You*, good boy.' She'd noted Leal taking the path of least resistance. 'Let's start this grading process with what you do.'

'Navigation,' he replied.

'What Powers do you have?'

He was silent. His inquisitor rolled her eyes and grabbed his nuts.

'Argh! *Telepathy*,' he squeaked and she let him go.

'Excellent.' She raised her brows and nodded. 'And what does Prince Charmless do?' She motioned to Yasper, and Leal hesitated. She grabbed his nuts again.

'Fuck!' Leal endured the agony, staring his adversary down.

'Levitation,' Yasper answered, whereupon she let Leal go and he collapsed to the floor.

'What else?' She turned her attention back to Yasper.

'What do you mean, what else? That's it.' He was insulted.

'Disappointing,' she decided, moving on to Swithin, who was hauled out of a puddle by two Valoureans, who held him fast. 'And what about you?'

'Kiss my arse, cu—'

Swithin took another blow to the gut.

'He brings people back from the dead.' Leal knew Swithin's pride wouldn't allow him to answer her, so he spoke up before he died.

'Oh, really?' She seemed delighted about that. 'A resurrectionist, that's rare.'

'But before you kill anyone seeking a demonstration,' Leal advised, 'I will add that he brings people back to life, but cannot heal their death wounds. Your general blew up the only man who could do that, with AMIE.'

'So there were others on board.' She slapped Leal's face hard for lying in the first place.

Leal wiped the blood from his face, numb to the taste as he'd swallowed nothing else since being taken captive. 'He's better off dead,' he uttered, defiant.

'You got that right,' she assured, before having them all dragged to their feet.

They were conveyed past an open back entrance of an institution that presented as a place of opulence and pleasure — at least for the Valoureans and Phemorian women who frequented it. The men, some taking pleasure in their service and others being coerced with torture and devices designed to assure compliance, appeared pretty much as the Valourean had defined Yasper earlier — breeding machines to populate this planet with more women. The Valourean in charge explained that they had the technology to ensure all the offspring of the Phemorian seeding stations remained female.

Beyond the pleasure house were the psychic containment cells, where the house whores were caged to be fed and stored until desired. Here the males of the AMIE crew were each thrown, naked, wet and shivering, into a dark concrete cell containing only a toilet.

'D ... *amn*.' Leal quivered, lifting himself off the freezing floor in the hope that the toilet seat might be a warmer perch, but the stainless steel was like ice. He hugged knees to chest to seek relief in his own body warmth. It seemed logical that this was part of the submission process — a warm bed under any conditions did seem an attractive option right now. The scenes he'd just witnessed replayed in his mind, chilling him to the core and his body shivered even more violently.

'Hey, Navigator!'

Leal recognised the voice, but it was not either of the men he'd been hauled in here with. He got to his feet, staggered to the door, and was devastated to see Mythric peering through the small barred window of the cell opposite. 'What are you doing here?'

'Never mind me,' Mythric stammered and slurred his words. 'What are you doing here?'

'The Qusay ordered her Valoureans to destroy the ship and take us hostage.' Leal was in too much pain to be delicate; he just delivered the devastating news frankly.

'They got you all?' Mythric sounded close to despair.

'Not all,' Leal uttered.

'The boss?' Mythric queried.

'No.'

'The captain?'

Leal found his emotion and choked on it a moment. 'The captain is dead ... he was on board the ship when —'

'That defies belief! Are you sure the Qusay gave the order?' Mythric was clearly gutted and unwilling to accept the truth.

'According to General Prochazka.' Leal was only repeating what he'd been told. 'Her orders were to do AMIE as much harm as possible and find Thurraya.'

'And did they find her?' Mythric was clearly concerned for his granddaughter.

'No.' Leal was pleased there was some good news. 'We assume she is with her father, who is also still at large, along with Aurora.'

'Praise the universe,' Mythric uttered, relieved to hear it. 'They haven't caught my lad.'

'Of course they haven't,' Leal found his humour. 'Who else would be the hero and save all our arses?'

'Argh!' Mythric cried out in pain and gripped the bars to support his stance.

'Have they had you in there?' Leal motioned towards the seeding station.

'No, they've had me otherwise detained, pumped full of pain enhancing crap and interrogated.' He nearly slipped from view, but maintained his grip on the bars and heaved himself up to speak once more. 'My nerves are a little shot.'

'What did they want to know?'

'No idea. Initially I tuned out, eventually I passed out. They dragged you in butt naked, so I assume they took your Juju stones?'

'Correct,' Leal was pissed to concede.

'Then I expect I'll be getting hauled up before her Majesty again, presently.'

'You've spoken with the Qusay?' Leal was shocked to hear this. 'Why has she turned on us?'

'Because she believes we have turned on her.'

The main entrance to the cell block was heard to open, followed by the sound of a battalion of Valoureans entering.

'Don't look so worried,' Mythric said. 'This will be for me.'

'If you know what's going on, then tell me.' Leal lowered his voice as the guards drew nearer. 'If I am to be a man whore, don't I at least deserve to know why?'

As the guards reached them, Mythric clammed up and Leal watched, guilty with relief, as they opened the door to Mythric's cell, and hauled him out, wincing in silent agony.

Leal envied the fact that Mythric was still half clothed. 'How come he gets trousers?'

"Cause he is the Qusay's personal pet,' the Valourean answered, slapping Mythric's behind, whereupon he wailed at last.

'Why him?' Leal thought it odd that the Qusay-Sabah Clarona would take a fancy to the man her sister married.

'Because he is of royal Sermetic stock, aren't you, precious?' She grabbed Mythric by the jaw and Leal wasn't sure if his comrade was hyperventilating from the pain or seething with anger, but he managed to bite his tongue and avoid a further beating. 'Take him away, clean him up.' She looked back to Leal and smiled. 'Are you nice and cold in there? Keep dreaming of a warm bed … because it is coming, I *promise*.' With a wink and a growl, she followed the battalion and left his field of view.

How bad could it be, he wondered. He was a single guy, which would spare him from a lot of the guilt Swithin and Yasper, as married men, would experience. Perhaps he could just close his eyes and think of Kassa? She filled most of his free brain time anyway. She was the first telepathist he'd ever known besides himself, and although the doctor had allowed him to flirt with her and on occasion flirted back, she hesitated to take his advances seriously because of their age difference. Yet, just the thought of her now thawed his frozen core and he felt warmer. What had become of her and the other women on the crew? At least the Phemorians had a reason to keep the men alive as breeding males, but what use would defunct female psychics be? Beyond being syphoned for information, they would be nothing but a threat to national security. 'Damn it!' He gripped the bars, wanting to rip them out and escape. 'This can't be how it ends!' His warm flow of tears turned cold as they streamed down over his cheeks.

Leal hadn't been with the AMIE project very long, and yet he felt more connected to the people on this crew than any of his own family. He believed in the cosmic connection the timekeeper claimed they all had; he just had to keep the faith and know that those crew still at large would be coming for them.

12

EXPLOIT

'That does feel better,' Taren admitted, rubbing her full stomach and finishing her tea. '*Now* my brain is functioning.'

'Yes, you are human,' Ringbalin empathised with a grin. 'And you've calmed down, which is always to one's advantage.'

'How could I not … with Mr Feel-good around?' Taren reached out and gripped his arm in appreciation. 'Thank the universe it was you who escaped …' She'd forgotten for a second that Lucian lay dead, and choking on the statement Taren bowed her head, wanting to retract the remark.

'It's under control,' Ringbalin assured her, gripping her arm with his free hand.

Hope and determination surged into her via their points of contact, and thus Taren raised her head and could smile.

'Just put one foot in front of the other and keep moving forward,' he suggested.

'But in which direction?' Taren appealed for his advice. 'Do I get my father involved in this and risk an international incident … i.e. a war? Do I attempt to rescue our crew alone, and then take on Satomi and her Valoureans?'

Ringbalin opened his mouth to advise.

'Or,' Taren added, 'do I attempt to free my mother from the celestial city and expose Satomi's coup, resulting in civil war on Phemoria?'

Again Ringbalin ventured to speak, but Taren's mind was on a roll.

'But I can't free Mother without first dealing with the curses. One, maybe two, components of which Satomi has in her possession, and the other is only Telmo knows where! If, of course, I even knew where Telmo was?'

'Which brings us back to the idea of finding Jalila Lamus and stealing the crown of Phemoria to ensure it is not disposed of incorrectly,' Ringbalin posed.

'I couldn't focus on that mission without knowing all the crew are safe.' They were priority number one.

'If we go, they will be waiting for us,' Ringbalin reasoned. 'And if we get caught there's no one left in this dimension to save us. Except your father,' he allowed. 'Which leads us back to war.'

'I can do this ...' Taren imagined herself invisible, and as she was still in skin contact with Ringbalin, he vanished also.

'Well, this is weird. *Helpful*,' he granted, as they both stared at the empty space where their bodies should have been. 'But also a *little* freaky.' Ringbalin loosened himself from her grip and appeared across the table from her once again. 'Whoa!'

'They can only catch us if they can find us,' Taren reappeared to say, noting Trance entering the mess hall.

'Thank goodness, *food*!' He made a move towards the facilities.

'What do you think you are doing?' Taren queried his exultation.

'Eating.' He stated the obvious. 'What, you don't feed your prisoners?'

'You are not my prisoner,' Taren argued. 'I thought we'd established that.'

'Your guests then?' Trance stood corrected.

'We don't have guests.' Taren grinned. 'Only working personnel.'

Ringbalin was suppressing his amusement as Trance had walked right into that one.

'All right! Fuck it. I'll work for you.' Trance had a little hissy fit. 'Can I eat now?' He continued his beeline to the food.

'Not so fast.' Taren's objection stalled him once again, and he turned his dark eyes back to her to hear her out. 'If you work for me you have to leave your attitude problem behind you. I only want your skills.'

'Believe it or not I am usually a very pleasant person,' Trance advised her calmly. 'That is, when I have not been kidnapped, forced to break into a crypt, and then possessed! Before narrowly escaping being sucked into another dimension, on an obscure planet, in some bum fuck part of the universe that no one has ever heard of.'

'You mean you're not enjoying the adventure?' Taren queried with a good serve of sarcasm.

'Hardly.' He headed towards the food, feeling at liberty to do so. 'I can assure you that staring at your arse has been the biggest highlight so far.'

'That's attitude,' Taren pointed out that he was breaching terms already.

Trance held a hand to his bleeding heart. 'But at least I am endearing.'

'Now, what were we saying before we were so rudely interrupted?' Taren diverted all attention to Ringbalin.

'I think Jalila Lamus would be helpful in freeing the crew and stealing the crown,' he proffered.

'And she has a thing for you,' Taren noted that was also to their favour.

But Ringbalin shied away from the notion. 'All women have a thing for me, I don't take it personally.'

'You haven't changed at all. With that attitude, the only thing you are ever going to lay is a flower bed,' Trance tossed in his thoughts.

'I'll do whatever is necessary to get our crew free.' Ringbalin ignored his childhood friend, appearing to feel he'd not matured very much since then.

A very large mercenary type of fellow suddenly appeared on their table, whereupon Taren and Ringbalin were both startled to standing.

'I did it!' he announced, as he and Taren made eye contact and recognised one another.

'Harry Cane.' Taren hadn't really given him a thought since she'd left him to his dream life on a remote island in Frujia. 'You don't have PK … how did you find me?'

'Apparently anyone with a Power has access to all of them,' Vadik advised. 'I was guarding a captive for your mercenary, Bob —'

'Bob!' Taren exclaimed, realising he was referring to Zeven.

'Who is Bob?' Trance wandered over, a little wary of the big man. 'Who is this?'

'Valik Corentin.' He stepped down off the table to introduce himself and was delighted when Trance backed right up.

'The Hurricane?' The younger man seemed rather starstruck and wary at once.

Vadik gave a hearty laugh at Trance's reaction. 'Good to know that my reputation still precedes me.'

'You're a fucking legend!' Trance emphasised that was no secret in psychic circles. 'Wanted by two out of four systems in the USS, making you the most wanted psychic alive.'

Taren felt the top of her arm to check her Juju stone was still in place and it was. No one should have been able to find her via psychic means who was not in possession of one of these stones. 'I don't get it,' she uttered aside to Ringbalin.

'He must be one of us,' Ringbalin reasoned, 'or at least on our side.'

'Of course I am,' Vadik cut in. 'Have you not been testing me in order to decide if I can join your crew?'

Taren raised both brows, speechless a moment. 'Is that what Bob said?'

'You didn't even know I was working with him, did you?' Vadik looked a little pissed. 'That lying little sack of shit! I've just spent days honing this fucking talent so that I could warn you they'd gone missing —'

'No, no. Bob speaks on my behalf,' she assured. 'And I happen to desperately need recruits at present, so your timing could not have been better.'

The angry expression faded from the big guy's face.

'We're going to jailbreak my crew from the Valourean prison and then we're going to steal the crown of Phemoria. Are you in?' Taren posed hopefully.

'A real mission, *finally*.' Vadik grinned. 'Shit yeah!'

Mythric was led by the Qusay's guards into the waiting room outside the Phemorian room of court, where he was met by another Valourean all dressed in purple. He knew General Prochazka by reputation only. She had her arse rested on the desk, her arms were folded, and her eyes were shooting daggers in his direction.

'Leave us,' she dismissed his escort, eyeing him over like an insect to be squashed. She waited for the door to close before she spoke. 'So … you are the one who made a whore of my queen and got her killed.'

'And you are the one who murdered my captain and destroyed our ship,' he replied with the same mix of calm and disgust.

'You heard about that?' She smiled, pleased by her recent accomplishments. 'Then you must also realise that your little psychic conspiracy with President Anselm is over.'

'If you say so,' Mythric replied, confident that was not the case.

'Did you really think Phemoria was just going to lie down and be Sermetica's bitch?' She was angered that she could not get a rise out of him.

'Forming a government is not submitting to anything but establishing a constitution,' Mythric pointed out. 'You would be on such a governing body. Do you not want a greater say in the future of Phemoria?'

'I serve the true Qusay, all else is treason!' she insisted. 'Ultimately Anselm seeks to give men the same psychic freedom as women! Personally, I would rather kill every man on Sermetica. Our ancestors should have done so a thousand years ago, then I would not need to be having this conversation.'

'So why did you aid the Princess Satomi to escape there?' Mythric was guessing — Satomi had always kept secret the identity of those who had aided her escape from the clutches of the Phemoray.

Prochazka's eyes narrowed; she was wary of the subject. 'She didn't confide in you, did she?'

'Well, the only other option is that you still serve the Phemoray,' Mythric concluded. The disdain on her face indicated that was certainly not the case. 'If you don't, you would have been the only person capable of getting Satomi off the planet without you finding out about it.' He trapped her and flattered her at once.

She nodded, appearing unimpressed. 'You don't get to speculate upon my agenda, you just cooperate with whatever my Qusay tells you to do, or I'll see you end your days alongside your redundant forefathers in the Pit of the Obstinate.'

'Then you shall only be adding to the damned force that you are trying to disperse,' he told her honestly, and received a back-handed slap to the face.

Okay that scared her, Mythric considered as the sting of her strike peaked and then ebbed.

'Want to speculate some more?' She invited him to provoke her.

'Were you the one who got Khalid out?'

A punch to the jaw sent him staggering back a few paces, but he managed to stay on his feet. *I'll take that as a yes*, he decided.

'I would not aid that abomination!' She vehemently denied it. 'He took the life of the true Qusay.'

'Khalid is not the abomination; it's the curse that attached itself to him the night he was conceived.' Mythric noted a twinkle of fear in the general's eye, a flash of woe, before her expression hardened once again. 'But I suppose you don't know anything about that eith ... er —' Mythric began to suffocate as his windpipe suddenly restricted.

'You don't know anything about me.' She let him breathe enough to speak.

'I ca-ant serve you, if I-I'm dead,' he wheezed.

Prochazka released her hold on his throat, whereupon his windpipe relaxed and he could again breathe freely.

'Better,' she decided. 'Now ... when you see the Qusay, you really should bear in mind that the lives of your crew mates are in your hands, so I would be very careful.'

That did complicate his options somewhat. 'If I cooperate they won't be harmed?' he clarified.

Prochazka roused half a grin. 'I didn't say that. And you are in no position to make deals.' She opened the doors to the courtroom with a thought. 'I shall be keeping a very close eye on your progress, Spyridon Vidor. Betray us, and I shall know of it.' She motioned to the door.

Lose the resentment, Mythric advised himself quietly, sucking up the situation to proceed as advised.

In the chamber the Qusay sat upon the throne wearing the form of her younger sister, Clarona, and a large number of Valoureans stood guard like beautiful, deadly adornments around the inner walls and doors.

As Mythric proceeded towards the Qusay, his diminished appearance seemed to escape her attention; there was not the slightest hint of remorse or compassion.

'Stop there,' she commanded and he obliged. 'Leave us,' she ordered her guard.

Her Valoureans turned with a stomp and proceeded to the closest exit doors, which closed in their wake.

This was unexpected, and although Mythric was pleased to be granted an opportunity to speak with Satomi alone, he was also wary.

'I have decided to give you the opportunity to make good on your claim to assist me.' Satomi motioned to the Juju stones still scattered on the floor of her room of court.

Mythric glanced down to the restraint on his ankle, which vanished before his eyes. 'You are going to trust me?'

'I have a little time before your Powers return, so we shall see,' she informed him as she stood. 'I have had a vision.' She assumed her true appearance before descending the stairs to appeal to him directly.

The sight of her true form was a vision to Mythric; she was as lovely as the day he'd met her. Yet he knew her transformation was only a cruel means to manipulate him as she had already made it clear that she no longer felt anything for him.

'I believe Khalid saved our granddaughter because she is the key to ending the curse of the Phemoray.' She came to a stop several paces in front of him. 'I believe he is getting close to her and her family with the intent to sacrifice her to the pit and claim the planet of his birth in the wake of the Phemoray's demise.'

Mythric was puzzled by her claim as it ran contrary to what Zeven believed, but then maybe their son was being deceived? 'You saw this? You saw Khalid murder Thurraya?'

'No,' she admitted. 'I saw Thurraya take her own life. But I ask you, what would possess such a sweet child to martyr herself in such a fashion when I have the Phemoray contained?'

'And the Soul Keep from Dead Man Downs,' Mythric suggested.

'But there is a third part to the curse,' Satomi continued, neither confirming nor denying the statement. 'The part that attached itself to Khalid during his failed attempt to slay Anselm … without it, I cannot dispel the other two curses for fear the remaining component will be used to resurrect these horrors against Phemoria. Do you know where this missing component is?'

'You speak of Chironjivi,' Mythric acknowledged that much. 'Our son advised me that the evil entity was attached to an amulet that he extracted from Khalid's hand. The cursed item has been contained and hidden, but he did not say where.'

Satomi appeared disappointed. 'You think *me* insane,' she stated and forced a laugh. 'You want me to trust that our son has not been somehow deluded by Khalid, in order to deliver our granddaughter straight into this demon's hands? Assure me that the future heir to the throne is completely safe with our nemesis,' she invited him to convince her.

Mythric was speechless; Zeven's bizarre story of adventures in other universes did seem more like a delusional mind implant than reality.

'In all honesty, Spyridon, you don't know who to believe, do you?' she asserted. 'Welcome to my dilemma.'

'If I help you, will you spare the AMIE crew from interrogation?' Mythric hoped to cut a deal.

'They are rebels conspiring with a usurper,' Satomi insisted.

'As were we!' Mythric stressed. 'They restored your life and rid your kingdom of the Phemoray.'

'Then stole my birthright, whilst aiding my murderous bastard brother and his curse, to only the spirits know what end?' Satomi emphasised. 'I have to get to the truth, do you not see that?'

'The crew don't know anything about our son's movements; only Taren and the captain knew anything —' Mythric's tense drifted into the past when referring to the captain and it made him step back from the situation a little. 'You knew Lucian was a good man; how could you give the order to take his life?'

'Unfortunately for the captain, he was married to my seditious little niece and abetting her to overthrow Phemorian sovereign rule,' Satomi justified.

'You had a hand in the overthrow of the Phemoray,' Mythric pointed out.

'Of course I did! The Phemoray were never meant to rule our Qusay, and their reign of terror and segregation had to end. But at that time I had no idea my niece planned to abdicate her right to the throne and force my sister into forming a democracy! Nor did I realise that I would be resurrected and find need to protest her intention. I am the true Qusay of Phemoria, I believe I know what is best for my planet and my people. My niece has not spent more than a few days here; how could she possibly be in a position to decide what is best for Phemoria? Just because she cannot stomach the sacrifice of leadership doesn't mean a democracy is the answer. Maladaan is a democracy, but the government is run by large corporations and thus they are the most corrupt leadership in the USS!'

She had a point, she had several valid points. 'But what if you are wrong, and you are torturing those who have been truly loyal to your cause?'

'I have only seen true loyalty in one soul since my resurrection, and we both know that soul is not on the AMIE crew.'

'Then just give me some time to prove my loyalty and their innocence,' Mythric appealed.

'I need answers and my general intends to get them,' she told him coolly. 'Bring me the missing component and our granddaughter, and I will reconsider my position.'

'A telepathist could retrieve the information from us far more easily than torture does.' Mythric wasn't a fool, he knew Satomi would not leave anyone living who knew about her coup.

'You should know from your time in the MSS that a telepath cannot read the thoughts of a restrained psychic as the restraining device interferes with the process,' Satomi explained.

'I was only ever involved with the capture side of the process, so I guess I'll have to take your word on that.' Mythric's gut was churning with resentment as he realised every quality he'd once loved about his wife was no longer apparent. She still looked as beautiful as ever she did, but the harsh, merciless façade she now wore as the Qusay of Phemoria was so very unbecoming — and it was not as if it was the Phemoray influencing her decision-making process. He thought his love for Satomi would never waver, but in this moment he had to wonder if he'd met her after she'd become Qusay, would he ever have loved her at all?

'So,' Satomi returned to her throne and was seated. 'Do you still wish to help me? I'll give you a full Phemorian day to complete your mission before I start killing what remains of your crew.'

Only a fool would tell her to stick her mission, as in effect she was giving him what he wanted — if not a chance to prove AMIE's crew were innocent, then a chance to help them escape — plus an opportunity to discover who was deluded in this scenario and who was not. 'Two days,' he appealed.

'Granted,' she concurred, and Mythric didn't have time to thank heavens for having that wish granted. 'Bring the remains of AMIE's rogue crew to me and I shall cease killing their comrades.'

'Wait,' Mythric queried her inference. 'You said I had two days before you kill anyone.'

'I never said that,' Satomi asserted, 'and now you are inspired to complete all my requests in one day. It shouldn't be too hard; just find my niece.'

Clearly, to argue terms was only going to make his predicament worse. He walked over to where all the Juju stones lay glistening and retrieved one. 'And if you get everything you want, what then?' He felt a surge of energy move through him upon exposure to the Juju. Contact with the celestial force washed away his ill will and gave him a burst of vitality that lessened the pain of his injuries.

'Then we will know the truth and can judge accordingly,' the Qusay reasoned. 'What you don't seem to have considered is that I am right. I am giving you the opportunity to save our son from himself and our granddaughter from Khalid and his curse.'

For the first time since Mythric had entered the room he detected true emotion in Satomi's voice at her first mention of their son — it seemed she'd not had all feeling for him swept from her consciousness as she claimed. If she was lying about that, then maybe she was lying about having her love for him erased too?

'Or maybe this is just an elaborate way for you to allow me to escape, before you really settle into the ruthless business of ruling Phemoria?' He took several steps closer, to more carefully assess her reaction.

'Do you wish to die, Spyridon?' She warned him against coming any closer.

'I did a moment ago … but now I do not,' he confessed with a little more exuberance.

Her eyes narrowed, wary of his change in mood. 'Then go, before I reconsider and toss you back to my general.'

'I will get to the bottom of this,' Mythric assured her. 'I will report back here this time tomorrow with a full account.'

'Successful is what you meant to say, I'm sure.' Clearly, Satomi was not open to further negotiation, yet something told him that there was more going on beneath the Qusay's cool façade than she was letting on. Regardless of whether she still cared for her family, if personal feelings clashed with political duty there was only so much she could do. She may have given the order to finish Lucian Gervaise and his project, but when push came to shove, was she really ruthless enough to slay her own family? If she was, then they may as well have left the Phemoray in power. What he truly regretted was that she felt she needed to be so heartless to achieve her aims.

Mythric envisioned himself fully dressed, and as his vision manifested it was clear his Power had been restored and he was fit and able to depart.

Absent the resentment caused by his recent torture and the captain's death, Mythric found himself sympathetic to Satomi's position. This was indeed the Satomi he had first met — alone, resourceful and very determined. But beneath that veil of sovereignty there was a soul as sweet as any he'd known and he hated the thought of that woman being quashed on the same resentful path her mother had been forced to take. He wanted to reassure her, and believe himself, that the situation would end well; it was all a misunderstanding and somehow their family would survive this unscathed. But only one of his kin could ultimately be right about Khalid and the void between his wife and their son was expanding fast! He feared that gap would soon be beyond bridging — if it was not already.

'Keep heart,' was all the encouragement he could muster in parting, and his sentiment only caused the Qusay's scowl to deepen.

'Heart does not factor into this; you either bring me what I ask for or your new friends die a sad and painful death.'

Mythric suppressed the urge to react to her threat, and held out the Juju stone towards her. 'We are all one,' he told her sincerely. 'If you would only touch one of these, you would realise that.'

'I don't know what magic my niece wove into those charms, but she is manipulating you all as surely as the Phemoray controlled my mother!' Satomi glared at him. 'Deny that you cannot think ill of Taren while you are wearing it?'

'Or anyone! I cannot lie, or do undue harm to any,' he pointed out, and the Qusay's expression was ever more bitter. 'The truth is you don't understand the true purpose of these stones.'

'And you do?' Satomi proffered.

'Was your spirit not right beside me when Taren gave it to me?' Mythric posed, although he'd always had trouble recalling that moment himself.

'My spirit was only drawn to you when you mourned me, which was not the case in the instance you mention,' she replied.

Still, the statement barely registered with Mythric, as after all these years of trying to recall the moment he'd received his Juju stone, he was finally recalling it with blinding clarity.

He remembered sitting in the teeming rain on Oceane, and being bathed by the celestial light there for the first time. Taren had delivered him to the virgin planet to be healed in the wake of a near fatal beating he'd received at the hands of Valoureans, and having been restored to full health from the brink of death, he'd felt high on life and at peace.

'*And how many names do you have?*' Taren asked and he'd picked himself up off the ground to answer the rather odd question, for she was not talking about aliases in this instance and at the time he'd known that.

'*Many. Although the one you may know me best by is —*'

'*Rhun,*' they both answered at once.

Mythric gasped; he didn't grasp the full significance of the memory, but he suspected that it might corroborate his son's story. However, here was a less than ideal place to speculate.

'Spyridon!' It was only when the Qusay roared that he realised that he'd not heard her calling for his attention.

'My apologies.' He realised he must have seemed a little vague, but in truth he was feeling both panicked and excited. 'I must go.'

'Agreed,' the Qusay concurred. 'The clock is ticking.'

Mythric had to speak with Zeven, and so brought to mind the last place he'd seen him.

Without her restraint casting a haze over her thoughts, Kalayna had figured out how to reverse the function of the psychic neutraliser so that it became a shield against psychic attack.

She had found it fairly easy to remove the device, and to disengage its primary function, whilst still having the signal light remain active to avoid suspicion. But after spending hours inspecting the circuitry, Kalayna had dreams that night that disclosed how some rewiring would completely reverse the system function.

Kalayna had experienced this kind of technological waking dream before. This was how she had discovered and fashioned the missing component that had restarted the oldest and only defunct inter-system gateway — located in the Oceane system. And now that she had envisioned the alterations, it made sound sense, from an engineering point of view, that the redesign would work.

By the time Ayliscia awoke, Kalayna had completed the conversion of both their devices. They had been bitching at each other and faking fights since they'd been thrown together, in the hope that they might swap Kalayna to another cell with another of their crew mates.

Ayliscia was a remote viewer like Aurora, and Kalayna felt if she had a Power, her technological mind was it. But neither of their talents was going to be able to free them all, as all the workings of the door locks were located on the outside of the cells, out of reach. They needed to get Kalayna in with Jazmay, as the ex-Valourean had PK and she could shapeshift.

As Kalayna replaced the device on her cell mate's ankle, Ayliscia was hurling abuse at her and bashing the shit out of her own hand. Then, grabbing Kalayna's tiny screwdriver, she stabbed her hand with it and smeared the blood under Kalayna's nose and across her cheek. 'Make this look good,' she whispered, as Kalayna stuffed her tools back into the waistband of her trousers. 'You ready?'

'Don't hold back.' Kalayna nodded, and was hauled out of the corner by her shirt, and hurled into the middle of the room.

'You fucking bitch!' Kalayna wiped some of the blood from her face. 'I'm sick of this shit! I want out!' she yelled, turning circles as if unaware of where the surveillance was.

'And I am sick of your whining! You don't have to worry about them killing you, I'll do it myself!' Ayliscia came after her, and Kalayna dodged.

'Get me out of here! She's fucking nuts!' Kalayna yelled through the tiny window, and seeing Kassa and Amie observing her through the tiny window of their cell across the way, she gave them a wink.

'No one is coming to save your precious little arse!' Ayliscia grabbed hold of her from behind and leaned in close to whisper, 'The guards are on their way. Good luck.'

Ayliscia yanked Kalayna from the door and spun her around to take a swing at her; Kalayna ducked and crash tackled Ayliscia to the floor, and much hair pulling and struggling ensued.

The door to their cell opened and they were violently separated by Valoureans. 'Get off!' Kalayna was dragged out into the corridor, whilst Ayliscia was held down on the floor by the foot of the guard accompanying.

'Don't move.' The guard backed up and closed the door.

'A private cell for you, then,' the Valourean suggested, as Kalayna held a hand over the bloodied side of her face. 'I need the doctor.' Kalayna motioned to the cell Kassa and Amie were in.

The guard peered inside at the two women. 'Which one is the doctor?'

'The brunette,' Kalayna informed before the women could speak up, but this was not the truth, and she hoped Amie and Kassa would not correct her on it. The doctor was actually a redhead and a telepath, which again was not really going to aid to open the cell doors. Kalayna didn't know much about Amie Gervaise, so she was taking a gamble and hoping her talent might be more beneficial to their cause.

The cell door was unlocked, and Kalayna was cast in.

'Doc, clean her up,' the Valourean commanded Amie.

'Why … does she need to look her best for interrogation?' came Amie's snide reply, which detracted from Kassa's bemusement.

Kalayna didn't know the crew very well, and clearly Kassa wondered if she'd got them confused, but she said nothing as she was hauled out and thrown in with Ayliscia.

'Some food would be good!' Amie yelled out the cell window after the Valoureans as they locked the door closed.

'Dead people don't need food,' the guard informed and left.

Amie turned to question Kalayna, who had retreated to sit on the toilet. But when she removed the restraint from her leg, and then held a finger to her lips, no further explanation was required.

'Well then.' Amie grabbed a towel and wet it down and moved in closer to her patient. 'Let's assess the damage then, shall we?' She raised the leg wearing the restraint and rested her foot on the seat between Kalayna's legs. The engineer got to work on converting it.

The hut Mythric once established on Oceane was completely abandoned. Mythric had hoped to find his son and family here, but there was no hint as to where they or the rest of the crew had fled, and with AMIE destroyed here had been his best guess. He tried willing himself to Zeven, Aurora, Thurraya, even Khalid, but when no shift in location was forthcoming, he began to fear that they may have been on board AMIE when she blew. That was the only explanation for why he could not locate them using psychic means. Unless, of course, Satomi was right, and Khalid was using some dark magic to keep them hidden.

'Damn all these curses!' He grew frustrated with speculation, knowing he was very pressed for time. 'Who do I believe?' He leaned on the railing of the covered verandah, watching the rain fall and hoping that the enlightened being that tended this planet might grant him some insight. 'Rhun,' he wrapped his mouth around the unusual name. 'Why do I know this name?'

He gasped as his memory flew back to the day he'd met Zeven in President Anselm's office. Zeven had come breezing through the door and, laying eyes on Mythric for the first time, had exclaimed, *Rhun? How did you get here?*

Was that the extent of the epiphany? Why did Zeven and Taren call him by this name? Why had he called himself by it? *Rhun. Who is Rhun? Am I Rhun?* Mythric paused, feeling the same anticipation as someone who had found the secret combination to unlock a mysterious door, but was he going to like what he found on the other side? *I AM Rhun.* He repeated the mantra many times, and the Juju stone began reverberating under his hand.

A barrage of memories of other lives in foreign climes flashed through his mind — like a recording on fast forward. Honing in on one instance in particular, his conscious perception was filled by a vision.

He was reclining in the seat of a large, white, egg-shaped capsule that was opened at the front, and before him stood a tiny woman.

No taller than a child, she was dressed in a dark blue hooded robe that covered her tiny form completely and directed his attention to her pale angelic face and her most striking feature — her large eyes of brilliant blue.

'You are sad,' she observed. 'It was as you remember?'

'Worse,' he admitted, his voice hoarse with hurt, and he swallowed hard as he looked at her to catch her reaction.

But she didn't bat an eyelid. 'Not to worry. We know what must be done. We are resolved.'

'I cannot allow it,' he insisted. 'I cannot in good conscience save my people, if this is the cost.'

'The choice is not yours to make.' Her tone was more gentle now. 'Our only worry is Wu Geng … the one you call Khalid. For thirty years, while you were collecting the rest of your timekeepers from among the Zhou, you left your one-time nemesis in our care. During that time we were the compassionate mentor Wu Geng has needed and never had. Our pupil has spiritually advanced beyond expectation under our guidance and we worry he will not cope well with the forthcoming events. We ask that you will protect our student from his own grief in the wake of this event.' She held his gaze in heartfelt appeal. 'It is all we ask in return for this service. Promise us …'

The vision passed and Mythric found himself again staring at the pouring rain; and in the wake of the experience he had mixed emotions. This could not have been some fantasy he'd dreamt up to validate his son's claim. He had no idea who or *what* the being was to whom he'd made this pledge, but Mythric knew his imagination had not spawned her, he just wasn't that creative. If

Zeven wasn't lying and they had pledged to protect Khalid from himself, did that then mean Satomi was wrong in her stance of wanting to kill them all?

'Not really,' he answered himself. From what he could tell, no one was in the wrong per se, which made it mighty difficult to pick a side. By his reasoning, they all had a common goal — destroy the curses. The trouble was no one trusted anyone else to do it.

From beneath the storm clouds in the distance Mythric spotted the lights of craft descending towards the great ocean that lay beyond this, the only small landmass on this planet, and the shape of the craft was unmistakeable.

'AMIE.' Mythric was stunned to see that the reports of her destruction had been false! Perhaps the death of the captain had also been a fabrication? He held an image of the captain in his mind and envisioned himself in his company, but the sound of the rainfall persisted as Mythric's will was again denied.

Taren Gervaise was of course the most obvious person to target next, but he dared not join her without knowing her current movements in case she was already running a mission to save the crew. Thus Mythric made the flight deck of AMIE his next target location — someone was flying that vessel and whoever it was surely had some insight to lend to his quest.

Before departing on her mission to free the crew, Taren parked AMIE deep underwater in the quiet, still depths of Oceane's waters. By her reasoning the Valoureans could not have found AMIE via psychic means due to the large hunk of Juju stone she had placed at the vessel's core as per Zeven's advice. The Phemorians must have used a picture of the defunct inter-system gateway to teleport their craft into the Oceane star system and then would have been able to locate the vessel the old-fashioned way, although the vessel had been cloaked and should not have been trackable by radar. At present the Phemorians believed the vessel was no more, so just in case they decided to check if Taren had restored it, she would conceal it below sea level, as AMIE was the only large craft in the

USS with this kind of deep sea capability. Hindsight was a killer; they should have taken this precaution days ago!

'No one could have foreseen anyone finding us so swiftly,' Ringbalin countered Taren's self lashing.

'I should have known, that day in her courtroom,' Taren commented. 'If shifters could take her form, then they obviously had inherited her Power also.'

'Satomi awarding all her shapeshifters all of her Powers was an unthinkable move,' Ringbalin said.

'Satomi did what?'

Taren's heart leapt to hear Mythric's voice as she dropped anchor and turned to find her uncle flabbergasted by the conversation he walked in on.

'It's true.' Taren raised herself from the pilot's seat — she had no idea how to fly this vessel; she had guided the descent using her telekinetic ability. 'I was confronted by a whole bunch of her in the courtroom. And whilst I was in Heavensgate informing my father of this, Valoureans —'

'— took the ship,' Mythric cut in. 'I've just come from prison on Phemoria, where I ran into Leal.'

'They're still alive?' Taren was relieved when Mythric nodded. His expression was not encouraging, however. 'But I thought you were with Zeven?' She was hoping to have some news of him, as her cousin's tenacity would be a very useful asset right now.

'Where is Zeven?' Mythric jumped at the opportunity to ask.

'You don't know then?' Taren realised.

'Know what?' Mythric appealed with a good serve of desperation.

'Hold on.' Taren hesitated to brief him, as her reasoning won out over the shock of seeing him. 'How did you escape from the clutches of the Valoureans?'

Everyone in the room took a step away from Mythric, except for Vadik, who took a threatening step towards him.

'Why are you here?' Mythric had assisted Taren to make Vadik disappear off the MSS radar, so he knew who he was.

'To protect the boss's interests,' Vadik advised in a distrustful manner.

'Satomi will be seeking Zeven and Thurraya.' Taren queried Mythric's motive, which to her mind was more in doubt than Vadik's loyalty at this point.

'Absolutely correct,' Mythric confirmed. 'She has given me one Phemorian day to find Thurraya, Chironjivi's curse, and bring the rest of the AMIE crew to her court, before she starts killing those members of our crew that she has incarcerated.'

Taren lost her ability to breathe as the threat sunk in. 'And if she has released you to do this, she shall be guarding her prisoners twice as closely.'

'That's exactly right,' Mythric concurred. 'So if you would like to assist me with any of this, I would be most obliged. Where are Zeven and my granddaughter?'

'They've been sucked into another dimension,' Trance piped up to inform him rather casually.

'Who are you?' Mythric queried.

'Another orphan your Grand Mai fostered,' Trance advised, but Mythric was already looking to Taren for answers.

'What is he talking about?' Mythric pushed.

'It's true. Zeven took Khalid to Oceane in the hope of healing him —'

'I know that part,' Mythric attempted to speed her explanation along.

'Khalid's blood opened a portal to another realm of existence. All in Zeven's company appear to have entered and not yet returned.'

'And you are not concerned by this?' Mythric was clearly alarmed.

'Of course I am concerned,' Taren stressed. 'Lucian has gone through the portal after them to investigate.'

'But word is that the captain was killed when the ship was destroyed?' Mythric attempted to sort fact from fiction.

'He was killed.' Taren swallowed hard in the wake of the bitter statement. 'We submitted his body to stasis, where Satomi's body once lay. His spirit was the only one of us who could traverse the collapsing portal between worlds. That was late yesterday, I've heard nothing since.'

Mythric's eyes glazed over as he processed the information. 'How am I going to deliver them to Phemoria tomorrow?'

'Who gives a fuck about tomorrow, if we rescue the hostages today!' Vadik voiced his view very clearly. 'They are not even going to see us!' Vadik did Taren's vanishing trick, and seconds later Mythric was startled by a tap from someone he couldn't see.

'You're invisible.' Mythric was stunned as Vadik had not possessed any of the kinetic abilities the last time they'd met. 'I must learn to do that.'

'It's really not that difficult,' Taren advised. 'You just have to remain focused.'

'I can see him,' Trance held up a finger to confess, whereupon Vadik made himself visible again so that his frown could be seen. 'The Valoureans will have clairvoyants among their ranks, so that plan is not foolproof.'

'Same with me?' Taren vanished, feeling she would fare better as she was wearing a Juju stone.

Trance frowned. 'I can't see your form just a whole lot of light.'

'Shit!' Taren appeared once more.

'You'd need a hands-off impressionist to mask your presence altogether,' Trance advised.

'Amie is an impressionist, but I don't know if she can do it remotely, without contact. I have done it too, but I need contact.' Taren pored over their options.

'Amie's Power will not return immediately upon having her restraint removed,' Mythric advised. 'Although the Juju does speed the restoration process.'

'Still,' Trance noted, 'you do have emo-boy here.' He motioned to Ringbalin. 'Who can just charm them all into submission.'

Taren smiled at this. 'It wouldn't be the first time.'

Ringbalin forced an unconfident grin, and pushed his glasses back up his nose. 'I don't remember any of those instances, so they don't really count. And if anything should happen to —'

They all stood awaiting his conclusion, as he rethought it.

'— anyone I care about,' he finally phrased his point, 'then I may not be so charming.'

'Even psychically restrained, our crew are very resourceful,' Taren returned the encouragement he'd given her earlier today. 'I'm sure we are not the only ones making plans for their release.'

'So we are doing this?' Vadik was still keen on the idea.

Taren looked to Mythric for his thoughts.

'In this other universe my son claims you have visited, what name was I known by?'

The query came right out of left field for Taren, but she was happy to answer. 'You had many lives there and many incarnations, but the one I remember best is Rhun.'

The information seemed to pain him and bring him joy all at once. 'The captain is mendable, just as Satomi was, if we can get Ringbalin and Swithin to him.' He got straight in his mind what Taren already knew, and he nodded to confirm his reasoning.

'The ship I have restored,' she added to assure him that she held no bitterness towards Satomi. 'I understand why she has done what she has, but I want you to know that were I in the same position, I would not have killed you to spite her.'

'And that is what sets your course of action apart from hers,' Mythric realised, finding his truth a little regrettable. 'The way I see it, Satomi can't do anything else she will regret if our crew are safe with us.'

The pain of Lucian's death was difficult to swallow, but Taren forced a smile and nodded to concur with his reasoning.

'I'm so sorry this has happened.' Mythric's eyes were brimming with tears. 'Could we just go back to that fateful dinner party and put Thurraya to bed early?'

'If only it were that simple.' Taren had contemplated the same thing herself. 'But I couldn't handle all this again, half of which I am still in the dark about! I have to trust Zeven is coming through for us. I've never seen him more passionate about anything as he has been about defending Khalid.'

'He doesn't know what has befallen us here.' Mythric was not so optimistic.

'If Lucian found him, he does.' Taren bit her lip. 'We just need to get our crew clear and buy us all some time.'

'You are just completely fucking insane, aren't you?' Trance fronted up to Taren to point out. '*My Lord Vidor*,' Trance motioned to Mythric, 'has just told you that he's supposed to deliver the remaining crew, i.e. *us*, to the Qusay of Phemoria, i.e. *his wife*, and you're still more than happy to allow him to aid you to break into a Phemorian prison to release your crew … does this not scream *trap* to you?'

'You don't have to worry, as you won't be coming,' she advised, thus his opinion ceased to matter.

'I thought you said you needed me.' Trance was deflated.

'When Lucian gets back, I will,' Taren clarified. 'Until then you can stay put in case the captain or Zeven try to make contact.'

'You're just going to leave me here?' He motioned out the front shield window to the deep depths of the ocean of an alien planet, where no one would ever find him. 'What if you are captured?'

'Well then, we'll be sure and let someone know you're here.'

'And what if you're all killed?' Trance was not reassured.

'Do you ever stop worrying about your own skin?' Vadik came and stood over Trance.

'You're really not helping me with that.' Trance shrank into a seat.

'How about I just kill you now and save you any further worry?' Vadik offered.

'I'm good.' Trance waved them goodbye and Vadik backed off to follow Taren from the flight deck to suit up for the mission. 'I suppose if I get really stuck I could just hack the system and teach myself how to fly this thing?' He turned his seat around to face the workstation before him, and began clicking away.

'You're a hacker?' Taren's interest was piqued as she returned to his company, grinning.

'No,' Trance admitted, both flattered and concerned by her sudden interest. 'But one of my spirit contacts was something of a hacktivist.'

Taren's expression was a little tortured as she slapped a hand down upon his shoulder. 'Looks like I can use you after all.'

*

In the remote wilds of Phemoria's deepest jungle, where it rained a good part of the year, lay the remains of a once grand civilisation. The origins of these ruins harked back to before the time of the sexual revolution and the male-dominated oppression that had spawned that revolt, to a time when the sexes had lived in harmony on Phemoria and worshipped nature, the sun and stars. The jungle had swallowed up much of the outer city dwellings, but the central palace still stood. Although looted and stripped of its riches long ago, the motif carved into the stone walls and columns still remained, as a reminder of how joyful and harmonious life had once been here.

The general thought the artwork sad and rolled her eyes every time she viewed the pictures of men and women lovingly entwined. 'Fucking deluded,' she would say. She hated this place, but as it was inaccessible to anyone who didn't have PK, and only very few Phemorians knew it existed at all, it was the perfect place to hide the Soul Keep. The main room of court here was very dark, which was a requirement if one did not want to weaken the ghostly crew's already depleted power.

As Prochazka entered the dark chamber, she desired all the torches therein to light up, and it was so. The general did not break her stride until she reached the centre of the chamber. 'You are all fucking useless ectoplasm!' she insisted as she came to a standstill and her voice echoed around the seemingly empty space.

A wind stirred in the still chamber, and then whipped around the room. '*Did you not find the vessel you sought, General?*' the entity asked in many harsh, muffled voices.

Once upon a time she could not see or hear the ghostly crew; she'd had to rely on that rotting pile of flesh and bone they'd once called their leader to convey their sentiments. Since then she had learned that the crew could make themselves seen or heard as desired; it was getting them to respond when they didn't wish to that was more difficult. But since the true Qusay had taken her advice and passed on her genetic code to all her shapeshifters, Prochazka included, she had many psychic abilities she'd not had access to before — like the kinetic arts and clairvoyance. Her psychic sight was underdeveloped and she only saw brief flashes of the spectres. She heard more than saw them.

'Yes, I did,' she replied winningly. 'But Thurraya Vidor and her parents were not on it!'

'*Not our fault,*' came the reply, as the spirits of the dead men circled around her.

'I have told you the true names of the ones I seek; why can you not locate them?' Prochazka demanded.

'*For the same reason you can't: their light is too bright, we cannot stand in its presence. We can spot their light shield but cannot see into it to define who or what is inside. And the planet they are hovering near is all light!*'

The reply only pissed her off. 'Then what use are you? I may as well cast this vat into the closest galactic centre and be rid of your curse!'

She had led them to believe that she had laid claim to their curse to further her own ends — and not to seek revenge for the last time they had betrayed her — and that was true, in so far as her ends were whatever served Phemoria.

'*We are weak, General,*' the horde defended. '*We need sustenance to fortify our darkness, only then do we stand a chance to penetrate the light on Oceane and see what lies beneath.*'

'Don't make me repeat myself,' she cautioned. 'I am not going to feed you Phemorians!'

'*Then don't feed us Phemorians,*' the ghosts suggested. '*There are three other planets full of females; you have prisoners at your disposal — exploit some of them for the sake of your mission.*'

'Men spill blood just as readily,' she suggested.

'*We have plenty of male souls already!*' they hissed in revolt. '*We need women, GIRLS! Little girls! Babies, even better!*'

'Fuck you and your fucked up perversions!' She served them all the finger, which just happened to be the digit sporting the ring that bound the ghostly crew to her in obedience. Once upon a time the ring had only protected her from the evil force, now it did as it was always supposed to do. She had learned from past failures and would not be hoodwinked again. She saw no point in continuing this conversation, and headed for the exit.

'A *patron is supposed to supply sustenance or how can service be rendered! If you seek to squander our power, we shall align to another more cooperative, to whom we can be of true service.*'

t'You can only serve one patron at once, Chironjivi taught me that.' Prochazka brushed off the threat. 'So while I have your ring, I guess you are all screwed.'

'*For you to seek us out you must also be pretty* screwed!' they bantered, still confident of swaying her moral code towards her own sex. '*See you soon, General,*' the ghostly crew taunted. '*When you run out of options.*'

As Prochazka strode out of the central palace chamber and into the natural light of the drizzly day, she extinguished the torches in her wake. The crew's taunt made her furious — she was fast running out of options.

Out of the crew she had captured, Spyridon Vidor was bound to know more about his son's movements than the rest of their AMIE captives, and her Valoureans had learned nothing from him. If he failed to deliver the Qusay the rest of the crew still at large then Prochazka held little hope that any of the AMIE prisoners would prove any more helpful in their hunt for Satomi's heir.

Still, she also knew better than to assume anything, or to sit idly by and wait for the outcome. Despite her Qusay's wish that the crew of AMIE be left alive in the wake of their interrogation, if one or two accidentally died or vanished Prochazka felt confident of being able to offer up a valid excuse for the bungle.

Upon returning to the security station inside the psychic prison complex where the women of AMIE were being held, the general consulted the Valoureans on duty. 'Are any of the prisoners giving you trouble?'

'This one, Kalayna Zuri,' her lieutenant advised, bringing up her file on the database. 'We've had to shift her to another cell as she claims she's not part of the crew, but was kidnapped by them.'

'Well, she won't be missed then,' Prochazka concluded happily. Observing Kalayna on camera, she decided this prisoner would serve her purposes nicely, and she certainly wasn't a native Phemorian. 'She looks to be the youngest also … very good. Have her brought to me.'

The general eyed over the remaining women, spotting Jazmay Cardea, who had resigned her commission in the Valoureans to pursue science studies on Maladaan years ago. 'Let's see how forthcoming the traitor is when witnessing her husband whored before her eyes.'

The lieutenant smiled, delighted by the mandate. 'I'll see to it personally, General.'

'I want some serious rifts shot through this crew,' Prochazka elaborated. 'Screw with their solidarity, do some serious emotional damage! Am I understood?'

The lieutenant's eyes widened at the passion behind the demand, but her enthusiasm didn't wane. 'I shall do my worst.'

1 3

EVIL TO BETRAY

Kalayna was just finishing up the conversion of Amie's neutraliser when the doors to their cell block were heard to open, and she shoved the said item in between her ample breasts and hid her tools, before joining Amie at the cell window to see what was happening.

There were eight Valoureans marching down the corridor, the first four of whom stopped outside Jazmay's cell. 'Time for you to see how well we are enjoying your man whore,' the lieutenant advised Jazmay as she unlocked the cell.

'You'll never have a clue about men,' came Jazmay's reply, as the Valoureans were seen to enter the cell she occupied with her son, Fari.

A scuffle ensued, and the second foursome of Valoureans stopped outside the cell to catch the action.

'Give me any problems and I shall bring your son with us.' The lieutenant's threat brought a swift conclusion to Jazmay's protest, although Fari insisted he did want to come.

Kalayna looked to Amie, who had a horrified expression on her face — clearly wondering whether she was next to see her husband abused before her eyes. 'It's okay, you are free,' Kalayna whispered, 'but Jazmay is not so fortunate.' As she reached inside her shirt to sneak Amie's device back to her, she noted the second quad of Valoureans were proceeding towards them, so she left it where it was.

285

'The general wants to see you,' advised the Valourean leading the group, and Kalayna was stunned to note they were referring to her.

'Me? Why me?' Kalayna wondered if they'd spotted her tinkering. Fortunately Amie was wearing long trousers and none of the guards noted her restraint was absent.

'Maybe she likes them young, dumb and full of complaints?' This guard waited outside the unlocked door and encouraged only Kalayna to exit.

Although she was fearful of her destination, Kalayna saw an opportunity to aid Jazmay, and so exited swiftly and took off up the corridor ahead of her guard. Out in front, Jazmay was exiting her cell on her own recognisance, whilst two guards awaited her further up the corridor, and two held back her son from following.

Was she really about to attack one of the best warriors on their crew? She was asking to have her lights knocked out. 'This is all your fault, you shapeshifting freak!'

Jazmay turned about, stunned to see Kalayna launching herself towards her.

With a high jump, knees tucked tight to her chest, Kalayna hit Jazmay with her full force and knocked her to the ground, pinning her arms to the floor with her knees. Shielded from sight by her masses of long thick hair, Kalayna shoved the converted neutraliser down between Jazmay's equally ample breasts.

'What the?' Jazmay was confused as, still making a good show of choking her, Kalayna leaned close to whisper.

'It will block your restraint.'

At least, reason denoted that the signal from her psychic amplifier would cancel out the signal of the neutraliser. As long as these devices were functioning and close, one did not need to be wearing one for it to have effect — they emitted a signal regardless; the band design was simply for locking the device on a prisoner.

Jazmay's eyes flashed wide in recognition as Kalayna was dragged off her by several Valoureans — spitting, kicking and cussing.

'What the fuck is wrong with you?' Jazmay still appeared confused and as the Valoureans pulled her back up to standing, she had daggers in her eyes. 'I won't forget this,' she threatened, as she was hauled out of the cell block ahead of Kalayna.

'Do I look like I give a shit?' Kalayna kicked out after her, but an elbow to the face snatched away all conscious thought.

If her ex-comrades in the Valoureans felt that they were going to drive a wedge between herself and her husband, Jazmay felt they had a rude shock in store. Clearly they were going to play the emotional torture card, which she could adjust her mind-set to withstand — it was Yasper's emotional and physical wellbeing that concerned her more.

She was driven clear across the huge prison complex to a grand building located on the outskirts. No one needed to tell her where they were going; Jazmay was familiar with the pleasure-house-cum-seeding-stable most frequented by the Qusay's guard. She had visited this place herself in her distant past, to use and abuse the men here, as that was a Phemorian's idea of pleasure. She looked back on herself at that time and considered how miserable she must have been to find pleasure in the pain of another. Perhaps she hadn't spiritually evolved too much since, as the idea of beating the shit out of the lieutenant who kept pushing her about was very appealing.

'You remember this place … traitor?' The lieutenant strapped Jazmay to the wall in one of the private torture chambers that was decked out like a luxurious bedroom, complete with restraints on the walls and all the furnishings.

'Are you going to try and impress me with your sexual prowess?' Jazmay made it clear that she found their efforts all rather droll. 'I'm sorry, but tough chicks just don't do it for me any more.'

Her captor gripped a handful of Jazmay's hair and yanked her head to one side. 'By the time I'm done with your man whore, he won't do it for you any more *either*.' With another jarring yank, the lieutenant let her go and backed up, her expression smug. 'I have something very special planned.'

As much as she wanted to wipe that look off her captor's face, Jazmay tried another tack. 'What do you want from us? If we knew anything about Thurraya's whereabouts, don't you think we would have told you to save AMIE and the captain? We don't know anything!'

'Which makes you both expendable!' The lieutenant grinned in conclusion. 'Lucky me.'

Jazmay could feel her blood starting to boil. 'Harm my husband in any way, and you will not live to regret it.'

Her captor had a chuckle at this, and then her expression soured. 'You really love him. *Sweet.* All the more fun for me.'

'Go fuck yourself!' Jazmay wanted to rip her limb from limb.

'Fortunately, I've made other plans.' She blew Jazmay a kiss and left the chamber along with her company.

As soon as Jazmay was alone she began testing her PK, by willing herself free. When that didn't work, she focused on a pitcher of water hoping to make it rise off the table, but nothing — not even a ripple in the water. As a shapeshifter she attempted to turn herself to water and slide out of her bonds, but again she had no success. She realised that Powers took a little time to return once freed from a neutraliser's restraint, but it had to be getting on to an hour since Kalayna had attacked her.

The doors opened and three Valoureans hauled Yasper, naked and shivering, into the room — the lieutenant was not with them.

'Ladies, as much as I love being in a room that is not a steady sub-zero temperature, I really have to decline the extracurricular activities,' he bantered, and it was heart-warming to Jazmay to see that Yasper still had his humour. 'My wife is really not going to be happy about this.' He attempted to resist being strapped to the bed, and copped a punch to the gut that winded him long enough to secure him in place.

'That's what we are hoping.' A Valourean directed his attention to Jazmay. 'You chat among yourselves; our lieutenant will be with you presently.' She backed off Yasper and left with the others.

'Aww shit, Jaz …' Yasper sounded more panicked than he had before he'd spotted her. 'I don't want you to witness this.'

Jazmay shrugged, as it seemed they had no choice in the matter; that pitcher of water still wasn't budging for her. 'Perhaps we can just pretend it's some sadomasochistic adventure we dreamt up for our anniversary?'

'I like your thinking,' Yasper nodded, forcing a grin. 'But I think this is favouring one of your fantasies, rather than one of mine.'

'So, indulge me,' she said, hoping to lessen the discomfort of the situation for him. 'I give you full consent to comply with whatever she asks of you. Don't try to resist,' she warned, knowing there were very painful ways to make him comply. 'Just close your eyes and pretend it's me.'

'Jaz!' Yasper objected.

'Please,' Jazmay begged him.

'And what if I cannot?' Yasper appealed. 'If the situation were reversed, you would fight.'

'Yet the outcome would still be the same, only far more damaging, *believe me!*' Jazmay was panicked as she had some idea of what was coming; Yasper didn't. 'You are more than the skin you are in; she may take the vehicle but don't let her break your spirit.'

Yasper was stunned to hear Jazmay speak in metaphysical terms, as she never had before. 'Okay, now I'm really worried.' He yanked at his bonds to test their strength but they held firm.

'Please, Yasper.' Jazmay could feel her own inner panic welling into tears, which would only alarm him more, and she breathed deep to suppress them. 'Oblige her.'

The door opened and a lone woman entered; she had the countenance of a Valourean, but she was not in uniform. Her jet-black hair was plastered up into a ponytail that sprouted from the top of her head, and she wore a long black leather coat and matching high heeled boots. 'Are we all comfortable?' she asked.

'I feel a little underdressed,' Yasper offered up an answer, as Jazmay seemed preoccupied with a pitcher of water on a side table by her.

'Did your wife tell you why you are here?' The femme fatale walked over to the bed and stepped on a button on the floor which raised the bed to an almost vertical position.

'Um …' Yasper found himself face to face with her. 'I think that is rather self-explanatory.'

She found this amusing, and cast a snide glance in Jazmay's direction. 'So she didn't confess?'

'Confess?' Yasper queried.

'That she still works for us,' the lieutenant informed him.

Yasper was a little shocked by the comment and looked to his wife to see her reaction.

'She's lying, Yas—'

The lieutenant grabbed his face to direct his attention towards her own gaze. 'She's been working for us all along … that is how we found the AMIE vessel so easily.' She stroked his naked form as the statement cast a shadow of doubt in his mind. They had not been able to fathom how the Phemorians had managed to find AMIE. 'She is the reason you find yourself in this *happy* situation.' She slapped his thigh with her free hand, and it stung just enough to piss him off. 'You must believe me.' She stared deep into his eyes, and he felt irked. Even though her claim was plausible, he resisted the urge to believe it.

'Yasper,' Jazmay demanded his attention, in a panic. 'Forget what I said before, don't look at her!'

Jasper turned his eyes to his wife, as the lieutenant's grip on his face still held fast. 'Make up your mind, hon.'

'She's an impressionist!'

Yasper suddenly realised that his lack of resistance to this woman's suggestion was not his own doubt at all; she was trying to implant that doubt in him.

'*Man* she sucked you in, didn't she? She knows what I am capable of and is only encouraging you towards a slow and painful death to serve her own vanity!' The dominatrix let him go, as he still refused to look at her. 'But you had best focus on me, because your life depends on it.' She opened wide her coat, and beneath it she wore a tight, crotchless leather catsuit that also exposed her ample breasts. But equally diverting were the needles, vials, jars and gadgets that were neatly placed in pockets and fasteners on the inside of the coat.

'Oh my badness!' Yasper was like an animal caught in headlights, as he took it all in, but her display did nothing to rouse his interest in mating with her.

'Oh come on?' She noted his lack of enthusiasm. 'Not even a little excited?'

'A bit overwhelmed to be honest.' Yasper diverted his eyes to the ceiling.

'Not to worry,' she advised. 'I have a little something that will firm up our engagement.'

Yasper, curious to her meaning, looked back to her and was actually a little relieved when she selected an opaque jar from her arsenal of much nastier looking weapons.

'No!' Jazmay's panicked appeal alarmed him anew. 'There are other ways —'

What the hell is it? Yasper's eyes became glued to the lieutenant as she selected a pair of large tweezers, popped the top of the jar, and used the tweezers to lift a spider from inside of it.

'Meet *Phoneutria Erectis*, which means murderous erection,' she advised with glee, as she held the large spider up so Yasper could observe it.

Brown in colour, the body of the creature was not overly huge, about two inches, but the legs on it were at least three inches each and rather hairy, which made it appear large. But the most striking feature was the scarlet coloured hair surrounding its fangs.

'She is the most venomous spider to be found on Phemoria,' the lieutenant continued the brief. 'Her neurotoxin causes a loss of muscle control, breathing problems, paralysis and eventual asphyxiation. But aside from the *intense pain*, her bite causes priapism in the human male.'

Yasper raised both brows, knowing he didn't want to ask what that meant, but his lack of reaction betrayed his ignorance, thus the lieutenant spelt it out for him.

'An *extremely* painful erection, that can last many hours.'

'Oh.' Yasper swallowed hard, beginning to see why his wife was so alarmed.

'If not treated with anti-venom, the bite is fatal, and even if treated, there is a very good chance you will be left impotent,' she concluded with glee. 'Then the only thing that's ever going to get you up again is another dose of her murderous venom. Please me, and you may live to fuck another day.'

As the lieutenant brought the spider closer, Yasper was justifiably nervous.

'Might I just have a minute's grace to reverse the situation of my own accord?' Yasper asked, looking anywhere to avoid eye contact with her.

'Of course. I want to help you,' she agreed far too easily. 'Just look into my eyes.'

Yasper looked to Jazmay, juggling his horrendous options in his mind — should he bear the physical pain of her torture, or lose all fond memory of his wife?

Jazmay, teary-eyed, appeared as much at a loss to choose as he was.

'Only a fool looks for help from the very person who betrayed him.' The woman in black turned his attention in her direction. 'Only I have the power to spare you this fate. Give yourself to me, look into my eyes and this shall be a far more pleasurable experience, I assure you.'

Yasper stopped resisting her, but did not look in her eyes — his sights were firmly planted on the spider wriggling between the tweezers in her hand, and it did not look happy.

'That's it.' She gestured with her free hand for him to raise his sights. 'Come to me, save yourself.'

With a deep breath for strength, Yasper kept his head bowed. 'I'd rather the slow and painful death.'

'Me too,' she whispered with a smile as she lowered the spider down onto his skin.

'Wake up!' A boot kick to the side woke Kalayna with a start and she groaned. Still, she was quick to roll away and find her feet, her head spinning from her leap back to consciousness as she stood.

Torches were lit all around her in a chamber that appeared more ancient than any she had ever seen in her young life. 'Where the hell am I?' She spotted General Prochazka, and backed away from her.

'You are not on the AMIE crew, is that correct?' the general queried.

Kalayna wondered whether a confirmation or a denial was the correct response to get her out of here. As magnificent as the ruins were, she had prickly chills all over her that were giving her the creeps. 'AMIE kidnapped me from the USS space program,' she replied.

'But you are not crew?' Prochazka sought further clarification.

'No.' Kalayna stuck by her story. 'I'm not even psychic.'

'And where were you born?'

Kalayna was puzzled as to why she should care. 'Frujia.'

'Excellent,' Prochazka concluded happily, slapping her hands together. 'She's all yours,' she announced.

Kalayna turned a circle to see if she could ascertain to whom the general was speaking. There was no one else in plain sight, but shadows aplenty where someone might hide. Upon turning back Kalayna discovered the general absent and herself alone in the chamber.

'Oh, shit,' she uttered under her breath, only now noting how silent it was — even her breathing seemed to have an echo. Out in front of her was an archway that appeared to lead upstairs and out into the daylight, so she made a move towards it.

'You're not leaving.'

The malign whisper of many harsh male voices increased Kalayna's chill factor tenfold, but turning around she saw no solid figure. Strange shadows on the walls encouraged her sights to drift upwards to the domed ceiling where the shadowy outlines of many men could be seen surrounding her!

Ghosts! she screamed in her mind, and the sound of depraved laughter made her limbs involuntarily freeze in fear.

A wind whipped up out of nowhere, swept around the chamber, and extinguished all the torches, the chamber falling into darkness.

'*Show us your tits, then.*'

She felt something brush by her, and as she turned about, her hair was tugged from behind, and her jacket pulled in another direction.

'Stop it!' She was flustered as her shoulder was exposed and she felt something bite into her flesh and draw blood.

'Argh!' both Kalayna and her invisible attacker yelled at once.

'*Light fucker!*' the spectre hollered and the attack stopped. '*That Phemorian bitch screwed us!*'

Kalayna recovered her sensibilities quickly, realising her psychic enhancer must have been working — and was awarding her protection. 'Ha ha.' She backed towards the only exit. 'Eat my radiance, arseholes!' She served them the finger with both hands and bolted for the exit.

'*You're not going anywhere!*' The entities resumed grasping at her clothes and hair. '*There's still loads of fun to be had!*'

So many hands pulling her back, slowed her escape. 'ARGH!' She turned in circles trying to disentangle herself from them as they grabbed at her arse, her crotch, her breasts — they smelt *awful* and their touch was like ice. 'Let go!'

'*Yes, be angry with us,*' they encouraged her.

Inside, Kalayna snapped — damned if she was going to give them anything they wanted. She detached herself from the frustration of the moment and allowed her mind to drift to a happier time … back to working on the inter-system gateway project with Telmo Decree. It was only since he'd gone missing that she realised how much she had come to adore his company, and how comforting seeing his friendly face right now would be.

The attack on her abruptly ceased, and she was rather stunned to learn that love was the weapon of choice here. 'I love my life,' she stated, and there came no snide comment in response. 'I love all things!' She took her first few cautious steps towards the door. 'Even those who would do me harm.'

'*Fuck off!*' the spectres insisted. '*Get out!*'

Kalayna took off towards the exit, feeling a force bearing down on her as she made it to the stairs — down the middle of which a steady stream of water flowed. Sticking to a side wall, she scampered upwards towards the light. Once she penetrated the light barrier the force on her trail ebbed and dissipated.

In the long corridor beyond, pillared down both sides, there were no windows; but a curving glass ceiling allowed natural light to illuminate the walkway where Kalayna collapsed to catch her breath and steady her nerves. Several of the glass ceiling tiles had broken over the course of time, and rain poured in streams through those spaces.

'Must be still on Phemoria,' Kalayna assumed, as it never rained on Sermetica. Frujia wasn't this cold anywhere, and if this was pure Maladaan air she was breathing, she'd be suffocating by now. But looking around at the beautiful romantic depictions on the walls, this was certainly not any Phemorian tourist destination she'd ever read about.

'Whoa …' Kalayna boggled at the artwork as she wandered down the corridor, avoiding the small waterfalls pouring from the ceiling and the vines hanging from the gaps and flourishing in all the moisture. The end of the gallery opened to an outdoor covered balcony, and as Kalayna stepped outside to view her location she discovered this annex had rather a high vantage point.

This was not just a palace in ruins, but an entire city — most of which had been swallowed by jungle. Beyond the crumbling city walls, way out to the horizon, there was nothing but forest, rain and storm clouds for as far as the eyes could see.

With so much storm activity, it was difficult to tell how long she had before nightfall, perhaps a few hours? 'Crap!' Kalayna knew she had no hope of walking out of here, and come sundown she would be dealing with roving ghostly perverts and the probable return of the general. Shrieks, coming from the forest, promised many other challenges as well.

The best way to ensure the alarm was not raised during a jailbreak was to take out the guards monitoring the security systems in the psychic containment wing of the prison. The AMIE rescue team could not just teleport themselves into the said area, however, as none of them knew what it looked like or knew anyone who might be therein. Fortunately, Vadik had been detained by the Phemorians before being recruited to run the mission that Taren and Mythric had thwarted many years ago, by making Vadik a better offer. Vadik had not been taken inside the security station, but had been marched past the door.

Once at the desired location, Taren used her PK to get past the security coded door and they all entered the room silently.

There were three guards therein, seated watching the monitors, and they all looked to the door bemused when no one entered and the door again closed. One of the occupants got up to investigate.

'Ouch!' A Valourean who was still seated grabbed the top of her arm, as did the guard seated beside her, and they both passed out.

Taren startled the roving guard when she appeared before her dressed as a Valourean. Placing a hand on her target's forehead she demanded that she 'blackout'.

Vadik let go of Trance, Mythric let go of Ringbalin, and they all appeared before her.

Vadik tossed aside the syringe in his hand and pulled the sleeping Valourean off her chair, planting Trance in it instead. 'Get on it!'

'Okay!' Trance landed with a thud, hands raised in submission. 'Just give me a second to contact my guy.' He closed his eyes.

'There she is!' Ringbalin spotted Ayliscia on one of the screens. 'I mean, there they are.' He noted Kassa in the cell with her, and pointed to the image in question. 'Where is this?'

Trance breathed deeply, gave a nod, looked to the system keyboard and held his hands above it. System files about their comrades presented on screen. 'Locating matches detained within this psychic containment block,' Trance advised, in a distinctly different voice, which startled them all a little. 'Five matches.'

The files of Fari, Ayliscia, Kassa, Kalayna and Amie appeared alongside one another.

'They are being held in PC block 3, cells four, five and six.'

'Where is Jazmay?' Taren queried. 'Where are the men?'

Mythric opened his mouth to advise, but Trance's spirit buddy beat him to it.

'Jazmay Cardea and the men of your crew are being held in the seeding stables, block 5.'

'The what?' Taren gasped on the query, looking to Mythric. 'They actually exist!'

Mythric nodded to confirm. 'You didn't believe that old "the Phemorians self-seed" myth, did you?'

'Why didn't you tell me?' Taren held her gut; the very notion made her sick and furious at once.

'Because I knew it would make you panic,' Mythric proffered, 'and we need you —'

'We should get them out first,' Taren decided, in a panic as predicted.

Mythric grabbed her arm to calm her down. 'We are here now, the coast is clear, and there is far less chance of us creating a big stir here. Once we break the men out of the seeding stable, this entire complex will be on full alert. Stick to the plan.'

Taren nodded, seeing the sound reasoning in that, but her gut was still churning. 'How many other prisoners are in PC cell block 3?' She looked back to their possessed cohort, wondering how many witnesses they needed to deal with.

'The system is registering five life forms in PC cell block 3,' Trance, in a trance, replied.

'Excellent.' Taren was pleased they only had guards to contend with, and leaned over Trance's shoulder to observe the screen in front of him. 'Show me how we get in there?'

As she presented as a Valourean, Taren had no problem striding around to the cell block in question, and Mythric and Vadik flanked her, invisible to sight. She was wearing a head mic with an earpiece like the ones all the Valoureans wore, and via this Trance was directing her to their destination.

'*Turn right, and you're there,*' he said.

The corridor that led into this high security psychic containment block was not governed by the same power-deadening technology as the cell block it led to, as such a measure would also disable the psychic aptitude of the Valoureans who guarded the several sets of doors that led to the prison. Taren had seen inside the cell block and could have teleported herself inside, but then she could not teleport herself or anyone else out — she had to get clear of the psychic containment block first. So rather than have to fight their way out with a psychically handicapped crew, Taren felt it better to fight their way in and ensure a clear escape route.

The first set of guards were knocked out easily by her invisible flanks, and Taren quickly imagined the pair standing back on guard, as they had been, causing them to rise back to standing with their eyes open.

Unconscious and eyes wide, these Valoureans didn't appear any different to when they were on full alert. They had been trained to maintain an unflinching stance, which worked very much to their rescue party's favour in this instance. Taren suppressed a satisfied smile as she triggered the security door to open with her PK and entered the next checkpoint.

Upon sighting Taren, one of the Valoureans pulled her weapon. 'Intruders,' she advised her fellow guard, who also pulled her pulse-laser weapon to fire at them — this Valourean was obviously clairvoyant, as clearly she saw Mythric and Vadik despite their invisibility.

'Mine,' Taren commanded the weapons to fly into her awaiting hands, which made both Valoureans gasp. 'Attention,' she commanded them to resume their guard, which they did, before they froze like statues. 'Here.' Taren cast the weapons to either side of her, and they vanished as they were caught by Mythric and Vadik respectively.

'*You have a problem,*' Trance whispered in Taren's ear, just as she was about to open the last set of security doors.

'What?'

'*I've just discovered there are security monitors inside this checkpoint monitoring the first two.*'

'They know I am here,' Taren concluded quietly, and advised her company at once.

'And so would the rest of the complex if I hadn't blocked the alert they sent out.'

'Thanks for the heads-up.' Even if they were clairvoyant, they could not perceive any psychic message that the equipment they were viewing did not pick up on. And, just in case they had psychic sight and they spotted Mythric and Vadik, Taren triggered the door lock and then teleported herself to the far door therein.

The doors parted and the Valoureans opened fire; obviously they were not clairvoyant and could not see the men as they stopped firing to search for an intruder.

'Looking for someone?' Taren queried, and startled them to an about-face. The men knocked them unconscious, and Taren directed the door they had just come through to close.

'Inconvenient.' Vadik motioned to the monitors that had betrayed them.

'Keep watch,' Taren instructed, removing the guard's code key from her belt, knowing she wouldn't be able to use her PK to open the doors inside this cell block. 'We'll be right back.'

As Taren inserted the key into the lock, Mythric lifted up the unconscious Valourean and parted her right eyelid wide for the retinal scanner. They were granted access.

In the cells at the end of this small block, they found their missing crew, and they were all very relieved to see them.

'We need to move quickly.' Taren ushered them out of the cells and into the corridor before noting something amiss. 'Where is Kalayna?'

'General Prochazka took her,' Amie said. 'We don't know where. I have tried to look for her remotely, but all I'm getting is darkness.'

'That's not good.' But Taren was puzzled by something else. 'The scan of this block said five life forms?' She left the group to go and check the vacant cells back up towards the door. The first two were empty, but in the third one lay the acting prime minister, Jalila Lamas.

'Jalila?' Taren called to her, and although her eyes flickered open, they closed again and she did not look well.

It was only after Taren unlocked and entered the cell that she noticed the large bump on her head. 'I feared you'd been sent to join your sister.' That she hadn't was a blessing indeed, provided she didn't die on them.

'What you got?' Mythric entered behind her.

'She's concussed, I think.'

Kassa Madri came around Mythric, and Taren moved out of the way so that the doctor could check her over.

'She needs specialised medical attention,' Kassa agreed.

'We have something better.' Taren turned to Mythric. 'Bring her with us.'

Mythric scooped Jalila up into his arms and followed Taren, along with those they'd freed, out into the first security checkpoint, where Vadik was waiting.

'All clear, boss,' he reported, smiling at the ladies and winking at young Fari.

'Whoa, you're huge!' Fari observed, sounding very impressed. 'But, once I get this band off, I bet I'm stronger!'

After closing the security door to the cell block behind them, Mythric vanished with Jalila. Those who remained linked hands, and between Taren and Vadik, everyone managed to teleport back to the security station.

When they appeared in the area they'd previously secured, Ringbalin stood awaiting them. 'Thank heavens you are all all right!' His welcoming smile was aimed at Ayliscia, who returned his affectionate gaze and took a step towards him.

'Ringbalin.' Mythric sat the semi-conscious prime minister in a chair.

'Oh dear.' The healer's attention was diverted to Jalila, and he moved to kneel before her. 'What happened?'

'Princess ... Satomi ...' she mumbled and cringed, attempting to hold her head, which clearly ailed her.

'Shhh … Never mind.' Ringbalin rested his hands on either side of her face, and her eyes closed as he focused on healing her injury.

The palms of Ringbalin's hands filled with light, and as the healing force was absorbed into Jalila's being, her painful expression melted into one of pure bliss. The swelling of the bump on her head reduced before their eyes and then vanished altogether.

'How is that now?' Ringbalin went to remove his hands, but Jalila was quick to place her hands over his and hold them where they were.

'Sensational.' Jalila opened her large, almond-shaped eyes and smiled at him. 'You are a wonder, Mr Malachi.'

Taren chanced a glance in Ayliscia's direction, and found the Phemorian marine biologist with arms folded and appearing none too happy.

'Have you found the others?' Amie grabbed Taren's arm to query her husband's whereabouts. Kassa and Fari were also eager to hear how the rest of the crew fared.

'We are going after them now,' Taren said.

'I'm coming with you,' Amie insisted.

'You're still restrained —' Taren began to point out.

'No,' Amie cut her off. 'Kalayna reversed the function on some of our devices. So, either I'm coming with you, or I'm screwing with your intention and coming anyway.'

'I'm also fully operational,' Ayliscia informed.

'You are familiar with the seeding stables here?' Taren queried.

Ayliscia noted all eyes upon her, including Ringbalin's, and her response was to the point. 'Anyone working for the Phemorian Secret Service or the Valoureans knows of it, but I was not a patron.'

'I know it, very well,' Jalila stood to advise. 'Allow me to guide you.'

'Why should we trust you?' Ayliscia objected.

'Because I am indebted to you on many levels.' Jalila looked to Taren to appeal. 'I believe our cause is still aligned and that we can help each other.'

Taren nodded to agree. 'Trance, is there anything on that database that advises of the acting prime minister's arrest?' Taren suspected that the Qusay and her general had not made this public knowledge.

After a quick scan, Trance replied, 'No data report. The cell in which you found her is listed as unoccupied.'

Taren really didn't want to make this call, but taking both Ayliscia and Jalila on this mission could prove problematic. 'Vadik, take Kassa, Fari, Trance and Ayliscia back to AMIE.'

Vadik nodded to agree, but Ayliscia was pissed. 'No, you need me.'

'Follow our movements from AMIE,' Taren instructed her. 'And let Vadik know if we get into any trouble.'

'I thought the ship was destroyed?' Fari queried.

'Not any more,' Taren assured him, ahead of envisioning Amie dressed in the same red leather Valourean uniform that she was.

Amie gasped at her own transformation.

'I gather they are being held in psychic containment cells?' Taren posed, and both Jalila and Mythric nodded in accord.

'Unless they are in the pleasure house itself,' Jalila said.

'In that case …' Taren looked to Mythric and Ringbalin who suddenly found themselves in handcuffs. 'I guess we are going in the front door.'

'Back door, for stock,' Jalila corrected, getting the drift of Taren's plan. 'Only clients come in the front door.'

'Stock?' Ringbalin didn't like the sound of that at all.

'Fear not,' Jalila advised. 'This is another institution that I fully intend to close down, as soon as I reclaim my position.'

Ringbalin forced a grin, pleased to hear this.

'I'm happy to stay and watch your back,' Trance's spirit friend said via the clairvoyant's body. 'I can hack into the other security stations from here.'

'And what if you are found?' Taren erred on the side of caution.

'I am not worried,' he said, sounding confident that he could protect himself. The spirit looked back to his monitor and brought up the transmission from the cameras monitoring the rear of block 5. 'No guards out back, coast is clear.'

'Go,' Taren urged, looking to Vadik, who held out his hands.

Those going back to AMIE joined hands with him and each other.

'Be careful,' Ayliscia urged Ringbalin, casting a distrustful glare in Jalila's direction, before she vanished with Kassa, Fari and Vadik.

It was a relief to see them depart, and Taren looked to those who remained. 'Ready?' She held out her hands, and her team formed a circle in response. 'Please, universe, let us find them before any harm does.'

Across from her stood Mythric, staring her gravely back, as they vanished to their target area.

General Prochazka was in her office, filing a sham death report on Kalayna Zuri, when one of her Valoureans called in a security breach in cell block C.

'Finally, Clarona's bastard shows herself.'

The general was at the scene in a heartbeat, but she was anything but thrilled by the apparent chaos that greeted her upon her arrival.

All the security doors between her and the cell block were wide open as Valoureans searched the cell block, and aided the guards to wake up.

'The prisoners are gone!' The guard who had sounded the alert came striding forwards from the cell block.

'Why is this the first I know of this?' the general demanded, furious, and was startled when an alarm began sounding. 'It's a bit fucking late!' she raged, just as the sprinkler system was triggered and water teemed from the ceiling, saturating them instantly.

'*Alert!*' a calm female voice advised through the internal intercom system. '*Security system malfunction. All personnel be advised that all security defences are down, prisoners may be at large.*'

Prochazka wasted no time in teleporting herself to the closest security station where she intended to flatten the person responsible for allowing this breach to transpire.

Upon landing she found three of her Valoureans unconscious, and one young man watching the chaos unfolding on the monitors with great amusement.

'You will pay!' Prochazka hurled a psychic force containing all her pent-up anger at the lad, yet the strike barely made him sway in his seat.

'You call that psychic force?' The young man, slight of build, had a surprisingly deep voice. He rose from his chair and released a wave of psychic force that knocked the general clean off her feet. Prochazka hit the internal metal wall of the station and blacked out.

At the back door of the seeding station the guards were happy to grant Jalila and her company entry.

'What a little doll,' the guard commented, eyeing Ringbalin over and playing with the fair strands of hair that were falling all over his face.

'That's what General Prochazka said,' Jalila replied.

The guard pouted, disappointed, and ceased toying with him. 'She always ruins the good ones.' She continued to gaze at him, mournfully.

'I feel quite sure the general will be paying this establishment a visit later today,' Jalila added, hoping to speed things along.

'Best make haste then,' the guard advised. 'Let me know when he becomes available for mass consumption.' She and her companion stepped aside to allow them to ascend the stairs to the holding area.

Poor Ringbalin was looking rather shocked and concerned at this point, and received a slap on the arse on the way past.

'I shall be seeing you,' she said, serving him a wink and a growl.

Mythric, already known to be the Qusay's favourite, was not woman-handled at all.

It was a great relief to be inside the complex, the exterior of which was rather large — it was not going to be easy to locate their four lost crew members.

'*I have a present for you,*' the voice of Trance's invading entity said through Taren's earpiece. '*Chaos.*'

Before she had time to ask his meaning, the alarm went off and the power went out.

'*Alert! Security system malfunction. All personnel be advised that all security defences are down, prisoners may be at large.*'

The reserve power kicked in and activated minimal lighting, which flashed red intermittent with darkness.

'I always was a fan of chaos theory,' Taren uttered by way of thanks to their hacktivist. 'Move it!' She led the sprint up the stairs.

Their rescue party came to a holding area with several cells, beyond which, Jalila advised, was the decontamination room, and the psychic containment prison beyond that. All the cell doors in this area were open and the cells were vacant.

Ringbalin was trailing his comrades when, from behind him, a hand clamped over his mouth and another around his waist. He was lifted right off his feet and hauled into an empty cell.

Leal heard the alarm in the distance, but thought himself hallucinating as he heard the lock on his cell door click open and then observed the door slide aside. A cold shiver ran through him as he expected the Valoureans had finally come to drag him away to the pleasure house.

A din rose in the prison; he could hear other inmates cheering, and then a few ran past his cell. He stood and approached the door cautiously, wary of a trap, and was startled when he was hit in the face by a pair of flying trousers.

'What are you waiting for?' Swithin asked. 'Let's get the fuck out of here!'

'But even if we escape this complex ...' Leal pulled on the pants, 'where the hell are we going to go? You can't teleport and —'

Swithin grabbed Leal's wrist and took off up the corridor. 'But I can run.'

'Where is Yasper?' Leal, having been released from Swithin's hold, was having trouble keeping up with him, as he was amazingly agile, ducking and weaving through other escaping prisoners and the handful of Valourean guards struggling to control them all.

'They took him, I don't know where.' Swithin threw his hands up.

They came to a crossroads at the end. Leal could see reinforcements heading this way from straight ahead, thus Swithin veered left towards the decontamination showers. 'This way!' Swithin urged, as Leal bolted faster to catch him up. 'It's clear, I already checked.' He grabbed his trousers to imply that's where he'd acquired them.

Leal glanced behind to see several Valoureans split from the reinforcements to pursue them. 'Not for long.'

Upon reaching the decontamination room, Swithin grabbed one of the hoses, although Leal had no idea why.

'No power!' Leal explained the pumps would be down also.

'Water is for pussies.' Swithin began swinging the large metal head of the defunct hose around to build momentum and smashed it into the head of the first Valourean who came through the door. She dropped like a rock to the floor, unconscious, causing a nice obstruction for the two Valoureans who followed.

'Ha!' Swithin grinned. 'What goes around comes around!'

'Duck!' Leal advised, and Swithin was quick to do so as following his comrade's example, Leal knocked out the second Valourean through the door.

The third Valourean came in firing, whereupon they both dived for cover behind a cement shower divider. When two more Valoureans entered from the opposing door that led to the dock, they both knew their number was up.

'Oh fuck!' Swithin uttered, resolved to meet his fate, until the Valourean firing at them suddenly stopped and froze like a statue.

'Swithin?' The sound of Amie's voice was a delightful shock to them both.

'That's my girl,' Swithin announced with pride and the pair were quick to join their allies. 'What took you so long?'

'Are you hurt?' Amie hugged her husband, briefly.

'We're good,' he said. 'Not so sure about Yasper, however. I think they took him into the house.'

'I'll find him,' Taren volunteered. 'And Jazmay, Kalayna and Zelimir —'

'The chief is dead, Prochazka killed him.' Swithin sounded surprised that no one had filled her in.

'Damn!' Taren winced at the news but there was no time for regret. 'Get these guys back to base,' she directed Mythric, only then noting that they were one team member down. 'Where's Ringbalin?' It didn't take her very long to figure. 'Oh shit!'

Jalila immediately turned tail to go after him, but Taren hauled her back.

'I'll get him, you go!' Taren ordered the prime minister to return with Mythric.

'But I'm —' Jalila was of the mind to argue.

'— wasting time!' Taren had zero patience and this was obviously apparent as Jalila complied with her request and returned to the team.

'I'll be back,' Mythric said.

'Home in on me,' Taren said as they parted ways, and Mythric vanished with them all.

With an about-face, Taren returned into the holding area, and noting one of the doors was now closed, she headed straight for it. Ringbalin was one of two very important keys needed to bring her husband back from the dead and his healing powers were dependent on his peaceful state of being. Her heart felt to be beating in her throat and she slid the door aside, making a silent plea to her guardian spirit that she would find her dear friend unharmed.

Ringbalin was seated in a chair. The Valourean who had fancied him had her head resting in his lap, and the healer stroked her hair as she wept.

I should have known. Taren breathed a sigh of relief as the Valourean continued to pour her heart out to him.

'I never wanted to be like this,' she said, looking up into his eyes. 'I wanted to be a dancer.'

'Well, it's not too late,' Ringbalin encouraged, 'you're still young.'

'You are *so* right,' she replied with complete adoration.

'*Okay* … therapy session is over.' Taren entered to retrieve her charge.

'I wish you the very best, Zeonetta.' Ringbalin rose to join Taren, and the Valourean did not object, but rose also.

'Thank you.' She kissed him tenderly on the cheek. 'I shall make you proud.'

'No.' Ringbalin took a couple of sideways steps towards Taren. 'You shall make yourself proud.'

Taren didn't know what situation might greet her upon going after Yasper, so she felt it best to return Ringbalin to AMIE first, and took hold of his hand to teleport him back.

'Don't forget Trance … or whoever he is at the moment,' Ringbalin thought to mention. 'The Valoureans must be aware he's occupying the security station by now.'

'Good point.' Taren's gut was churning; there were only so many places she could be at once. 'We'll pick him up on the way through.'

When they arrived back in the security station in complex 3, Taren was stunned to find General Prochazka unconscious on the floor, and Trance snoozing on the desk, whilst the chaos he'd created played out on the screens before him.

'What on earth happened here?' Taren mumbled.

'Let's not ask questions,' Ringbalin uttered, as they both noted the general beginning to stir.

'So where is Kalayna now?' Taren grabbed Trance's shoulder, hoping he might have some answers.

'Hah!' He objected to waking to a situation in which he found himself staring at the slumbering head of the Qusay's guard. 'What the fuck, Reggie? You made me assault the general of the Valoureans, seriously?' Then noting the hand on his shoulder, he was almost too afraid to turn and discover who it belonged to. He saw the Valourean attire and a pang of shock made his body reverberate, before he realised it was Taren. 'Are you trying to

scare the shit out of me?' He was angered by the scare. 'Get us out
of —'

Taren slapped a hand over his mouth to shut him up. Obviously the hacker was no longer with them, and Trance by himself was useless — she was not going to discover anyone's whereabouts this way. Nor did she fancy her chances of torturing the information out of the general.

With three crew members still missing, she didn't have the time to pamper Trance's ego to get him to cooperate; swifter action was required.

In the flight deck of AMIE they found a not entirely happy reunion going on, but all were pleased to see Ringbalin safely returned.

'You are so lucky.' Ayliscia let go of Jalila's hair, and smiled sweetly at Ringbalin, as did Jalila, as though nothing had transpired between them.

'I was just about to come after you, but,' Mythric motioned to the two Phemorian women to explain the delay.

'Three crew still missing.' Taren didn't stop to draw breath. 'We should seek Yasper and Jazmay first.'

'Leave that to me,' Mythric appealed. 'You find Kalayna.'

Taren held a soft spot for Yasper as he had been her first love, but considering the situation in which they expected to find him, perhaps it was better to send a male to retrieve him.

'If I get caught I'll fare better far with the Qusay than you will,' Mythric added, seeing how torn she was.

'Not now you've betrayed her again,' Taren cautioned, but as Mythric's look of appeal was still unflinching, she nodded to agree to his plan.

14

SERENDIPITY

The soft touch of the creature's legs making contact with the skin on his chest sent a shiver down Yasper's spine and goosebumps rose all over him in a wave of fear.

The spider stopped moving, wary of the change in its landscape.

'She senses your fear … and your intent to be rid of her,' his torturer whispered.

Yasper's breath shallowed to minimise movement, his eyes glued to the spider as it stared back at him. *Don't be fearful,* he countered her suggestion in his mind, *I mean you no harm.* But Yasper's survival instincts were not heeding his affirmations, as adrenaline caused his temperature to rise and cold sweat began to ooze through his pores and trickle down his skin.

'Did I mention she detests moisture?'

Every word she uttered disturbed him and the spider, sensing this, lowered its body in temporary retreat and shifted its feet about to avoid the drops rolling towards it.

'She is giving you a warning. She does not want to harm you, but she senses you are a threat.'

An alarm sounding startled Yasper and the spider reared up on its back legs to expose its scarlet red fangs poised ready to attack. The lights went out and Yasper prepared himself for the strike of the predator on his chest.

'Alert! Security system malfunction. All personnel be advised that all security defences are down, prisoners may be at large.'

Minimal lighting was restored and began flashing red in warning, and the spider had not flinched from its attack stance.

His captor turned towards the door, and spotting a water jug floating, her suspicious glare turned towards Jazmay.

The spider struck out at Yasper but was airborne before it made skin contact. The horror of the near miss skyrocketed to relief as he witnessed the creature land on the chest of his tormentor. Highly agitated by the scare of its flight, the spider delivered a full payload of venom into her left breast.

The Valourean screamed in agony, batting the spider clean across the room, and opening her coat to search for the antidote.

Jazmay broke free of her bonds, and Yasper's bonds fell away from him also as his wife rushed over to hug him.

'I'm okay, Jaz,' he assured her. 'Get us out of here.'

Jazmay looked back to find their tormentor in a panic as she loaded the contents of a vial into a syringe. 'I warned you, Lieutenant.'

The syringe and vial shattered in her hands.

The lieutenant screamed in frustration, and shot daggers with her eyes in their direction. But as she moved to raise herself, she found her nerves were already too shot to retaliate. In that moment her warrior façade vanished and only a helpless young woman remained. 'Help me.'

'Not a chance!' Jazmay sneered, taking hold of her husband's hand to teleport him to safety, but he unexpectedly withdrew his hand.

'We can't leave her to die.' Yasper was nearly as surprised by his resolve as Jazmay was.

'You didn't buy into that shit she was whispering into your ear!' Jazmay was rather furious.

'If you were wearing your Juju right now … if I were … it would never let us do this.' Yasper explained his reasoning. 'If you are not one of them any more, then prove it.'

'Fuck!' Jazmay belted the air in frustration and stamped her foot, then manifested a full syringe. She stomped over to the lieutenant and mercilessly stabbed the needle into the dying Valourean's chest.

Having administered the anti-venom, she withdrew the needle and cast it aside. 'Remember, the next time you want to torture a man, that you now owe your life to one.' Jazmay returned to her husband, still furious. 'Happy now?'

'Thank you,' called the Valourean, over and over, reduced to tears by their mercy, but Jazmay didn't care for her gratitude.

'Can we leave?'

'You did good, Jaz.' Yasper was proud of her spiritual evolution and just how far she had come since her time in service to the Valoureans, even if she wasn't. 'But there is one more thing.'

Jazmay rolled her eyes, and beckoned him with a hand to name it.

'Do you think I can possibly get some trousers?'

Jazmay finally roused a smile. 'Perhaps temporarily.'

When Taren thought of Kalayna and was teleported, she was relieved to be able to safely assume that the young engineer was still alive.

Rain teemed down on her upon arrival and but for how cold it was, she would have assumed she had landed on Oceane. A thunderstorm flashed across the sky as she looked out over a vast city in ruin being reclaimed by the jungle.

'Taren?' Kalayna called, and the next thing Taren knew she was being crash-hugged by the saturated girl. 'Praise the universe, you came!'

'Where the hell are we?' Taren wondered.

'Never mind about that,' Kalayna urged. 'We need to —'

They heard a very loud growl, and it was quite close.

'Go,' Kalayna whispered in conclusion, pointing up to the perpendicular wall above the entrance door to the palace where dark shadows loomed.

As the lightning flashed, Taren saw several wildcats waiting to pounce.

'Suction cats.' Taren recognised the species from her school studies, and they only frequented the wilds of one planet. 'We are still on Phemoria.' She found this most curious, and with a wave of her hand the cats froze.

'Thank fuck for that!' Kalayna breathed a short sigh of relief.

'How did you get out here?' Taren asked, curious about the ruins.

'General Prochazka brought me out here to feed me to some demons.' Kalayna warned they were not out of the woods yet. 'We need to leave, as they're still here.'

'Where?' Taren queried, and as Kalayna pointed towards the exit from the terrace, Taren had to smile.

'You've found it.' Taren made haste towards the opening to inside.

'Found what?' Kalayna panicked, not wanting to follow, but not daring to hesitate either. 'You don't want to go in there! They hate women!'

'I know!' Taren said with glee. 'But I also know what they fear.'

'Really?' Kalayna ran to catch her up.

'Here,' Taren manifested a Juju stone and gave it to Kalayna, who was momentarily stunned by the light, colour and energy it exuded.

'I was wondering what all the fuss about these stones was.' Kalayna was having a few revelations of her own. 'The Phemorians went to great pains not to touch these when they took them from the rest of the crew.'

'They fear I have put a curse on them,' Taren explained as they wove their way down the corridor, avoiding the broken sections of the roof, through which small waterfalls flowed. 'And that those who hold them are compelled to follow my orders without question.'

Kalayna halted. 'Is that true?'

Taren waylaid, trying not to look offended. 'Let's see, shall we? Kalayna, go on ahead and take care of these demons for me, will you?'

'No fucking way.' Kalayna backed up, horrified by the thought.

'I rest my case.' Taren grinned and kept walking.

'Oh.' Kalayna was relieved to be convinced. 'I meant no offence.' She ran to catch up with her only company.

'None taken.' Taren came to the stairs, down which the water flowed. 'You are not obliged to follow me anywhere.'

'Considering the alternatives,' Kalayna posed, 'I'm your Siamese twin right now.'

'Then let's go bag ourselves a bunch of pirates.' Taren headed down the side of the stairway and Kalayna was close behind.

As Taren set foot in the chamber the shrill from the ghosts therein was absolutely deafening. They cussed Taren, calling her every horrid name ever known to the United Star Systems, and threatened her with a horrible end if she did not leave.

But their attempts to scare Taren off only made her more confident. 'Oh come now, lads, surely you are not threatened by a couple of girls? I brought you a present.' Taren held out a large chunk of Juju stone, and they began shrieking anew, and as she focused on loving thoughts the Juju glowed brighter and brighter, and the ghostly spectres retreated to behind the throne. 'So that's where it is.' Taren grabbed Kalayna with her free hand and made haste in that direction.

'What are you looking for?'

Taren dragged Kalayna up the stairs to circle around behind the large set of thrones where they found an ancient vat that reeked of death and made their skin crawl.

'The Soul Keep.' Taren had never seen it, but the ghosts couldn't shelter from her light anywhere but in their source.

'Oh crap, it stinks!' Kalayna covered her mouth to resist the urge to be sick.

'Touch that and you will regret it!' Prochazka called in warning to announce her arrival.

Taren was quick to defy the threat. With Kalayna still in tow she made contact with the item in dispute, and conjured a picture in her mind's eye of the one place Prochazka dared not follow.

With AMIE destroyed, Oceane was the only place Jazmay could conceive of where Taren might hide the few members of the crew who avoided capture. Still, Jazmay had only been here once, as had

Yasper, and although Oceane may only have had one landmass, it was a bloody large landmass when travelling by foot. How were they ever going to find anyone?

'Maybe we should just forget trying to find everyone and take a little time for ourselves.' Yasper took hold of Jazmay, feeling very amorous.

'Don't be distracted by the atmosphere.' Jazmay felt rather amorous herself; every day on Oceane felt like spring on steroids. 'The others are still trapped on Phemoria.'

'We don't know that; they might have escaped during the security breach,' Yasper pointed out. 'Actually our lot probably caused it.'

'Then where is everyone?' Jazmay held him off to get an answer.

'You know, you get more and more like Taren every day,' Yasper noted. 'Can we please just take a breath and appreciate the fact we are both still alive?'

'Our son is still in custody.' Jazmay's resolve hardened and the reminder sobered Yasper somewhat too.

'No, we have him.' The couple were startled and elated to find Mythric had appeared by them in the pouring rain.

'Mythric!' Jazmay was so thrilled by the news and to see another crew member that she kissed him. 'Thank you!'

'We?' Yasper queried.

'Taren led the mission and we got everyone out,' Mythric further advised, annoyed by trying to talk through the water teeming upon them. 'You do know I erected a shelter here?'

Both Jazmay and Yasper shook their heads.

'Follow me.' Mythric vanished.

Jazmay grabbed Yasper's hand and focused on Mythric to pursue him.

'That's better.' Mythric shook himself off, and with a thought was bone dry — Jazmay followed suit and dried Yasper off at the same time.

'So where is everyone?' Jazmay had expected to find them here.

'On AMIE.' Mythric grinned.

'Taren reconstructed her,' Jazmay figured with a smile of relief.

'So where is she?' Yasper asked, excited.

'Deep beneath the ocean here.' Mythric pointed outside.

'And Taren?' Yasper queried further, happy to know she'd not perished in the explosion.

'I'm here.'

They looked to find Taren and Kalayna on the balcony, as something fell from the sky beyond the balcony and landed with a huge splash in the water behind them. There followed a deafening shriek of protest, and as all present ran out to view the cause of the disturbance, the shrill noise died away, as a vat disappeared below the water.

'The Soul Keep.' Mythric grinned at Taren, impressed. 'You found it.'

'Well, technically Kalayna found it.' Taren passed the credit to their newest team member.

'Good job!' Mythric gave Kalayna a hug, as she looked completely shell-shocked and in need of one.

'You guys got out.' Kalayna was gratified to see Jazmay and Yasper.

'Thanks to you.' Jazmay pulled the revised psychic restraining device from between her breasts. 'You saved both our arses.'

'You have no idea!' Yasper seconded that statement.

'So it worked!' Kalayna took hold of the device and looked to Taren. 'You know I do believe I might be able to adapt this technology into a handheld pulse laser weapon.'

Taren was very pleased to hear this. 'That would certainly aid us in dealing with the Valoureans' new, improved army.'

'Is that what you intend to do, confront the Qusay directly?' Mythric's up-vibe departed.

'I do not intend to do anything until I get word from Zeven,' Taren replied. 'He has one element of the curse. I have one …' She motioned to the water. 'And the Phemorians have the other. So, for the moment, it is stalemate. None of us can do anything without all three.'

Mythric nodded to concur with her appraisal. 'I should report to the Qusay as promised.'

'Please, no.' Taren gripped his hand to prevent his departure. 'Why?'

'Because I vowed I would report what I know.' Mythric was determined. 'If she knows the truth about Zeven's whereabouts —'

'She'll just believe Khalid has them trapped somewhere on this planet,' Taren concluded.

'Well isn't that the truth?' Mythric argued. 'Neither of us can truly say whether there is foul play afoot or not.'

'Then just wait until we have brought Lucian back from the dead,' Taren appealed, swallowing her emotion. 'If he managed to find Zeven, he will be able to shed some truth on this for both of us.'

Mythric nodded in accord, and looked back to Jazmay and Yasper, who were both dumbfounded.

'What has Khalid to do with all of this?' Yasper voiced their woe. 'Please don't tell me Zeven *was* the one who broke Khalid out of prison. Is that the reason why the Qusay Clarona is so pissed at us?'

'It's not my mother we are dealing with any more.' Taren realised just how much explaining she had to do. 'Satomi has instigated a coup d'état on Phemoria.'

'You're shitting me?' Yasper was overwhelmed by the influx of information. 'So it was Satomi who gave the order that killed my father.' His angry sights turned to Mythric, who held his hands up in truce.

'I doubt very much it was Satomi's wish to kill Zelimir,' Taren intervened. 'It was his long and illustrious history of torturing Phemorian spies, Yasper … it caught up with him.'

'But my father changed his ways,' Yasper appealed, only now fully feeling the grief of his father's loss.

'You and I know that,' Taren countered. 'The Phemorians do not.'

'The way I see it, this is all on Zeven,' Jazmay voiced her view. 'Why are you still defending him, when you see what his actions have done? We were *all* nearly killed.'

Yasper had to agree, and wanted to know what Taren had been hiding from them all. 'Has Zeven gone rogue?' He was fit to explode if Zeven had been acting on his own recognisance.

'If he has,' Taren answered him cautiously, 'then your brother is his right-hand man and is equally to blame.'

Yasper had near forgotten about his long-lost sibling and calmed a little. 'Well, what the fuck are they doing?'

'That is why I am about to resurrect my husband to find out,' Taren replied calmly, well accustomed to Yasper's mood swings. He may have been a warrior, but it was also his nature to be optimistic. 'I want answers as much as you do. Jumping to conclusions is only going to land us in more strife.'

'Telmo is no idiot.' Kalayna came forth in support of her old offsider. 'He knew we needed to shut down the inter-system gateway before any of us. I thought he'd gone insane, but … as it turns out he prevented a major international incident and saved both our lives. Despite what we've all been through, I believe that if he has chosen to support Zeven with his quest, then that quest must be vitally important.'

Taren nodded. 'The future event they are seeking to prevent is the very event I brought this crew together to deal with. If they play their cards right that event will never come to pass and our primary objective will have been realised.'

Yasper was overwhelmed. Wiping his hand down his face to gather his thoughts, he concluded, 'Then I guess a little torture and a few deaths would be a small price to pay.' He let go of his angst and need to place blame.

'No more secrets,' Taren promised. 'Once Lucian is back on board, I'll tell you everything I know.'

All present nodded to accept her word as compensation for now.

'Then let's go get our captain back,' Mythric suggested, and the resolve spurred them all to better spirits.

Once the entire crew was reunited in the mess hall on AMIE, their multitude of problems and suspicions were briefly forgotten as everyone rejoiced in their union and deliverance. Jazmay and Yasper were reunited with their boy, Fari, and Kalayna was patted on the back by many of the female crew for her bravery and assistance during their incarceration. It pleased Taren to see that she was fast making friends on AMIE and that they now realised why Kalayna was such an integral addition to the crew.

Only Swithin appeared to have a bone to pick. 'Where is my brother's body?' He approached Taren to learn what she knew. 'Please tell me he wasn't blown to pieces in that explosion.'

Taren's eyes immediately welled with tears of joy. 'He didn't …' she shook her head, so pleased to be able to reassure Swithin. 'He's on Sermetica, residing in the same unit from which you raised Satomi.'

Swithin burst into a huge smile, and hugged Taren — spinning her around and yahooing like a madman. 'Then what are we waiting for?' He dropped Taren and looked to Ringbalin, who was chatting with Mythric and avoiding the females in the room. 'Are you up for this?'

'Ready when you are.' Ringbalin was over-eager, and Taren suspected he was looking to escape this room at any cost.

'Ditto.' Mythric joined the huddle and the four of them gripped wrists and vanished to Sermetica.

In the family crypt beneath the House of Vidor on Sermetica, Taren and her resurrection team were met by an alarming sight.

A dozen Valoureans stood guard around the stasis unit in which Lucian's body lay, and General Prochazka was seated casually on top of it — legs crossed.

'I told you you'd be sorry.' Prochazka grinned.

Taren's first reaction was to get her team mates out of there, but Prochazka slid a hand down over the power switch to the module.

'I wouldn't make any rash moves if I were you,' she threatened. The fact she was seated on the unit meant if Taren tried to teleport it back to AMIE, the general would go with it. Taren didn't want her knowing they had taken up residence on their old vessel, nor did she want her on Oceane near where they had hidden the Soul Keep. 'Besides,' Prochazka continued, 'I am here to talk terms for a truce.'

'A truce?' Taren was sceptical.

'Not my idea, of course.' She sounded very put out by the notion. 'But my Qusay feels that this dispute is getting us nowhere.'

'Agreed.' Taren demonstrated that she was prepared to hear her out by letting go of her team mates — Mythric did also.

'Very good.' Prochazka took her finger off the power switch and twisted around to gaze down at the captain therein. 'He was very attractive, your husband; he's enough to make one necrophilic.'

It seemed this general always knew exactly what to say to piss her off, and Taren took a breath to blow off her annoyance. 'What are your terms?' she queried as if she shouldn't guess.

'Return what you stole from me,' she advised. 'You do not have the means to control its powers.'

'Well, if you do wield such power,' Taren posed, 'and you have not brought it to bear at this meeting, you must have realised that I do have the means to contain that power. For the moment it can do no harm and no more women need to be sacrificed to sustain it. You already hold one part of this curse in the crown of Phemoria, and I think we both know all three parts of the curse must be brought together in order to put all these demons to their eternal rest. I will vow to you that AMIE will not attempt to retrieve that part of the curse from your possession, as a sign of good faith. And when the missing part is found, we shall bring them all to Phemoria, where all of us can bear witness to an end to their interference in the affairs of this world.'

'And what of Khalid?' Prochazka raised the prickly subject. 'He must also be brought to Phemoria to answer to his crimes against our Qusay.'

'It was the demon Chironjivi who committed those crimes; Khalid was just the tool he used to do it.' Taren put forth Zeven's assessment.

'We shall be the judges of that,' Prochazka advised. 'You must deliver him to us.'

'I cannot promise to deliver something I do not have in my possession,' Taren replied.

'No deal.' Prochazka moved her finger back to the power switch of the module.

'Finding Khalid and the rest of our missing crew, including Thurraya and her family, is our top priority,' Taren assured to waylay her. 'The captain is the only one who may have any idea how they fare. Finish him, and we may never find them.'

Prochazka's eyes narrowed. 'And when you do? Will you bring your crew, Khalid and the Princess Thurraya to Phemoria, to answer to the Qusay for your actions?'

Taren looked to her team mates and even Swithin, the most sceptical and self-preserving person on the crew, was nodding in encouragement. 'Yes,' she replied.

'What guarantee do we have that you will keep this promise?' Prochazka wasn't convinced.

'A hostage.' Mythric stepped forwards to volunteer.

'A lying spy!' The general gave half a laugh. 'I'd rather eat off my own hand. I'll take the pretty little one.' She pointed towards Ringbalin, whose big blue eyes opened wide in alarm.

'No,' Taren refused. 'I need him to help resurrect the captain.'

'I will wait.' Prochazka shrugged off the protest.

'Ringbalin is vital to my crew's survival.' Taren's resolve hardened. 'No deal.'

Prochazka shrugged, indifferent. 'Then war it is; your man whore dies.'

'I will go.' Ringbalin stepped up to speak for himself.

Taren looked to him, stunned — Ringbalin went into mourning if he was separated from his greenhouse for more than a day! 'Who knows how long our search will take, Balin, how —'

'I know,' he assured her, and then shrugged. 'I trust you can take care of my greenhouse.'

'What guarantee do I have that he will not be harmed?' Taren turned back to the general, not happy with the arrangement. Apart from being their healer and horticulturalist, he was also one of her dearest friends.

'He will have to wear a psychic restraint, of course,' Prochazka advised. 'But beyond that, we will regard him as a guest of state, and he can freely communicate with you.'

'That doesn't sound so bad,' Ringbalin stated as Taren looked to him mournfully. 'I'm sure I could do wonders for the royal garden.'

'He can live in the garden if he wishes.' Prochazka grew impatient. 'Don't worry, your precious little pet will be safe enough.'

Taren was really starting to feel her fatigue and it wasn't helping her patience any. 'He is not a pet!' she barked. This was exactly the mind-set that worried her.

'Then stop treating him like one!' Prochazka barked back. 'He's a grown man, isn't he?'

'All good!' Ringbalin stepped into the argument, cheery as always. 'It would be my honour to serve both AMIE and Phemoria in this treaty.'

'I guess we have a deal then,' Taren breathed down her resentment for the sake of keeping the peace.

'Not quite.' Prochazka sat back. 'Will Sermetica be interfering in our business?'

'Anselm is none too happy about my mother's spiritual exile,' Taren outlined.

'Your mother is perfectly safe,' Prochazka posed. 'And will be returned, along with all our other sisters, when the curses have been put down.'

'I shall encourage my father to reserve judgement and action until that time,' Taren agreed.

'And what of after her deliverance?' Prochazka took the long view. 'Do you accept that the true Qusay is already on the throne?'

'I do,' Taren answered without hesitation, which surprised Mythric.

'Do you promise to honour her rule and not incite political rebellion?' Prochazka probed. 'Or ever again protest against the matriarchal rule of your great foremothers?'

This was a difficult one for Taren as she was no longer heir, but agreeing meant cementing her young niece, Thurraya, as heir to the Phemorian throne. She looked to Mythric, who was considering the negotiations as seriously as she was, and after a moment he gave a slight, very pained nod.

'I promise I shall never interfere with the rulership of Phemoria henceforth,' Taren conceded.

'Then we have ourselves a truce.' General Prochazka stood and descended the stairs to stand with her Valoureans. 'Agreed?'

'Agreed.' Taren forced a grin, but was truly relieved when the Valoureans and their leader stepped aside, leaving them a clear path to Lucian's resting place.

'Go ahead, don't be shy.' The general motioned them to their target. 'We are all friends now. Let's see you do your stuff.'

'Is it just me,' Swithin uttered aside to Taren as they scaled the stairs, 'or does something feel a little off here?'

'Maybe Satomi has come round?' Mythric suggested.

'Let's just get Lucian out of here, ASAP.' Taren gazed inside at his lifeless form, saddened by the sight and yet elated to have made it back here with the team she needed.

Ringbalin held her shoulder in silent reassurance, as Mythric deactivated the status unit, and they all stood back as the lid opened, releasing the chilled air from inside.

'Good to see you, baby brother,' Swithin uttered as he moved to lay his hands on the captain.

'Maybe we should do this simultaneously,' Ringbalin suggested, already holding his hands together and building a glowing energy force between them, just as Swithin was.

'Good call,' Swithin agreed with a nod to confirm he was ready. 'In three, two, one.'

They both laid hands on the captain at once, and after a breathless moment for them all, Lucian came gasping back to life.

'Welcome back, Captain.' Swithin grinned at his brother, who was gazing about, trying to assess where he was.

'I'm back!' he realised, appearing not entirely happy about that. 'How long was I gone?'

'A few days,' Taren stepped in to answer and reassure her husband.

'Felt like ten minutes.' He frowned, wanting to sit up, and Taren lent him a hand. 'I could have used a little more time.'

'And what does one get up to when one is dead, Captain?'
Prochazka drew his attention.

Lucian clammed up at the sight of his murderer, and Prochazka
laughed. 'I am not here to finish you off again. Your wife and I have
just struck a bargain for your life.'

Lucian looked to Taren, who appeared guilty as charged.

'Which did not include interrogating our captain,' Taren
pointed out.

'No,' Prochazka agreed. 'I shall leave it to you to meet the rest of
the details of our treaty. Give me my hostage and I shall go.'

'Hostage?' Lucian was wide awake now, and glaring at his wife.

'It's all right, Captain.' Ringbalin placed a hand on his shoulder
to calm him, and Lucian smiled, then passed out, collapsing back
into the unit.

'Give her your stone,' Prochazka insisted.

Ringbalin removed the band containing his Juju from beneath
the long sleeve of his T-shirt and handed it to Taren. 'Maybe you'll
create a few new weird and wonderful species while I'm gone?' He
made light of their parting, but Taren could barely breathe through
her sorrow.

'Balin,' she went to speak, but choked on the words, as a
psychic restraining device appeared, clamped and locked around
Ringbalin's ankle.

'I know you'll miss me, but that's just my thing.' He shrugged
and smiled. 'I don't take it personally, you shouldn't either.'

Taren shook her head; it was more than psychic expertise that
made everyone adore him.

'Take care, kid.' Swithin ruffled Ringbalin's hair as the healer
moved past him, and Mythric pulled him up.

'Enough already!' Prochazka objected. 'All this fucking
sentiment is making my brain bleed!'

The two men just smiled at each other as Prochazka hauled
Ringbalin over to join her Valoureans, who all towered over him.

'I want regular reports,' Prochazka stipulated.

'I want regular visiting rights,' Taren demanded back.

'Quid pro quo?' Prochazka suggested.

'Done,' Taren agreed.

'I shall be seeing you, Princess,' Prochazka sneered as she vanished with Ringbalin and her soldiers.

'Oh fuck, what have I done!' Taren immediately began hyperventilating in the wake of the confrontation.

'You did what you had to do to get our captain back.' Mythric grabbed hold of her, hoping to calm her down. 'Ringbalin will be fine, you know that.'

'No, I don't! He's never been without his gift before!' Taren shook off the comfort, feeling she did not deserve it.

'At least you can rely on him not to do anything stupid,' Swithin posed. 'Which makes him a better choice than either of us.'

'This isn't a joke!' Taren blasted.

'After where I've just come from, don't you think I fucking know that?' Swithin replied soberly.

'And it's not just Ringbalin,' Taren stressed. 'I've saved your lives only to place them all in future jeopardy!'

'What … like they aren't anyway?' Swithin reasoned. 'Truces get broken all the time, don't worry about it.' He waved it off. 'Saving one hostage is nothing compared to the jailbreak you just pulled. For now we have what we need, everyone is safe, mission accomplished.' He drew his hands apart in finality to imply that was the bottom line.

With a few deep breaths, Taren pulled herself together, confident that when she was rested enough to have her brain functioning, she might see the situation in a better light.

'Let's get the captain back home, hey?' Mythric was eager to leave this place. Too many bad memories were stored in this crypt for his liking.

She really wasn't looking forward to explaining this truce and Ringbalin's absence to the rest of the crew — she was going to have a couple of really distressed Phemorians on her hands and that was never a good thing.

Prochazka appeared before Satomi's throne, unannounced, as the Qusay was awaiting her return.

'How did you fare?' Satomi queried, remaining seated in her chair of state. 'Did she agree to our terms?'

'Of course,' Prochazka reported. 'It is always easy to agree to terms you have no intention of keeping. But I demanded a hostage to hold in good faith, to ensure the deal did not look suspiciously sweet.'

'Which crew member?' Satomi was curious.

'The gardener,' Prochazka said. 'He seemed the least trouble to maintain.'

'Don't let Mr Malachi fool you,' Satomi advocated. 'He could charm his way out from beneath even you, General.'

'He is restrained,' she advised, not worried.

'But Malachi is regarded fondly by the crew, and so was a good choice,' Satomi awarded. 'He'll serve our purposes nicely.'

'Of course, Spyridon Vidor was with your niece. Clearly his allegiance lies with her.' Prochazka appeared to have a sour taste in her mouth.

'Fortunately, we were counting on that.' Satomi was pleased to turn a betrayal to victory. 'He did exactly as I predicted. And if he hadn't, we would not have been able to implant a spy amid their ranks.' She smiled pleased with the payoff. 'So, from now on no more trust required, no more lies or betrayals. As soon as my rogue son shows up with my granddaughter, Khalid, and his curse, we will know of it.'

PART 4

UNIFICATION

15

INTERCONNECT

Mission Log — Day? (Feels like the same day, but it probably isn't.)

This place is like a living, breathing dream, constantly changing to suit the observer's will, both spoken and thought.

Telmo was right, this is not so much a different plane of existence, as a buffer between the world we left behind and another world that preceded ours, that is again slowly manifesting — although only certain aspects of that manifestation will be evidenced in the physical world in the form of the nature and habitable atmosphere. The civilisation of Karmandi will only be able to be accessed by the souls residing in our physical plane of existence when they have evolved to a point where their consciousness and vibratory rate is in harmony with that of the Dropa. Those humans will find themselves drawn to Oceane, and only they will be able to tolerate the vibratory frequencies of this place. At that time the Dropa will guide those souls towards the Eternity Gate, and on to the next stage of their cosmic journey in the next universal scheme in the ascending spiral towards oneness.

'Much like Shamballa of Earth in the universe parallel,' Telmo had noted.

Not I, or any in my party, can see Karmandi as it truly is. For, as advanced in consciousness as we like to think we are, the home of the Dropa is beyond our comprehension, and they deliberately present themselves to us in a form we can fathom. Clearly, even the Zagriata have a lot of growing to do.

The sudden appearance of the captain's spirit here, news of his death, the AMIE vessel's destruction and the incarceration of the crew on my mother's orders, is deeply shocking to all of us, and only hardens my resolve to seek out the ousted Qusay Clarona in the celestial city of the Phemoray. In order to do this I must shed my physical form and astrally project myself to them, a feat that is one of my wife's talents, but was never one of mine. Yet the nature of this place is to grant my desire, and on the next semi-causal level of existence, Aurora and I are one being, Sammael, hence my perceived disability is as illusory as our physical separation. On a purely causal level we are one with all the Zagriata, in the form of Azazèl-mindos-coomra-dorchi, the being overseeing the development of life on this planet; this means every one of us has access to the talents of all our soul-group. Telmo taught me this back on Kila; that's how the timekeepers managed to shift their consciousness back into past life incarnations, by tapping into that pool of skills and combining them.

As much as I wish to head straight home and aid Tory in combating my mother's attack on our crew, this is a rare opportunity to make contact with the occupants of the Phemorians' celestial city and find out exactly how they feel about their banishment and the current developments on Phemoria. Perhaps they can advise us how to deal with my mother's revolution?

I am also aware that we are currently residing in a time-warp of sorts, and that there is no measure to calculate how long any sidetrack might delay our return to the physical realm. I would have sought the captain's counsel, only he vanished shortly after delivering his news. I feared his soul had left for his next incarnation, but the Dropa assure me that the captain has merely returned to his last one. Just like my mother, he has been resurrected and will hopefully remember our meeting and advise the timekeeper of our situation. Yet, in order for the captain to be restored to the land of the living, several members of the crew are needed. Was the captain mistaken about the capture of the crew at the hands of the Valoureans?

Acutely aware that the more I procrastinate the more time will be flitting away back home, I must choose a course of action.

Like waking from a dream, Zeven found himself in a much smaller, dimly lit space, where several beds were laid out before him. He looked about to find most of his company appearing just as disorientated.

'This feels real.' Zeven looked to Telmo for comment, wondering if they'd been returned to the physical world. He hoped not, as Khalid was missing.

'What is reality, but a perception?' Telmo said with a smile, taking a seat on one of the beds. 'We need somewhere to leave these bodies while we travel to the celestial city, so I guess you decided we are going.'

'I did?' Zeven was unsure. 'I know for a fact I was considering going alone.'

Telmo observed the situation. 'Then why are there three beds?'

'I gather you've decided you are coming?' Zeven looked to his wife, realising it wasn't only his will being served here, this was a group manifestation.

'As a matter of fact, yes.' Aurora took a seat on the last of the beds, leaving only the one Zeven would use. 'I thought I could guide you out.'

Zeven folded his arms, not opposed exactly, more sceptical. 'And how do we find this place that none of us have been to?'

'The once Qusay, Clarona.' Telmo grinned and so did Zeven.

'We finally know someone who is there,' he concluded happily. 'And who shall watch Thurraya?' Zeven wasn't game to leave his daughter by herself in this realm.

'Ahura,' his daughter said, pointing to the spirit who manifested alongside her. 'We are going adventuring.' She held up her bright little kitten to include it in the group.

'I don't intend to be long,' Zeven said, going down on one knee before her. 'So don't wander too far, okay?'

Thurraya found this very amusing. 'Oh, Dad … nowhere is *too* far here.' She kissed his cheek and vanished with her spirit guide and her pet.

'Time is of the essence,' Telmo said from his reclined position.

'But what about Khalid?' Zeven came and sat down, unwilling to depart without his charge.

'I doubt very much that his presence would be beneficial to this particular quest as it is unclear how much these Phemorians know about Khalid. Yet, it *is* clear that a rift still exists between them and the Dropa,' Telmo outlined. 'We will be the first masculine consciousnesses ever to enter the celestial city, which is going to put enough pressure on our quest as it is. Remember these souls have been forced into spiritual exile; they are not ascended to that state of being by their own enlightenment. So, even though they are spirit, they can still demonstrate hostile behaviour.'

Zeven was still not comfortable with the arrangement. 'But Khalid —'

'— has not been home for a very long time,' Telmo spoke up over the protest, eager to get on. 'He obviously has other business to attend here. So, let us trust that these ascended beings have a better grip on *the plan* than we do, and just get on and do our part. If Khalid was meant to be here, he would be.'

'You'd better be right about that.' Zeven finally laid his body down.

'Am I ever wrong?' Telmo retorted.

'There's always a first time.' Zeven resented how cocky he was, but Telmo only grinned.

'We could lose weeks, months, *years*, while you two resolve your power struggle, or I could get on with my tutorial?' Aurora posed.

'Go right ahead.' Telmo gave her leave. 'I'll wait.'

'You know how to do this?' Aurora assumed.

'Of course he does, he's Taliesin!' Zeven overstated.

'Pardon?' Aurora frowned.

'Never mind.' Zeven waved off a trip down memory lane. 'Please continue.'

Aurora explained that there were a few stages to the technique to having an out-of-body experience, and the first of these was to completely relax both the body and the mind by focusing on one's breathing.

At stage two they entered the state bordering sleep, and Aurora explained the easiest way for Zeven, as a beginner, to avoid collapsing fully into this state was to hold a forearm upright — as his arm would fall and jog his consciousness back to a more alert awareness within this semi-hypnotic state.

At this point, stage three, light patterns formed in the blackness behind Zeven's eyes. Aurora advised him to ignore these, as they were simply neural discharges. Instead, he was to sink deeper into his relaxed state and become aware of a vibration that would now beset his body. This vibration could be used as a tool to aid separation of his light-body from his physical form, and to utilise it Aurora asked him to mentally push the vibration into his head, then down to his toes, and to repeat this several times until he felt a wave-like motion up and down his form — he was now ready to leave his body.

All attention focused on floating upward, Zeven waited for the vibration to pool at his toes and caught the wave on its upwards rush, which propelled his light-body right out of the top of his physical form.

A flare of light. The sensation of a warm breeze blowing against him. Sunlight on his face, warm and revitalising. The smell of dewy undergrowth mixed with sea spray and fresh air. The crashing sound of waves on a shore, and sand between his toes.

Khalid opened his eyes to drink in the view that was reflective of the paradise they'd left on Frujia. All his senses were amplified, acutely tuned into the present moment. There was an exchange of energy flowing between himself and everything around him, and he felt like he'd come 'home'.

'As close as you can come, still hindered by that form.'

To one side of him was the spirit of Dorje Pema, which transformed into an apparition of a human female and solidified into a physical form.

To Khalid's eyes she was the most heavenly creature he'd ever laid eyes upon. Her white flowing dress sparkled in the sunshine and billowed on the breeze, her long dark hair also.

'You are my Qusay?' he managed to say without stammering or drooling.

'More a manifestation of her energy,' she smiled, turning a circle to show off her creation. 'Is it pleasing?'

'Beyond expression,' he replied. 'And your name?'

'We have a name, but to hear it would surely spark memories that would draw you back to us before you achieve what you will. To see us, or remember us, as we truly are, you must first shed that body,' she enlightened. 'And as you cannot come to us yet, we come to you.'

'I am most grateful, but ...' He tore his attention from her, to note they were alone. 'Where —'

'They have gone to the celestial city of the Phemorians ...' she advised. 'So you are at liberty to remember the one thing you seem to have forgotten during your time away.' She held her hands out to him, palms up, and Khalid was compelled to rest the palms of his own hands against hers.

Her mauve eyes, so reflective of the royal women of Phemoria, were mesmerising and held his gaze. 'What have I forgotten?' His heart welled with an ache that almost choked him.

'How much you are loved.' She leaned in and rested her forehead against his, and through these points of contact streams of pure joy poured into his essence. The tsunami of energy washed through him, cleansing every dark corner of his mind and being, filling it instead with the memory of a higher state of actuality. His heart felt to be exploding in his chest, his gut filled with butterflies, his spine tingled and his entire body was vibrating so fiercely, it brought tears of relief to his eyes. In his mind's eye all he could see was light — golden, bubbling cascades of it, that had no coherent memories attached, just a sense of happiness, belonging and a complete absence of limitation.

'This is home,' she said. 'And it awaits your return with great anticipation.'

When she took a step away Khalid was left reeling and for a moment couldn't open his eyes as he wished to dwell in this blissful state a while longer. There was no telling how long before he would experience it again.

'There is something else we wish to tell you that we feel is a vital truth that will aid your quest.' She did not appear so joyful about it.

'Any aid you can give, I would greatly appreciate.' Khalid gave her permission to bring him back down to earth.

Her look was mournful. 'It concerns the night you were conceived ...'

Zeven had seen himself leave his physical body behind, yet it seemed that no matter what body a soul was wearing, it felt as solid and realistic as the plane it inhabited. He wasn't too sure what he expected a celestial city to look like, perhaps changeable, semi-transparent and filled with spirit types. But it wasn't like that at all.

In answer to his desire to join the Qusay-Sabah Clarona, he and his company had found themselves in an elegant room that opened onto an enclosed bridge that extended out and joined this building with the next of the mega ghost city — but the view!

The ethereal metropolis was far more impressive and remarkable than the city that concealed it. The hidden city appeared to interpenetrate the existing Phemorian city capital, which had been named Tonissia, which meant 'twin', or 'twofold city'. Here the celestial city and its occupants appeared solid, and the physical city of Tonissia appeared less so. What was rather disturbing was how fast the physical world and its inhabitants appeared to be moving, by comparison to its etheric counterpart — a day and night flashed by in a moment.

'We don't get many tourists here.'

Zeven and his company turned about to see the exiled Qusay of Phemoria seated close by, and several other Phemorian women stood around her — one who was the very image of Jalila Lamus.

'Especially of your gender.'

'Forgive the intrusion, Highness,' Zeven bowed his head to her, and Aurora and Telmo followed his lead. 'But we bring news of your daughter, and the coup on Phemoria.'

'My daughter is aware of my exile?' Clarona appeared very relieved to learn this.

'Yes, Majesty,' Zeven concurred, not looking up. 'And she seeks a means to free you from your exile, without causing a war or a revolution.'

'Please rise,' Clarona granted, keen to look them all in the eye. 'Who are you, and how did you get here?' The Qusay did not sound annoyed, but rather relieved to see them.

'My name is Zaman Vidor, son of Spyridon Vidor of the royal house of Sermetica, and your sister, the Princess Satomi.'

'Impossible; that babe was killed.' Clarona was stunned to meet a nephew she never knew she had.

'Not on Maiara Vidor's watch,' Zeven outlined. 'It was also the late Dowager Duchess of Vidor who preserved my mother's body and ultimately saved her life. Although I wonder now, with all her great foresight, if she saw all that has now come to pass because of it?' He couldn't help but sound ashamed.

'You do not support your mother's claim?' Clarona assumed from his tone.

'I do not,' Zeven stated in no uncertain terms. 'She claims a right to your throne as the eldest daughter, yet she ran from that responsibility, and having been dead for thirty years she is the eldest daughter no more.'

Clarona could not suppress her amused smile. 'You make a valid argument,' she acknowledged. 'And your companions?'

'This is my wife, Aurora, and my advisor, Telmo Decree.'

The Qusay served them a rather strained smile of greeting. 'Your wife,' she repeated, curious. 'And do you have children?'

'A daughter, six years old,' Zeven replied, knowing exactly why the question had been asked.

'An heir to Satomi's claim,' Clarona concluded, very concerned to learn this.

'Over my dead body,' Zeven assured the exiled Qusay, who appeared unsure if she should be reassured or insulted.

'And where is this child now?' Clarona probed.

'She is with the Old Ones, and it is they, the Dropa, who aided us to seek you, Highness.' Zeven hoped his means would not prove even more offensive.

The statement was shocking to her. 'It is my understanding that the Old Ones still resent the citizens of this city, even though it was they who betrayed us.'

'Forgive my saying so, Highness, but I believe that everyone involved in the incident in question was deceived, the Dropa most of all.'

The Qusay's tolerance departed. 'They sent a monster to impregnate my mother, who was found guilty by his own admission!'

'From my own investigations into this matter, I believe that monster was summoned into Phemoria by someone inside the royal palace,' Zeven ventured. 'The same someone who aided both your sister, and the boy child of that horrid union, to escape Phemoria.'

'What?' Clarona stood. 'Who would dare betray their Qusay? The Phemoray would have known.'

'Not if the perpetrator had some sort of psychic protection,' Telmo proffered.

'And perhaps the intention was not to betray the Qusay,' Zeven said. 'Maybe they sought to aid the Qusay by ridding her of the Phemoray on the one night that the crown was removed from her head?'

The suggestion stumped Clarona, for it was true, the only time the Phemoray would permit the crown to be removed from the head of the Qusay was during mating, as the Phemoray could not tolerate men. 'Who?' she probed.

'I have no answer to that as I have not been at liberty to accustom myself with many of the occupants of your court,' Zeven was sorry to advise. 'But surely there are very few people with the power and guts to arrange such instances.'

'If I might speak,' Aurora held up a finger in question, and the Qusay granted her request with a nod. 'I met with Taren shortly after Satomi's coup and she mentioned that she had met the general of the Valoureans and felt that she fit the profile of the person Zeven has been seeking.'

'General Prochazka,' Clarona named the woman in question and looked to the woman alongside her, who was clearly Jalila's twin. She nodded to second the reasoning.

'As head of the Valoureans, Prochazka would have been on guard the night that our last Qusay lost her sanity. She was the one charged with killing the boy child who resulted from that union,' the Qusay's advisor reasoned.

'And now she is aiding Satomi, who trusts her completely.' Clarona was deeply concerned. 'She could be intending to seize power.'

'Or merely seeking to right past mistakes before they come to light?' Zeven suggested. 'If the curses and Khalid Mansur are destroyed, there shall be nothing to inform the Qusay Satomi that her main ally was the one who gave Khalid his freedom. Again, this is postulation, but who else could possibly have managed it?'

Clarona shook her head, unable to come up with an alternative and sank to a seat once more.

'Destroying the curse of the Phemoray and the crew from Dead Man Downs on Sermetica is one of AMIE's primary objectives,' Zeven went on. 'But Khalid is innocent of any crime committed whilst under the influence of Chironjivi's curse, and I will not allow either him or his father to carry the blame any longer — the truth must be known.'

'Chironjivi?' Clarona queried. 'Do you refer to the last prince of Phemoria?'

'The very one,' Zeven enlightened.

'But he perished —' The exiled queen abandoned her protest as Zeven and his comrades all shook their heads. 'Does no one simply die any more?' Clarona emphasised her frustration.

'It would seem Chironjivi learned a few of his mother's tricks and summoned up a curse, very similar to that of the Phemoray, by sacrificing the lives of the damned men on board his vessel before it crashed. Both the last prince and his curse survived. And as soon as Khalid was old enough to serve them, this unnatural apparition sought him out and masqueraded as his father, implanting an amulet in him as a child that compelled him do the curse's bidding.'

'I was never told of this.' Clarona was shocked and frustrated. 'The Phemoray kept me ignorant about a great many things.'

'As I said,' Zeven concluded, 'we have all been deceived.'

For a moment Clarona pondered the situation, but was none the happier for it. 'I wish I could help with these struggles, but there is no release for any of us here without first putting the curse of the Phemoray to rest. Satomi must not be allowed to destroy the crown, or every soul in this etheric city will perish,' Clarona informed him.

'I am aware of this,' Zeven assured her, as he remembered how the curse had been lifted last time around. 'Taren also knows this, and will not allow any harm to befall the item before it can be dealt with accordingly. As soon as our talks are complete, and with aid from the Dropa, I intend to return to the physical world and aid the AMIE crew.'

'The Old Ones are aiding you … us, why?' Clarona was suspicious.

'Because they know what you now know,' Zeven replied. 'That the fault in this situation rests squarely on the shoulders of no one person living.'

'Except Prochazka,' the Qusay's advisor was quick to say.

'If our speculation proves correct.' Zeven couldn't concur with any certainty.

'Prochazka is ruthless,' Clarona said, knowing the subject better than her company. 'She will die before she admits to crimes that she is prepared to go to such lengths to keep hidden.'

Telmo held up a finger, having had a revelation. 'While it is true that there was no way to release the occupants of this city while the Phemoray held sway here and a rift existed between you and the Dropa … that is not necessarily the case now.' Telmo chuckled as he observed the occupants of this city going about their everyday life, performing habitually psychic feats that those among the *Zagriata* were still striving to master. 'Provided, that is, that the occupants of this city desire to be released?'

It wasn't only Zeven who was perplexed by his advisor's epiphany.

'None of us came here by choice,' Clarona spoke for the women around her, who all stood tall to support her response. 'If you can unlock this prison, there is not a soul here that shall not gladly return to the life they were meant to live.'

16

THE WAITING GAME

Lucian was slumbering peacefully in the medical chambers, his vitals being monitored closely by Dr Madri. Taren returned to Oceane with Vadik who, with his command over the elements, encapsulated the Soul Keep in the same metal compound used for the case currently containing the Phemorian crown, the canister that held Chironjivi's trinket, and in the walls of every psychic containment prison in the USS. Until Zeven and his company returned with the final component of the curse, two members of the crew would stay stationed in the hut on Oceane in shifts to keep an eye on the Soul Keep and the area where their crew mates had vanished from this world. Vadik being the only crew member who was not completely exhausted in the wake of the day's events, volunteered to take the first watch alone.

The news of Ringbalin being taken hostage by Phemoria of his own volition was not received well by any of the crew.

Ayliscia did not openly display an attachment to the outcome. 'I will attend to Module C in his absence.' The look on the Phemorian's face was one of resentment and was aimed more at Jalila than Taren, yet there was a tinge of relief there as well.

The decision to postpone the rest of the debrief was unanimous.

Taren hit her sleeping pod and didn't wake for two days.

*

340

When Leal was summoned to report to the medical quarters for a check-up in the aftermath of the crew's incarceration, he was a little nervous. What really ailed him was not going to show up on any of the doctor's equipment — but as a fellow telepath, Kassa was bound to pick up on it anyway. Honestly, he'd gone beyond the point of caring about embarrassment or rejection — his recent experiences had taught him that in their line of work, they could be dead tomorrow. If he didn't go after what he wanted today then the opportunity might never come again, and he would rather live with rejection than regret.

He entered the waiting room and buzzed Kassa's surgery intercom to let her know he was here.

'Be right with you. Take a seat,' came her reply.

As Leal was rested, showered and way too agitated to sit down, he wandered about the small room, observing the pictures on the wall. None of these images were quite how he'd remembered them, but they were lovely nonetheless.

It blew his mind that Taren had reconstructed this entire ship from memory. Even the clothes in his wardrobe were the same, although brand new and not quite as comfortable. But he wasn't complaining — at least Taren remembered his favourite jacket in the finest detail, so her powers of observation were pretty damn impressive.

The door to the surgery opened and the captain was dismissed from therein.

'Not too shabby for a dead man,' Kassa was saying, as she saw Lucian out.

'I still rather smell like one though.' Lucian had a whiff of himself and cringed, but smelled something more pleasant as he entered the waiting room and spotted Leal. 'At least your next patient smells much better than I do.'

Maybe I went a little overboard with the aftershave? Leal considered, feeling a blush rising in his face, which was always far too noticeable with his fair complexion.

Fortunately his company were focused on each other. 'If a bad odour is all you have to complain about in the wake of your resurrection, you're doing well.' Kassa grinned at Lucian and looked to Leal briefly. 'Just give me two ticks to clean up in here.'

'That's a polite way of saying get rid of the horrid smell,' Lucian clarified, chagrined. Kassa did not dispute this, but merely grinned as she closed the door.

'Good to see you, Captain.' Leal shook Lucian's hand. 'The last time I was in your company, I felt sure it was the last time I would be in your company.'

Lucian smiled broadly, obviously pleased to see him also. 'Prochazka did quite a dance on your face,' the captain said, referring to Leal's numerous cuts, bumps and bruises.

'Where's Ringbalin when you need him?' Leal's jest quashed the mood somewhat, and the captain appeared a little vexed as their handshake ended. 'So I look that bad, huh?' Leal changed the subject.

'Not at all,' Lucian was diplomatic. 'Very macho.' The captain cocked an eye, and glanced back to the surgery from where he'd just come, ahead of rousing a smile once again. 'Well, good luck in there,' he said. 'I'm off to find a shower and smell a little less macho.'

'It's for the best.' Leal held his nose to cover the awkward moment, and watched the captain leave. Leal never gave a damn what he looked or smelled like normally and he felt sure the captain had picked up on his ulterior agenda this morning, but like the true gentlemen that he was, Lucian said nothing of it.

The door to the surgery opened once again and Kassa smiled warmly in greeting. 'I'm ready when you are, kiddo.' She disappeared back inside, and failed to notice him cringe.

'Kiddo' was a general term of endearment that Kassa used on everyone on board AMIE, a subtle reminder that she was one of the most senior members of the crew. And with Zelimir Ronan gone, she was the most senior crew member! Still, Leal really hated when she referred to him thus; it only emphasised the difference in their ages, and made his purpose here this morning just that much more awkward.

Maybe today is not the day? He felt his confidence fraying before he'd even stepped in the room.

'On the bed, let's take a look at you,' Kassa instructed as he entered, laying out clean implements on a table in preparation for the examination. 'I want to examine those lacerations on your head.'

Leal stripped off his jacket and tossed it on a chair, then jumped up to a seat on the bed as instructed.

Kassa dragged her table around nearer to him, and took up her ophthalmoscope to check his eyes and ears. 'Where are you feeling the most pain?'

That was a loaded question, as if he chose to tell the truth she had to know he wasn't joking. The memory of being trapped in a cell on Phemoria with no idea what had become of Kassa was enough motivation.

'Here.' He held a hand to his heart, choking on the emotion the confession triggered in him.

Kassa's jovial mood sobered. 'What did they do?' The doctor was immediately more choked up than he was. 'I'm sorry.' She stepped away, held a hand over her mouth and gasped back her emotion. 'You don't have to answer that.'

He gripped the wrist of the hand she was using to cover her face, feeling a little guilty for upsetting her unduly. 'They locked me up away from you,' he confessed the worst of it.

Kassa looked to him, hopeful. 'That's all?' She gasped as he allowed her to perceive and feel the memory that had inspired his candour in this moment.

'That's all it took,' he assured.

'I was so worried —' they both confessed at once, smiling through their tears, when, much to Leal's delight Kassa placed her implement aside and overwhelmed him with a deep heartfelt embrace.

'I've been such an idiot! I could have lost you.' She disclosed her true feelings for once, and pulled away to divulge a few secrets of her own. 'Before we'd even met I knew you were the one for me, but I just couldn't bring myself to believe I could possibly be that fortunate.'

Leal was in complete shock — elating though this news was, he couldn't quite believe what he was hearing. 'What are you talking about?'

'It was something I picked up on the first time I met Zeven — I didn't know what the vision was … a premonition, or a fanciful thought or —' She shrugged. 'And then when I met you that same day, and you were so young, I just ...' She threw her hands up in conclusion.

'I'm not that young.' He smiled, rather delighted by her discomfort.

'But that was before I found out that Zeven had been jumping timelines and what have you.' Kassa's frustration ebbed, and her amazed expression returned. 'And now I see that maybe that vision was a memory, lost in those timelines somewhere.'

'What memory?' Leal grinned, seeing how uncomfortable the query made her. 'What did you see?'

Kassa smiled, overwhelmed by the question, and shook her head. 'You don't need to know the details. Besides, circumstances alter when the timekeepers do their thing, we all know that.'

Leal took hold of both her hands, and hooked his feet around her legs to pull her towards him. 'You're right, I don't need to know.' He let her off the hook. 'Let's get married?'

Kassa was stunned, and not just by the question. 'You knew what I saw. You saw it too?' She slapped his chest, onto his game.

'Have I not been beaten enough?' he appealed, to quell her protest.

'I'm sorry.' She stroked his chest in comfort instead, and sniffled back her tears. 'You were saying?'

'The point is ... all I could think about in that prison was you.' He knew he'd made that painfully clear. 'So answer the question.'

Kassa breathed deep to process his proposal more seriously. 'But children —'

'I don't want children,' Leal insisted. 'Just you.'

'Don't you think we should at least go on a date first?' Kassa proposed, and Leal tried not to appear put off by her reserve. 'With half the crew still missing, right now is probably not the best time for a wedding.' She clearly didn't want to disappoint him, she was just being practical, as was her way. 'However ... some time alone together could be just what the doctor ordered.' She grinned suggestively, which he found encouraging.

'Well ... you're the doctor.' He held her face and wiped the stray tears from her eyes, drawing her into the kiss he'd been dreaming about since the day they'd first met. 'And I do like that prescription.'

As soon as Taren was back on deck she wasted no time summoning the crew together for a full debrief — all except for Trance and Vadik who were at the cabin on watch.

The feeling in the room was a mixture of relief and gratitude to be home, tainted by the all too obvious absence of the crew members still unaccounted for, and the uncertainty of their return.

First up, Lucian raised his concerns in regard to Ringbalin's role as hostage for the Phemorians, but when Mythric and Swithin outlined the situation in which they had found themselves, the captain admitted that he would have probably done the same in Taren's place.

Yasper took issue with his father's death. He wanted Zelimir's body returned for cremation, as his father's state of decomposition would make it impossible to resurrect him at this point. Taren vowed she would ask after Zelimir's remains when she next met with the general to give a report.

Just about all the crew had a beef with Zeven's mission to rescue Khalid from himself and no matter how many times Taren explained the situation, or how much she voiced her complete faith in her cousin's actions, the general view remained unaltered.

'You know I adore the short man,' Jazmay spoke up to give Swithin's voice a rest, as he was the most fiercely outspoken on the subject. 'But the fact is, you don't really seem to know what his motives are, and him going AWOL without us, is just plain reckless! He endangered all our lives.'

'Like you all haven't done that at some point!' Taren blew a fuse. 'If this is what it takes to prevent an inter-universal disaster then *sorry*, but I support it one hundred per cent.'

'If we were all dead, would you still be saying that?' Swithin challenged, coolly.

'Please don't make me answer what ifs,' Taren simmered down. 'Let's just deal with what *is*. What happened was not Zeven's fault; he took every precaution to ensure the safety of this crew and the future. If anyone is to blame it is me; if I'd not ignored Thurraya's repeated requests to know where her father was, she would not have been compelled to pop off and see him.'

'Well, I ain't going to blame a six-year-old girl,' Swithin gave up his beef. 'But Starman had better fucking come through!'

Taren nodded to accept his point, but was truly drained in the wake of the onslaught. She half expected a hug from her husband, but Lucian kept his distance.

'Anything else you need brought to our attention?' Lucian invited everyone to air any other complaints or information for discussion.

Leal raised a finger and Lucian gave him the nod to speak. 'I don't believe anyone mentioned why Zelimir was slain so swiftly.'

'How do you mean?' Taren was curious, thinking it was Ronan's MSS history that had forced Prochazka's hand.

'The ring!' Yasper clicked his fingers, remembering the instance in question. 'My father questioned Prochazka about a ring she was wearing.'

'Where in *wretchedness* did you get it?' Leal quoted. 'Which seemed a poignant remark from someone who could see auras.'

'That confirms it,' Taren uttered under her breath. 'That's how she controls them and how she found this ship so damn quickly.'

'Is that helpful?' Yasper queried. 'I'd like to think my father didn't get his brains blown out for no good reason.'

'Yasper?' Jazmay hugged their son to her, obviously feeling he didn't need to be reminded.

'Mother.' Fari pushed her away. 'I'm not a kid,' he insisted.

'It wasn't your fault,' Jazmay went down on her haunches to assure him.

'I know.' The boy exhibited his mother's same detachment from emotion. 'I wasn't holding the gun.'

Jazmay was a little taken aback by his view, but satisfied he was not just putting on a brave front, she let it be. 'I really don't think this discussion is appropriate for a seven-year-old.'

'No, Ma! Don't get me dismissed!' he objected.

'The information is very helpful,' Taren assured them all, especially Fari. 'It confirms a hunch I had; your grandfather's word is gold to me.'

'Now, you're going to send me to bed, aren't you?' Fari drew in the corners of his mouth, and exhaled heavily.

'Dismissed.' Taren was sorry to be so predictable.

Fari rolled his eyes as his father turned him towards the door and slapped his behind to get him moving. 'I'll be in to say goodnight shortly.' Yasper watched his son flounce out of the mess.

Mythric raised a finger. 'I too am fairly sure Prochazka is at the bottom of all this. But something she said has me puzzled.' He frowned as he recalled. 'She promised that she would be keeping a very close eye on my progress and if I betray them she would know of it. But then immediately following, Satomi gave me back my Juju stone.'

'Which shields you from being perceived or found via psychic means.' Taren got his drift.

'I'm fairly sure the general was aware of what Satomi was about to do, and Prochazka is not the type to make idle threats.' Mythric raised both brows in question. 'So how else might she perceive my movements?'

'A spy,' Swithin concluded, as his mind was the most devious.

'Exactly,' Mythric put it to Taren. 'I am thinking that perhaps one of the people we rescued may not be who we think they are, but a shifter.'

That statement set everyone on edge, but not Ayliscia. 'Or perhaps the spy is exactly who they appear to be.' Her wary sights looked back to Jalila.

'I was near dead when you found me,' Jalila defended. 'Perhaps you are the impostor, if you feel the need to point a finger at someone else?'

'I had someone with me the entire time we were captive,' Ayliscia argued.

'True,' Kassa concurred.

'You, however,' Ayliscia continued, 'knew we had a healer and that the timekeeper would not allow you to die.'

'Ladies!' Lucian called time on the argument. 'At this point the claim is supposition. We have no proof of leaked information, and until we do there is no crime here.'

Taren looked around the room, feeling in her gut that Mythric might be right; she needed to be careful who she trusted with important information. 'Just out of curiosity, is there anyone else who can vouch they had company the entire time they were captive?'

Amie and Kassa raised their hands. None of the men present, including Mythric, could raise theirs. This left only Lucian and Vadik in the clear. Jazmay and Kalayna had also been separated from their crew mates, and even Trance had been left alone for a time.

'So now we go back to being kept out of the loop,' Swithin grumbled, 'because you can't trust us!'

'If anyone in this room was wearing the guise of another I would see it,' Lucian pointed out, as he was clairvoyant. 'And I can assure you that you are all who you appear to be.'

This was a relief to all present, Taren most of all. She had just brought all the crew into her confidence and didn't wish to exclude half of them again.

'That doesn't mean one of us won't voluntarily hand over information,' Ayliscia cautioned. 'And who better than a telepath to do it?'

Your view is noted,' Lucian assured the biologist. 'And if no one else has any concerns at present ...' He put it to the room, who were all looking ready to depart and shook their heads in decline. 'Then we are done here. Jazmay, would you drop Yasper and Swithin over to the hut, to relieve Trance and Vadik for a spell? I'll run my second sight over them when they return and be sure they are all clear also.'

'You got it,' she concurred.

'I'll need to grab some things.' Swithin raised himself and headed out.

'I better say goodnight to the lad.' Yasper followed, along with Jazmay and most of the crew, but not Mythric. He sank to a seat, and as Taren knew why, she remained also.

'You still haven't told us what news of Zeven?' Mythric folded his arms, feeling he was owed that much. 'Did you locate him?'

'I did,' Lucian admitted now that they were alone. 'And he was right about Khalid, his soul belongs to the Old Ones, who Zeven refers to as the Dropa. It was they who built the inter-system gateways to pave the way for our civilisations to flourish. Khalid was meant to be born female and bring enlightenment and balance back into the Phemorian culture by pacifying the curses created during the time of the sexual revolution. For many of the souls who took part in those events were also Dropa and needed to be freed from their earthly delusions and fears in order to rejoin their source. So the Dropa formed an alliance with the Phemoray, promising the offspring of the unions of Dropa men with their Qusays would produce even more powerful progeny. When this plan went awry, and as Khalid was what they term a Sharrujahan —'

'What … like their leader?' Mythric guessed.

Lucian cringed, not satisfied that this was an accurate translation. 'The Dropa are one and so don't really have a leader. It means something more like "most excellent expression of their being" perhaps? "Most beloved expression" or something to that effect.'

'So when the Dropa lost their Sharrujahan, they …?' Taren got them back on track, fascinated by the theology behind their evolution in this universe as it was far and away the least documented topic in the USS.

'They called upon the Grigori for help getting their soul minds out.'

Lucian's claim made Taren gasp, and she felt as though her heart had shot into her throat, bringing tears to her eyes. 'That makes perfect sense,' she rasped.

'To you maybe.' Mythric was cynical. 'Who are the Grigori?'

'Our watchers,' Lucian said. 'The beings who mediate between us and the being residing over this planet; the one that gives your Juju its power.'

'You picked up a good deal in ten minutes.' Taren, listening to Lucian speak in terms metaphysical, fell in love with him all over again — she found this side of him seriously attractive!

'*Okay* …' Mythric rolled with that. 'But what has all this to do with Zeven?'

'He is being guided by the Grigori also, and the Dropa, perhaps more clearly than any of us.' Lucian's view was a great relief to Taren.

'But where is the rest of my family? When are they coming back?' Mythric probed, losing patience. 'Are they coming back?'

'I was dragged back to the land of the living before Zeven reached any resolve,' the captain was sorry to inform. 'I know he was contemplating trying to make contact with your mother in the celestial city, Taren.'

'But if your ten-minute stay cost you two days,' Taren fretted, 'a sidetrack like that could stretch out to be months, even years!'

'I didn't say that's what he would do,' Lucian clarified. 'As I also know, Khalid was keen to return here and fulfil his reason for being born.'

'Which would involve doing what to my wife?' Mythric's past adverse experiences with Khalid came back to haunt.

'These are highly spiritual beings we are talking about,' Lucian stressed. 'They are creators, not destroyers.'

'Was it not members of their soul-group that started all of this in the first place?' Mythric's comprehension skills were sharp as always.

'Extreme trauma can make a malefactor out of the purest of souls,' Lucian reasoned. 'In the last universe, one little tantrum from you got your entire civilisation wiped out!'

Surprisingly, Mythric was not as sceptical now, as if he knew there was truth in the outrageous statement.

'Wait a second, you both remember what happened during the last mission that Zeven claimed we went on?' Taren was shocked — were more crew members AWOL?

'I had a few visions while I was on Oceane,' Mythric confessed with some discomfort. 'I know I made Zeven pledge to help save Khalid, as I had pledged the same to a being who claimed to be one of the Dropa.'

'Holy shit!' Taren gasped, looking back to Lucian for his explanation.

'I was enlightened to these events at the time of my death,' Lucian explained morbidly.

'So you can both confirm Zeven is telling the truth!' Taren was overcome with joy, and when Lucian nodded to confirm this, she hugged him. Lucian's embrace was not so heartfelt, however.

'Is there something you're not telling me?' Taren wondered why he was so distant. Was it just because Mythric was present? Being openly affectionate had never bothered Lucian before.

'Nope. That's about all I learned before I got brought back.' Lucian left Taren to approach Mythric. 'But I can assure you that your family are perfectly safe, and that Zeven, by all accounts, appears to know what he's doing.'

Mythric nodded, and having a lot to digest, he rose and shook Lucian's hand. 'Many thanks.'

'Any plans to visit your wife?' The captain queried his intentions.

'Not at this point,' Mythric replied. 'But I will be sure and let you know if that changes.'

'Much obliged.' Lucian watched him leave.

When the captain turned his attention back to her, Taren expected that he was about to explain the cold shoulder she was getting.

'Kalayna asked if I'd pay her a visit in the tech room, so I'll catch you a little later.' He headed off towards the door.

'I get that you're mad with me, what I don't get is why?' Taren's appeal waylaid his exit.

'There's no point discussing it until this crisis is over,' he said shortly.

'But that could be years away.' Taren entreated him to show a little mercy.

'Look, I'm not mad at you,' he explained. 'I just need a little distance to process.'

Now Taren was really panicked. 'What on earth happened? Did I betray you? Get you killed?'

'Not me,' he said, choking down his emotion. 'But this week was not the first time you traded the safety of another to save my life.'

'What?' Taren couldn't believe he was going to guilt her out over that. 'Don't you think I feel bad enough about Ringbalin? He volunteered!'

'At least he was in a position to.' Lucian's response was cutting, even though Taren didn't really understand what it meant; it was the resentment underlying his comeback that hurt. 'I'm sorry, please forget I said that.' He attempted to wave off the entire matter. 'Death was just a little confronting, I'll be right in a few days.'

Taren could feel her tears welling again, and they were anything but joyous now. 'It's a bit unfair to chastise me, when you won't tell me why.'

'After the crisis,' he repeated. 'Don't forget I've already experienced these instances a few times now and I know for a fact that you will prefer it this way.' He left for his next appointment.

In the wake of the clash, Taren was completely shell-shocked. They'd had differences of opinion before today, but never had she felt such true resentment directed at her from Lucian's quarter. She was starting to wish she'd gone AWOL when Telmo and Zeven did. She had four years to wait before she would be able to clearly recall the events that had her crew so divided. She could only hope that the unification of the last universe would not cost them the same in this one.

The waiting game began and the truce held firm. Taren met with Prochazka each month to report the same lack of contact with her missing crew, and every time Prochazka accepted her account without question. This was disconcerting. Did the general have a spy in their midst to confirm these reports, or another means of observing them altogether?

Taren had been taught to see auras during her first visit to the universe parallel, but unused, this skill had become a little rusty. She needed to really focus on her target, who also needed to be still and in good natural light, in order to get her lazy third eye sight to function. Her attempts to perceive the general's ring and see whatever Zelimir had seen, without her obviously staring at the item, had proved impossible thus far.

But at least Taren had been able to retrieve Zelimir's remains for cremation and burial in space, as there was no planet that Zelimir Ronan called home at the time of his death. Zelimir had been born and raised on Maladaan, whose government had betrayed him. As the industrial capital of the USS, any natural beauty to be found on the planet had been destroyed long before Zelimir had been born. No one dared breathe the air outside of the completely enclosed cities, so it was no place to rest in peace.

The meetings with the general were never very long; Taren suspected that the presence of the Juju she wore would have a draining, even sickening, effect on Prochazka — if the ring she wore was as evil as the charm that was once implanted in Khalid. Whilst connected to the curse, Khalid had become violently sick when exposed to the Juju, when he'd never known a sick day in his life before that.

Despite her lack of news, Taren was permitted to visit Ringbalin where he worked and lived — in the royal gardens. She need not have feared for her friend's wellbeing as the horticulturist-cum-biologist appeared to be thriving in his new environment, just as his environment was thriving around him.

'Are you quite sure that restraining device is working?' Taren had asked, admiring how well the garden was growing as Ringbalin gave her the tour.

'Absolutely,' he assured her, well pleased. 'I haven't had one woman so much as smile at me in the entire time I've been here. A Valourean even slapped me down for looking at her the other day.' He was most excited about that, and Taren had to laugh.

'I could replace that restraint with a fake,' Taren teased, as without it on a planet of women he'd be doomed!

'Please no!' he was quick to refuse. 'I'm thinking I might even keep this on when they finally let me go back home. At least then I might know when someone is attracted to me and not my power.' Ringbalin was only half-joking about this.

'Even restrained, I still adore you.' Taren leaned her head on his shoulder and grinned. 'And so does the garden!'

Although he smiled at her viewpoint, clearly it was no consolation.

He always asked after Module C, and Taren would pass on any concerns Ayliscia was having, and although neither one of the biologists specifically asked about the other, Taren kept them up to date with each other's news.

*

Another regular meeting on Taren's agenda was with President Anselm, who was as dissatisfied with the circumstance of their stalemate as everyone involved, but as there was clearly no getting to the truth before Zeven Gudrun and his crew showed up, her father was staying his hand at this point. Despite passing on what Lucian had said about Khalid and the Dropa, Anselm was also wrestling with the concept of forgiving Khalid for the part he'd played in Maiara's death. Yet, as Taren pointed out, Anselm had forgiven her mother her curse and Khalid's circumstance was no different.

All talks pertaining to the psychic rights bill were put on hold. Maladaan was really their primary concern in regard to psychic persecution, and chances were that President Tallak would never sign the psychic rights bill in any case. Unless, of course, he was left with no other choice, and/or the agreement could somehow be seen as being advantageous to Maladaan and the majority of her people, through which the paranoia and hatred of psychics ran rampant.

As frustrating as waiting for Zeven to reappear was, it had given AMIE time to focus on the problem of Maladaan, and of how they might be brought to the negotiating table on the issue of psychic rights. As Zeven had previously advised, the answer to this problem lay with Kalayna.

Not only had Kalayna adapted the psychic restraint technology into a handheld weapon, but having got their hands on one of the photon cameras the MSS were using to identify anyone with the Powers on Maladaan, she'd come to the conclusion that the timekeepers could destroy all these cameras with a thought.

Taren agreed with this assessment, but equally obvious was the fact that the MSS would only produce more cameras to replace the ones they destroyed.

'But this design of the photon chamber in this camera is based on technology that you designed,' Kalayna pointed out.

'Are you suggesting we steal the blueprints?' Taren felt the pro-psychic movement going on in the United Systems at present would surely end up with the blame.

'I'm suggesting we alter the blueprints and create a design flaw that is undetectable. Just like the Old Ones did when they shut down the inter-system gateway to the Oceane system. It's only taken us a few thousand years to figure that one out!' Kalayna enlightened. 'That's what happens when people don't fully understand the technology they are dealing with.'

'I can see exactly where you're coming from,' Taren awarded. 'Perhaps we could even design a flaw that interferes with a high photon count?'

'That way anyone with Powers won't be detected, and the user of the camera will be none the wiser,' Kalayna agreed. 'I can also design a flaw for you to install in all the photon cameras currently in circulation, to make them burn out after a certain amount of use and that way it looks like —'

'— a manufacturing flaw.' Taren smiled, appeased. 'Of course, if we alter my original blueprints, no one else will be able to get the photonics chamber to work.'

'Not without you,' Kalayna advised, and then shrugged to boast, 'Or someone like me. Good luck filling that order on Maladaan.'

This plan meant no all-out war to ban the use of the photon camera on Maladaan, so the rest of the United Systems would not have to become involved. As nothing was being stolen, there was no visible crime being committed, nor was there anything to prosecute.

Taren was impressed. 'Have I mentioned how great it is to have you on crew?'

Kalayna beamed with a satisfied smile. 'The best news is that we should be able to execute this mission without ever leaving AMIE.'

Taren nodded to concur that was the case. 'They cannot catch a thief who was never there.'

The event of the photon cameras' demise on Maladaan would be suppressed by the MSS and the government on Maladaan. For Maladaan's president, Woodford Tallak, the introduction of the photon camera psychic detection system had earned him a good deal of public support. The camera was part of his political agenda to fight against psychic supremacy, and was his direct response to the USS-proposed psychics' rights bill, which left no doubt as to where Maladaan stood on the issue.

Even with the photon camera and psychic restraining devices, the MSS still had a big problem capturing many of the psychics they spotted with the camera and getting them safely restrained. Kalayna's latest invention would fill that void and it was Taren's hope that her father could use it as leverage to, if not decriminalise the use of psychic power on Maladaan, at least to ensure that rather than being imprisoned, psychics could be deported to one of the other planets they hoped would eventually sign the psychic bill of rights.

These developments played a large part in staying Anselm's hand in regard to putting down Satomi's coup on Phemoria and reinstating Qusay-Sabah Clarona. For the technology also gave Anselm an assurance that when the time came, they had the means to take down Satomi and her psychic army.

The advent of Kalayna's new weapon was kept under wraps; as far as the rest of the crew were concerned she was still working on it. Lucian, as captain, had volunteered to be Kalayna's test subject and the trial revealed a direct hit would induce a loss of psychic power for one standard USS hour — about the same amount of time it took for a psychic neutraliser's effect to wear off. Only Taren, Lucian and Kalayna knew of this.

The three newest members of their crew each took to life with AMIE very differently. Vadik's adjustment had been the easiest. He'd taken up permanent residence in the hut on Oceane. Even though the coast had remained clear and nothing much ever happened there, he was a good watchman who preferred the isolation and being close to nature. This meant that the other crew members only needed to be at the hut to keep watch while Vadik slept.

Since all the action had died down and his life was no longer under constant threat, Trance was less annoying, but he still found life on board AMIE far from ideal. Shortly after the captain was again in office, Trance arranged a meeting to appeal to be returned home — pointing out that the captain had been restored to life and he was no longer needed to act as a medium. The request was granted, and Taren was instructed to return Trance to the House of Vidor.

As her relationship with Lucian was already rather volatile, Taren did not argue the decision when she was called to the captain's office and advised of Trance's dismissal. She just delivered the medium back to the grand empty kitchen she'd found him in.

'You think I went behind your back?' Trance noted that she was a little aloof.

'Lucian calls the shots on AMIE.' Taren reasoned that he'd not done anything wrong. 'You fulfilled the mission I recruited you for, and I am most obliged to you for that.' It wasn't that she was annoyed at Trance, it was her husband's distance that was underlying her irritated mood.

Now Trance was annoyed. 'I know you think that we with the Powers all want to fight for our freedom and so forth … But seriously … I'm happy to hide the damn Power and just live life.'

'Whatever floats your boat.' To Taren the thought of a mundane life was exactly that.

Trance leaned forwards on the bench, and raised his eyes to her in appeal. 'Are you aware you have a massive passive aggressive, judgemental streak?'

'I'm not judging you.' Taren was a little upset by his observation, mainly because it was surprisingly accurate in this instance. 'It may not be safe for you here any more.'

'Ha!' Trance held up a finger as he suppressed his amusement. 'After what you subjected me to, you're worried it is not safe here?'

'You knocked out Prochazka; she's not going to forget that,' Taren said.

'So you say,' Trance scoffed, as he didn't recall anything that went on when channelling another's spirit.

'Whether or not you knocked her out, I'm pretty sure she saw you.' She watched Trance remove the piece of Juju stone she'd given him. 'You should keep that for protection; at least it will stop anyone finding you via psychic means.'

'And if they find me via normal means this stone is evidence that directly links me to AMIE.' Trance handed it over. 'Besides they say it makes the wearer do anything you tell them to do.'

Taren rolled her eyes. 'Did Kalayna tell you that? It's total rubbish —'

'It certainly worked on me —' Trance choked a little on the statement, and then shrugged off the brief emotion to be back to his pompous self. 'It was fun while you were single, but staring at that arse and knowing there is a husband attached, is just plain frustrating. Especially considering that he does not seem to appreciate what he has.'

Taren didn't know how to respond to that. 'It's … complicated right now.'

'Really?' Trance found this amusing. 'Well the way you two live, you'd best un-complicate it, before one of you ends up dead again. I mean, when is the last time you took time out together to have a life?'

Taren found this amusing; it seemed a trivial thing when there was so much going on in the world.

'You think that's a joke?' Trance was a little dumbfounded by her reaction. 'I'm no marriage counsellor, but when a guy has a girl like you and he's avoiding her, there is something *seriously* wrong.'

'I know there's something wrong!' Taren stressed. 'But he won't tell me — Oh, never mind.' She declined going into detail.

'I'm just saying.' Trance held his hands up in truce. 'There is more to life than saving the universe, and you never seem to stop. Everyone else on your crew takes breaks,' he pointed out.

'I'll get there.' Taren bowed out of the discussion.

'Hey, don't get me wrong … I'd love for your marriage to fall apart, and if it does, you know where to find me.' Trance grinned.

Taren refrained from rolling her eyes, but was amused by his cheek. 'Thanks again for all your help.'

'Don't mention it,' he said graciously, before reverting back to his regular self-serving tone. 'To *anyone, ever.*'

*

'All done,' Taren manifested in the captain's office to report. 'Trance is safely home.'

Lucian was seated in his chair, gazing out the large windows and into the deep ocean beyond. 'He told me about his missions with you during my absence,' he said, not looking to her.

Taren felt she knew where this dialogue was headed. 'Another innocent life I endangered to bring you back.'

'True.' Lucian rose and looked to her. 'But that's not what we spoke about. In fact, Mr Ducer did most of the talking ... I got my butt kicked for being such an ingrate.'

Taren was shocked to learn this. 'Oh dear.'

Lucian nodded to concur, as he wandered around his desk to speak with her more directly. 'He pointed out that I am married to one of the most remarkable women in existence, and that I should consider myself damn lucky that you hadn't returned me to my grave by now and found yourself someone with a bit more fucking backbone.'

The heartfelt sentiment behind Lucian's confession filled her eyes with tears, but as it was delivered with a good serve of Trance's deadpan humour, it warmed her heart and made her smile as well. 'That's a little harsh.' She sniffled back her emotion so she could see.

'Not really,' Lucian disagreed. 'You managed to restore the ship, rescue most of the crew, resurrect me, *and* you have created a truce that *seems* to be holding. You could not possibly have done a better job than that.'

'But Ringbalin —'

Lucian shook his head. 'I was wrong. At the time I didn't realise he had two Phemorian women fighting over him. I now believe he may have had an ulterior motive for volunteering.'

'I didn't think you knew about that.' Taren's smile was beaming, there was no suppressing how good it felt to be back in Lucian's favour — the ill will that had been between seemed to have been completely swept away.

'Well, Jalila volunteered for kitchen duty,' he outlined, 'and apparently Ayliscia didn't take kindly to her having access —'

'— to Module C.' Taren got the picture. 'I shall investigate.'

'That's beside the point.' Lucian looked to her with his big dark eyes, and he really didn't need to say anything else.

'Whenever you can tell me whatever I did to upset you,' Taren spoke first, 'I promise you … if it is within my power to rectify it, I will.'

Lucian grinned broadly at this, which gave her hope that she would be able to redeem herself. 'I believe you.'

'Oh damn, now I'm really curious.' Taren was a little discomforted by just how much his mood improved, as he took her in hand and drew her closer.

'Just forget it.' He kissed her and it felt like the weight of the world was suddenly lifted from her shoulders. 'As I will surely *not* forget,' Lucian added as he let her go.

'Fine.' Taren ignored the tease. 'I shall be happy to oblige.'

Lucian suppressed a chuckle, and Taren served him a perplexed look. 'I'm done processing,' he announced happily. 'Date night tonight?'

'Date night every night for a while.' She headed out to go investigate the squabble over Module C, when the door in front of her locked closed and her smile broadened.

'Oh, look at that!'

Taren did an about-face to see Lucian gesturing out the window.

'Night,' he concluded, merrily.

It was quite some time later that Taren finally made it down to Module C, and she was pleased to find Ayliscia still up and working.

'Is it that time *already?*' The biologist was referring to Taren's regular report from Ringbalin, as she brushed herself off and stood.

'No, that's next week,' Taren corrected, subconsciously hitting her fist into her hand to get to the point. 'It's about Jalila.'

'She complained to the captain.' Ayliscia rolled her eyes, her harsh Phemorian accent made thicker by her disdain. 'Kitchen duty, what a joke! She'll poison us all!' She folded her arms.

'We need all hands on deck right now,' Taren appealed for her to be a little helpful. 'And working in the kitchen sometimes you need some fresh herbs or —'

'*Herbs* ha!' Ayliscia came closer to whisper her concerns. 'I found her up in the booth.' She pointed to the climate control centre where Ringbalin chose to live. '*Sniffing* his clothes! The woman is a pervert!'

When Taren suppressed her amusement, Ayliscia assured her it was true.

'Ya!' She raised her brows and her eyes boggled. 'Is sick, right?'

'Well, Ringbalin's energy is a bit addictive,' Taren attempted to explain it.

'I hadn't noticed.'

Ayliscia was so stone-faced that Taren would have thought it the truth. But she had known enough Phemorians to realise this was a simple intimidation tactic that usually worked for them.

'Then why are you so pissed that Jalila is so taken with him?'

'Because she's a pervert!' Ayliscia stressed, as if Taren hadn't been listening.

'Ringbalin is a big boy,' Taren felt forced to conclude, and backed up. 'And Jalila is —'

'A *spy*,' Ayliscia insisted.

'Well, I'm sure she won't find anything damning in Ringbalin's drawers,' Taren pointed out.

'He doesn't know what she's really like.' Ayliscia's tone finally softened and had a hint of sincerity in it. 'None of you know! I worked for her.'

'And you've changed since then,' Taren pointed out. 'You must allow that she may have too.'

'Why must I?' Ayliscia was annoyed and gripped her armband, which appeared to be paining her.

'You can't physically change the past, at least not easily.' Taren warranted that it was possible. 'But way back in the day when I actually had time to do scientific research, I proved that the easiest way to heal the past was to simply change your mind-set in the present. Not only does that prevent the mistakes of the past repeating themselves, but it makes for a much more promising future.'

'Pretty words.' Ayliscia understood they were meant to inspire her. 'But what do they mean?'

'If Jalila was a bitch to you in the past, then you teach her how to be a better person *now*, when you are in the position to set the example.' Taren simplified the premise.

'How?' Ayliscia emphasised how perplexing the challenge was, but her arm appeared to have stopped bothering her, as she let it go.

Taren looked around Module C, remembering how many times she'd sought sanctuary here. 'There's a lot of love in this place,' she commented fondly. 'Just treat Jalila as Ringbalin has treated you.'

Ayliscia was panicked. 'I don't think I can do that.'

'But you could try?' Taren posed, and Ayliscia finally consented with a nod.

'But Jalila is banned from the booth,' Ayliscia insisted.

'Good deal.' Taren smiled, thankful. 'I'll ask Jalila to report to you in her spare time. Make her work — I mean, make *it* work.' She subtly implied that there could be a silver lining.

'I certainly will do this,' Ayliscia agreed, in much better spirits.

In the kitchen of the mess hall, Taren tracked down Jalila who was finding her way around the foreign room with some help from Kalayna — as she'd gotten quite familiar with the work space before she'd been captured.

It was odd to see the dignitary in casual clothes but, even when she was covered in flour, her make-up was still perfect. 'I'm getting cooking lessons ...' Jalila looked rather happy about it, batting her long dark lashes. 'Fancy?'

Taren had a chuckle at the scene. 'I can hardly wait to taste the results. I just dropped by to inform you that shouldn't have any more trouble getting into Module C. In fact, if you've got some free time Ayliscia could use a hand in there.'

'Sure,' she agreed, appearing happy to help. 'What did you do ... threaten her with death?'

'I merely pointed out that you are just trying to pull your weight,'

Taren advised diplomatically. 'But, she did ask that the weather control centre remain off-limits.'

Jalila flushed red at the request. 'I can't believe it, she mentioned the shirts.'

Taren wasn't a very good liar, so she nodded.

'Whose shirts?' Kalayna had to know the gossip. 'Ringbalin's?' she guessed.

Jalila's grin, as guilty as sin, confirmed it. 'It was just a little whiff, seriously,' she explained, thinking Ayliscia was being childish. 'I just wanted to feel some of that energy, that's all.'

'I used to do that with Telmo's shirts,' Kalayna confessed, with a chuckle. 'When he was around to wear them. All his scent has worn off them now.' She pouted mournfully, and Jalila sympathised, pulling a sad face.

'I've done it too.' Taren raised a hand to confess, and then seeing the shock on both women's faces she added, 'To my husband's shirts, obviously, not Ringbalin's.'

Upon hearing this both women relaxed.

'So what's the big deal?' Kalayna wondered. 'Unless … Ayliscia has a thing for Ringbalin too! Does she?' Both women were wide-eyed as they looked to Taren for an answer.

'Don't ask me.' Taren waived all comment. 'Once I wanted to fix everyone else's relationships, but now I'm older and wiser, I just stay focused on my own.'

'I thought Ayliscia was just holding a grudge from our good old days,' Jalila commented to Kalayna, as the girl was more interested. 'But now I see there could be more to it.'

'I didn't say that.' Taren threw her hands up and backed out of the speculation. 'I'll see you both at dinner.' She made a quick exit.

That was the last thing on her to do list today, but before Taren went and found her husband to commence date night part two, she felt compelled to pop back to the House of Vidor on Sermetica and thank Trance for his wee bit of interference in her personal affairs. He'd been completely right on calling her out on her judgemental streak and she now felt like a complete heel for thinking him to be self-serving and a pain in the butt, for clearly he was neither.

Taren had never seen the House of Vidor on Sermetica in its entirety, gardens and all, but for the next few hours, she scoured the entire house, in search of its custodian, but Trance was nowhere to be found. Trance was the only live-in servant of the house, and as it was the wee hours of the morning on Sermetica, there were no house staff in attendance to query about his movements. Still, she had a very bad feeling about his disappearance, and she took her suspicions straight to Lucian.

'He's missing!' she fretted, having explained where she had been for the past few hours.

'He could have just gone out,' Lucian reasoned. 'Or run off somewhere to lay low for a while.'

'Well he is a cautious fellow.' Taren thought that more likely. 'But what if Prochazka —'

'Throwing around allegations is really not going to help your truce any,' he warned.

'Maybe I should just teleport to him rather than to his home, and check he is okay?' Taren wanted to believe that option so badly.

'And what if the Phemorians have him in a psychic containment cell?' Lucian knew why she hadn't tried that already. 'Like it or not, when Trance opted off this crew he ceased to be our responsibility.'

'Then why do I still feel responsible?' she appealed, collapsing herself against Lucian for a hug.

'Because you feel responsible for *everything*.' He kissed her forehead and rested his head against hers. 'But you're not. Everyone chooses their own path; you have to let them walk it. Even if there are dire consequences to pay; those lessons are meant to be learned — you can't judge fate, you can't stop consequence.' He had second thoughts about that last statement. 'Well, not for everyone, all the time.'

'Is there nothing to be done then?' She'd managed to get a whole crew out of a Phemorian prison, but Lucian was right, the Phemorians would not be happy to be accused, or to catch her sneaking around in their prison complex again.

'All we can do, as with everything else at present, is keep our eyes and ears open, and wait.'

17

BACK TO THE FUTURE

The hut on Oceane was the only place Mythric felt at peace these days, and he and Vadik had been permanently stationed here for some time now. All the men and women on the crew had families or wives to be with and jobs to do on board AMIE. Mythric, as a strategist, was not of much use at this time, nor did he have anything better to do, with his family all missing and his wife repeatedly refusing his requests for an audience.

So much time had elapsed since Zeven's disappearance and Satomi's coup on Phemoria that Mythric's hope of seeing any of them again waned with each passing month. This vigil they kept on Oceane may have been a farce, but being in the light of Azazèl-mindos-coomra-dorchi and being battered by its constant rainbow storm, was the only thing that kept him sane, patient, buoyant.

It had been daylight for a couple of hours and Vadik was resting, so Mythric stripped off his shirt and walked down to sit on the stairs in the warm rain and have his morning shower. Same as every day, the temperature was warm, the rain was constant, the view was unaltered. Or was it?

Mythric noted the colour orange springing from the rocks yonder, which stood out against the deep grey shale and deep green of the huge tundrell plants that thrived here. 'What is that?' Through the rain it was difficult to tell, so he jumped in the water and waded over to the site of the anomaly.

Upon closer inspection Mythric found what he thought were little, round, orange, sponge-like flowers, multiplying between a crevice in the rock. The further out into the light and rain they were positioned, the bigger they were blooming — or perhaps expanding was a better word, as they absorbed more water. He nudged the largest of these with his finger, and two little black eyes popped open and they ogled one another.

'Whoa! You're not a flower.'

Although it was cleverly disguised as one — complete with a little lime green tuft upon the top of its bright orange body, which made it appear rather cute. Whatever they were, they weren't growing out of the rock; they were crawling out, and spreading themselves over the surface.

'Where did you come from?' Mythric peered down into the crevice — perhaps there was a whole subterranean world on Oceane that they had never even considered? Between the mass of migrating sponge-slugs, down deep where one would expect to see darkness, he was surprised to see light! And that light appeared to be growing more intense the longer he looked.

The ground under foot began to rumble and as he staggered back a few paces, Mythric witnessed light shoot out of the gap in the rock in thin white streams. This burst made the ground rumble even harder and the light was succeeded by an electric blue light-filled ooze that began to gush from the rock like lava and pour into the water. As the glowing substance moved towards him, Mythric didn't wait to see what happened next. He high-tailed it back to the hut to wake his fellow crew mate and ensure he wasn't dreaming this.

'This is it!' Vadik was already up on the verandah by the time Mythric reached it.

'Are you sure?' It hadn't occurred to Mythric that this was the event they'd been waiting for.

'Damn sure.' Vadik's eyes were glued to the expanding light phenomenon. 'I have mastery over all four elements, and that —' he pointed to the bright blue ooze spreading through the water and cutting through the air like cracks in rock '— is the only element I don't control: ether.'

The etheric matter tore through reality causing ruptures of light so intense the men had to shield their eyes. A hurricane-force wind exploded outwards from the centre of the disturbance, blowing Mythric and Vadik off their feet and back into the hut, before the roof collapsed on top of them.

'We need to get out of here!' Mythric yelled to Vadik, from whom he'd been separated by roof debris.

The hut itself was swaying on its footings and felt like it would collapse at any moment, but then the rumbling of the ground ceased. All was quiet for a moment, before the damage done to the hut suddenly righted itself and Mythric found himself seated against the back wall. 'You okay?'

Vadik peeled himself off the floor not far away. 'I could have done without being beamed on the skull.' The big guy rubbed his head.

'Hello! Anyone home?'

The call came from outside and had both men on their feet and back on the verandah in a heartbeat.

'Greetings!' Zeven announced his return with good cheer as he scaled the stairs to join them, with Telmo, Khalid, Aurora and Thurraya in tow.

'Bob!' Vadik waved, as Mythric raced towards Zeven and crash-hugged him straight back into the water.

'Greetings?' Mythric emphasised as they both surfaced to face each other. 'It's been three fucking years!'

'What!' Zeven looked to Telmo, annoyed.

'It's not my fault how long the negotiations took,' Telmo replied with a shrug.

'What negotiations?' Mythric queried, but Zeven was wading out of the water to talk with Telmo.

'What if we've missed the mission?' Zeven climbed the stairs to confront his advisor.

'To what mission do you refer?' Telmo raised both brows.

'The one we executed from the universe parallel, you idiot!' Zeven wiped the water from his eyes, annoyed.

'It's not going to happen,' Telmo shrugged calmly, and as Zeven appeared unsure whether to be angry or perplexed, he expanded on the reply. 'It's already happened in the timeline we altered. That's why I told you not to boast about it, or arrange any meetings you couldn't fulfil ... idiot!'

'What? Really?' Zeven frowned, as he tried to figure if Telmo was right or not.

'And it's a good thing too; we've got other fish to fry now.' Telmo looked to Mythric who had scaled the stairs and was hugging his daughter-in-law and granddaughter. 'Do we still have a crew?'

'Thanks to Taren.' Mythric had a scolding tone in his voice. His attention turned back to Zeven. 'That was a hell of a situation you left her to deal with.'

'Is everyone okay?' Aurora requested to know.

'All, but Zelimir,' Mythric was sad to advise. 'Prochazka killed him when she took the ship.'

'How unfortunate.' Aurora was deflated by the news.

'That's sad for Fari.' Thurraya's expression was woeful, but her little kitten popping its head out from inside her jacket made her smile again.

'I didn't *leave* ...' Zeven deflected his father's implication, 'I was swept away!'

'My fault.' Khalid raised a hand; he was still standing in the rain, apart from the family reunion.

The sight of his most hated enemy, healthy and breathing, made Mythric's stomach knot and the arm beneath his Juju stone ached in equal measure to his rising hatred. 'It's always your fault,' he replied spitefully.

For a moment there was silence, as everyone held their breath awaiting the inevitable clash.

No matter how hard he tried, Mythric could not hold his anger here on Oceane, the truth always won out. 'Except for in the last universe, when everything was my fault,' Mythric admitted, releasing the ill will — the pain in his arm ebbing with it — as the frowns of his company melted into smiles of relief.

'You remember?' Zeven placed a hand on his father's shoulder, pleased to hear it. 'Then you know I'm right about Khalid?'

Mythric nodded, though the fact was rather mournful to him now.

'We're going to fix this,' Zeven assured him.

'I don't see how.' Mythric wished he could believe that. 'You don't even know what we're dealing with.'

'So take me to Taren and let's get it sorted out,' Zeven suggested. 'Where is she?'

'On AMIE.' Mythric grabbed Zeven before he could disappear. 'But I would not go publicly announcing your return to anyone, as Prochazka may have planted a spy on board. Only the captain and Taren must know,' he insisted. 'Let me go ahead and find them; I can arrange for them to be somewhere alone to meet with you.'

With a nod, Zeven concurred. 'I'll await your word.'

It was a glorious day on Phemoria, the sky was mauve and clear, and the warm, dry weather felt to be settling in for its short season. But the lovely day and surrounds of the royal garden brought the Qusay little joy. All she could think about today, or any day, was the lack of progress she was making towards ending the curses she'd overthrown her sister to see destroyed. She was tired of wearing her sister's persona, weary of waiting for a resolution, and missing the family who had betrayed her. Perhaps Prochazka and her niece were both wrong in thinking her son and his family would ever return from whence Khalid had led them, but wherever that was, every attempt to locate them had proved fruitless. They had to be hiding on Oceane somewhere, but be damned if Satomi was sending her finest warriors down onto that planet to be infected with her niece's madness.

General Prochazka had been overseeing the development of bio-technology that would protect them from any such infection, and ground penetrating radar designed to detect Osmium, that would end this stalemate very soon. Intel received from the spy on board the AMIE vessel had also been very beneficial in preparing Tonissia's defences for what Prochazka termed 'the final assault'. Yes, they were fully aware that her niece had reconstructed the vessel Prochazka had destroyed — they had expected that she would. And as the captain had been restored to life, Satomi's coup had come at little cost to the crew of AMIE — she could not say the same of herself, however. When all was said and done, her family's friends and associates had little to hold against her; in fact, she imagined they would be thanking her in the end, for freeing them from the delusion spell Khalid had cast upon them all. Yet, time had caused her to doubt whether the opportunity to prove them wrong would ever, in fact, arise?

In recent years it seemed AMIE had turned their attention and resources towards disrupting psychic exploitation and persecution on Maladaan. Of course there was no evidence to point to Taren Lennox and her crew as the perpetrators who had tampered with the photon detection system that the MSS had been using to identify psychics. But an unfortunate series of events that had evidenced faults in the devices and reproduction flaws that could not be identified or explained made it clear to Satomi that the AMIE crew were behind the problems. After all, the device had been illegally adapted from a photon chamber Taren Lennox had designed, and this wee spot of espionage was costing President Tallak the confidence of his people. The presidential office had tried to cover up the recent failures in his psychic defence system, but the truth of the matter had been leaked to the public, who were now forcing an early election on Maladaan that Tallak was expected to lose.

The notion rousted a smile from Satomi. She may have resented her niece for the coup she had attempted to execute on Phemoria, but she did admire her dedication to the cause of psychic freedom in the USS; and Taren had managed to keep Sermetica minding its own affairs for the past three years and off Phemoria's back. Phemoria certainly held no love for Maladaan, so Satomi felt in no way compelled to enlighten President Tallak to the source of his woes; but it was a nice ace of information to have up her sleeve should her niece try to cross her in future.

Perhaps she was in a good mood after all.

Her radiant surrounds were certainly helping lift her spirits; the fragrance of the garden was just divine — acquiring AMIE's green-thumbed healer had been something of a coup in itself. Prochazka had certainly chosen her hostage wisely as the young gardener had not been one spot of bother during his entire stay with them.

She stopped to observe him yonder, preparing a new garden bed, whistling to himself as he turned the soil and fertilised it with mulch. He had pots of seedlings all lined up in rows, ready to plant in the bed he was preparing, and Satomi considered he was about the happiest person she'd ever seen.

'You do very fine work, Mr Malachi.' Her comment startled him, and when he saw her he dropped what he was doing and bowed deeply to her.

'Thank you, Majesty.'

'I did not mean to disrupt your productivity,' she advised, whereupon he immediately retrieved his shovel and continued to turn the soil. 'Do you miss your people and your garden in space?'

Clearly Ringbalin considered this a loaded question, as he ticked his head to one side, to consider his answer. 'I am happy doing what I can to aid the peace,' he said, and then cracked a smile. 'I'm just thankful you assigned me to the garden and not the seeding stables.'

Satomi found his jest most amusing. 'Seeding stables are a myth; I could hardly send you somewhere that does not exist.'

Ringbalin stopped what he was doing, and served her a peculiar look. 'Your Majesty shut them down?' He appeared most delighted by his assumption.

'I cannot shut down what does not exist,' she scoffed, her amusement waning, as the young gardener appeared suddenly discomforted.

'As you say, Majesty.' Ringbalin bowed again and got back to work.

A seed of panic planted in her gut. 'Am I wrong?' She appealed to him for correction.

'It is not for me to advise you of what takes place in your own jurisdiction,' Ringbalin was hesitant.

'Tell me why you do not believe my assurance?' She was now seriously concerned.

'Because we rescued the men of our crew from a seeding stable three years ago.' He squinted and shielded his eyes to look her in the face, and she could tell he was not lying.

'I was never told of this.' She gasped on the premise. 'Spyridon too?'

'I believe the Valoureans held him there for a time,' Ringbalin was sorry to advise.

'No!' Satomi gasped again, one hand over her mouth to hide her horror, the other over her heart as she imagined what her husband must have been put through before he was dragged before her. 'He must think me a monster. I only said to interrogate him! I wanted him to suffer, but not like that.'

'You set him free,' Ringbalin reminded her, hoping to quell her anguish.

'Where is it?' Satomi let her anger take over, and gathered her wits quickly.

'Ah … block five of your prison complex.' He turned away and began to rake faster, in the hope of being left to mind his own business.

The shock came over her in waves, but she had enough sense to ensure her witness was within eyeshot until she got to the bottom of this deception. 'Come with me,' she held out a hand to him.

'Majesty,' Ringbalin hesitated. 'Are you sure you want to go there?'

'Oh yes.' Satomi was quietly seething; what else had Prochazka failed to tell her about? 'The truth is always best.'

When the Qusay walked into the reception area of the seeding stable with Ringbalin in tow, just the state of the naked men waiting around the lounging area to be of service was enough confirmation of Ringbalin's claim — clearly the ruler was appalled.

'Majesty.' The woman behind the desk stood and bowed. She was not young like the Valoureans who frequented the place, but was very surprised to see the Qusay on her doorstep. 'Can we assist your Highness in some way?' She smiled winningly, glancing

Ringbalin up and down, obviously assuming the Qusay had some personal interest in him.

'Are you the proprietor of this establishment?' the Qusay enquired in an aloof fashion.

'I run it for your Valoureans, yes.' Her response was evasive.

The Qusay picked up on this and her eyes narrowed. 'For General Prochazka.'

'Well, of course,' the proprietor emphasised that went without saying.

'Of course.' Satomi forced a smile, and her expression hardened like stone. 'I am shutting down this establishment, effective immediately!'

The Valoureans and their whores relaxing in the large lounge area beyond the reception had began to gather around, and a grumble of discontent rose from among them.

'Majesty, please!' the proprietor appealed on behalf of all. 'You cannot, it's all perfectly legal —'

'I am the law!' Satomi roared in response and her discontent burst forth in the form of a wave of force that made everyone take a step backwards. 'This is not legal!' she stressed in disgust. 'This is not even human.' She gazed around the room, taking in the evidence of abuse and torture, and there was not a soul in the room who dared breathe a whisper. 'I want all memory of this place erased from these men. Then they will be nursed back to health by every Valourean who has frequented this place and then shipped back to wherever it was they came from.' Satomi pointed to the closest Valourean. 'Get on that work-station and get me the ledgers.'

'Yes, Majesty.' The soldier jumped right to it.

'If any one of these men fail to exit Phemoria safely, I'll have the head of the woman responsible,' the Qusay decreed.

'How do you know your Valourean won't corrupt the files?' one of the men stepped forwards to query.

'Trance?' Ringbalin was shocked to see he was a captive of the house. 'What are you doing here?'

'Prochazka caught up with me some years back.' He shrugged.

'Take your hands off those keys,' Satomi ordered the Valourean behind the reception desk, and she held her hands up in the air.

'Years! You've been in this place all that time?' Ringbalin was filled with sympathy for his friend. 'Are you all right?'

'Been shagged a few times, obviously.' Trance didn't seem too traumatised by it all. 'But they never had to get out the spiders on me, and it beats prison, I guess.'

'The spiders!' The Qusay was becoming more furious by the minute.

'I can get those files for you,' Trance proffered, congenially, despite the fact he was butt naked. 'But um.' He motioned to the restraining device on his ankle, and it vanished. 'It might take a little while for my abilities to kick back in. I'm a medium,' he explained. 'I have a hacker friend on the other side.'

'I would be very much obliged to you both.' She accepted his offer graciously. 'Get this man some clothes, get them all some clothes, and blankets. *Chop, chop!*'

'Much obliged.' Trance graciously accepted her ruling as he threw on the clothes he was handed.

The establishment was now a frenzy of activity. Valoureans rushed to dress and carry out their Qusay's orders as the ruler directed the proprietor to walk ahead of her. 'Let's go and see what takes place behind closed doors here, shall we?'

When Mythric returned with the all clear to see the captain, he advised it would be best if Thurraya was not brought aboard yet.

'But I want to see Fari!' Thurraya was quite upset by the directive. 'And show him kitty.'

'Soon,' Aurora assured her. 'I'll stay with her.'

'Telmo, I might need you to explain stuff,' Zeven warranted that he should come along. 'Khalid, you too.' Despite Mythric's refrain, he didn't trust leaving Khalid alone in his father's company.

'I'll stay with the girls and Vadik,' Mythric confirmed, as they made it a rule to always have someone with PK at the hut at all times. As the vibrational frequencies of the being that sheltered them on this planet interfered with their communications systems, it was necessary to have someone in the hut who could pop back and forth with reports, and combat any emergencies, or execute an evacuation if the need arose.

'I'll be back soon.' Zeven kissed his wife, daughter and her pet goodbye. 'Promise me you'll stay put and do as Mummy tells you.'

'I absolutely promise,' Thurraya emphasised that she had learned her lesson in that regard.

'Good girl.' Zeven ruffled her hair and moved to join Telmo and Khalid. 'Captain's office.' He named their destination as they gripped each other's wrists and vanished from the premises.

When they arrived in Lucian's office the captain couldn't have been more pleased to see them. 'Your timing is bloody perfect,' Lucian emphasised, as he came forth and shook Zeven's hand. 'It's the thirteenth hour, but better late than never.'

'Where is Taren?' Zeven was expecting to find her here too.

'Debating options with Anselm,' Lucian advised. 'We've caused some political strife on Maladaan that we had planned to deal with long ago, before things became so heated. We've been waiting for you to deliver the last part of the curse, so we can be rid of them and restore the Qusay Clarona to the throne so that Phemoria, Frujia and Sermetica can sign the rights bill. Then we hope to lure Maladaan to the negotiating table by offering them something they need.'

'And what is that?' Zeven queried.

'Top secret for the present,' the captain advised. 'I believe both Taren and President Anselm will be very pleased to see you. You should go, she's in private conference with him right now. Telmo can fill me in.'

'Actually,' Telmo bowed away from the duty, 'best not, as I have a few errands to run.'

'Errands?' Lucian was baffled. 'Well if those "errands" have anything to do with Phemoria, be aware that they are holding one of our crew hostage until we deliver the curses to their Qusay.'

'Mother,' Zeven stated with disappointment. 'Which crew member?'

'Ringbalin,' Lucian replied. 'They have put him to work in the royal garden.'

'I remember,' Telmo confirmed. 'The charming gardener.'

'You might want to give him a heads-up to lay low,' the captain requested.

'As you say,' Telmo concurred and vanished.

'But what —' Lucian pointed to the void where Telmo had been and looked back to Zeven. 'What errands?'

'If you have a spy on board, that's also best kept secret for now. But believe me, it's important,' Zeven advised. 'Probably best that I leave Khalid here with you, if that's okay?'

Lucian frowned and smiled at once; it was not like him to be undiplomatic despite any doubts he might have. 'Of course.'

'He won't bite,' Zeven guaranteed as he backed up to take his leave.

'I know that.' Lucian tried not to sound offended. 'I remember Wu Geng. I'm more concerned about you still keeping secrets.' Lucian folded his arms.

'Not for long.' As time was fleeting, Zeven focused on teleporting himself to Taren.

'We need to offer Tallak the technology now!' Anselm was telling Taren, when Zeven arrived in the president's private home office. 'If an election is forced and Tallak loses then someone even more right wing could end up in power —' Anselm's attention shifted from his daughter as he spotted Zeven in the room.

'And better the demon you know,' Zeven concluded on Anselm's behalf.

When Taren laid eyes on him, clearly she doubted her own perception a second. 'Zeven? You're here!'

'I surely am.' He held his arms wide to pre-empt the hug from his cousin that he promptly received.

'What took you so long?' She squeezed him, clearly as relieved as the captain had been to see him.

'I had a bit of political tip-toeing to do myself.' He grinned as she pulled back to hold him at arm's length.

'Do you have the third part of the curse?' she queried. 'And Thurraya, is she safe?'

'Yes, all good,' Zeven was pleased to inform her.

Taren's sights turned back to Anselm, who appeared like he should have known better.

'Well then,' he allowed, regaining some cheer. 'I guess we do this your way; back to plan A. But we really don't have much time up our sleeves. We need to restore your mother to power now.'

'That process is already in motion,' Zeven said.

The wait for her father to return seemed to be taking ages! After some lunch, Thurraya sat in her grandfather's lap telling him about her adventures in Karmandi with Ahura.

'He said that whatever ails you, the sprites of nature can heal it,' she conveyed what she'd learned.

'Did he now?' Mythric was delighted by her tutorial.

'Even here in the real world I see them sometimes,' she assured him.

'Well, speaking of nature,' Mythric lifted her up off his lap and raising himself, sat her back down, 'I need to answer its call right now.'

Thurraya understood his meaning and chuckled.

'I'll be back.' Mythric backed up towards the door outside. 'Stay right there.'

'I will, Grandpa,' she assured — it seemed like no one actually believed she'd learned her lesson.

Her mother was sleeping in a chair close by, and Vadik was keeping watch out front, so she hopped down on the floor to play with her kitten.

'You're so cute!' she told it, as she watched it play with a wood chip it had found on the floor and gave a heavy sigh. 'I wish Fari could see you.'

*

In a flash of etheric light, Thurraya found herself in the tech room on AMIE.

Ooops. I didn't mean that! She mentally denied responsibility for the location shift.

Fari, years older than when she'd last seen him, was standing in front of her at a work bench looking over some papers. 'Fari?' She stood to greet him. 'You got big!'

Fari, startled at first, smiled, pleased to see her. 'You're just the same,' he replied.

'What are you doing in here?' Thurraya wondered, as the tech room was not one of their usual haunts.

'Kalayna's been building some neat stuff in here,' he said, 'and she lets me build stuff too, 'cause I get bored.'

As much as she wanted to stay and chat, Thurraya knew she should not be here. 'I'd better get back, before my charge wears off.'

'Hey wait!' Fari waylaid her. 'I've got a new trick, wanna see?'

'Sure,' Thurraya allowed, and a second later Fari had turned into a cat! 'That's cool!' she emphasised, clapping as he transformed back into himself.

'You try,' he urged, holding out his hand to her.

As Thurraya was an adaptor, she couldn't resist the chance to really be a cat, and taking hold of his hand she made that wish and the next thing she knew she was tiny and walking around all covered in black fur. *This is fun!* She rolled around, loving the feel of her furry little body, then she felt the cold metal band clap around her neck. When she tried to return to her true form she couldn't, and she couldn't get the band off. She was trapped!

Fari, this isn't funny! she tried to say, but all that came out of her mouth were meows.

When Fari picked her up, she tried to wriggle and scratch, but she was too little. 'You're coming with me, Princess,' he informed with a grin, as he dropped her in a box and closed the lid.

General Prochazka was leaving her office to answer a summons to the Qusay's room of court — news of her Qusay's raid on the seeding stable here in Tonissia had already reached her, as many of the Valoureans were none too happy about Satomi's decree to turn it into a nursing home for men, and neither was she.

But as Prochazka opened her door to depart, her AMIE spy was waiting with a box in hand. 'What are you doing here?' she queried the boy, who immediately transformed into her true Valourean form.

'Mission accomplished, General.' She held out the box in her hands in offering. 'The Princess Thurraya.'

Prochazka took the box and looking inside she smiled broadly. 'Are you sure it's her?'

'No question,' the Valourean replied. 'Only she could do this.'

'It was a clever move to get her to transform,' Prochazka awarded. 'They won't be able to track her.' Prochazka gloated over her timely little prize. 'You can hardly fulfil my Qusay's prophecy like this,' she told the kitten who was trying desperately to scale the walls of her container. 'Much safer this way.' She closed the lid and handed the box back to her spy. 'Tell no one else its true identity. Find a more secure cage, and give her to my lieutenant to guard in my absence. All she need know is that her life depends on keeping this creature safe.'

'You are going somewhere, General?' the Valourean queried, as Prochazka did not often leave the palace.

Prochazka's mood had picked up considerably; there was nothing to forestall victory now. 'I'm off to do a spot of fishing.'

Her subordinate clearly found this hard to believe, but did not query the general's good cheer.

'Excellent work,' Prochazka awarded her spy in parting. 'Remind me to give you a promotion.'

'Shall I return to AMIE?' she posed. 'I have been able to fly under the radar all this time as I was not suspected, but if I'm brought before their captain for questioning he may finally engage his psychic sight to view me and I will be discovered.'

'I agree.' Prochazka considered their options. 'The kid is in psychic containment, so they cannot retrieve him directly, but have the lieutenant double the guard in that block.'

'Thank you, General.' She nodded her head in respect, and left to do the general's bidding.

Prochazka knew she was about to get a dressing down about being deceitful, but she was not concerned — if she could pacify the Phemoray for a hundred years, she could certainly deal with one of Satomi's little tantrums.

'You asked to see me, Highness?' The general strode into the courtroom to face the music, and bowed before the Qusay, who appeared most displeased.

'Why was I not told about the seeding stables?' she demanded. 'After the way in which I died, did you really think I would approve?'

'The stables have been an institution on this planet since before you were born —' Prochazka began.

'Instituted by the Phemoray!' Satomi rebutted the excuse. 'We are supposed to be rectifying their evil ways on this planet, not continuing them!'

Prochazka raised both brows, unaffected by her Qusay's ire. 'I have been serving this royal house for hundreds of years. I am given orders, and I achieve results. How I fulfil those orders and keep the Valoureans loyal to the crown has never been questioned. If you wish to know the grisly details, Highness, you need only ask.'

'Is it true you took Spyridon Vidor and the other men from AMIE there?' Satomi ran with the general's recommendation.

'It seemed a shame to waste all those psychic genes.' Prochazka was not angered about being questioned, but for the first time in her career she felt ashamed of her Qusay. The one thing the general had in common with the Phemoray was a hatred of men, spurred on by her own remorse for ever trusting a male to help her take the Phemoray down. 'They are only men after all.' She challenged her queen's priorities.

'You think treating men with the same disrespect they once showed us makes us superior in some way?' Her Qusay was clearly upset, which only made Prochazka more angry.

'It's called retribution,' she defended.

'It is abuse!' Her Qusay stood, enraged. 'In a thousand years, have we not evolved at all? What other little secrets are you hiding from me?'

The question sent Prochazka's temper skyrocketing. 'I am not the one keeping secrets.' Prochazka turned the interrogation around. 'When you allowed me to absorb your genetic code and pass it on to other shifters, I did not only acquire your power but your memory also.' She raised her brows to see if the Qusay could guess what her concern was.

Her Qusay stood tall to defy any accusation. 'What of it?'

'Deny that this coup was not executed for the sake of Phemoria, but rather for your family!' Prochazka had had enough of the games.

'That,' Satomi challenged, 'is a treasonous remark.'

'Only if it's false.' Prochazka was confident it wasn't. 'It is your intention to lay down your life to end the curses, to spare your granddaughter that fate, knowing that the end of the Phemoray will return your sister to this world, where she will reclaim her throne.' The general gave half a laugh. 'Can you see why this might be a concern for me? I aided you to win your throne back; what happens to me and the rest of the Valoureans when you abdicate?'

The Qusay wasn't faltering in her stance, but like all kind-hearted martyrs she had no poker face. The truth lay in the fear behind her eyes. 'Valoureans!' The Qusay commanded them to attention. 'Arrest General Prochazka for treason.'

The Qusay's guards moved in on the general.

'I have not committed treason yet.' The general's claim confused the troops, who refrained from seizing their leader without hearing her out. 'You all have Satomi's memory to reference; search it and know for yourselves that she will betray us all.'

As expected, within moments all the Valoureans began to look to their Qusay with a fierce disdain.

'Fear not,' the general assured the assembly, as a restraining device clamped around her Qusay's ankle and locked closed at Prochazka's mental command. Satomi returned to her true form and the general continued, 'I have taken measures to ensure that Clarona shall never return to claim this throne and see us all imprisoned or worse!'

'No,' Satomi objected. 'You can't shut the life support in the vault off, thousands of our fellow countrywomen would die —'

'A thousand psychic warriors more powerful than any of us here,' Prochazka reminded the Valoureans. 'You may rest assured, Clarona will return with a formidable army at her back! But I now have the means to control the Phemoray. Instead of having them command us, we shall command them!' She held high the ring on her finger, and her Valoureans cheered this notion.

'That ring doesn't control the Phemoray, but the cursed crew of Dead Man Downs on Sermetica,' Satomi interjected. 'The very men our foremothers banished from this planet during the sexual revolution. Once it was protected by a golden energy that gave the general control over the curse, but that golden shield is fast fading along with her dedication to me, the true Qusay she swore to serve,' she warned. 'If she releases those curses they will control her, not the other way around.'

'True, in part,' Prochazka admitted, and the Valoureans were perplexed by their general's candour. 'That curse is contained in a smelting vat,' she explained, 'and all the souls contained therein are beholden to this ring. Is that not true, Majesty?'

'That is true,' Satomi admitted, as she had been present when the spirits of the vat had agreed to serve Prochazka.

'The remaining two parts of the curse are also attached to metal items,' Prochazka pointed out. 'Can you see where I might be going with this?'

'You can't seriously be considering combining them!' Satomi was horrified. 'They must be destroyed!'

'Under my control these demons will make Phemoria the most feared planet in the USS!' Prochazka announced, and the Valoureans all cheered her intention.

'I did not sanction this, nor would I *ever*.' Satomi made it clear she thought her deluded. 'Your love of Power has defeated even your love of Phemoria. Those curses will *eat you alive* and *control you*, just as they have controlled all those who have attempted to preside over them in the past!'

'I know more about the dark arts than Queen Thurraya did herself! I have made the subject a life study. I was ignorant once, but now I shall have my revenge. When you came to me and begged for my help to take your throne, I thought that you would put your people first. But when I realised your true intent and discovered that you had not had your feelings for your man whore and that bastard you bore together erased, it was clear that other measures would have to be taken to ensure the continued dominance of women on Phemoria.'

'If you saw my memories of my husband and our son,' Satomi's sentiment was filling her eyes with tears, which made Prochazka become rather nauseous, 'you must know that however misguided, they are not the beasts you make them out to be.'

'I took the liberty of having those sentiments *erased* before I passed on your Power to these women, so they are not infected with your weakness,' the general spat at her in disgust. 'If you would rather die for your family and leave your home planet absent a Qusay of age, I shall grant that wish.'

Satomi gasped as Prochazka exerted her will to make the Qusay freeze and be silent. '*Now* I am inciting rebellion. Your granddaughter will prove much easier to control.' The general grabbed a blade from the arsenal of weapons on her belt and slashed Satomi's throat open with it. 'You are the true Qusay no longer.' She watched the life and blood gush from Satomi's body, and let her drop to the floor. 'Long live Qusay Thurraya the second,' Prochazka uttered. 'I shall adore her, and that love shall be my shield.' Prochazka turned to instruct the dazed Valoureans, 'Watch her … and make sure no one resurrects her again. Shoot anyone who enters this room who is not me. I'll be back within the hour.'

She had hoped to string Satomi along a while yet, and her death did add some urgency to this mission — it wasn't going to take long for the crew of AMIE to come looking for their lost brats — but they would prove no competition to her once this undertaking was complete.

In the Qusay's private chamber just beyond her room of court, Trance and Ringbalin were seated at a table with the workstation retrieved from the seeding station, compiling files on the establishment as instructed.

Ringbalin was enjoying the afternoon tea that had been laid out for them, but he felt very uncomfortable in the luxurious surrounds, aware of how dirty his clothes were. 'I really don't see why I am here?'

'The chick in charge said to say put,' advised the entity that had taken over his old friend. 'Pass me one of those pink tarts.'

Ringbalin was happy to, as he wasn't serving any other purpose. 'Ringbalin Malachi.'

The call startled him and he turned in his chair to find a young fellow, much the same colouring as himself, but larger and rather more handsome.

'Whoa!' commented the hacker, shielding his eyes from the visitor. 'What the fuck? Can you turn the aura down? It's massive!'

The fellow did have a rather positive glow about him, but Ringbalin couldn't see auras, so he was not bothered. 'Who are you?' He stood to address the newcomer.

'Telmo Dacre.' He shook Ringbalin's hand.

'Yasper's brother,' Ringbalin acknowledged, having heard he was working with Zeven.

'Yes indeed,' Telmo warranted.

'So Zeven is back.' Ringbalin was hopeful this meant he might be going home soon.

'I am about our captain's urgent business.' Telmo would not confirm or deny the statement, but looked to the dark fellow behind the workstation. 'And who is your friend?'

'This is Trance, but he's not here right now; he's channelling Reggie at present who used to be a hacker before the MSS caught up with him.'

'How synchronous.' Telmo grinned.

'Hold on a second.' Trance became mesmerised as he gazed about the room. 'It's not just your light-body, it's many light-bodies.' A delighted smile swept over his face. 'So many beautiful women.'

'All what women?' Ringbalin couldn't see anyone but Telmo where Trance was looking.

'Hey, aren't you the chick giving the orders here?' Trance queried into empty space. 'Have you died?'

'No,' Telmo informed Trance. 'The woman on the throne at present is only posing as the Qusay-Sabah Clarona, the spirit you see before you is the real Qusay.'

'That is true,' Ringbalin conveyed to his associate. 'It is the Qusay-Sabah Clarona's sister, Satomi, who is ruling in her stead.'

'The plot thickens,' said Reggie, in a detached fashion.

'But the Qusay's ghost is here?' Ringbalin sought clarification.

'The bodies of the anointed Qusay and all these women are being held captive elsewhere in the city. In a vault, designed and built under guidance of the Phemoray,' Telmo explained. 'That's why I am here —'

They all heard cheering coming from the Qusay's room of court.

'What's happening in there, I wonder?' Ringbalin wasn't game to find out.

'It's a good question,' Telmo warranted, most curious.

'Any Valourean with Trance's skill will see if so much as a ghost sticks their head in that room,' Ringbalin cautioned the company he couldn't see.

'You need to lose that.' Telmo noted Ringbalin's restraint, and it vanished.

'No, please,' Ringbalin panicked. 'I'd rather keep it.'

'*You'd rather* have your Power at your disposal this day,' Telmo warranted. 'I promise you.'

Trance clicked his fingers to draw their attention. 'I found a security camera feed to reception.' He swung the screen about so that they could view the scene unfolding in the court room. 'I think you may have another coup on your hands.'

They had turned the hut on Oceane upside down looking for Thurraya, and when Mythric could not teleport himself to her and Aurora could not find her with her remote vision, their concern tripled.

'She would not have left this kitten behind if she's gone anywhere of her own accord.' Aurora was cuddling the animal, which was unsettled by her panic. 'Someone has taken her, I know it. We need to report this to the captain —'

'Hey, guys,' Vadik waved them onto the verandah and pointed to an incoming craft. 'Is that one of ours?'

'Since when do we bother using craft?' Mythric made haste to investigate, and it only took him a second to identify the vessel. 'Phemorians.'

'They took Thurraya!' Aurora freaked out.

A red beam shot down from the craft and began scanning the ground in front of the hut. 'Then why are they still here?' Mythric grabbed both his comrades. 'This hut is a target, we need to move!' He teleported them to a rocky mound that overlooked the base.

There was a cave in a ledge here where they could conceal themselves. A heartbeat later the hut was blown to pieces but the red beam continued its search.

'They're here for the curses,' Mythric realised, as the search beam locked onto the large plinth of a rock Zeven and Telmo had brought back from the otherworld with them and the item vanished. 'Shit! I can't retrieve the canister hidden inside that boulder as I have no idea what it looks like. When did they develop particle manipulation?'

'I know what it looks like.' Vadik focused on producing the said item, to no avail. 'Maybe I'm not practised enough with PK?'

'If they are storing the item in a particle state that would prevent anyone with PK retrieving it until it was reconstituted.'

'I don't care about the damned curses!' Aurora lost it. 'We need to find my daughter!'

'They won't harm her,' Mythric insisted. 'Moving the Soul Keep is far more urgent. Not to AMIE ...' Mythric raked his brain to think of a temporary safe haven.

'Take her back, report,' Vadik insisted. 'I'll distract these guys and take the rock containing the Soul Keep to the hut on Frujia.'

'You sure?' Mythric wasn't questioning his ability. 'You have to be touching it to teleport it with you.'

'I know what it looks like, I can teleport it to me.' Vadik stepped out of the cramped shelter and began summoning up a whirlwind. 'Go!' Vadik urged.

Mythric grabbed Aurora, who was still clinging to her daughter's pet, and headed for the captain's office.

Upon their return to AMIE, Taren and Zeven were met with utter chaos. Aurora was in tears as she informed Zeven that their daughter was missing. Jazmay and Yasper were also ropable as Fari could not be found either.

'If Satomi's spy was posing as my son,' Jazmay seethed, 'then Fari has been in a Phemorian prison for three years!'

'I let Fari tinker in the tech room,' Kalayna confessed, as she placed all the prototypes of the weapon she had crafted on the captain's desk. 'The Phemorians may know all about our new weapon and could use it against us.' Kalayna outlined the worse case scenario, sorry to add to the captain's problems.

'Get back to Vadik,' Lucian instructed Mythric. 'See if he managed to spirit away the Soul Keep before the Phemorians got their hands on it.'

'I was only gone an hour!' Taren was shocked by just how many disasters had erupted in that time.

'They got Chironjivi's curse, and I believe they are storing it in a particle state so that it cannot be retrieved.' Mythric brought Taren up to speed.

'Go!' Lucian insisted, and Mythric vanished.

'Thus ends our truce.' Taren had hoped to have time to plan and execute this rebellion carefully, but it seemed the universe had other ideas.

'Telmo!' Kalayna was overjoyed to see him appear in the room and ran to embrace him. 'It's been so long, I thought I'd never see you again.'

'I need you,' he told her.

'I need you too,' she replied, teary-eyed, thinking his confession romantic.

'There is some fairly alien technology I need your advice on.' He explained that his need was more a practical one.

'Oh.' Kalayna was a little deflated. 'Sure, I'll grab my belt.'

Telmo manifested the said tool belt in his hand and gave it to her.

'When did you learn to do that?' Kalayna strapped her belt on.

'Long story.' Telmo declined going into detail at this time.

'You are Telmo?' Yasper was stunned to finally meet him. 'You are my —'

'Brother,' Telmo concluded. 'And as pleased as I am to meet you, sentiment must wait.'

'Obviously,' Kalayna rolled her eyes.

'What are you doing here?' Zeven queried, expecting him to be otherwise detained.

'Prochazka has killed Satomi and taken control of the palace and the Valoureans,' he reported. 'She intends to shut down the vault, and to combine the three curses to use for her own ends.'

'No!' Aurora looked to Zeven, who was mortified on many levels. 'That makes Thurraya Qusay of Phemoria!'

'My mother is in that vault,' Taren protested.

'And my sister,' Jalila seconded Taren's dismay. 'We cannot allow them to succeed —'

'Satomi is dead?' Mythric turned pale, having arrived back in the room unnoticed.

'Did you find Vadik?' the captain queried.

'Parts of him.' Mythric was clearly unnerved. 'The Phemorians now have all three parts of the curse in their possession.' He sat down to process the horror.

'Damn,' Zeven stressed under his breath. 'He was a good man.'

'If he's in pieces, I can't resurrect him,' Swithin was sorry to advise Taren and the captain, as he knelt in front of Mythric.

'But Satomi I can do,' Swithin encouraged Mythric to keep the faith. 'If we are quick.'

'Load up, everyone.' Taren wasn't prepared to waste another second procrastinating. 'If Prochazka is chasing curses, she is not in the palace, so we have a small window of opportunity to seize it. Kassa, Ayliscia and Aurora, stay with the ship.'

'No bloody way!' Aurora passed her kitten to Kassa and claimed one of Kalayna's weapons from the captain's desk. 'Ayliscia can be the remote viewer on this one, I am coming with you.'

'And me?' Khalid queried those in charge.

'Haven't you done enough!' Mythric found his determination and as he stood Swithin had to hold him back from lashing out at Khalid.

'Not nearly,' he replied calmly. 'If those old prophecies are correct, then the curse of the Phemoray cannot be banished until I return to Phemoria.'

'He's right.' Zeven looked to Jalila. 'The secret Phemorian prophecy you spoke of.'

Jalila concurred with a nod. 'When the first prince of Phemoria returns, the rule of Phemoray will end.'

'I am not the first true prince.' Zeven referred her to Khalid. 'He is the one you've been searching for.'

Jalila's eyes opened wide in wonder.

'Then you are with us,' Taren advised Khalid.

'No!' Mythric was strongly opposed.

'If you cannot work with the agenda, then you stay here.' Taren gave him an ultimatum.

Mythric smothered his protest, grabbed one of the new weapons from the captain's desk, and joined the crew returning to the chamber behind the queen's room of court on Tonissia.

'What is taking so long?' Ringbalin stressed in a whisper, as he paced out his frustration. Satomi was dead in the next room and there wasn't a thing he could do about it, and that being the case they no longer had the Qusay's consent to be in the palace.

'The Qusay suggests that stressing will not aid your Powers to return any quicker,' Trance passed on Clarona's message to Ringbalin. 'Now if you would all shut up and let me focus that would be — Uh-oh.'

'What now?' Ringbalin approached the table where Trance was holding his hands over the keypad, the keys of which were furiously responding to his instructions.

'I just intercepted an order from General Prochazka to shut the vault down,' he advised. 'But it probably won't be long before she checks in to ensure the order was carried out.'

This news did not aid Ringbalin in his attempt to remain calm. 'We're —'

'Shhh,' Trance insisted, looking to the empty space beside him. 'Hard to say,' he commented at last, and Ringbalin assumed he was conversing with the Qusay's spirit form. 'Clearly this vault has a self-contained system, so you need to get Trance inside it. I can only interfere with the outer defences from here.' He listened for a moment and then nodded. 'You go ahead as Telmo instructed, I won't say a word and neither will he.'

Ringbalin wondered why he was being signalled to. 'Say a word about what?'

'Seeing the Qusay,' Reggie conveyed.

'But I haven't seen her?' Ringbalin was perplexed.

'That's the spirit,' Reggie confirmed with a wink from Trance.

'What?' Ringbalin frowned as his friend looked back to his monitor.

'Hold on.' He paused from his work and motioned Ringbalin around to have a look. 'Didn't we rescue this kid last time we pulled a prison break here?'

Ringbalin recognised Fari. 'Yes, we did.'

'So why is he still listed as a psychic captive?' Trance posed.

'Balin,' Taren announced their arrival.

'Boss, thank heavens.' Ringbalin breathed a huge sigh of relief to see her, motioning to Trance.

'Trance? What are you doing here?' Her attention shifted his way.

'Nope, not here,' Reggie's deep, droll voice advised, as most of the team circled around behind his chair to see what he was up to.

'This is Reggie.' Ringbalin did the introductions, as he'd obviously been the only person to enquire after the spirit's true identity.

'You found Fari.' Jazmay read the file on the hacker's screen. 'They are keeping him in the same cell block we were in before. I know where that is.' She looked to Taren, seeking permission to go.

'One second,' Taren begged her patience. 'Are there any other children in psychic containment here?'

Trance did a quick search. 'Nope.'

'I thought as much.' Taren suspected Prochazka would be keeping Thurraya's presence a secret.

'I'll go with Jaz and Yasper to get Fari out,' Zeven volunteered. 'With any luck they might have thrown them in together.'

'Me too.' Aurora joined her husband.

'There are three sets of guards to get through and the third guard post has monitors that observe the first two … they will see you coming,' Taren warned.

'Then we'll take out the third station first,' Zeven suggested. 'You've been there, Jaz?'

Jazmay nodded.

'Let's rumble.' Zeven rallied his troops.

The four of them stood back to back, all touching each other, with their new weapons drawn and Jazmay teleported them to their target area.

Double the guard meant Fari's rescue team were met by four Valoureans at the third guard door that led into psychic containment block C. One blast from Kalayna's new weapon ensured none of them could use any form of psychic attack on them, and with a thought Zeven knocked them all unconscious.

Jazmay wasted no time retrieving the keys from the slumbering guard and, raising the unconscious guard up to the eye scanner, she unlocked the door to the psychic containment area and an alarm sounded.

'Go find him!' Zeven urged Jazmay and Aurora, as he and Yasper turned towards the outer guard doors and prepared for the onslaught.

'Perhaps we should have taken out the other two guard stations first,' Zeven noted.

'Hindsight is a bitch,' Yasper uttered, as the outer doors to the second guard post opened and the four Valoureans therein came running at them.

'Fari!' Jazmay called as she ran from cell to cell, peering through the small window in each door in search of her son. 'Damn it all!' Jazmay kicked the door of the last cell. 'He's not here!'

'He must be!' Yasper was frustrated as he knocked out the remaining Valoureans from the last onslaught.

'We should leave,' Zeven suggested, as the alarm switched off, and it became all too calm and quiet.

'Not until I find a conscious Valourean who can tell me where my son is.' Jazmay stormed determinedly past them towards the last set of guard doors, and Zeven and the rest of the team pursued her.

The doors parted without any prompting from them and it was General Prochazka's lieutenant who confronted them.

'You bitch!' Jazmay flew at her.

But Yasper pulled her back, noting that the lieutenant stood alone, weapons holstered; the Valourean guard was unconscious around her.

'If you are looking for your boy, I know where he is. Follow me,' she advised with a smile.

'Straight into a trap!' Jazmay was not as eager to steam ahead now.

At the sound of a force moving towards them, Zeven raised all the unconscious Valoureans up to stand at their posts, before a large battalion of Valoureans rounded the corner to confront them.

Jazmay reached for her weapon, but again Yasper stayed her hand.

'Wait,' he whispered, as the lieutenant halted the group.

'False alarm,' she told them. 'These people are with me. Return to your posts.'

Some of the women appeared a little hesitant to walk away when they'd been expecting a fight.

'General's business!' The lieutenant encouraged them all to disperse, whereupon the Valoureans did an about-face and left. 'This way,' she invited politely.

As they were led into the private quarters of the Qusay's guard, Zeven was a little concerned. 'Are you sure we are going the right way?'

'Relax.' Their escort opened the doors and they entered to find the halls completely vacated. 'Your timing could not have been more perfect,' the lieutenant explained. 'With the palace on high alert, all hands are on deck and not in here.'

They came to a door that read 'Lieutenant Paturi' and opening the door she led inside.

'Hey, Sovee.' Fari waved from the bed where he was seated watching television, and playing with a kitten. 'What is going on out there?' The boy spotted his parents following her in. 'Mum! Dad!' He rose and sprang into Jazmay's waiting embrace.

'Are you all right?' Jazmay looked him over, tearing up to find him appearing so well, as she vanished the restraint from his ankle.

''Course I am.' Fari wiped her tears away, appearing confused as to why she was so upset. 'I've been here with your friend, Sovee, since the Valoureans took you from our cell. It's been pretty fun, except she made me do schoolwork.'

Jazmay looked to the lieutenant, who smiled sincerely. 'I didn't forget.'

'How did you get away with this?' Yasper's mind boggled.

'There is a lot you can get away with when you are in charge.' The lieutenant was getting teary herself. 'He's really amazing, I'm going to miss him.'

'No, you're not,' Jazmay breathed through her emotion. 'Because you're coming with us. Prochazka will have your head for this.'

The lieutenant shook her head to disagree. 'Not if we take her out.'

'There was another child,' Aurora couldn't wait any longer to enquire. 'A little girl, have you seen her?'

'Not a little girl,' she advised, motioning to the kitten that was trying to climb its way up Zeven's leg.

'Thurraya?' Zeven lifted the animal up and noting the restraint around its neck, he realised it might well be. 'That's why we couldn't find her.' With a thought he got rid of the restraint and gave her a cuddle. The kitten began purring madly, and butting its head up against his.

'Our daughter is a cat?' Aurora was mortified as Zeven passed the kitten over. 'For how long?'

'About an hour.' Zeven wasn't worried, she only had to be near Jazmay, another shifter, and she would resume her normal form. 'We should get back to the others.'

'Don't you think we should take the children straight back to AMIE?' Aurora asked. 'There's a revolution about to go down here; we don't want them in the middle of that.'

'Back on the ship there is minimal crew, minimal protection, I say they are better off with us.' Zeven put it to them all, and Yasper and Jazmay nodded to agree. Aurora, still unsure, went with the majority.

What Zeven couldn't say was that he knew from living through these instances before that Thurraya had a vital role to play in dispersing the curses at the heart of all this trouble. That was going to be far more harrowing for Aurora than her daughter's kidnapping.

Behind the monitor, observing the throne room where Satomi lay in a pool of blood under Valourean guard, the rest of the crew were debating how they were going to get to her, and a diversion seemed the best option. Without knowing if Prochazka's spy had stolen the blueprints for their prototype a direct assault could have debilitating consequences — a more cautious approach was required.

'I cannot prevent the power being cut to the vault from this workstation,' Reggie advised via Trance. 'But that complex does have internal backup generators that will kick in if the power goes out … *those* will have to be shut down manually, so if we can fortify that area, we could hinder the shut-down process.' He looked to Taren. 'The walls of the complex and the control room are made of Osmium —'

'So you cannot teleport in there,' Taren concluded. 'Makes sense, if the only way out of that vault for any soul is via the portal of the Phemoray, which they are not here to create.'

'In and out on foot is the only way for you living folk. If we can lock it from the inside,' Reggie posed, 'that should secure the vault.'

'I can rewire the doors,' Kalayna volunteered.

'Once I'm inside,' Reggie added, 'I can probably switch the system over to the generators before the Valoureans shut off the power, to ensure there is no break in the power supply, as that could prove fatal for all inside.'

'This system was designed and built by the Phemoray,' Telmo pointed out. 'I very much doubt you will have seen anything like it before.'

'And you have?' Reggie obviously felt that Telmo appeared a little young to have garnered much experience.

'You'd be surprised what I've seen in my travels,' Telmo replied with a grin.

'I know the system rather intimately.' Jalila came forward. 'And my sister is in that vault.'

'All four of you go,' Taren gave Telmo, Kalayna, Trance and Jalila leave. 'Leave this monitor.' Taren materialised in her hand a compact, state-of-the-art workstation and handed it to Trance. He appeared delighted with his new toy.

'I know the way,' Jalila said.

'You'll need this.' Taren conjured up a copy of the ring Jalila had once used to open the complex, an item that had been taken from her when she was incarcerated.

'Much obliged.' Telmo claimed the item from her.

'What are you going to do about the guard?' Taren wondered, as none of the trio were really warriors. 'When they see Jalila —'

'They won't suspect a thing, I promise you. I have a few new tricks up my sleeve,' Telmo asserted, 'I don't expect any trouble.'

'This is all taking too long!' Mythric was at his wit's end.

'Until Ringbalin is back to himself, there is no point going in.' Taren discouraged her uncle from doing anything rash.

Ringbalin was seated in front of a dying plant that Taren had conjured up for him, focusing his energy on making it heal. 'Nothing is happening!'

'Don't stress,' Lucian advised. 'Find a happy place and then try.'

'I've tried already.' Ringbalin's failed attempts were driving him to tears.

'I think I may be able to help.' Jalila broke from the group she was about to depart with.

'Not another delay?' Mythric objected.

'This won't take long.' The telepathist kneeled beside Ringbalin's chair and looked him in the eye. 'I have spent the past three years in your greenhouse, and I can tell you there is more blooming in there than meets the eye.' Jalila placed a palm against his forehead and Ringbalin was overwhelmed, but lost his compulsion to pull away and completely surrendered.

'What the —' Mythric was about to protest, but Taren's frown dissuaded him.

When she removed her hand, Jalila pulled back, biting her lip, hopeful.

Ringbalin opened his eyes, appearing sedated. But given a moment to process, he was suddenly amazed. 'She really said all those things?' he asked Jalila, who nodded, brows raised to confirm.

'But I wasn't even there to influence her!' Ringbalin's excitement suddenly snowballed.

'That's right.' Jalila grinned.

'So that means … she —' Ringbalin choked on the revelation.

'You got it.' Jalila winked, stood, and backed up to motion to the plant. 'You might want to try that again.'

'Oh, my goodness!' The young man could barely contain his excitement and cupped his hands around the failing sapling. It greened within moments. 'I'm back!'

'Thank our lucky stars!' Taren looked to Jalila and smiled in gratitude for a good deed well played.

Jalila shrugged off her sacrifice. 'There's plenty more fish in the sea.' Her mournful intonation betrayed her true feelings on the matter, and she returned to her team.

Taren felt they both knew Ringbalin was one of a kind.

'Be careful out there,' Taren warned. 'We still don't know where Prochazka is.'

'Duly noted,' Telmo concurred. 'We shall be cautious.' He joined hands with his team and the four of them disappeared.

'Okay, Ringbalin is operational.' Mythric appealed, 'Can we go in now?'

Taren opened her mouth to reply, when Zeven and his crew reappeared with Prochazka's lieutenant in tow.

'Have you lost your mind?' Mythric objected to the Valourean's presence.

'She's on our side,' Jazmay declared, putting Fari down.

'Thank goodness you found him!' Taren was pleased to see the boy.

'Prochazka's ship has returned,' advised the Valourean newcomer. 'She has sent Valoureans to shut down power in the vault and ordered me to clean up the mess in the throne room.'

'Mess?' Mythric, offended, grabbed the Valourean by the arm and hauled her over to the workstation, so she could see for herself what that mess was.

Upon laying sight on the dead woman, she gasped. 'That is the Princess Satomi? But how can that be? Where is the Qusay-Sabah Clarona?'

'In the vault,' Taren enlightened.

The lieutenant's eyes boggled. 'But the general is completely devoted to Phemoria. Why would she do this?'

'Where is she now?' Lucian felt was the more pertinent question.

'She said she had some other business to attend, but would not expand on those details,' Lieutenant Paturi relayed.

'And all the curses will be with her,' Taren uttered aside to the captain. 'If she combines —'

'No one of us is going to be able to take on Prochazka and three curses.' The captain knew her too well. 'Let's deal with one crisis at a time.'

'What's with the feral?' Swithin pointed to the kitten Aurora was struggling to keep in her arms.

'That's my daughter, if you don't mind,' Zeven bantered, as the kitten got its way and jumped to the floor to go scampering off to Khalid.

To avoid the kitten clawing its way up his trousers, Khalid picked her up and she settled in his arms.

'That's it!' Mythric moved to retrieve his granddaughter, who hissed at his intention.

'Leave her!' Zeven demanded. 'She's safer with him than anyone.'

Mythric turned on Zeven, and had Ringbalin not stepped in between the two, Taren would have had an all-in brawl on her hands; but the healer was generating so much good will, the men both took a step back.

'Satomi.' He reminded them both of where they should be focusing their energy.

Taren changed into the attire of a Valourean with a thought, along with heavy make-up to aid disguising her appearance and Jazmay followed suit.

'Has Prochazka said anything to you about a new weapon?' Taren queried.

'No, nothing,' the lieutenant claimed.

'That could be a lie.' Swithin was dubious.

'Well, we don't have time to doubt her, so don't get shot,' the captain suggested, 'or pull weapons at all if you don't have to.'

Taren and her team nodded to confirm, and fell in behind the lieutenant as she headed to the doors that led to the courtroom of the Qusay of Phemoria.

The captain headed over to view the live feed from the courtroom on the monitor. 'Let's just hope that they can get Satomi back here with a minimum of fuss, or we'll be seeing a whole lot more Valourean uniforms.'

Telmo's company were alarmed to find themselves standing before a huge, elaborate set of ancient vault-like doors with nowhere to hide as ten Valoureans turned their sights their way.

'This is his idea of being cautious?'

Telmo picked up on Jalila's distress; clearly she felt overexposed. 'Don't mind us,' instructed Telmo, projecting the suggestion that he was General Prochazka to the guards. 'Eyes front and centre, if you please.'

When the guards immediately responded to Telmo's instruction, Kalayna and Trance were both gobsmacked, but Jalila as a telepathist picked up on his game and smiled, knowing the guards saw them as fellow Valoureans.

'I need to learn that trick,' commented Reggie as they proceeded to the door unobstructed. The hacktivist had stayed in possession of Trance's body for the mission, as the moment he vacated, Trance would lose consciousness.

'Just call him General,' Jalila uttered aside quietly to Trance, as they proceeded to the door. 'That's who they think he is right now.'

'*Skills!*' Reggie admitted he was impressed as Telmo observed the locking mechanism on the vault.

'An impressionist too; you have many talents.' Jalila's sights turned to Telmo, who was rather more rugged-looking than Ringbalin, but rather like him.

'When I first learned, it was known as a glamour,' he advised pulling out the ring Taren had given him and inserting the signet head into the centre of the ornate lock. He turned it clockwise and a loud *chink* made Kalayna and Trance flinch, as they still felt rather exposed.

'Relax, will you please,' he said.

When Telmo removed the ring, the large metal doors of the vault opened inwards to a grandiose, vaulted stone arched hallway.

'Oh my fucking stars,' uttered Reggie, as pools of oil at the bases of each pillared arch burst into flame in consecutive order, all the way down the long hall.

Kalayna looked to Telmo and Jalila, completely lost for words.

But eager to have a steel door between them and the Qusay's guard, Telmo took hold of her arm and guided Kalayna quickly inside after Reggie and Jalila. Once the ring he was holding entered the hallway the doors began to close.

'Vault guard, Captain Vishketah.'

Their attention diverted to a member of the Valourean guard, speaking into her headset. '*General Prochazka?*' She looked to Telmo with daggers in her eyes, and was already running towards the door, which was not closing fast enough!

With a wave of his hand Telmo gave the doors a psychic nudge. The Valourean pulled her weapon and managed to get a shot off, which missed Telmo by a hair's breadth. Jalila was not so fortunate; she hit the ground as the doors slammed closed, locking the Qusay's guard out.

'That will hold them until Prochazka gets here with the real key,' he advised Kalayna, who was gripping him rather tightly around the waist from behind.

'Sorry.' She released him, as their attention turned to their downed team member.

'The captain obviously didn't have time to change the function on her gun,' Reggie advised via Trance, who was down on one knee checking Jalila's vital signs. 'She's unconscious, is all.' He gathered her up in his arms and, with some effort, rose to standing. 'I'll take her; you guys get the door.' He turned and wandered towards the similar set of metal doors at the far end of the passage.

'So much for having a guide.' Telmo looked up to observe the imposing architecture of the ceiling in the corridor. 'Quite impressive though?'

'I'll say,' Kalayna concurred, and Telmo glanced aside to find her eyes were fixed on him. 'You sure know how to woo a girl.' She smiled winningly as she pulled a socket wrench from her belt and wandered over to take a look at the bolts on the door mechanism.

'I remember wanting to woo you, very much,' Telmo admitted. 'But you were never very interested … you were still pining for some Kale guy?' It was easy to joke about it now, with umpteen years of experience between him and then. 'But besides being a little bit dense now and then, Zeven is a remarkable person, so I understand the attraction.'

'Ah!' She waved that off. 'Over that, long time. My disinterest might have had a bit more to do with your reputation for seducing your colleagues.' Kalayna attached the socket to her ratchet and got to work on the door mechanism.

'I slept with a female professor at my university who stole my ideas to further her own career; she got me into the space program in exchange for me not exposing her as a fraud! At the time, I thought that rather chivalrous.' Which, in retrospect it clearly wasn't. 'She did make a fortune from my power converter.'

'So you forgot me during your travels. Did you find yourself someone special out there?' She pretended to be more interested in her work than the answer to her question.

'I didn't forget you. I just stopped caring about impressing you,' he confessed. 'And started trying to impress myself instead.'

'That seems to be working for you.' Kalayna served him a cheeky grin as she dropped the last of the bolts on the ground and removed the cover to the circuit wiring for the door. 'This doesn't look so alien,' she remarked, snipping a few wires.

'This is just the outer defences.' Telmo smiled as he watched her work; he'd missed this every day since he'd been conned into universe jumping with the timekeeper. He and Kalayna had been lovers, but that reality had been voided when he'd followed Zeven and gone AWOL in this timeline.

'Even with the key, they aren't getting this door open now.' Kalayna holstered her tools. 'They'll have to pry it apart.'

'Good job. That buys us some time.' Telmo headed off after Trance, who was halfway down the hall and chatting away to himself.

'Who is he talking to?' Kalayna caught up to Telmo.

'The souls of all the ladies whose lives we are aiming to protect, I expect. As a spirit being himself, Reggie sees them all clearly; to me they appear as tiny spheres of light, at least they do on this level of demonstration.'

'But I thought they were all trapped in some celestial city and couldn't be freed until after the curse of the Phemoray is lifted?' Kalayna was stunned to learn this.

'That's what everybody thinks,' he concurred.

'But why didn't you tell Taren or the captain?' Kalayna queried his secrecy.

'Because I was instructed not to.'

'Instructed by whom?' Kalayna obviously couldn't think of a higher authority than the captain and his wife.

'By the Old Ones.'

His claim stopped the interrogation for a moment, as Kalayna processed. 'As in the beings who built the inter-system gateways!' She could barely breathe for her excitement.

'Yes,' Telmo granted, knowing just how envious that was going to make her.

'You met them?' she asked and thumped his shoulder at once. 'Why didn't you take me with you?'

He blocked her strike this time and gripped her arm gently. 'I didn't say I was never going back to Karmandi.'

Kalayna's eyes grew wide in awe, and he could see the questions fighting for precedence in her mind — the Kalayna from this timeline was seeing him in a very different light now and he couldn't deny that was delightful. It was a shame that she could not remember their romantic attachment any more, but he did enjoy getting to tease her interest all over again.

'Is that like a city?' she asked as he let her go and kept walking.

'*Like* a city, yes.'

'If not a city, then what?' Kalayna hounded him, more playful than ever he'd seen her.

When they'd worked alone together on repairing the defunct inter-system gateway, she'd always kept their relationship very professional. It just figured that she'd pick the middle of a disaster to decide to be amicable.

'Will you take me there?' Kalayna pleaded.

'Being the amazing soul you are, you are bound to be drawn to Karmandi all by yourself,' he teased, eyeing up the door before them that appeared to open in the same fashion as the first.

Kalayna appeared torn between feeling flattered and rejected.

'Can we hurry this along,' Reggie droned. 'Trance is not really built for carrying Phemorians around.'

'So where's all the alien technology you were boasting ab—' Kalayna froze in awe as the massive doors parted onto a high balcony overlooking an expansive underground cavity, where towering racks of stasis pods hung in seemingly endless rows. All the light-beings who were accompanying them, raced out into the vast space in search of their own pods.

Despite the overawing sight, Telmo was more preoccupied with how they were to get down into the complex. There were no doors or stairs leading from the balcony.

'What's the bet the control room is at the other end of this compound?' Telmo wandered over to one of the smaller balconies that annexed off the main one.

'Absolutely correct, I've seen the layout,' Reggie confirmed.

'So how do we get there, if we don't know what it looks like?' Kalayna was eyeing off the ceiling that was shrouded by darkness; most of the lighting streamed from the rows of pods and there was light at the far end, which was too far away to see the source.

The plate in the middle of the little annex balcony drew Telmo's attention and when he placed a hand upon it, the plate lit up. 'Ha ha, very clever, this is like Nefilim technology,' he commented to himself, 'but of course it would be.'

'Who are the Nefilim?' Kalayna neared to see what the fascination was.

'A race of beings that parented humanity in the last universal scheme, much as the Dropa parented humanity in this one.' Telmo sat to remove his boots.

'The Dropa?' Kalayna quizzed.

'The Old Ones,' Telmo clarified. 'I suspect there might be a soul connection there. Even though the Dropa and the Nefilim occupied the same space/time back in that universe, time is really a simultaneous event, and as we are ultimately all one, that really has to be the case, now, doesn't it?' He looked to Kalayna, whose expression was somewhere between admiration and utter bewilderment.

'I have no idea what you just said,' Kalayna admitted.

'Just thinking out loud.' He smiled to assure her she wasn't expected to understand. 'The question was rhetorical.' Telmo tossed his shoes under the bench in the small annex balcony, and directed Kalayna in the same direction. 'Hop on.'

'You say that like we are going for a ride.' The instruction made Kalayna appear wary, as she looked over the edge to see it was a long way down.

'Trust me,' he suggested, looking to Trance. 'Are you coming?'

'Sure, I got nothing to lose, I'm already dead.' Reggie lumbered over with his load. 'And Trance could use a seat!'

'Thanks for that vote of confidence, team.' Telmo waited for them to settle on the seats provided around the back half of the annex, before stepping onto the central plate, which lit up again under his feet.

'Whoa!' Both his passengers panicked as the annex detached from the main balcony and hovered in midair.

Telmo's next thought turned the craft around, so he could see where he was headed. 'Well, this sure beats walking.' Telmo was enjoying the the experience, but his passengers were a little more wary.

'Just don't lose your concentration.' Kalayna was trying not to look down.

Trance was gazing out at all the pods before them, with a mournful look on his face. 'Of all the horrid things done in the name of the Phemoray, this must be the worst. So many beautiful women with lives in limbo.' His eyes turned to the woman in his arms.

'It is time for a huge wake up call on Phemoria,' Telmo agreed.

'And we're the alarm.' Reggie grinned as Telmo focused his will on moving forwards and their hovercraft began moving at speed.

'Speaking of alarm! AHHHH!' Kalayna's shriek echoed through the chamber as they were whooshed towards the light at the distant end.

In the Qusay's room of court, the Valoureans guarding the chamber pointed all their weapons in their direction — Taren was pleased to note that none of them appeared to be of the same design as Kalayna's weapon — but upon spotting the lieutenant they lowered their guard. She was of the mind to use her PK and just freeze the entire guard where they stood.

'Lieutenant Paturi,' the Valourean in charge acknowledged her.

'Captain Vudil,' the lieutenant began. 'I'm here —'

'I know why you are here,' the captain confirmed. 'The general has already advised us of your orders. We are required elsewhere, so we are to leave you to your clean up.'

The lieutenant gave a firm nod, and the Valoureans filed out of the room, closing the doors behind them.

'Unbelievable!' Jazmay mentally commanded all the locks to close in their wake to secure the room, even though many of the Valoureans had been given Satomi's ability to teleport now.

'My thoughts exactly ...' said Taren. 'Maybe I should have restrained them all while we had the chance, but why risk raising the alarm if we don't have to?' The ease of taking the chamber was unnerving, as the men of the crew ventured through the doors at the back of the room to join them.

'What just happened?' Lucian sounded as wary as she felt.

'It's either a miracle or a trap.' Taren frowned and shook her head, unsure.

'I should have come back.' Mythric collapsed to his knees at Satomi's head, no doubt reliving the last time he'd found her thus. Fortunately Khalid had not entered the court chamber with everyone else as Mythric's grief would have surely been let loose upon him.

'The Qusay refused you an audience; you didn't have much choice.' Aurora placed a hand on Mythric's shoulder in comfort and crouched beside him.

'I should have snuck in,' Mythric cursed himself in retrospect. 'Why did I bring her back ... not for this misery! Should I restore her life now?' Mythric hated to query what he wanted, knowing it would be easier on everyone if they didn't.

'Satomi's spirit is here,' the captain felt compelled to advise Mythric, who was both relieved and wary to learn this. 'She wants you to know she never intended to remain Qusay, she did this to save the family from Khalid's delusion, but —' the captain paused to hear the rest. 'But she can see now that she was the one deluded, and Zeven was right.'

The news came as a great relief. 'Do it,' Mythric urged Swithin and Ringbalin who were both close by, awaiting his word.

'She feels she is not worthy,' Lucian forestalled them.

'That is not the question here,' the captain told her. 'The question is, do you wish to come back?'

No one drew a breath as they awaited the answer, and Taren's heart went out to Mythric, who'd had such a rough trot with loving this woman — she hoped Satomi appreciated that.

'More than words can express,' Lucian relayed her answer, and everyone began breathing once more, the rescue team springing into action.

'Don't move her,' Swithin warned the grieving husband, as he went down on one knee beside her, and Ringbalin positioned himself on the other side of her. 'Together?' Swithin suggested, and Ringbalin gave an encouraging nod.

Zeven was standing back, out of the way, when he noticed the kitten go scampering past him, heading for Jazmay. Some meowing got her retrieved from the floor, but no sooner had the shifter taken the wee animal in hand than Thurraya had transformed back into her true form.

'Thanks, Jaz!' she said, breaking free of her hold, then racing back towards her father. 'You have to come!' She dragged him back towards the Qusay's private chambers.

'I can't just —' Zeven motioned back to his dead mother, upon whom everyone else's attention was focused at this time.

'You must!' she implored, still dragging him away with all her six-year-old might.

'Okay.' He grabbed her up and ran with her into the room.

'Oh no, he's already gone?' She jumped from her father's arms, and looked about the room to be sure, spotting Fari heading out a servant's entrance. 'Khalid left?'

'Yep, just vanished,' Fari shrugged.

'Where do you think you are going?' Zeven queried.

'General Prochazka just ordered the vault doors to be welded shut!' Fari pointed to the monitor as his source.

'How do you know?' Zeven rushed over to see for himself. 'This is a closed Valourean security network! How did you get in here?'

'I guess I didn't spend all my time with Sovee doing homework.' The lad grinned mischievously.

'We have people in there.' Zeven looked back to the screen and by the time he looked up from reading the order, the boy was gone.

'You have to take me to the Pit of the Obstinate right now!' Thurraya neared to grab his hand.

'I have to find Fari,' Zeven emphasised.

'I probably have enough charge already to take myself,' she considered.

'No, baby, please —' Zeven waylaid her, gripping hold of her wrist — at least if she went somewhere he'd go too. 'Just tell me why.'

'Khalid is going to face Prochazka and the curses, and I am the only one who can protect him!' she insisted.

Zeven was horrified, and yet from his own experience he knew Thurraya was integral to neutralising the curses.

'I am the adaptor, the only one, do you see? This is why I came into this world.'

'One of many reasons,' he corrected, also remembering what the Dropa had said about his daughter. 'But yes, I see.' He glanced back to the door leading to the room of court, feeling that he should really consult Aurora on this one.

'She will only be distressed,' Thurraya guessed his hesitation. 'We must go now!'

Before Satomi's eyes had opened, Mythric had dispersed all the blood from the scene, not wanting her to awaken to the grizzly sight. Her wounds had vanished during resurrection, the colour had returned to her flesh, and now that she was breathing peacefully, Swithin and Ringbalin sat back to admire their work.

'She's all yours,' Swithin advised with a wink.

Mythric took Swithin's place by her side as Satomi awoke with a start and a gasp.

'*Spyridon.*' She was relieved to see him and gripped his shirt in panic. 'I was deceived,' she rasped.

'I know,' he concurred in a forgiving tone.

'Clarona!' She panicked. 'The vault.'

'We are on it,' he assured, stroking her head.

'This coup was to protect Thurraya, and I only exposed her to more danger!' Satomi was frustrated by her misjudgement.

'She's safe, we have her,' he said.

Aurora looked away from the intimate scene to note her husband missing. 'Where is Zeven?' She wandered back towards the rear chamber doors as the lieutenant hushed everyone to silence, pointing to her headset. 'General Prochazka,' she spoke into the mouthpiece as the room hushed, and Taren moved in close to listen in on the transmission.

'*Are you in the room of court?*'

'Yes, General,' she replied.

'*Any sign of the AMIE crew?*'

'No, General. All is as it should be here.'

'*Is it?*'

The comment alarmed both Taren and the lieutenant, who looked to each other wide-eyed and wary.

It was at that moment Taren noted the new steel plate set in the middle of the chamber. 'What is that?'

The doors to the back room closed in front of Aurora and trapped her in the room of court with the others. 'No!' She slammed the door with her hands in protest and tugged at the knobs that were now firmly fixed in place and would not turn.

'*I cannot abide disloyalty, Lieutenant.*'

'Uh-oh!' the Valourean mouthed in trepidation, pointing to the camera on the wall through which they had been viewing this room, and Taren backed up to hear.

'*I was going to ensure you were out of range, but now I shan't bother.*'

'Out of range ... of what?'

A beam of light shot down from the ceiling in the centre of the room and a blast of force bounced off the metallic plate and exploded outward, sending everyone flying into the walls. Taren cracked her head, and blacked out as she slid to the floor.

18

MOTHER OF ALL CURSES

It was coming on to dusk, but there was no mist this time of year on Phemoria, so visibility was still quite good. From behind a large tree trunk of the dead forest that led to the Pit of the Obstinate, Khalid observed the scene unfolding with some trepidation.

Atop of the stairs that led to the platform where a sacrificial altar stood open to the pit beyond, the smelter that was the Soul Keep had been placed and was heating up rapidly. As the solid metal contents were reduced into a red-hot molten liquid, the spirits of the demon crew shot out of the Keep and flew above it, revelling in their release from their Osmium encapsulation.

Prochazka was seated on the stairs speaking into her headset; the case containing the cursed crown of the Phemoray was still locked closed and positioned under one of her feet. Between her knees she held the metal coffer containing the curse of Chironjivi, which she kept picking up and shaking, just for the hell of it.

'*We knew you'd come for us, Mistress,*' the crew from Dead Man Downs caroused. '*Let's kill all those light fuckers —*'

'Quiet!' She wrapped her hand around her mic and held up the middle finger on the other hand on which she wore their ring. 'I give the orders and you obey.' The general released her clasp on the mic to resume communications with her Valoureans back at the palace. 'Captain. Wait ten minutes for the charge to dissipate then kill them all and retrieve the princess.' She ended the call, using the remote in her hand.

'*Whoo-hoo! Most wise, Mistress.*' The spirits laughed and cheered. '*What's in those containers?*' they asked, and Prochazka found her grin.

'I'll get to that in a moment. Now, one more word and I'll stick you back on that light-filled planet I fished you out from.'

She looked back to her remote and placed another call. 'Captain Vishketah, report?' The general listened. 'How are you coming with the doors? ... Have you cut the power? ... If the switches are not responding, cut the damn wires! I want it off! ... I am well aware the generators can only be shut down from the inside, but the fuel feed is exterior, so cut it off!'

Prochazka ended the call, frustrated. 'Must I do every damn thing myself?'

'*Send us, Mistress, let us lift the burden.*'

She drew a deep breath for patience, and replaced the remote on her belt. She took the metal coffer in one hand, grabbed up the case in the other, turned and scaled the stairs. 'I need you here.'

'*What's the plan?*' The spirits were wary — you didn't need to heat the smelter to conjure their presence.

'A little trip down memory lane.' Prochazka placed the case and the metal coffer down by the Soul Keep and backed up to the stairs, a ring of fire appearing and encircling all three items. The demon crew became agitated when they discovered they could not move beyond the circle.

'*What trick is this? We cannot help you if we are trapped.*'

'Did you really think I had forgotten your betrayal ... or that I need your help to do anything any more?' she sneered in revulsion and delight. 'In the case is the crown of the Phemoray you promised to destroy for me, and now you shall regret for all eternity that you did not.'

The case containing the cursed crown flew open, and although the naked eye would have seen nothing extraordinary result, Khalid's third eye vision was acute since his time in Karmandi, and he saw the seething mass of hateful, tortured souls rising to oppose the crew of Dead Man Downs.

'*How are you here?*' they hissed in spite. Then, realising they were trapped in a confined space with the equally spiteful male energy, they screeched in protest.

'*She brought us.*' The crew directed the Phemoray and the blame to the general, who waved.

'Welcome to the festivities, ladies,' she gloated at their discomfort.

'*General! Get us out of here this instant!*'

'I don't take orders from you any more.' She flashed a grin as the crown of Phemoria rose to hover over the smelter. 'Nor will any, ever again.' She allowed the crown to fall into the molten metal. The thought form screamed, burst into flame, and split apart into many entities, who proceeded to chase and attack the crew from Dead Man Downs.

'*It was Chironjivi who deceived you, we were only following his orders,*' they defended. '*He is the one who screwed up your queen.*'

'That is why I brought him to the party too.' The general motioned to the metal coffer, which unlatched and popped open. A cloud of ash rose into the air, but it was contained within the circle of the flames.

'*Finally come to join us, Captain?*' the spirit crew taunted. '*Now you Phemorian whores are really in trouble.*'

'*It just gives us the chance to finish what we started,*' the Phemoray retorted.

When it could find no living soul to cling to, the ashes formed a shadow of a man. Observing the conflict around him, he looked beyond it to the culprit. '*You're not my son ... but I know you,*' it discerned and then laughed. '*You're the silly bitch who left your queen wide open to be taken by me. You're the reason I have a son!*'

The Phemoray ceased their feuding and looked back to the general. '*It was you who betrayed us!*' they hissed, all their ire now aimed at her.

'And I will do it again.' Prochazka was silently fuming, her jaw clenched in anger as she manifested a large ancient text in her hand and forced a smile. 'Recognise this?'

Chironjivi stopped laughing. '*Mother's grimoire.*'

'Correct.' Her smile was more sincere.

'Where did you find that?' The Phemoray were most curious, and a little fearful.

'Does it matter? Thurraya obviously took great pains to ensure you never knew of its existence,' Prochazka gloated. 'It is the ultimate text on controlling the disembodied — that would be you — and now the book that began your twisted reign will end it!'

All the spirits had ceased their agitated movement and gone very quiet.

'Did you know there are sub-planes existent where pesky souls can be banished for all eternity?' she queried with glee, opening the book to the said page, and then looking up to her captive audience. 'What's wrong? Am I not *amusing* you any more? Do you not fancy spending the rest of time fighting out your woes with the souls that you've consumed all your wretched time hating?'

'She's bluffing!' Chironjivi wasn't convinced, but he didn't sound too bothered either.

'Am I?' she challenged. 'It took years of research and digging into classified files to find the crew manifest for the *Insurrecto*, but I found it. It took even more delving to find the names of every female soul sacrificed to this pit and later summoned unto our crown by Thurraya. But, with those names I can banish you all! There is seal I have drawn into the ground beneath the Keep, a symbol that only I know, and this sigil will be your prison.'

The spirits turned very hostile, and the particles forming Chironjivi's grey form spread apart to make him appear huge. *'We could make you more powerful than you ever dreamt —'*

'I've heard that before!' Prochazka looked away and squeezed the hand that hosted the demon's ring into a fist — something was ailing her and Khalid knew her torment all too well.

'We can destroy any who oppose us,' Chironjivi appealed.

'Time for you to join your crew.' She looked to the canister and from it rose the amulet Zeven had torn from Khalid's hand.

Chironjivi was the soul who had created the Soul Keep, he had witnessed the entire rite, so Khalid was hoping to use the amulet to dig into Chironjivi's memory in order to reverse the curse.

'Stop!' Khalid ran from the shadows to the base of the stairs, and Prochazka turned to confront him.

'No, you stop!' Prochazka suggested, snapping the book closed. 'I have all the curses contained, but with a thought I will set them free to wreak havoc where they will.'

'That's my boy!' Chironjivi was pleased to see Khalid. *'Go on then, provoke her.'*

'You are the one!' Prochazka's interest in her unexpected company was piqued; she drew a pulse laser weapon and aimed it at him. 'You are Khalid Mansur?'

'I am.' He held his hands palm outwards in submission.

'How did you find me?'

'I saw this place in a beautiful dream I had,' he explained, and clearly the general thought he was being sarcastic.

'There is nothing beautiful about this place,' she scoffed.

'There could be,' Khalid said with great sincerity. 'You have gathered everything we need to make it so.'

Prochazka was perplexed. 'You want to see your father and his demons banished?'

'He is not my father,' he advised amicably. 'He's just a twisted, tormented being who tricked us both into taking the wrong path.'

'No,' Prochazka disagreed. 'I am on the *right* path, and *you* … killed my Qusay.'

'You killed your Qusay,' Khalid pointed out. 'And ordered the death of another.'

Prochazka was perplexed by this, as if she had only just realised the strange irony in her bitter hatred for this man who owed her his life. 'I acted in the best interest of Phemoria,' she justified, although she appeared pained about it.

'In the best interest of Phemoria? Or in the best interest of not being discovered as the woman who saved the first true prince of the Phemorian royal line?' Khalid suspected the truth would piss her off, and the look of contempt she served him certainly reflected that sentiment, and yet, she was still considering the question.

'He's trying to trick you,' the spirit crew hissed. *'Let us deal with him.'*

'*No, General, raise our crown from the flames and we shall serve you*,' the Phemoray appealed.

'I know you think you are in control of … *this*,' Khalid waved a hand about, referring to the seething mass of hatred. 'I was attached to it for nearly all this earthly life, but they twist your perspective to suit themselves. While you wear that ring, no decision you make is truly your own.'

'I cast a protection spell on this ring.' Prochazka held up the grimoire as her source. 'They cannot control me so long as I stay true to Phemoria.'

'Which leads back to my original question.' Khalid appealed for her to consider that. 'Because if that condition has been broken then you are no longer protected and all their negativity and angst will be influencing every move you make. Chironjivi is a black hole that thrives on the fear, hatred and horror of women; you really don't want to feed him thought forms like the Phemoray?'

'*I said provoke her, not counsel her!*' Chironjivi objected. '*You're just confusing the fucking issue!*'

'I know they've lied to you, cheated you, hurt you!' Khalid ignored the spirits and stayed focused on Prochazka. 'But despite all that, you have served Phemoria to the best of your ability. You have the power to banish all these souls to damnation, including those of your foremothers, at the risk of being tempted to summon them back, or someone else discovering the means to do so. Or, we could free these souls from these curses so that they can all move on to the next phase of their spiritual evolution, and ensure they never get the opportunity to enforce their archaic mind-set on anyone of influence again.'

Prochazka was reluctant. 'You are asking me to forgive them their crimes against myself, my Qusay and my people?' That was clearly difficult; emotionally Prochazka was starting to crack. Tears were welling in her eyes and she didn't like it.

'Just take off the ring before you answer,' Khalid appealed. 'You don't need to control them with it, you've cast a circle of protection.'

'*It's a trick*,' hissed the crew.

'*He is an abomination who should never have been born.*' The Phemoray were so full of spite that they would rather side with their nemesis than accept that a man might have their best interests at heart.

'*What the fuck is wrong with you, boy?*' Chironjivi snarled. '*Have those light fuckers made a pussy out of you? Stop talking rubbish and take her out!*'

'Don't listen to them, all they know is hatred and mistrust.' Khalid endeavoured to stay focused on the general.

'That's all *I* know.' Her expression hardened.

'*We'd rather be damned to fight for all eternity than to forgive those fucking bitches!*' the crew snarled.

'*You haven't seen the half of it!*' the Phemoray threatened the crew right back.

Their words only infuriated the general. 'There is no forgiveness in this world, it's not in them, and it's not in me. They deserve one another.' She let her hold over Chironjivi's amulet lapse and it dropped into the smelter, drawing in his dark soul, the crew of Dead Man Downs and the Phemoray along with it. The ash shadow lost its form, snowing down upon the furnace, and then silence.

Prochazka's gaze turned back to Khalid, her weapon still aimed at him. 'I really can't allow anyone to witness the banishing ri—'

A rumbling was heard from deep in the belly of the smelter.

'Ahhhhh!' Prochazka struggled to hold her weapon, as the ring upon her finger began to glow and burn.

Inside the vault's control tower, Telmo's team had located the primary operations centre. Like their transport here, the system was psychically controlled. There was a telepathic control plate that sat within a pulpit-like structure. This overlooked the room of pods through a huge glass wall that faced inwards towards the complex.

'Where am I supposed to connect to this thing?' Reggie asked, cord in hand; he'd looked over the entire pulpit, but its surface was entirely smooth.

Telmo placed his hand on the control plate, and it remained dead as a doornail. 'Access denied,' he assumed, looking back to

Reggie. 'You can't just dive in and control it like you do with your workstation?'

'Well, I could if I knew what the fuck I was looking at?' Reggie defended his skills. 'Besides, I don't actually touch the keys and this is a telepathic touch pad, so that ain't going to work. What about her?' He motioned to Jalila unconscious on the lounge.

They fetched her over and placed her hand on the plate, but there was no response either.

'Where is the genie room?' Kalayna proffered. 'I can switch the power manually from there.'

'There's a lift yonder that will take us there,' Reggie advised, heading off with her.

'Wait up!' There was still one little sphere of light hanging around Reggie, and Telmo assumed it was the spirit of the Qusay-Sabah Clarona. 'That will help keep them alive,' Telmo outlined, 'but it's not going to get these pods to bring their hosts out of status and open. What does her Majesty suggest?'

'Her Majesty is not here,' Reggie replied. 'She remained outside the complex.'

'Then who is that?' He pointed to the sphere, as it came to settle on Jalila.

'I think you are about to find out.' Reggie ran to catch the lift that Kalayna was already inside of.

'You should take the hovercraft, it will be faster,' Telmo suggested, and Kalayna held the door.

'I feel safer in the lift,' she advised, releasing the hold button.

As the lift doors closed, Telmo's attention reverted to the lounge where Jalila woke up and immediately stood. 'Jalila, thank goodness —'

'I am Jafera.' She moved past him to take up a position behind the control plate. 'We met during your spirit walk —'

'Jalila's sister,' Telmo recalled, although she'd not been formally introduced. 'Do you think you can —'

She placed her hand on the plate of the device and it lit up. Seconds later, the interior lights in the pods began to turn on, row by row from the centre out, until the whole chamber was ablaze with light.

'Is the system designed to take this kind of strain?' Telmo noted lights flickering. 'If we overload it, I doubt very much that the generators will fare any better.'

'No one has ever awoken all the occupants at once,' Jafera admitted, appearing determined to proceed all the same. 'But there is only one more function this system needs to perform.' She issued the command to open the pods and Telmo focused his psychokinetic will on the same cause.

A split second later the lights fused and Telmo found himself standing in darkness. 'Did it work?' He watched all the spheres of light disappearing, unsure if this was a good sign or not, when something fell against him and slid to the floor with a thud.

'No!' Kalayna stamped her feet as the elevator stopped mid-descent and fell into darkness.

'Guess we should have taken the hovercraft?' Reggie appraised on her behalf. 'The generators will kick in in a second.'

They waited in the dark impatiently.

'Any moment now.'

'It doesn't matter.' Kalayna slid to the floor and thumped it with her hand. 'If Telmo hasn't got those pods open, all those women will be dead!'

Reggie was quiet for a time; clearly he didn't know how to respond to that. 'I am dead. It's not so bad.'

Clarona may have been in a spirit form but she was not entirely without means to defend her throne; she'd jammed all the power switches feeding power to the vault into an 'on' position, and hindered her guards from interfering with the power wires. All she needed was one Valourean who was a medium, and so far none of the guard charged with shutting down the vault had acknowledged her presence. Still, it was becoming plainly clear to them that something supernatural was in the room hindering their efforts.

'Maybe our sisters are protecting themselves?' suggested one Valourean to her captain.

'That's impossible.' The captain didn't sound convinced by her own statement. 'Not without the aid of the Phemoray.'

'We all know what happened the last time the vault was shut down,' the Valourean ventured to say. 'Why are we being ordered to murder our own sisters when the Phemoray are no longer in charge?'

'A *very good question*,' Clarona awarded, hoping the captain was as astute as her subordinate.

'Get a medium in here, now!' Captain Vishketah ordered through her headset.

Finally! Clarona was exulted when a Valourean entered whom she knew to be qualified. *'Do you see me?'*

'Qusay!' The clairvoyant knelt and alarmed her comrades.

'Qusay?' the captain queried, turning pale.

'Yes,' confirmed the medium, 'I see the spirit form of the Qusay Clarona right there!'

'But?' The captain couldn't understand it. 'Why would our Qusay be in spirit form?'

'Because my body is trapped in the vault you are trying to shut down! Prochazka put me there!'

The medium conveyed this to her superior, who gasped and got straight on her headset to alert the rest of the queen's guard. 'In the name of the Qusay-Sabah Clarona, General Prochazka is to be apprehended, all her orders and powers of command are revoked!'

An alert sounded from the control panel. 'Power out in the vault, Captain,' the Valourean monitoring the system was alarmed to advise.

'Then reboot!' the captain ordered, and then spoke into her headset. 'Get the vault open —' She paused, looking shocked. 'It is open!' She marvelled at the stroke of luck. 'Did you say a little *boy*?'

Clarona felt her control over her spirit form lapsing. *'Oh no …'* Her conscious awareness slipped into darkness.

*

The sound of moaning stirred Taren, and when she moved, her entire body cried out in agony and her own moans joined the chorus in the room. Her muscles ached, her head was throbbing and her heart was beating way too fast. 'Argh!' She managed to roll over, and realised where she was: the blast had landed her here on the outer wall of the Qusay's room of court.

'What the fuck was that?' Swithin peeled himself off the floor in front of the throne where he'd been thrown and dragged himself up onto it. 'I feel like I've had the life sucked right out of me.'

Ringbalin, close by him, nodded in complete empathy with that assessment.

Clearly all of them were experiencing the same lethargy.

'My power is zapped,' Jazmay droned, having made it to a seated position.

Upon hearing this Taren tried to exert her Powers to help get herself upright, and her fear was confirmed. 'Prochazka has taken Kalayna's weapon to a whole new level ...' Taren pulled her Juju stone from her armband, to note that it now looked like a regular piece of shale. 'Oh damn.'

They had no protection whatsoever! If the blast had been powerful enough to neutralise their Juju stones, only heaven knew how long their Powers would be impaired.

'We have to get out of here.' Taren managed to stagger her way up to standing, but it was an effort even to talk. 'They will kill us all.'

Even the threat of death couldn't roust enough energy from the crew to drag their heavy bodies off the floor, some of them were still not even conscious, and the thought of rallying them all caused Taren to stagger in her stance — all she wanted was to fall down and sleep for a year!

'Get up!' Lucian made it to his feet and gave Yasper a nudge with his foot to get him conscious. 'That's an order.'

'Thurraya!' Aurora grabbed the doorknob of the door she'd been thrown against, and hauled herself up to check the door was still locked. 'Open this door!' She slammed her hands against it when it would not open.

The sound of all the doors unbolting at once sent an alarming cold shiver through Taren's entire being. *Too late.*

Time and perception slipped into slow motion as the doors to the courtroom burst open, and Valoureans entered, laser guns blazing.

Aurora, being so close to the door, was hit point blank in the forehead — her brains shooting out the back of her skull as she fell to the ground.

Mythric turned and wrapped his arms around Satomi, and was shot three times in the back before he collapsed to the floor on top of her.

Jazmay pulled her weapons, and managed to stun three of the Valoureans, before her weapons were drawn into the hands of her enemy, who then shot her in the chest.

In the horror of the moment, her heart and mind both screaming in objection to the twist of fate she was helpless to prevent, Taren had a blinding moment of clarity — she had to protect the healers.

Swithin had already jumped behind the huge throne he'd been seated upon and was returning fire. Amie was shot as she ran to join him.

Ringbalin stood stunned, like an animal caught in headlights awaiting its death.

Taren drew her weapons as she threw herself at him. 'Live!' She pressed the guns into his arms and barged him out of the line of fire and behind the cover of the throne. Her body rebounded violently from several shocking impacts in her back that tore right through her body, and she fell face-first back to the ground.

'Taren!' she heard Lucian calling from somewhere behind her, but all she could see in her eye line across the floor was Ringbalin's mournful face as he cried in protest to her deed.

Her body, emotions and mental reasoning felt frozen — she was numb to the pain of her injuries, and even to the outcome of their struggle. Yet, as her perspective suddenly shifted and she was flipped onto her back to find Lucian leaning over her, she panicked. 'Take … cover …'

He was trying to tell her something, but she couldn't hear him;

there was so much yelling going on in the room, everyone was shouting.

'… it's *over* —'

She heard that much. Was he giving up?

'Look!' Lucian directed her to someone else who was now crouching over her, and with her last conscious breath Taren recognised the face. *Mother.*

'Why did you land us so far away from our target?' Thurraya complained as they traversed the dead forest in near darkness. She was dragging him forwards in the direction he'd said they needed to go, as he had a firm grip on her hand.

'Because I want to observe what we are walking into,' he explained, having a mental battle about running with the whim of a six-year-old girl while there was a crisis going down in the palace.

'Hold on.' She stopped still and looked to the silhouette of the trees ahead against the fading light of the evening sky. 'This place is significant.'

'Significant?' Not really the kind of word that was part of his daughter's everyday vocabulary. He felt his daughter tremble, but it was not from cold. 'You've never been here before,' he advised. 'Not in this timeline, anyway.'

'Yes I have,' she replied, her trembling intensifying. 'A very *long* time ago.' She withdrew her hand from Zeven's grasp with a single tug that was beyond her tiny capability. 'The pit where we finished our bloody revolution is just through those trees.' She pointed in the direction of the sacrificial altar that was not yet in eye shot.

'Thurraya?' Zeven suddenly got the feeling that he was not addressing his daughter any more.

'This is the Cathedral of Trees,' she said mournfully. 'Once the most renowned and beautiful natural formations on this planet, or anywhere in the United Systems! It was a place of worship to our ancestors for countless eons, before my generation damned its vibrational energy with our wars and hatred of one another.'

Now Zeven *knew* it wasn't his daughter he was reasoning with.

Prior experience had taught him that the conscious awareness of the late queen of Phemoria had been lying dormant in her young namesake, in wait for the opportunity to set her past mistakes to right.

'But as dead as it appears to mortal eyes, there are still elementals here,' she noted, 'waiting patiently in the sub-planes to restore the balance.'

'Thurraya is an adaptor, yet she talks about elementals all the time.' Zeven had wondered about this. 'Does she get this talent from you?'

'She draws her power from her environs,' she replied, 'and nature has more Powers than any human.' She strode off towards the edge of the tree line.

'Please.' Zeven was hot on her heels. 'That's my six-year-old daughter you are using to seek recompense with. If you intend to slit her throat in order that you might lead the souls of your people out of here, I need other people present to save her life when you de—' Zeven was struck dumb as he caught sight of their destination.

The sacrificial platform was ablaze in a ring of fire. The Soul Keep bubbled away in the centre, and a huge flaming entity was rising from the molten liquid as Prochazka and Khalid cowered before it.

'—part,' Zeven finished his sentence, stunned beyond rational thought for a moment. 'She combined the curses.' The notion sent shockwaves through his being, and then a sudden shock of pain stabbed through his arm where his Juju stone was placed. 'Argh!' The pain paralysed him, and as an intense feeling of dread swept over him, it took a few deep breaths to prevent himself being sick. 'Something very bad has happened.' Was this woeful premonition a result of the scene before him?

This was not at all how this situation had looked the last time they'd gathered here to banish the Phemoray, and Zeven's first instinct was to grab his daughter and get her the hell out of there.

'Thurraya.' He looked down to explain his misgivings to find her absent. 'Oh, shit no.' He turned his harrowed sights to the event unfolding in the distance, where his daughter had reappeared in between Khalid and the general. 'I'm there.' He shifted location just as swiftly.

'Stay back.'

Zeven had no sooner arrived on the scene than his daughter rebounded him out of the way, using his own PK against him.

'Will you kill your Qusay?' The child confronted the general, who was gripping the grimoire under one arm, whilst her other hand, crippled in agony by the ring burning hot on her skin, struggled to maintain her aim at Khalid — the girl was blocking her line of sight.

'Thurraya,' Prochazka uttered — although they had never met, Prochazka clearly recognised her and diverted her aim. 'You should not be here, Highness.'

'This child should not be your Highness,' Thurraya retorted, 'but since you have made it so, I command you to yield!'

'*Kill her!*' the entity of fire raged. '*Then we will have done away with them all.*'

'You need to leave.' Prochazka raised her weapon, her hand trembling as it struggled against her intention.

'No!' Zeven got himself to his feet and moved to intervene, but an unseen force was holding him back and Khalid also.

'If you kill this child, you wipe out the royal line you swore to protect, then the curse will have you. I penned that book you are holding as safeguard against a situation like this unfolding.' Ray eyed it over with regret. 'I was deluded to think I could wield such power over the dead without recompense, and the price Phemoria has paid for my foolishness is already insurmountable. Hence I have returned to this world to relieve you of the burden that should never have been yours to carry.'

'Thurraya … slayer of men?' Prochazka's eyes boggled and welled with tears, at a child's suggestion that she was addressing the great sorceress incarnate.

'Not a title I am proud of any more.' She glanced back to Khalid and Zeven. 'There are some amazing men incarnate at this time, and I was wrong to judge them all by the standards of the king I slayed.'

'*She is a lying little bitch! My father was a great man!*' the entity fumed. *It will be my pleasure to send my mother to her grave all over again … so do it!*'

'*Argh!*' Prochazka resisted the demon's painful compulsion to comply, and dropped the book to the ground.

'Yes,' Thurraya encouraged her. 'Now drop your weapon and give me the ring, lest you become another victim of this curse.'

Prochazka shook her head. 'I have this.'

'*That's a girl.*' The demon felt he had the upper hand.

'You are too important to risk,' Prochazka told Thurraya, even as battling her inner demons brought tears to her eyes.

'This curse is not contained,' Thurraya warned. 'Part of it is still on your finger, you must toss it to the flames!'

Prochazka wept when she realised the oversight, and then laughed in the face of her own undoing. 'My first priority has always been Phemoria.'

'I know,' Thurraya replied in earnest. 'This moment would never have been possible, were it not for your devotion to freeing your Qusay from the curse that I unwittingly unleashed. Phemoria is in your debt.'

'*Kill her or I will consume you,*' Chironjivi threatened, and when the general dropped the weapon and served him the finger, her entire hand burst into flame, and she cried out in agony. The flaming limb reached out towards Thurraya.

'No!' Prochazka threw herself backwards to the ground, to struggle with the entity that was fast consuming her. The ring was melting into her burning flesh, and was impossible to remove. 'You want me?' Prochazka raised her half-flaming body to its feet and turned to confront her attacker. 'Then consume this, motherfucker!' She took a running jump and launched herself into the molten vat.

'*NO!*' the entity wailed — there was nothing this curse hated worse than the blood of a fearless martyr — and as her body disappeared into the smelter, the entity diminished significantly.

'Thurraya!' Zeven continued to bounce off the invisible barrier, wanting to shield his daughter from the gruelling sight.

'Fear not,' she called back to him, seemingly serene as she watched the flaming entity flailing and cursing its loss of control. 'Our success is assured now; the good general has supplied us all the names we need to reverse this curse.' She walked over and retrieved

the grimoire from the ground where it had fallen, and then looked
back to Khalid. 'I believe between us there is not a soul who cannot
be accounted for.'

Khalid moved passed the barrier to join Thurraya, and yet
Zeven was still restrained.

'I want to know what your intentions are regarding my daughter.'
Zeven felt unprepared for what he knew was coming.

'Chironjivi,' Thurraya turned to the smelter and held out her
hand. 'Come to mother.'

A tiny drop of liquid rose from the smelter and cooled into the
amulet that had once bound the evil entity to Khalid, then the
item flew into Thurraya's possession.

'What are you doing?' Zeven objected, as Prochazka had just given
her life to contain the curse. 'Khalid, you have to do something!'

'I am doing what I know is best.' Khalid took possession of the
amulet.

Thurraya looked back to Zeven, disturbed by his objections.
'Your daughter shall remember nothing of this rite, I promise.'

'She won't if she's dead, you mean?' Zeven barged the invisible
barrier, only to be bounced back.

'Best that there are no witnesses,' Thurraya outlined, as Zeven's
consciousness suddenly took leave.

As Zeven stirred he was looking at the stars in the night sky,
sparkling brightly, as they darted all over the place. *What?* He shook
his head and looked again, and the moving stars vanished. Only
the usual nightscape of fixed stars were glistening about the moons
shedding light upon the landscape. 'Weird.' He sat up and realised
where he was. *Thurraya!* The thought compelled him to his feet.

The smelter was in darkness now, all the commotion had died
down and Khalid was kneeling by the sacrificial altar, where a
single tiny body was laid.

'What have you done?' Zeven scaled the stairs and pulled Khalid
away from her; he went down beside her in his stead. 'Thurraya?'
She was very still.

'She's only sleeping,' Khalid advised. 'We've spent hours drawing the individual souls and their offerings from the furnace to free them from the curse and then we burned the grimoire. When we were done, I dismissed the spirit of the first true Qusay to its eternal rest … Ray is just a little exhausted from the channelling.'

Zeven gave a deep sigh of relief on one level, but this was a worry on another. 'But if you dismissed Thurraya's spirit, who shall lead the souls of the dead out of here?' As he asked this, Zeven wondered if these souls were the moving stars he thought he'd seen upon his return to consciousness.

'I shall lead them,' Khalid advised, sounding completely at peace with that decision.

'What? *No*, you can't!' Zeven objected, realising it meant the end of the road for their friendship.

'Why not?' Khalid challenged with a grin. 'Afraid you'll miss me?'

'I *will* miss you,' Zeven insisted. 'Isn't there another way —'

Khalid shook his head. 'This is the only reason I came back from Karmandi … now I can return.'

'Aw, man,' Zeven was disappointed. 'I saved your life just so I can watch you off yourself?'

'I'm not going to *off* myself.' Khalid found this amusing.

'You're not expecting me to do it?' Zeven hoped. ''Cause killing was never really my thing.'

Khalid was laughing out loud now and Zeven had no idea what was so amusing.

'Look, I know I'm a little cosmically challenged,' he freely admitted, whereby Khalid laughed even harder. 'You wanna tell me what's so funny?'

'Nothing really, you've been a good friend, Grigorian,' Khalid granted. 'Without you I would never have remembered any of our adventures, or who I really am.'

'Our time in the last universe was pretty radical.' Zeven grinned as he reminisced.

'Our time in the dark universe was even more so,' Khalid added.

'But you weren't one of the Grigori?' Not to the best of Zeven's recollections.

'No,' Khalid concurred. 'Not one of the Grigori.' Khalid shook off his physical form, as easily as Ahura once had, and the light-filled apparition of undulating colour who remained was so brilliant that Zeven was forced to shield his eyes. *I'll be waiting for you in Karmandi.*

'Samyaza?' As Zeven lowered his hands to take a guess, the site fell back into darkness and he was left with his sleeping daughter and an empty metal smelter. As his eyes adjusted to the moonlight, he noted how quiet it was here — even the insects avoided this place.

There was nothing to indicate that any huge transformation had taken place here this night, but being here no longer made his skin crawl — on the contrary the ambience was quite serene. The Juju stone on his arm was not aching any more, his daughter was alive, Khalid had found his people and there was now nothing to hinder Azazèl-mindos-coomra-dorchi from withdrawing to another universe unencumbered one year from now.

'So that's that then.' There had been quite a few moments recently when he felt he might live to regret his decision to go AWOL without his timekeeper's assistance, but his primary objective had been achieved and for that Zeven was very grateful.

Still, as he gathered up his daughter to return to the palace to report the banishment of the curses — and the heroic demise of General Prochazka and Khalid Mansur — he was saddened to realise that this victory also meant that his adventures through time, and across universes, had come to an end. The timekeepers had served their purpose.

When Zeven had made that first jump into the past with Taren and Jazmay they had been clueless as to how long and hard they would have to work to set the history of the USS back to rights. As wondrous and diverse as those travels had been, Zeven was damn sure none of them would risk such an endeavour again. It was time now to be content to allow human consciousness and causality to run their own natural course.

BACK FROM THE PAST

Through the lingering light haze of her quantum jump, which had numbed all her senses as efficiently as a deep sleep might, Taren's waking consciousness detected a disturbing distant sound that was both foreign and yet familiar. In a rush of awareness the sound grew louder.

As alien as the sound of a crying baby was to Taren, the intensity of the wail woke her nonetheless. Her breasts ached with a vengeance, as if they had been pumped full of air and were fit to burst, and upon inspection, she was horrified to find they had doubled in size and her T-shirt was dripping wet.

Lucian stirred beside her, and reaching across he gave Taren a nudge. 'The baby,' he mumbled, and sank back into sleep.

'The baby?' Taren finally put two and two together, and was horrified. 'We have a baby?' She sat up and shook her husband furiously.

'What?' Lucian protested to being forced into a fully conscious state.

'We have a baby?'

'I know,' he mumbled, 'and boy, he sounds hungry.'

'It's a boy?' she stated, stunned and enlightened at once.

'Well yeah.' He sat up to support his dozing form on his elbows, and yawned.

'Holy shit!' Taren panicked, as she had returned to her form on AMIE only one week before Khalid was due to cause the disaster that had cast many of them into another universe.

'Oh!' Lucian was enlightened and amused at once. 'You're back.'

'Yeah, I'm back,' Taren stressed. 'Only there appears to be a lot more of me now.' She referred to her swollen breasts, and all Lucian could do was laugh. 'How is this funny? We face off against Khalid in less than a week!'

'Well,' Lucian controlled his mirth. 'Look on the bright side, you missed the birth.'

'Yeah!' she emphasised, nearly hysterical. 'I missed the pregnancy, birth and everything I probably learned about being a parent! I don't even know our son's name!'

'Danon,' he informed, to calm her.

'Dan.' She smiled, delighted, being that Ji Dan would have been the father of this child.

'You approve, I take it?' Lucian climbed out of bed to fetch the soul in question, as Taren was quite obviously too petrified to do it, and once lifted from his cot, Danon fell silent.

'Does he do anything?' she asked in a panic, knowing Zeven's daughter had been performing psychic feats from a very young age.

'Well he cries, belches, creates a lot of dirty nappies,' Lucian advised as he carried the bundle over to where she was seated on the bed. 'But far and away his favourite pastime is gorging himself on your breasts.' Lucian held the child out to her.

'Seriously?' Taren was momentarily stunned by the request. 'I've never done this.'

'You've been doing it for months,' he downplayed her fear, and placed the child in her lap.

The sight of the dark-haired babe, sucking so hard on its own fist that it appeared it might devour it, broke her heart wide open, and as she held him close, he went into a frenzy, trying to nuzzle his way through her shirt. Then she raised the barrier and within moments, Danon had latched onto her aching breast and began sucking madly, which came as a relief to both mother and child.

'Told you so.' Lucian kissed her forehead, and she was overcome by the serene bliss of the moment.

'When I asked does he do anything,' Taren recalled her earlier query, 'I mean does he have any psychic talent?'

'Not that we've noticed,' Lucian said. 'But give me a break, he's only three months old. He hasn't even got teeth yet.'

'Oh, I'm not in a hurry to find out,' Taren assured him. 'We've got enough to worry about.'

Lucian had to chuckle. 'And you don't know the half of it yet.'

Taren's brief bliss departed, and she was panicked again. 'What could possibly be more shocking than this?' She referred to the child in her arms, but Lucian appeared to wish to defer that news for the present.

'I think you should just take a moment to catch your breath.' He sat down beside Taren to admire her and their babe. 'Whatever we did out there, where you've been … awesome job,' he awarded her her due. 'Danon is safe here with us, and not stuck in another time and universe. I was wrong to doubt —'

'No —' She felt he had just cause to.

'Regardless,' he persevered. 'You did the right thing, and that's all you need to know.' Lucian bent down and kissed his son's forehead, and then looked back to Taren. 'As far as the rest of what evolved here in your absence … well … that shall reveal itself soon enough.'

'I don't think so,' Taren insisted. 'I need to know what we are up against now! A week is not a long time.'

'I tell you what, why don't you take a shower, and I'll call a crew meeting,' Lucian proffered winningly.

Taren had a whiff of herself and decided. 'Good call, this parenting business is rather on the nose.'

Lucian grabbed up his communicator and placed a call. 'It's Lucian, she's back. And ah, best warn Yasper to expect Jazmay.'

'Telmo and Zeven are meeting us here today also, don't forget,' Taren relayed, noting Danon had lost interest in feeding and was getting grumbly.

'That's nice,' said Lucian, sounding a little uncomfortable about the news.

'What do I do with him now?' Taren held Danon out in front of her, and he released a huge belch.

'That's the one.' Lucian took the baby off her hands. 'Good job.' He kissed her forehead. 'Shower.'

Taren had to admit she was really impressed with how good Lucian was with Danon; he seemed to be a natural at parenting. She wasn't sure that she was going to be as proficient at it.

'Why Danon?' Taren wondered at their choice of name, as she accompanied Lucian and the baby to the mess hall for the crew meeting.

'I remembered Ancient Zhou and thought you would approve,' Lucian explained with a shrug, admiring their boy.

'I do approve,' Taren assured him with a smile, which quickly faded. 'But I thought we agreed to do children after we saw the being of the field safely gone, and Khalid back in prison?'

Lucian was amused. 'You really don't remember anything that happened these last few years, do you?'

'Well I've lived through it before a few times,' she was saying as they entered the mess, to find the entire crew assembled beneath a 'Welcome back' sign, and there were quite a few more of them than she remembered.

Mythric, Amie and Jazmay were all holding baby girls and Zeven had his arms full with twin boys — all the same age as Danon. Thurraya was proudly holding up a little aqua blue cat.

'What the hell happened?' Taren was smiling at how amused the crew were by her surprise.

'That's what I said! I had another kid! Who knew?' Jazmay seconded her surprise, and she observed the sleeping infant. 'Pretty cute kid,' she warranted.

'What are we going to do with all these babies when we take on Khalid?' Taren wondered what had got into everyone.

Most of the crew burst out laughing, but Zeven handed over the boys to Aurora to come forwards and explain. 'Timekeeper, I have a confession to make.'

'Oh no.' Taren was wary. 'What did you do?'

'Well, I helped.' Telmo came forwards to own his part in the affair.

'I haven't told her what we did yet,' Zeven objected.

'The curses have been banished, Khalid has left this world and returned to his own people, and your parents apologise that they could not be here today, but they are on Frujia signing the psychic bill of rights.' Telmo gave her the fast version.

'This is supposed to be my confession,' Zeven protested. 'I'm the one who decided to go AWOL and save Khalid.'

'You did what?' The control freak in Taren panicked.

'Did I mention we also took care of the photon-camera problem on Maladaan?' Telmo added, to quell her wrath.

'But that's everything on the list.' Taren realised there was absolutely nothing to panic about. 'You achieved all that? Truly?' Taren was hoping this wasn't all some horrible hoax, or some lovely dream she was having before she awoke in a nightmare.

'I did.' Zeven suppressed a grin in an attempt to be modest. 'And I kept a mission log of everything that happened, in the time you missed.' He braced himself to get yelled at but Taren just had to hug him.

'Well done, you!' She was bursting with gratitude. 'To know I don't have to face another disaster this week is the most incredible gift, I can't tell you.'

'Oh … you helped with all this,' Zeven assured her.

'A LOT!' Mythric emphasised.

'A WHOLE LOT!' Ringbalin was smiling broadly at her, as was everyone.

'But I still don't understand where all these babies came from?' Taren looked about; there was barely a couple on board who hadn't added a family member, and her sights came to rest on Ringbalin as he was holding up a finger. 'That's kinda my fault. I got a little over zealous healing you all after the battle of the curses … you fell pregnant at once.'

'I don't remember that.' Taren was perturbed, wishing that she could.

'No matter,' Ringbalin smiled to reassure her. 'It led to the release of all the Phemorian souls languishing in the celestial city of the Phemoray, who are now free to live out their lives as the universe intended.'

'We fixed that too?' Taren was speechless with joy and disbelief.

'With a lot of help from Jalila Lamus and her twin sister, Jafera,' Ringbalin added, to be fair. 'Both women have taken rather a shine to Trance, who is now running the Phemorian defence department. So, I don't think he'll be returning to Sermetica any time soon.'

Taren was smiling and frowning at the tale. 'Who is Trance?'

'It will take a little while for past and present consciousness to meld,' Lucian said, taking her in his free arm. 'But you've lived through these events, so sooner or later they'll come back to you. But until they do, all you really need to know is that … this time next week, we'll be waving Azazèl-mindos-coomra-dorchi farewell for the last time, with a drink in-hand to toast the being bon voyage!'

Taren placed her arms about both her husband and her son, and kissed them both. 'Best plan *ever.*'

BIBLIOGRAPHY

Once again my main references for this book were other books from my past trilogies as the events of these books directly relate to the events in this one.

The Light-field (Book 3: Triad of Being)
Dreaming Of Zhou Gong (Book 1: The Timekeepers)
The Eternity Gate (Book 2: The Timekeepers)

www.ingramcontent.com/pod-product-compliance
Lightning Source LLC
Chambersburg PA
CBHW020518110726
47899CB00004B/1161